Carnivalesque Inversion in the Fiction of Kurt Vonnegut

This book is part of the Peter Lang Humanities list.
Every volume is peer reviewed and meets
the highest quality standards for content and production.

PETER LANG
New York • Berlin • Brussels • Lausanne • Oxford

Emma Saggers

Carnivalesque Inversion in the Fiction of Kurt Vonnegut

PETER LANG
New York • Berlin • Brussels • Lausanne • Oxford

Library of Congress Cataloging-in-Publication Data

Names: Saggers, Emma, author.
Title: Carnivalesque inversion in the fiction of Kurt Vonnegut / Emma Saggers.
Description: New York: Peter Lang, 2023 | Includes bibliographical references and index.
Identifiers: LCCN 2022019684 (print) | LCCN 2022019685 (ebook) |
ISBN 9781433188213 (hardback) | ISBN 9781433188428 (ebook) |
ISBN 9781433188435 (epub)
Subjects: LCSH: Vonnegut, Kurt—Criticism and interpretation. | Vonnegut,
Kurt. Player piano. | Vonnegut, Kurt. Cat's cradle. | Vonnegut, Kurt.
Slaughterhouse-five. | Technology in literature. | Religion in
literature. | War in literature. | Bakhtin, M. M. (Mikhail
Mikhaïlovich), 1895-1975—Philosophy. | LCGFT: Literary criticism.
Classification: LCC PS3572.O5 Z84 2023 (print) | LCC PS3572.O5 (ebook) |
DDC 813/.54—dc23/eng/20220613
LC record available at https://lccn.loc.gov/2022019684
LC ebook record available at https://lccn.loc.gov/2022019685
DOI 10.3726/b18382

Bibliographic information published by **Die Deutsche Nationalbibliothek**.
Die Deutsche Nationalbibliothek lists this publication in the "Deutsche
Nationalbibliografie"; detailed bibliographic data are available
on the Internet at http://dnb.d-nb.de/.

Peter Lang Publishing, Inc., New York
80 Broad Street, 5th floor, New York, NY 10004
www.peterlang.com

For Lee, Holly, and Charlotte.

Contents

Acknowledgments

Kurt Vonnegut, excerpts from *A Man Without a Country*. Copyright © 2010 by Kurt Vonnegut. Reprinted with the permission of The Permissions Company, LLC on behalf of Seven Stories Press, sevenstories.com.
© Kurt Vonnegut, 2006, *A Man Without a Country*, Bloomsbury Publishing Plc.

From *Rabelais and His World* by Mikhail Bakhtin. Trans. Hélène Iswolsky, Indiana University Press, 1984, Bloomington, Indiana USA. With Permission of The MIT Press.

From *THE DIALOGIC IMAGINATION: FOUR ESSAYS* by M.M. Bakhtin, edited by Michael Holquist, translated by Caryl Emerson and Michael Holquist, Copyright (c) 1981. Courtesy of the University of Texas Press.

Excerpt(s) from *PALM SUNDAY: AN AUTOBIOGRAPHICAL COLLAGE* by Kurt Vonnegut, copyright © 1981 by Kurt Vonnegut. Used by permission of Dell Publishing, an imprint of Random House, a division of Penguin Random House LLC. All rights reserved.
From *PALM SUNDAY* by Kurt Vonnegut. Copyright © 1981 by the Ramjac Corporation, used by permission of The Wylie Agency LLC.

Introduction

*

    As our contemporary generation navigates a changing world, we face a host of renewed challenges as climate change, the pandemic, and continued conflict around the globe cause humanitarian adversity and hardships. The future for humanity can feel uncertain, but what we can be sure of is that there is an ever-growing need for humanity to adapt and change. As the need grows to modify and reshape our human social structures, so too does the gulf widen between people who cannot find common ground on how to successfully meet the challenges. With continued advances in technology, our generation can communicate with each other like no other, but that does not always seem to make it easier to find shared human collaboration. The future does not have to be all bleak and unaccommodating so long as we can overcome our differences and meet the problems as a united and collective human front. To understand and learn how past human generations dealt with their collective challenges, we can look to writers such as Kurt Vonnegut who engaged his personal experiences of global conflict and social change within his writing. He was a witness to history and that gave him a unique perspective of how human beings can behave at their most challenged and vulnerable, not always acting in their own best interests. His aim was to teach us the way to a better and kinder future, inclusive for all human individuals. Vonnegut was concerned about his contemporary America and how it could evolve as a nation in the future. He believed that America could be the guiding force for good and lead the world against the oncoming challenges he knew future humanity would face. Contemporary Modern America can look to Kurt Vonnegut for answers on how best to navigate their changing world, avoiding the mistakes of the past.

With a career that spanned over half a century, Kurt Vonnegut was a writer who observed some of the most important fundamental changes in human history. He was the product of the twentieth century, an era that saw a social, political, and religious change at an accelerated speed. He was immersed in a world struggling with ideological tensions and rapid scientific and technological advancements. The fundamental beliefs of religion and the hierarchy of social structures that had previously been accepted as the norm were now being challenged. The Suffragette Movement, the Civil Rights Movement, the Great Depression, the Second World War, the Cold War, and the Vietnam War are some of those significant movements and events that Vonnegut's life would bear witness to. Born in the roaring twenties, in 1922, he was born into a world coming to terms with The Great War, the war having only ended four years earlier in November 1918, a war so terrible and destructive to human life that it was often referred to as "the war to end all wars," a phrase borrowed and adapted from the author H.G. Wells.[1] Unfortunately, this was not destined to be true and just twenty-one years later, in September 1939, the Second World War would begin. Allied forces, including Britain, France, and Russia, fought a total war against the Axis, including Germany, Italy, and Japan. The United States was to join the war later, at the end of 1941, after the Japanese attack on Pearl Harbor. It was in January 1943 that Vonnegut decided to drop out of Cornell University to enlist in the United States Army. He was to be an Army private in the fight against a Nazi-occupied Europe and to become a part of world history in the fight against fascism. He later commented that it was, "'clearly a war that had to be fought and there are very few of those in history. It was worth fighting.'"[2] What he encountered in that war would influence him and his writing for the rest of his life.

Vonnegut became a writer preoccupied with engaging the reader in the cultural, political, and social world around them. His writing has serious intentions

---

1 H.G. Wells published several articles at the beginning of World War One that were collected and published as a book: *The War That Will End War*, Duffield & Company, 1914, New York.

2 Kurt Vonnegut interview with Charles J. Shields, March 13, 2007, from: Charles J. Shields, "One of the Biggest Fools on the Hill 1940–1943," from *And So It Goes: Kurt Vonnegut, A Life*, Henry Holt and Co., 2011, New York, p. 48.

to educate the reader on the importance of individual human beings. Vonnegut valued freedom of speech and the ability to speak the truth with sincerity. It was the sincerity of Vonnegut's writing style that enabled him to critique the contemporary world that he witnessed in flux following the war, and at the beginning of his professional writing career, and it is this sincerity that empowered him to read the changes that he continued to bear witness to until his death in 2007. To Vonnegut, it was important to reflect the world as he saw it and from a humanist perspective, this meant that the reality of his interpretation was often painful. The only way for Vonnegut to write a sincere book was to be truthful in reflecting on what he saw wrong in the world: "Shakespeare was as poor a storyteller ... But there's a reason we recognize *Hamlet* as a masterpiece: it's that Shakespeare told us the truth, and people so rarely tell us the truth."[3] Vonnegut understood that "If you write an insincere book, the reader will see right through you."[4]

Vonnegut's aim was never to offer his readers a strict alternative to the defects he found in modern society, but rather to draw attention to the problems he found so the reader was made aware of them. His personal history was turbulent, and his experiences during the Second World War, particularly his survival of the Dresden firebombing as a prisoner of war in 1945, impacted his writing in considerable ways. Vonnegut felt marginalized with the label of a Science Fiction writer and this was a great exasperation to him: "I wondered in what way I'd offended that I would not get credit for being a serious writer."[5] There can be no denying that his fiction contains elements traditionally associated with the Science Fiction genre, a genre that throughout much of his life could be argued to have been stigmatized as a form of writing not to be taken seriously. If the reader considers some of his life experiences, such as his knowledge of science from beginning a biochemistry degree at Cornell University, his experiences of war, his brother's scientific work to develop weather modification, as well as the premature deaths of close relatives, including one to a freak train accident, it can be no wonder to the reader that his fiction should contain fantastical elements of science and technology. He was on a quest to understand the absurd nature of human experience through the fantastic reality of everyday life. As Peter Reed discusses: "His fiction struggles to cope with a world of tragi-comic disparities, a universe that defies causality, whose absurdity lends the fantastic

---

3 Kurt Vonnegut, "Here Is a Lesson in Creative Writing," *A Man Without a Country*, Seven Stories Press, 2005, New York, p. 37.

4 Kurt Vonnegut & Lee Stringer, *Like Shaking Hands With God: A Conversation about Writing*, Washington Square Press, 1999, New York, p. 63.

5 Kurt Vonnegut, "Do You Know What a Twerp is?," *A Man Without a Country*, p.16.

equal plausibility with the mundane."[6] Vonnegut was exposed to the worst and the most extraordinary events life has to offer, whilst living through the fastest acceleration of scientific and technological advancement in the history of humanity. Much of what he encountered in his earlier life sounds fantastical and feels like it should be in a work of fiction. To Vonnegut, fiction and the real world are intertwined, the elements of Science Fiction happen every day, we just need to look at the changes in technology we have witnessed in our own lifetimes. Science and technology are at the core of human existence, so why would we leave them out of serious fiction?

Much of scientific exploration and experimentation begins with the seemingly fantastical. Men landing on the moon seemed unattainable before 1969, and today we see rockets propelling astronauts to the International Space Station that have the capability to land back on earth to be used for the next mission, something that would have seemed unimaginable in the past. Vonnegut's experiences with science and technology, particularly during the Second World War, convinced him that society does not always consider what is best for humanity's future. He witnessed the devastating consequences science and technology can have on human life, and he lived with the psychological consequences. Science and technology have the power for good, to enhance human existence, or the capability to destroy it. Vonnegut's experiences seemed to suggest that the latter was on the cusp of inevitability, the very thing he would spend his writing career petitioning people to understand and avert.

Vonnegut's writing is fantastical; it considers the extraordinary with sincerity, as though the events described are the everyday mundane. It does not matter to Vonnegut that we do not encounter aliens daily, or that humanity, as far as we can tell, does not hop and skip through time on a regular basis. He is more concerned with the possibility that advancements in society, often considered progressive, are not always for the betterment of humanity, and that reality is not always the "truth" we might have been told. What he witnessed in our contemporary world did not tally comfortably with the human conscience. He believed in the good of humanity and that by working together humanity can achieve wonderful advancements for future generations. He, therefore, embraced science, and he embraced technology, but only if both are used in conjunction with the purposes of advancing humanity collectively. He did not see scientific

---

6 Peter Reed, "Kurt Vonnegut's Fantastic Faces," *The Journal of the Fantastic in the Arts*, Vol. 10, no. 1(37), Winter 1998, p. 77.

advancement for the good of the corporate purse or the manipulation of the masses as a positive thing.

It is not the purpose of this text to question the validity of Science Fiction as a serious literary form, but the elements traditionally associated with Science Fiction in Vonnegut's work must be addressed for his writing to be released for more rigorous consideration. Yes, Vonnegut incorporates elements of Science Fiction, but it is not his intention to write a Science Fiction novel that incorporates a world autonomous from our own. He uses the elements of science, technology, time travel, and alien encounters to sensationalize. If it is the realist novel's aim to reproduce the everyday on the page and to give an honest account, it is Vonnegut's aim to reproduce the absurdity of the everyday; his honest account requires the reader to question and acknowledge the preposterous elements of human life. In the introduction to *A Companion to Science Fiction*, David Seed discusses the issues surrounding science fiction writers and considers whether authors can conform to a generic term.[7] He asserts that there appears to be a need for writers to have to be fitted into a specific genre, that it has become a convention that writers must be writing under a particular classification, they cannot simply write under the category of "Fiction" alone. Seed evokes the postmodern writer Brian McHale to support his arguments as McHale suggests that Science Fiction began to use elements of the postmodern and mainstream culture increasingly following the Second World War. He proposes that McHale starts from the foundation that fiction must belong to a category and never admits that a work can be a "multigeneric work that could move in and out of SF."[8] Seed contends that writers can embrace elements of science fiction without having to be considered authors of the genre; he argues that: "The best critical writing on SF approaches the fiction in relation to the images and narratives of related cultural practices."[9] It is not about the "Science Fiction" but about what the writing tells us about our own cultural practices. Seed continues that Science fiction is an exploration of a culture where we "cross-relate the familiar to the strangely new."[10] Vonnegut certainly fits this mold, as the main purpose of his writing is to convince the reader to question what is taking place around them in society.

On the other hand, Seed begins to list what he sees as important elements of the science fiction novel, "The concept of world-building is an intrinsic part

---

7 David Seed Ed., "Introduction: Approaching Science Fiction," *A Companion to Science Fiction*, Blackwell Publishing, 2008, Oxford UK, p. 3.
8 David Seed, *A Companion to Science Fiction*, p.3.
9 David Seed, *A Companion to Science Fiction*, p.3.
10 David Seed, *A Companion to Science Fiction*, p.4.

of the construction."[11] Vonnegut can be considered to fulfill this element of the genre in part because he is building future worlds, or possible timelines, for what could happen in the future of our society and culture. In his novel *Sirens of Titan* (1959) Vonnegut clearly endeavors to world-build with his use of an inhabited planet Mars, but in *Breakfast of Champions* (1973), he is more preoccupied with the notions of reader awareness rather than world-building. The point of Vonnegut's novels is that they all relate to the world that we exist in, not a world different and "other" from our own. They are possibilities for where our own Earth-bound existence might lead to with the advancement of science and technology. He is creating futures for us to consider and critique, futures that could be possible from the point our society is at now. Vonnegut invites us to consider our own modern world experience in relation to what could happen if we are not actively engaged, to challenge the limitations of our own self-obsession, and to put the future of the planet and humanity collectively before the rewards of now. He is not asking us to consider the cultural development of a fictional world but to consider the possibilities for our own world.

Working within the terms that Seed sets out, authors can be considered multi-generic, and it is under these terms that this text will consider Vonnegut as an author who incorporates and manipulates elements of the science fiction genre. Vonnegut is a writer who moves in and out of science fiction to add coherence to his contemporary critique. He is a writer that can remain genre-less and who is able to integrate the multi-voiced nature of what it is to be an individual in our contemporary world. Vonnegut commented on his science fiction categorization by critics, saying: "'I have been a sore-headed occupant of a file drawer labelled "science fiction" ever since, and I would like out, particularly since so many serious critics regularly mistake the drawer for a tall white fixture in a comfort station.'"[12] Vonnegut felt antagonized by his label as a science fiction writer because he felt the genre was not given serious consideration, he was writing serious social commentary in his fiction that was being sidelined. He had never intended to become a genre writer but did not deny the elements of science fiction in his work; what he did deny was the generalizations that it brought.

Vonnegut uses the fantastical, or sensational, in his novels and short stories to encourage the reader to establish their own reading of society. His main technique

---

11 David Seed, *A Companion to Science Fiction*, p.4.
12 Karen & Charles Wood. "The Vonnegut Effect: Science Fiction and Beyond," Jerome Klinkowitz & John Somer. Eds. *Kurt Vonnegut Jr: The Vonnegut Statement*, Granada Publishing/ Panther Books Ltd, 1975, St. Albans, Herts. p.135.

for this realization is the use of the satirical, defined in the Cambridge Dictionary as: "a way of criticizing people or ideas in a humorous way, especially in order to make a political point."[13] Vonnegut manipulates his subject in such a way as to render it comical and to emphasize the absurdity of the traditionally accepted notions in our social constructions. Vonnegut relies on the reader participating in his fiction, in their ability to read into what at first can seem obvious, or comical: "It's important to retreat from the hoopla on television, and what television says matters and what we're all supposed to talk about. And of course literature is the only art that requires our audience to be performers."[14] Vonnegut requires his readers to step back from the manipulations of media and the acceptance of everything at face value, that is, he requires readers to think for themselves and to consider possibilities.

Stylistically, Vonnegut offers a treasure trove for the reader: He manipulates conventions and creates subversions in his novels that the reader is expected to keep up with. He gives the reader responsibility; he treats them as individuals capable of considering the possibilities and therefore qualified to draw their own conclusions. For Vonnegut, the reader's ability is important, they must be able to understand the fundamental stylistic devices that he incorporates into his prose: "You have to be able to read and you have to be able to read awfully well. You have to read so well that you get irony! I'll say one thing meaning another, and you'll get it."[15] Vonnegut assumes a depth of knowledge in the reader, socially, politically, and historically, which allows the satirical expression to be understood by the reader so they "get the joke." The reader must understand the "ironic" elements in Vonnegut's narratives and comprehend that the situations presented often happen differently from the expected or accepted. Vonnegut empowers his readers to a meditative state where they possess the ability to question their cultural complicity. Vonnegut sees himself as a literary catalyst, always aiming to present the world as he sees it, trying to release the reader from the perception of a normal, accepted reality to an awareness of alternative meaning. It is through Vonnegut's use of satirical expression, and the use of irony, where the actual meaning can differ from the literal meaning, that the "subversive" becomes the most important way of assessing and analyzing his work. The satirical therefore becomes the main technique Vonnegut uses to subvert any sense

13 Definition of satire from the Cambridge Academic Content Dictionary, Cambridge University Press, 2021, dictionary.cambridge.org/us/dictionary/english/satire, Accessed August 28, 2022.
14 Kurt Vonnegut & Lee Stringer, *Like Shaking Hands With God: A Conversation about Writing*, p. 17.
15 Kurt Vonnegut & Lee Stringer, *Like Shaking Hands With God: A Conversation about Writing*, p. 17.

of social normality in his novels, and his consistent use of fantastical elements gives his prose an absurd edge. In *The American Absurd* Robert Hipkiss defines the nature of absurdity as "the human condition as one in which man is caught between the extremes of birth and death, phenomena which he cannot possibly hope to understand … ."[16] It is Hipkiss' "impossibility of human freedom"[17] that Vonnegut aims to counteract, to remove the veil that he sees engulfing people's understanding of what is happening to them in a modern media exploited world.

This text will analyze three novels by Kurt Vonnegut from the theoretical perspective of Mikhail Bakhtin: *Player Piano* (1952), *Cat's Cradle* (1963), and *Slaughterhouse-Five* (1969). It will concentrate on Bakhtin's theories on carnivalesque inversion from *Rabelais and his World* (1968) and will further consider his theoretical perspectives on the text as a site of struggle from *The Dialogic Imagination* (1981), and the practical application of his theories with the novel as polyphonic from *Problems of Dostoevsky's Poetics* (1963). Postmodernism will be addressed, but as with the genre classification of "Science Fiction" previously discussed, this work does not aim to consider at length Kurt Vonnegut as a postmodern writer. The term postmodern cannot be ignored when discussing Vonnegut's development of techniques of subversion, as the term relates to the post-world war period Vonnegut was writing in, and it is a term that defines writing that strives to make sense of a disjointed world. It is a period of writing that marks the fluid transition of ideas from the fixed state to the fluctuating, a time when the security of the world was changing, and roles were reversing. This element of change and social oscillation is also characteristic of the subversive elements in Bakhtin's carnivalesque inversion and is fundamental to Vonnegut's use of subversion in his narratives.

Bakhtin and Vonnegut were both writing at a time when social structures, attitudes, and beliefs were changing, and the accepted order of what had come before was being questioned and challenged. Both men wrote in an era, post-1918, that had been changed by war and revolution, and they appear to be trying to make sense of a world where no answers are now possible. The traditional structures had been overturned and society was struggling to create new and fixed definitions. Both authors reflect ideas and theories that allow an environment that incorporates a multi-layered and multi-voiced world. Vonnegut mimics the world he sees around himself and Bakhtin can theorize how that world works. Bakhtin's main work, although conceptualized and written early in the twentieth

---

16 Robert A. Hipkiss, *The American Absurd: Pynchon, Vonnegut, and Barth*, Associated Faculty Press Inc., 1984, New York, p. 1.
17 Robert A. Hipkiss, *The American Absurd: Pynchon, Vonnegut, and Barth*, p. 1.

century, was not rediscovered fully until the 1960s when it made a valuable reemergence, and neatly coincides with Vonnegut's own writing career. With the breadth of his writing spanning both philosophy and literary theory, Bakhtin saw "literary texts as a testing-ground for his ethical and philosophical concerns."[18] The postmodern era of authors like Vonnegut, Heller, and Pynchon was redefining the mode of writing, and critical theorists such as Bakhtin, Barthes, and Foucault were working to understand the non-formalist, post-structural world. Being men willing to consider the complexities of society came at a price. Bakhtin was persecuted by the Stalinist Russian State and his work was prevented from being published,[19] just as Vonnegut's work was withdrawn from public libraries and schools in America. When society struggles with social and cultural change it often seeks to suppress the voices that question and highlight the inadequacy that might be found in the current system.

Bakhtin's theories were chosen for this text because of the similarities that his work has with Vonnegut's writing. Vonnegut's work is complicated, multidimensional, and allows for the characters, reader, and authorial voice to be overtly present in the text; this style of writing clearly presents the dialogical and heteroglot nature of Bakhtin's concepts. In a sense, Vonnegut can embody and exemplify the literary theories of Bakhtin. Their comparison does not end here, in their quest to understand the social world around them they reflect its complexity in its entirety. This means that their work can at times become contradictory and open-ended, not really giving a distinct answer to work with. Both men offer ideas and concepts but in the carnivalesque and dialogic nature of their work, the reader is the sum of their understanding, after all, no text can be read the same twice: "what one says about Bakhtin is never what Bakhtin himself says … no study of Bakhtin's work can ever function 'within Bakhtin' or even 'from within Bakhtin's thought.'"[20] Both men are also writing in their "own times" reflecting the attitudes and social norms they would have been accustomed to. Bakhtin chooses to write about what might seem to us in the modern world as archaic by selecting a renaissance narrative to exercise his theoretical concepts on the carnival. However, both men seem to suggest that being human is always full of complexity and contradiction, which does not seem to change over history or time.

---

18 Sue Vice, *Introducing Bakhtin*, Manchester University Press, 1997, Manchester UK, p. 2.

19 David Lodge, with Nigel Wood, Ed., "Mikhail Bakhtin," *Modern Criticism and Theory: A Reader*, Second Edition, Longman, 2000, Harlow, Essex, p. 104.

20 Anthony Wall and Clive Thompson, "Cleaning Up Bakhtin's Carnival Act," *Diacritics* 23.2, Summer 1993, p. 48—also quoted in Sue Vice, *Introducing Bakhtin*, p. 2.

Concentrating on Bakhtin, as with the previous discourse on the use of genre to categorize texts, Mikhail Bakhtin's own conceptualization of genre is in-depth and charts the progress of the novel historically in two specific routes: "juxtaposing the epic on one side—elevated, stylistically fixed, incapable of laughter—against the novel on the other—low, stylistically mobile and diverse, serio-comic."[21] Bakhtin looks at genre in terms of the "novel genre," or the novel as a whole, and how the novel can incorporate many forms of genre, emulating many at one time. In *Problems of Dostoevsky's Poetics* Bakhtin states:

> Neither the hero, nor the idea, nor the very polyphonic principle for structuring the whole can be fitted into the generic and plot-compositional forms of the bio-logical novel, a socio-psychological novel, a novel of the everyday life or a family novel, that is, into forms dominant …[22]

Bakhtin's application of his own theoretical ideas distinctly highlights Dostoevsky as a writer who does not conform to a specific genre, but who in the essence of the "polyphonic principle" is able to incorporate many dimensions in his work. In this vein, Vonnegut can also be considered in the same light, as polyphonic, as an author able to emulate many generic structures in his writing. Again, there is a sense that Vonnegut has become multi-generic or multi-voiced in his stylistic and subject choices.

In *Rabelais and his World*, Bakhtin explores how language is used in texts to create the act of resistance against controlling social norms, and it is this resistance that Vonnegut is offering to his readers. Bakhtin asserts that the traditional and historical act of the festive carnival was used to invert the prevalent hierarchy of social class structures in society. Through the act of people wearing a mask to obscure their true identities, the established and accepted social hierarchy was rendered redundant and exposed as an illusion: a servant could be transformed into a master, or a pauper into a lord, and vice versa. Traditionally, the carnival allowed people to exercise their frustrations with their individual situations, but the system required them to revert to their normal role when the carnival was at an end, and they felt a release from their social vexation. This reveals that the class system or social hierarchy is illusionary because structures believed to be imposed

21 Simon Dentith, "Bakhtin and the Novel," *An Introductory Reader: Bakhtinian Thought*, Routledge, 1996, London UK, p. 49.
22 Mikhail Bakhtin, "Characteristics of Genre and Plot Composition in Dostoevsky's Works," *Problems of Dostoevsky's Poetics*, Ed. & Trans. Caryl Emerson, University of Minnesota Press, 1984, Minneapolis, MN, p. 101.

by higher authority could be changed and manipulated. It is only the illusion of reality that holds us in a social class system because we, the people, are the ones that have been led to believe and accept that condition without question. The function of the carnival allows a person to be free, to allow them to see past the constructs of society:

> All the symbols of the carnival idiom are filled with this pathos of change and renewal, with the sense of gay relativity of prevailing truths and authorities. We find here a characteristic logic, the peculiar logic of the "inside out' (*á l'envers*), of the 'turnabout,' of a continual shifting from top to bottom, from front to rear, of numerous parodies and travesties, humiliations, profanations, comic crownings and un-crownings. A second life, a second world of folk culture is thus constructed; it is to a certain extent a parody of the extracarnival life, a 'world inside out.'[23]

The element of carnival becomes an important reflective catalyst to enable an inversion from the passive acceptance of the "normal" to an awareness of the conformity that lies behind it, to the knowledge that any idea of concrete and fixed ideal of society is imaginary. The carnivalesque inversion becomes the "epitome of incompleteness"[24] because the complete and fixed definitions become incomplete and undefinable, and reality and illusion embody the "continual shifting from top to bottom." Bakhtin sees the carnival premise leading to a new form of communication because what was once accepted is now impossible, therefore we can no longer communicate by the same means. The new communication becomes mocking and satirical in order to "turnabout" the old form of communication, allowing for the shifting of meaning. There must be a lowering of the language with the extraction of the earthly from the spiritual. It is this "turnabout" that Vonnegut achieves in his prose; he aims to give the reader a deeper understanding of the world they participate in. Vonnegut's voice is that of a serious social commentator, his social and political discourse cuts through the widely accepted to expose the underlying foundations of our beliefs. Vonnegut can create the new form of communication that Bakhtin describes. Vonnegut is writing to subvert the accepted generalizations presented by our society as fact, the carnivalesque inversion of which is the "temporary liberation from the prevailing truth and from the established order."[25] In effect, the novel becomes the carnival:

23 Mikhail Bakhtin, "Introduction," *Rabelais and His World*, Trans. Hélène Iswolsky, Indiana University Press, 1984, Bloomington, IN, p. 11.
24 Mikhail Bakhtin, "Introduction," *Rabelais and His World*, p. 26.
25 Mikhail Bakhtin, "Introduction," *Rabelais and His World*, p. 10.

it is not a spectacle seen by the people; they live in it ... While carnival lasts, there is no other life outside it. During carnival time life is subject only to its laws, that is, the law of its own freedom.[26]

In the act of reading, the reader submits to the laws and freedoms explicit in the novel, and because of this "there is no other life outside it." Therefore, the participation of the reader has ultimate importance to Vonnegut, they are an integral element of the narrative working. They must engage in the text and in understanding the subtle implications of the satirical nature of the narrative for it to work. The reader contributes to the creation of the carnivalesque inversion, just as a person might participate in a physical carnival by wearing a costume or mask. The reader is integral to the realization and effectiveness of the subversion taking place.

The novel that takes on the form of the carnival is therefore able to manipulate language in the narrative in such a way as to enable communication with the reader on a new level. The narrative itself then becomes a new form of communication because it becomes a carnivalesque inversion that empowers the reader to a different understanding of their social/political environment:

> the carnival-grotesque form exercises the same function: to consecrate inventive freedom, to permit the combination of a variety of different elements and their rapprochement, to liberate from the prevailing point of view of the world, from conventions and established truths, from clichés, from all that is humdrum and universally accepted. This carnival spirit offers the chance to have a new outlook on the world, to realize the relative nature of all that exists, and to enter a completely new order of things.[27]

The carnivalesque offers a new way of understanding the world outside of the narrative, and therefore encourages free thought in the reader. Vonnegut understands the limited capabilities of human interaction and emphasizes the inadequacies of our preconceived ideas, our "conventions and established truths." His use of satire and the sensationalizing elements in his texts, work to release the reader from socially educated restraints, therefore empowering the reader to a new form of communication and order. The reader is given the power over their society because they must decide how to continue forward with their newfound liberation and knowledge. Vonnegut's use of the Carnival further allows the

---

26 Mikhail Bakhtin, "Introduction," *Rabelais and His World,*, p. 7.
27 Mikhail Bakhtin, "Introduction," *Rabelais and His World*, p. 34.

reader to comprehend ideological tensions present in society, and we can also relate this to Bakhtin's work in *The Dialogic Imagination*. Bakhtin stresses that novels are not written in vacuous spaces, in isolation from the social and political world around them. They are in fact, multi-layered reflections of the complex world that they represent.

In the four essays contained in *The Dialogic Imagination*, Bakhtin suggests the novel form is dialogic. The dialogic element means the narrative is constantly being informed by what has come before and is in a continuous dialogue with the language with which it comes into contact. Everything in the text can be understood as being a part of a greater body of understanding. In a similar way, cultures can be considered continually influenced by external cultures; as multiculturalism spreads globally, capital cities become prime examples of "melting pots" of cultures living, interacting, and evolving together. In this way, novels become sites of interaction, and are therefore subject to differing opinions from the characters, authors, and readers:

> Everything means, is understood, as a part of a greater whole—there is a constant interaction between meanings, all of which have the potential of conditioning others. Which will affect the other, how it will do so and in what degree is what is actually settled at the moment of utterance. This dialogic imperative, mandated by the pre-existence of the language world relative to any of its current inhabitants, insures that there can be no actual monologue.[28]

The dialogic nature of society implies that there are so many cultural, historical, sociological, and ideological meanings within our world, that there can be no fixed definition of what life represents. Narrative, and the novel form, is a classic example of this interaction as they have differing implications for different readers, all contributing to the multi-voiced and dialogical nature of interpretation. Vonnegut offers the reader the opportunity of freedom from their own inward-looking interpretation, as his satirical texts, although presuming some form of cultural understanding by means of words, do not offer an absolute dogmatic rendering of life for everyone. He is there to carnivalize and therefore invert the 'fixed' definitions offered to us within our world. He wants his reader to think for themselves, to consider the implications of everything they are told. The dialogic world is dominated by what Bakhtin refers to as "heteroglossia," or: "the base

---

28 Mikhail Bakhtin, "Glossary," *The Dialogic Imagination*, Ed. Michael Holquist. Trans. Caryl Emerson & Michael Holquist, University of Texas Press, 1981, Austin, TX, p. 426.

condition governing the operation of meaning in any utterance. It is that which insures the primacy of context over text."[29] Explained, this means that:

> At any given time, in any given place, there will be a set of conditions—social, historical, meteorological, physiological—that will insure that a word uttered in that place and at that time will have meaning different than it would have under any other conditions; all utterances are heteroglot.[30]

The moment a person reads a narrative, they bring to it all the sociological and ideological conditioning they have encountered. This means that texts are fluid and must be analyzed with the knowledge that they incorporate any ideas already perceived and understood by the reader. They are sites for interactive communication, with no idea being greater than another. Within "Discourse in the Novel," Bakhtin gives "prose discourse" the same value as everyday speech, scientific speech, or other means of speech communication. People, or readers, communicate readily, but again this does not take place in a vacuum. People are influenced by their culture, the place they live in a country, and the cultures they encounter; these influences are transferred to the novel discourse:

> Speech of characters are merely those fundamental compositional unities with whose help heteroglossia can enter the novel; each of them permits a multiplicity of social voices and a wide variety of their links and interrelationships (always more or less dialogized). These distinctive links and interrelationships between utterances and languages, this movement of the theme through different languages and speech types, its dispersion into the rivulets and droplets of social heteroglossia, its dialogization—this is the basic distinguishing feature of the stylistics of the novel.[31]

The idea of the novel as a site for struggle begins to become evident as Bakhtin investigates elements of the novel discourse and considers the elements that can influence and shape its formulation. In the same way, we can consider Vonnegut with similar actions, looking closely at the text to reveal how social and cultural heteroglossia can be considered to influence his work. He communicates in a way that encourages conflict and struggle for the reader, he wants them to question their natural instincts, their cultural norms, and he wants them to experience more ideas than they had before reading the text. He is encouraging the idea of

29 Mikhail Bakhtin, "Glossary," *The Dialogic Imagination*, p. 428.
30 Mikhail Bakhtin, "Glossary," *The Dialogic Imagination*, p. 428.
31 Mikhail Bakhtin, "Discourse in the Novel," *The Dialogic Imagination*, p. 263.

ideologization, that there is a multiplicity of interpretation, and it is through this medium that he can suggest difference and change.

In another of his theoretical works, *Problems of Dostoevsky's Poetics*, Bakhtin considers the novel as polyphonic, or to be multi-voiced. This is closely related to the narrative being dialogic, and a "world dominated by heteroglossia."[32] He considers characters to have autonomy, having their own distinct voices, independent of the narrator or author:

> A character's word about himself and his world is just as fully weighted as the author's word usually is; it is not subordinated to the character's objectified image as merely one of his characteristics, nor does it serve as a mouthpiece for the author's voice. It possesses extraordinary independence in the structure of the work; it sounds, as it were, *alongside* the author's word and in a special way combines both with it and with the full and equally valid voices of other characters.[33]

Novels, in effect, have many simultaneous voices, including that of the reader. Each reader has their own history, experiences, and political persuasions, which influence them in the act of reading which adds to the literary experience. Not only does the novel become a site for resistance from within, but each reader can interpret the language used differently, the novel further becoming a site of struggle under the influence of social dialogue. This idea of polyphony, and the idea of characters as autonomous, can be seen in many of the novels by Vonnegut.

In Vonnegut's Novel, *Breakfast of Champions*, the reader encounters a character autonomous from the narrator, who speaks directly to the narrator conversing about his own causality and death. This is further suggested in his novel, *Slaughterhouse-Five*, where the idea of an alien encounter introduces the reader to a different world with distinct cultural practices and beliefs independent of their own. The juxtaposition of ideas challenging the authenticity of our own social systems forces the reader to consider the implications. The "alien" other is autonomous from our Earth-bound perspectives so does not have to follow the laws that govern our own world. The novels become polyphonic as they are representative of many ideals, suggesting to the reader that there are many interpretations. Vonnegut's narratives can clearly be defined in terms of Bakhtin's polyphony and are reflective of the multi-voiced nature of cultural societies. The foundations for Bakhtin's polyphony in narrative stem from musical theory, and the idea that

---

32 Mikhail Bakhtin, "Glossary," *The Dialogic Imagination*, p. 426.
33 Mikhail Bakhtin, "Dostoevsky's Polyphonic Novel and Its Treatment in Critical Literature," *Problems of Dostoevsky's Poetics*, p. 7.

music is composed from several different instruments, all with their individual characteristics, coming together as one to create something beautiful and more complete. In this sense, novels become great narrative compositions, combining many different layers and disciplines: "**No matter how** corrupt, greedy, and heartless our government, our corporations, our media, and our religious and charitable institutions may become, the music will still be wonderful."[34]

It has already been asserted that Vonnegut is multi-generic, and that he incorporates many different genres within his writing to critique contemporary culture. It is also clear that Vonnegut's narratives can also be considered dialogic, dominated by the heteroglot nature of a world full of implication and interpretation. Vonnegut can now also be considered polyphonic, as he manipulates the conventions of writing, exploiting different voices over the body of his work to incorporate the complicated interactions taking place in society. He does not concentrate on his style specifically but alternates it depending on the requirements of the novel subject. The characters often speak authoritatively, narrators speak directly to the reader, and characters become self-aware. Vonnegut also explores the concepts of style and structure: for example, in his novel *Hocus Pocus* (1990), he brings the reader's attention to the fact that he has written the novel on various scraps of paper, and this is reflected in his prose with frequent breaks in the narrative. It implies an authentic feeling in the text, reflecting on the experiences of the reader. This structural experimentation happens in many of Vonnegut's texts, and he often includes many historical and literary signifiers to engage the reader in active participation in the novels. He needs the reader to consider all the possibilities and gives them plenty of examples to think about and make links to.

Not only does Vonnegut fit comfortably within the dialogic interpretation, but we can also see that Vonnegut fits comfortably with Bakhtin's idea of the chronotope. A chronotope, or "time-space"—"the intrinsic connectedness of temporal and spatial relationships that are artistically expressed in literature,"[35] can be seen to be manipulated and exposed in many of Vonnegut's novels. Bakhtin states that:

> In the literary artistic chronotope, spatial and temporal indicators are fused into one carefully thought-out, concrete whole. Time, as it were, thickens, takes on flesh, becomes artistically visible; likewise, space becomes charged and responsive to the movements of time, plot and history.[36]

---

34 Kurt Vonnegut, "I Turned Eighty-Two on November 11," *A Man Without a Country*, p. 66—emphasis in original text.

35 Mikhail Bakhtin, "Forms of Time and of the Chronotope in the Novel," *The Dialogic Imagination*, p. 84.

36 Mikhail Bakhtin, "Forms of Time and of the Chronotope in the Novel," *The Dialogic Imagination*, p. 84.

The literary form incorporates specific time-space relationships within a text, for example, Bakhtin refers to the chronotopes of adventure time (Ancient Greek literature), everyday time, autobiographical and biographical time, and further explores elements such as folklore and historic time. The novel becomes a site for the formation of a concrete "other," a narrative world that incorporates elements of time and space other than that of the author or reader which gives the text the presentation of a believable reality. Just as the narrative is created by the implementation of multiple chronotopes, the reader also adds their own time and space, the actuality of the time that they are reading in, and all their own experiences in time and space to the equation. The text is complicated and representative of the world around us:

> within the limits of a single work and within the total literary output of a single author we may notice a number of different chronotopes and complex interactions among them, specific to a given work or author... Chronotopes are mutually inclusive, they co-exist, they may be interwoven with, replace or oppose each other, contradict one another or find themselves in ever more complex interrelationships.[37]

This idea of complexity is especially evident in Vonnegut's novel *Slaughterhouse-Five*. The differing "time-space" of the novel, of the characters, the narrator, Vonnegut himself, and the readers, add to the dialogic nature of the text. The chronotopes of the past time experiences of Billy, the protagonist, with his present time, and with his future time, interact with the experiences we know happened to Vonnegut, together with our own reading of World War Two, and the differing time and space chronotopes of the alien "other," the Tralfamadorians. Vonnegut manipulates these to reflect the often disjointed, or "stream of consciousness" element of what it is to experience life as a human being. Time, including memory, interacts in the novels and adds to the complex nature of the world Vonnegut is presenting to the reader. The elements of time and space, past, present, and future are representative of everyday life. Life is complicated and Vonnegut knows it.

Vonnegut's novels explicitly demonstrate many of the fundamental aspects considered by Bakhtin to be present in the novel form. Vonnegut is an experimental author, willing to push the boundaries of popular accepted rules and regulations to accentuate the futility of their existence. He uses his narratives as a

---

37 Mikhail Bakhtin, "Forms of Time and of the Chronotope in the Novel," *The Dialogic Imagination*, p. 252.

site for struggle, to force the reader into a realization that cultural and social rules are not as fixed and definite as they had once been taught.

Having considered the theoretical basis set out by Bakhtin, it is evident that Vonnegut could also be considered as a postmodern writer. Again, it is not the purpose of this text to critique this in-depth but there is value in acknowledging that Vonnegut contributes to the body of "Postmodernism." Characteristics generally associated with this, including fragmentation, time distortion, paradox, and a sense of unanswered questions, can all be found in Vonnegut's work. His experiences during the Second World War certainly left an indelible mark on him, and many fictions written after this time bear the hallmarks of dislocation and duplicity; the world wars adding to a sense of disrupted reality, or a sense of the futility of the human condition. In her book, *The Politics of Postmodernism*, Linda Hutcheon suggests that the initial concern of postmodernism "is to de-naturalize some of the dominant features of our way of life; to point out those entities that we unthinkingly experience as 'natural'... are in fact 'cultural; made by us, not given to us.'"[38] It is in this sense that Vonnegut illuminates the cultural rules of society, his aim to question what we, as humankind on Earth, accept as the natural way of life. He invites us to question our fundamental beliefs, all that we believe unquestionable, and to consider the philosophical elements of life. In this way, Vonnegut's narratives incorporate the interaction of the elements of postmodernist fiction outlined by Brian Edwards as:

> interrogation of totalities, concern with ontological questions, displacement of fixed referents, emphasis upon innovation ... Treating reality, history, identity, culture and reference not as unified discourses but as fields of discursive practices, postmodernist fiction emphasizes particularly the operations of play in language, aesthetics and cultural constructions.[39]

Vonnegut creates grotesque laughter in his writing by his employment of the main carnivalesque inversion characteristics, satire and irony. He aims to show the reader that the environment that they are living in is not as definite as it might appear. Vonnegut exposes the contradictions that we are continually exposed to every day. He highlights that we collectively experience contradictions in our social sphere on a scale that renders us immune to their presence, or we are

---

38 Linda Hutcheon, "Representing the Postmodern," *The Politics of Postmodernism*, Routledge, 1989, London UK, p. 2.

39 Brian Edwards, "The Play in Postmodernism," *Theories of Play and Postmodern Fiction*, Garland Publishing, 1998, New York, p. 86.

overwhelmed by what is needed to change them. We are exposed to and bombarded with ideals of how we should live in every aspect of our lives, many of the cultural ideals promoting the idea that "we" live in the "right" way, even though this is only a perceived ideal that we should be aware of. Vonnegut uses carnivalesque inversion to engage his reader to acknowledge that there are alternative views and perceptions to their own. He pursues those differing perspectives and ideals in his writing to teach us how to recognize the social propaganda we are exposed to in our own society. Vonnegut's use of satire and irony are so important because they are the means by which the carnivalesque inversion takes place, they are the techniques that allow the reader to see beyond dogmatic perception.

Throughout Vonnegut's novels there is consistent use of the idea of the "other" that can create an environment where the reader is able to look in on society. This idea of the "other" takes on different forms depending on the novel that the reader is engaged in. For example, in *Player Piano* the idea of the "other" takes on the form of control through machines. This is the novel that sets out what a technologically advanced world may be like to live in and encourages the reader to be conscious of the direction that advancement of technology might take. Secondly, the idea of the "other" in *Cat's Cradle* is through the creation of a new religion that concentrates on the inevitability and acceptance of humanity being doomed to destroy itself. This novel seeks to investigate the advancement of technology as a way of destroying civilization and analyzes the fundamental basics that society and religion are based on. The third creation of "other," in *Slaughterhouse-Five*, is the idea of an alien encounter as a way of seeing outside of humanity and being able to look in to see the authenticity of human concepts. The idea of space travel and alien/human interaction as a normal experience is a concept that is repeated in later Vonnegut novels. He uses this idea to be able to see the absurdity of society and the restrictions that accepted scientific and sociological identities put on the individual.

Vonnegut's writing engages a satirical intensity in relation to the idea of the "other" because their appearance is unusual to the reader, often feeling strange and out of place. These "others" appear unrealistic and not based on comfortable reality, akin to a science fiction narrative. However, the role and effect of these inconvenient ideas are that they create laughter that can mirror and reflect the inadequacy of our own perceptions. At first, they appear to be ludicrous but closer consideration shows that they are nearer to our own accepted ideals and perceptions than originally realized. They become Vonnegut's prophetic view into a future that could be fulfilled if humanity continues the course, he believed it to be traveling. The Prophet Vonnegut is trying to steer his readers to a better world, where invisible forces that control people for profits and wars no longer repress society. The use of the carnivalesque by Vonnegut seems the natural choice as the technique for inverting how the reader sees themselves interacting within their society, and how he can invert their misconceptions about their own reality. Vonnegut seeks to give the individual back their democratic right and control from governmental and social forms that serve the minority. The carnivalesque allows for a satirical laughter that can parody society and how it conducts itself. A caricature of experience is expressed that contradicts the social ideals that people are nurtured to accept, releasing the ability for freedom of thought.

Another idea that is repeated throughout Vonnegut's writing is the self-conscious experience of the act of reading, and of the act of writing, an ideal example of this is the character of Kilgore Trout. Through the characterization of Trout, Vonnegut can explore both the novel form and the role of a character within that form, and simultaneously allow the reader to become self-aware in the act of reading. The self-awareness of the character acts as a support for the reader, they can reflect on their own awareness of accepted perceptions in relation to the wider issues and themes that Vonnegut draws attention to in his narratives. The reader becomes aware of their act of reading, they read with awareness rather than becoming lost in the passive act of the story world. The reader becomes self-aware of their growing realization of the reality around them, so the novels themselves, as acts of writing, become a carnivalesque inversion. The act of reading is used by Vonnegut to manifest the inversion of the carnival ideal, both the narrative and Trout's character are written fiction, therefore highlighting how we are manipulated in society by fictional ideas and concepts. The novel form is dialogic and multi-layered, and it becomes apparent that: "all these parodies on genres and generic styles ('languages') enter the great and diverse world of verbal forms that ridicule the straightforward, serious word in all its generic guises."[40] Allowing self-aware characters and self-aware readers creates an environment where nothing can be accepted as absolute, the reader must maintain an open-minded and critical awareness where they question everything. Nothing can be considered straightforward.

Vonnegut explores several themes within his novels and short stories, many of which are reoccurring throughout his body of work. The three themes that this text will explore are religion, technology, and war. Vonnegut's novels often feel like metafictional questions that ask what socially thematic concepts are,

---

40   Mikhail Bakhtin, "From the Prehistory of Novelistic Discourse," *The Dialogic Imagination*, p. 52.

how they relate to humanity, and if they contribute to the human experience in a positive way. Vonnegut investigates the human condition to ask the ontological questions: What makes our perceived world the way it is, and what happens to the accepted norms of our reality when they are taken into the sphere of ridiculousness? Vonnegut underscores the belief that the planet we live on is our world, all the ideals and accepted norms that our civilization incorporates are, to human beings, the best idea of reality. Vonnegut strives to take our ideals and perceived social structures and make them useless, or at least to show us their inadequacy. He transfers our idea of "normal" to the future where those accepted norms can no longer function and are rendered void. He exposes the carnivalistic nature of society by a realization that there can be no fixed definitions, that there is no "natural" right way.

Vonnegut begins to expose the "big" ideas as fraudulent. War is exposed as a catastrophic waste of human life that only leads to the ultimate destruction of everything that makes our lives worthwhile. Religion is left with a sense of shame and lies when it allows and condones the futile destruction of human life: "There is no reason good can't triumph over evil, if only angels will get organized along the lines of the mafia."[41] Technology is exposed as dangerous, and in need of restriction and oversight because of the power it can yield for destroying humanity and all life on Earth.

Vonnegut wants his reader to become aware of what and who they are, and in doing this he wants them to create their own awareness of the world around them. Vonnegut writes dialogic narratives that encourage many voices and narratives that work simultaneously. The reader becomes another device in Vonnegut's investigation, and Vonnegut himself brings his own distinct voice to the novels. The authorial voice and the encouragement of the reader's self-awareness means that they become conscious of Vonnegut the writer. It would be difficult to read any novel by Kurt Vonnegut without a sense of how history may have touched the man, just from the thematic ideas presented in the writing. It is another dialogic element or voice that contributes to the novel's heteroglossic nature and that allows the carnivalesque inversion to take place. Vonnegut is looking for an explanation for human history, and for his own personal historical experiences. His novels seek an answer to why the world is as it is, and why it defaults to such self-destructive behavior. Vonnegut's novels become the essence of democracy because they do not prescribe a life view that he thinks people should adopt.

41 Kurt Vonnegut, "There Is No Reason," Illustration, *A Man Without a Country*, p. xii.

Vonnegut offers the skills to pursue enlightenment for the individual, and he wants the reader to decide for themselves what their enlightenment will look like. The reader is left with the sense that there is no definite ideal perception, that humanity might never really understand what reality is, and that we must be open to everyone's view of the ideal and somehow make it work for ALL. Vonnegut asserts in both his fiction and non-fiction that he does not have any of the answers, possibly suggesting that in his opinion there really are none.

Vonnegut's writing spans a lifetime and incorporates a large body of work in terms of both fiction and non-fiction. The reader can observe the Bakhtinian elements within Vonnegut's fictional work from his early short stories at the beginning of the 1950s, his first novel publication, *Player Piano*, in 1952, and throughout his work until his last published novel, *Timequake*, in 1997. This text explores some of Vonnegut's earlier novels in relation to the carnivalesque inversion that is apparent during his professional writing career and shows how characteristic the dialogic nature of his work has been since the beginning. In many ways his later novels become more overtly carnivalesque as he becomes more comfortable with manipulating novel writing forms and structures. Perhaps this element of his work overtime could suggest an increased need for readers to take note of what he is trying to teach them about the world. He becomes more fantastical in order to grab the attention of the reader as he becomes older and wiser, aware that society might still be making the same mistakes it always has, with little optimism for change. With Vonnegut continually embracing the dialogic and heteroglot nature of writing throughout his career, we can see the continued and urgent need for the structures and restrictions of the social/political world still in need of change and evolution. Vonnegut found himself frustrated by a world manipulated by politics, money, media, and the social structures that one could argue have not changed, even after many wars. He worried for the safety of individual humans, as well as humanity as a species. It is impossible to closely analyze every Vonnegut short story and novel over the course of one academic publication, so with this in mind, this text will concentrate on the three main novels already disclosed, and touch on other novels as appropriate. The three novels cover explicitly some of the main themes of Vonnegut's body of work and are excellent examples of how his work follows the pattern of the carnivalesque from the very beginning.

Chapter One concentrates on the novel *Player Piano* and how technology could have a detrimental effect on the progress of human civilization. It will consider how society might allow the accumulation of wealth to become its overriding goal to the extent that it enables the trivialization of human worth. It considers how valuable technology is to the human experience, and what happens to civilization if humans are forced to surrender everything that gives their lives meaning. It contemplates the balance between technological advancement and the well-being of humanity. It also considers *Player Piano* as the first full-length example of Vonnegut's carnivalesque writing style and how this forms the basis for his later novels.

Chapter Two examines the theme of religion in the novel *Cat's Cradle*. It considers how religion is presented in society and how fundamental opinion can become embedded in our social and cultural structures. It addresses the element of Christianity in the text and how the fictitious religion of Bokononism can flourish even though it is blatantly founded on lies. It will further consider the cultural shift in belief from religion to science apparent at the time that Vonnegut was writing, juxtaposing the two ideals and highlighting the destructive forces of absolute belief and fundamental opinion. It also considers how any ideological thinking in society can be considered a type of religion when taken to extremes, and that no "ideal" should be given absolute and unfettered power.

Chapter Three analyses the novel *Slaughterhouse-Five*, looking closely at the representation of war, and its effects on the mental state of those that are forced to encounter it. It will engage with the "ideals" of war presented in society juxtaposed with the experience of physically taking part in war. It considers the detrimental effects of war on human beings and how our society has become more interested in fighting wars than in protecting the lives and futures of human beings. It seeks to highlight the value of a differing opinion, incorporating the importance of alien "other" in the novel as a form of looking at how detached society has become. The chapter discusses how Vonnegut implores his readers to care for the individual human being, and not just allow masses of innocent people to be killed through needless violence.

Vonnegut's novels, short stories, and non-fiction political/social commentary represent a lifetime of working towards a better future for all human beings. Vonnegut's personal aim was to critique and question the American social, political, and religious structures prevalent throughout his life, structures that he felt had moved away from America's founding principles of equality and freedom. Vonnegut believed America has always possessed the possibility to become a blueprint for the rest of the world, a role model for the liberation and equality of all human beings, but he knew that it needs consistent work and attention. His writings were his plea to Americans, and to humanity, to learn from their mistakes, to look back through history, and attend to the future. To Vonnegut there is always a hope that humanity will prevail, that "no matter how ghastly or ludicrous or glorious or whatever,"[42] human behavior

---

42 Kurt Vonnegut, "Introduction," *Palm Sunday: An Autobiographical Collage*, Dial Press, 2011, New York, p. xiii.

could always be innocent. In the politically fluid landscape of modern America, Kurt Vonnegut offers his readers the mirror of cultural self-reflection, and to lay bare the fundamental limits of the American inward-looking mentality. Vonnegut challenges his reader to envisage an America that overcomes adversity and polarized political opinion and to hold human beings at its core. To Vonnegut, human beings are the future of America, and no amount of money will change that fact, it is the only thing we can be sure of.

1

Technology: *Player Piano*

"Today we have contraptions like nuclear submarines armed with Poseidon missiles that have H-bombs in their warheads. And we have contraptions like computers that cheat you out of becoming."[1]

*

Player Piano (1952), the first published novel by Kurt Vonnegut, is a dystopian narrative reflecting the technological and social advancements witnessed in the early twentieth century. It is also the foundational novel that sets a precedence for the carnivalesque style that Vonnegut adopted throughout his work. At the time of its publication, two world wars had passed and Vonnegut himself, having served in the latter, had witnessed some of the most devastating forms of technological development. The *Encyclopedia Britannica* records the monumental changes and advancements in human technology in the decades following 1900 as having: "witnessed more advance over a wide range of activities than the whole of previously recorded history. The airplane, the rocket and interplanetary probes, electronics, atomic power, antibiotics, insecticides, and a host of new

---

1 Kurt Vonnegut, "I Have Been Called a Luddite," *A Man Without a Country*, p. 56.

materials have all been invented."[2] Inventions, it states, have created "possibilities and dangers" which would have been unthinkable to the previous generations. It is the "possibilities and dangers" presented to humanity and society that Vonnegut begins to explore within this novel. His own experiences with technology, together with his educational background in the Sciences, inform his ability to ask the difficult question as to whether technological advancement is always positive for human development.

The novel is set in an imaginative near future, following a third world war, and reads as a parable to those who are willing to listen: "*This book is not a book about what is, but a book about what could be.*"[3] Vonnegut incorporates the techniques of carnivalization to manipulate an everyday sense of belonging and normality, to project a society that appears realistically close to that of a 1950s America, yet an alternate reality that seems "almost" unimaginable. This gives the reader the opportunity to invest in the imagined society as something that is plausible, a society they might imagine their grandchildren being exposed to but allows them time to question and consider the possibilities. They can question if this is a feasible world, and if it is, do they want it to become their reality.

The technological advancements that Vonnegut was exposed to left him with little doubt that technology cannot always be considered progressive; in a letter home after rehabilitation from being a prisoner of war he stated to his family that "Bayonets aren't much good against tanks."[4] He understood what technology meant for war and he understood what technology could mean to society, in his later years stating that Bill Gates might as well be saying "'Hey, don't worry about making your soul grow. I'll sell you a new program and, instead, let your computer grow year after year after year …'"[5] His recognition of the possible implications that broad advancements in technology could bring made him stand sentry on humanity's behalf. His implicit agenda was to raise awareness of the potential threats and to ensure that humanity can make informed decisions. He wanted people to acknowledge that some decisions have the capacity to change not only the course of humanity but the course of the entire planet. He was concerned with what technological changes meant for the individual person, the

2 Robert Angus Buchanan, "History of Technology," *Encyclopedia Britannica*, November 18, 2020, www.britannica.com/technology/history-of-technology, accessed August 28, 2022.

3 Kurt Vonnegut, "Foreword," *Player Piano*, Dial Press, 2006.

4 Kurt Vonnegut & Dan Wakefield, Letter from K. Vonnegut, Jr., 12102964 U.S. Army to Kurt Vonnegut Sr. and Family, May 29, 1945, Le Havre, from "The Forties," *Kurt Vonnegut Letters*, Ed. Dan Wakefield, Delacorte Press, 2012, New York, p. 7.

5 Kurt Vonnegut & Lee Stringer, *Like Shaking Hands with God: A Conversation about Writing*, p. 33.

freedom they might be excluded from, as well as how society might be forced to adapt and change.

Vonnegut witnessed firsthand what destructive forces could be unleashed by technological weaponry during war, and he understood that the human body could not stand up to the power it unleashed both physically and mentally. On returning from active service and adapting to normal life in the following years, his position as an employee at General Electric furthered his interest in the increasing use of technology in society, and the effect it could have on human beings, individually and collectively. He saw the ability to write about what he bore witness to as vitally important, especially since there is the suggestion in his work that many people accept technology without thought or question, or without ever considering the implications for the future. The notion of his novels being science fiction, because they included technology, was a puzzle to him:

> I was working in Schenectady for General Electric, completely surrounded by machines and ideas for machines, so I wrote a novel about people and machines, and machines frequently got the best of it, as machines will … And I learned from the reviewers that I was a science-fiction writer.[6]

Technological machines were an everyday aspect of his life and are the reality of everyday life for many individuals. He believed that he was writing a novel that represented the experience of life as a human being: "I supposed that I was writing a novel about life, about things I could not avoid seeing and hearing … The feeling persists that no one can simultaneously be a respectable writer and understand how a refrigerator works."[7] It seemed incredulous to Vonnegut that although technology is something that people use and incorporate into their lives every day, writers are not allowed to include it, or draw any attention to it, in their writing.

For Vonnegut, writing about a world where technology is ignored is not reflective of a social truth: "novels that leave out technology misrepresent life as badly as Victorians misrepresented life by leaving out sex."[8] It makes no sense to "leave out" an element that has played such an important role in the lives of so many human beings throughout the planet. Technology, from before the stone age and beyond, has always been instrumental in human history, its progression,

---

6 Kurt Vonnegut, "Science Fiction," *Wampeters, Foma & Granfalloons*, Jonathan Cape, 1975, London, p. 29.

7 Kurt Vonnegut, "Science Fiction," *Wampeters, Foma & Granfalloons*, pp. 29–30.

8 Kurt Vonnegut, "Do You Know What a Twerp Is?" *A Man Without a Country*, p. 17.

and the simple day-to-day fight for survival. The historic human experience is to improve our quality of life by scientific advancement, something that continues to this day. To avoid that experience and daily occurrence is to ignore a vast swath of human life. Technology today might look vastly different from our ancestor's technology, but it is an instrumental part of being a human being and the quest for humans to make their lives easier and more efficient. Without the progression of technology our world would look quite different, as a world without sex and reproduction could not sustain itself. At the point in human history that Vonnegut was writing from, and what he had learned from his own experiences, science-based technology was only going to become more and more predominant and integrated into the human experience as time went on. It was not an option to leave out such an important element of human life but an imperative to consider where our progression might take us in the future.

Scientific understanding and advancement, since the beginning of the twentieth century, were accelerating and Vonnegut could see that this was different from the technological advancements that had come before. He recognized the horrifying reality that the technology of the modern world had the capacity to destroy itself, a capacity never reached before. Vonnegut's exploration of what the accelerating scientific technological advancements mean for human society is instrumental in *Player Piano*, as he navigates an understanding of where it could lead us. Do humans and society control technology or does technology begin to control human beings and society? In his biography of Kurt Vonnegut, *And So It Goes: Kurt Vonnegut, A Life*, Charles Shields refers to *Player Piano* as "a contest between society and technology."[9] There is a tension that exists between the two elements, and it is this tension that Vonnegut uses to create the carnivalesque narrative. Bakhtin refers to the structural tensions of society as a "two-world condition"[10]: there is the upper echelon of society, the "serious official,"[11] where the political power is held, and then the lower echelon, on which the higher is formed, the "nonofficial … extrapolitical."[12] These oppositions manifest themselves to create carnival tensions in the narrative. The power in Vonnegut's imagined society is held by the technology and those that control it; power is surrendered to them by the rest of society who are the majority, and they are kept subservient by technology's control.

---

9 Charles J. Shields, "The Dead Engineer, 1951–1958," *And So It Goes: Kurt Vonnegut, A Life*, p. 120.
10 Mikhail Bakhtin, "Introduction," *Rabelais and His World*, p. 6.
11 Mikhail Bakhtin, "Introduction," *Rabelais and His World*, p. 5.
12 Mikhail Bakhtin, "Introduction," *Rabelais and His World*, p. 6.

His carnivalesque interaction is evident throughout the text both as an overt representation of culture and the structure of the society, but also in a more subtle way by interactions and representations of characters, and the interplay of "parade" throughout the narrative. The narrative structure of the novel is also representative of the two-world condition as two cultures are represented against one another, the world of Ilium, or the new technological America, against the pre-mechanized culture of the Kolhouri Sect. The use of chapters represents the cultural divide of understanding as Vonnegut intermittently interchanges the focus from the main protagonist Paul to the Shah of Bratpuhr. The details that Vonnegut incorporates within the two are symptomatic of a carnivalization, the use of opposite spheres of society, on a global scale, being pushed together to interact. The visits and interactions of the Shah often lead to satirical laughter which emphasizes the polarization of the social perspectives and reinforces a heteroglot element to the text. The parade throughout the novel, again becoming a point where all the elements of the text converge, all the characters, including Paul and the Shah, come together in the climax of the carnival parade spectacle.

Vonnegut's choice of title, *Player Piano*, is loaded with connotations representative of the cultural dynamics taking place within the text. The Player Piano[13] is a piano that plays music automatically through the engineering of a mechanical device placed within its body. A special roll inside the mechanism allows music to be changed by means of perforated paper and can play music perfectly. Its popularity was concentrated in the latter half of the nineteenth century and early twentieth century but declined considerably in the 1930s when the popularity of the radio and the phonograph began to replace it. Having understood what the object is and what it achieves, we can see as readers that this mechanical device was meant to be there to make the lives of humans easier and more entertaining. However, in creating such a device the enjoyment of both learning to play the instrument and the achievement of playing is taken away. Why would anyone take the time to learn to play an instrument when they can easily have one played for them with little effort on their part? Technology is controlling what decisions a person might make; there is no need to pursue personal growth when technology provides the prepackaged answer of the piano that plays for you. If we consider the traditional perception of playing an instrument pre-twentieth century, it was predominantly considered a sign of "good birth and good education."[14] In

---

13 The Editors of The Encyclopedia Britannica, The Encyclopedia Britannica Inc., 2021, www.britannica.com/art/player-piano. Accessed August 28 2022.

14 The Victoria & Albert Museum, "The History of Musical Etiquette," 2016, www.vam.ac.uk/content/articles/t/history-of-musical-etiquette. Accessed August 2016.

a sense, the mass production of the instrument followed by its mechanization renders the piano altered and its social function changed to an object of entertainment and social control. Those that control society and technology do not want the masses to be elevated to "good birth and good education," so they have rendered the acquisition of knowledge diluted and changed entertainment into a form of social distraction.

Another example of this might be considered the introduction of the television which can also be seen as an object of entertainment to control the masses: "The institution of television controls us at a distance. It emanates from some place far away, yet it makes its presence constantly felt in our everyday lives."[15] It provides us with the experience of self-improvement or distraction without having to engage with the work involved in educating ourselves. It distracts us from the boredom of realizing we are not achieving our own self-worth with hard work and attainment. Vonnegut said of television "if you die horribly on television, you will not have died in vain. You will have entertained us."[16] Just as Vonnegut viewed the television as a device of mass entertainment, the player piano could also be seen as an object that distracts the lower social orders, keeping them amused and distracted. A mechanical piano emulates human ability, it is a machine designed for the amusement and entertainment of human beings, yet in emulating them it has rendered their ability useless. As the player piano's technology progressed, it began to play more complex pieces, pieces requiring technical skill and interpretation, previously only capable of being played by a human being. Mechanization, followed by technological advancement, allowed it to adapt and get better. One of the only reasons its popularity began to decline was because further technological advancement was made, listening to music became easier and easier through radio and the phonograph. Technological advancement appears to increase entertainment and distraction, yet human attainment seems to be stifled and reduced.

The title of the novel allows Vonnegut to engage the reader to question what is going on in the text and society at large. It is reflective of the overall content, and it throws up several questions that the reader is forced to begin to acknowledge as they navigate the narrative. Is technological advancement always a good thing? Does some technological advancement complement the human experience? What does it say about human beings if they are always trying to make

---

15 Ellen Seiter, Hans Borchers, Gabriele Kreutzner, & Eva-Maria Warth, "Introduction," *Remote Control: Television, Audiences, and Cultural Power*, Routledge, 1989, New York, p. 2.

16 Vonnegut, Kurt, "Cold Turkey," *In These Times*, May 10, 2004, inthesetimes.com/article/cold-turkey, Accessed August 28, 2022.

their lives easier? Are they willing to surrender what makes them intrinsically human, and what happens when they have nothing left of themselves? Already, Vonnegut's interaction with the reader is complex, he is suggesting the reader consider the bigger picture from the outset and to question what they see in front of them.

The deliberate choice of the title emulates the world that the reader encounters in the narrative and is synonymous with the experiences of the main character, Dr. Paul Proteus. The player piano becomes the metaphor reflecting how the imaginary future of the main character functions and how technology distracts from the truth of human society. Proteus begins to recognize that the "utopia" he thought he was living is an illusion, and the technological ideals he was once invested in are disintegrating to reveal an alternate truth he struggles to come to terms with. He begins to question the very idioms his society is founded upon. He begins to question the meaning of life, and what it is to be human. The straightforward and logical society he believed he lived in is revealed to be complicated and devoid of freedom. Nothing is as straightforward as it may first appear, a theme continued in the text when the physical player piano appears in the narrative in Homestead. Vonnegut purposefully places the reader in the same situation presented to the protagonist of the narrative and forces them to consider the repercussions of unchecked technological advancement. They need to engage and experience the feelings that Paul Proteus works through in order to reach the same epiphany.

The third-person narration begins ten years after the last war, the third world war, and is a world divided. It is evident to the reader that this divide, or segregation, is purposeful and denotes a hierarchical structure:

> In the northwest are the managers and engineers and civil servants and a few professional people; in the northeast are the machines; and in the south, across the Iroquois River, is the area known locally as Homestead, where almost all of the people live.[17]

Most individuals in the society live in the area known as Homestead, whose name is suggestive of a place colloquial and rustic. The connotations of the word evoke a sense of the original European settlers coming to the new world, as the imagery associated with the name suggests primitive living and a "back-to-basics" type of existence. In the reality of the narrative, the "Homestead" population

---

17 Kurt Vonnegut, *Player Piano*, p. 1.

does not struggle to make a living and are given everything adequate for life in society, and they supposedly want for nothing:

> the house and contents and car were all paid for by regular deductions from Edgar's ... paycheck, along with premiums on his combination health, life, and old age security insurance, and that the furnishings and equipment were replaced from time to time with newer models as Edgar—or the payroll machines, rather—completed payments on the old ones. 'He had a *complete* security package.' (PP, 165–166)

The problem is not necessarily with how the Homestead population lives, it is the restrictions put on them, the limits to their perceived capabilities, and limits to the decisions they can undertake for their own lives. The individuals of Homestead are beholden to the machines of society, they continually pay for advancements in their lives via decisions made by them. Even though they have an average standard of living, and have no deficits in terms of functioning requirements, they have few choices and have no effect on their life outcomes. They have a complete "security package" but little mental and emotional security, only really existing in society as the consumers of production.

It is evident from the text that the third world war experienced in the narrative was difficult, with so many people being away from home fighting for their country, "managers and engineers learned to get along without their men and women, who went to fight" (PP, 1). Little information is known about the war from the text, only that it had taken place. Not having any capable manpower forced the managers and engineers to come up with innovative ways to keep production moving, it was "the know-how that won the war. Democracy owned its life to know-how" (PP, 1). There is a sense of irony here, the mentioning of democracy on the very first page in relation to saving it, coupled with the mentioning of riots and thousands being "jailed under the antisabotage laws" (PP. 1) when people returned from fighting. The managers and engineers considered themselves the ones who won the war, not the masses who fought in the war. This does not sound very democratic, and it is evident that this society is not as straightforward and happy as it might first appear. If continual production is needed for society to function, and the human beings in the novel have been replaced by machines in order to maintain that continual production, what happens when they return from fighting in the war? What is the long-term outcome for human beings that are being slowly replaced by machinery and technology over time? Machines are a constant, they work efficiently to produce the products they are designed for, making human beings redundant in the process. It is in this way that the managers and engineers, having been left with the responsibility of keeping the "home-front" working and viable, were left to their own devices in the narrative. In doing so, society handed over the responsibility and effective government to those left behind, and a transferal of power happened without the democratic acceptance or acknowledgment of the people. Individuals were ignorant of what they were allowing to happen out of necessity. They were unable to say no, so when they did return and did not like what they were welcomed back to, they had effectively become voiceless. The traditional pre-war structure of society was then seen as inefficient and obsolete, production had been streamlined out of necessity, but in doing so, surplus humanity was left with no jobs or value, "One horsepower equals about twenty-two manpower—*big* manpower" (PP, 52). Democracy had also become obsolete as machines took over the choices for humanity and what was most efficient in terms of production, the masses of society being denied any representation. Vonnegut saw a culture where humans were increasingly being replaced by machinery under the guise of efficiency and profitability from a perceived necessity; he saw a future where humans no longer have a voice in society but are there to become consumers of production only.

The most efficient way for the new society to align itself with the surplus population was to create a system whereby those most valuable to the machines and production were sorted from those who could offer little support and value. In this sense, society is based on contribution to technological advancement, an area seen as naturally suited to the managers and engineers in the narrative. Society was therefore forced to find something to occupy the perceived lower order of society, the people not able to contribute directly to the knowledge needed to progress technological advancement, but here to consume the production. Many jobs formerly filled by people who contributed to the production of products needed by society were now rendered useless, and those roles were filled by machines. Unless something was found for them to do, they were likely to cause trouble and to endeavor to cause harm to the very machines that had rendered their lives meaningless. In the ten years since the war had ended in the novel, "dope addiction, alcoholism, and suicide went up proportionately" (PP. 54) as people were struggling to find value and fulfillment in their lives. People were disaffected and unhappy and Vonnegut suggests that their only form of defense was to try to sabotage the machines working on their behalf. The people were not willing to accept the "new" social structure without a fight: "it's just a hell of a time to be alive … this goddam messy business of people having to get used to new ideas" (PP, 37). Their demonstrations and rallies to show their dissatisfaction had been met with resistance and incarceration. The new system's answer to the problems was computerized assessment and segregation, rendering individual human beings down to a set of numbers.

The introduction of the EPICAC, "an electronic computing machine—[or] a brain" (PP, 116), during the war had helped the managers and engineers to keep production going with the loss of manpower and was credited with helping to win the war. Following the end of the conflict, the machine had been updated, and further updated, making EPICAC I "little more than an appendix or tonsil" (PP, 117), and now "EPICAC XIV could consider simultaneously hundreds or even thousands of sides of a question utterly fairly" (PP, 117). The EPICAC was seen as the holy grail of all machines, and ironically is personified throughout as though "a new, unique individual had been born" (PP, 118). Human capabilities were seen as limited which made the capabilities of the machines more valuable, and although the value of the machine was higher than that of the individual, they were still assigned the characteristics of humanity. The machines lacked all the emotional capabilities and nuances of humankind, they are "wholly free of reason-muddying emotions … never forgot anything … was dead right about everything" (PP, 117). Vonnegut is teasing the reader here, carnivalizing the situation to render it silly and ironic. Here is a machine that is spoken of like an individual yet has none of the characteristics intrinsic to being an individual, it was incapable of being a human being. The fact that it was always right about everything is also ironic as the reader can see from the suggestions in the text that human beings were not all happy in society. Production may have been efficient, but the mental well-being of individuals was at a low. The machine was not right about everything, but perhaps Vonnegut is suggesting here that EPICAC was in fact "dead" because it did not understand humanity or have the capacity to make the best decisions for their future.

The EPICAC machine decided everything for humanity, decided "everything America and her customers could have and how much it would cost" (PP, 118). Importantly, it also decided what "I.Q. and aptitude levels would separate the useful men from the useless ones" (PP, 118) and this was intrinsic to how society functioned. Young people took the "National General Classification Tests" (PP, 30), and depending on their scores they either went to college to learn something useful or they were forced to choose between the "Army or the Reconstruction and Reclamation Corps" (PP, 25). To work with the machines a person had to have a graduate degree, although the openings for college courses were extremely limited, "only twenty-seven openings, and six hundred kids trying for them" (PP, 30). You had to be of a certain intelligence, dictated by the machine, but there were few spaces available. If you graduated from college and worked with the machines, you lived on the north side of the city, where the machines were housed. If you joined the Army or Reconstruction and Reclamation Corps, or the Reeks and Wrecks, as it was nicknamed, you lived on the south side of the city, where most of the people lived. From the indication in the text regarding the social problems of violence toward the machines at the beginning of the novel, the obvious choice was to house the threat, or the people, away from the heart of technology, which was the machines.

The organization of Vonnegut's new America reflects the social conditions described by Bakhtin, and the reader encounters the "two-world condition": the North side of the city representing the "officialdom" and the south representing "a second life outside officialdom."[18] The form of revolution, as parade, that takes place being the natural folk response to the inequality that the society presents, as discussed later in the chapter. Not only is Vonnegut using this careful juxtaposition of the social class divide created by the unchecked power of technology, but he is also examining two social ideologies, Capitalism and Communism. It would be too easy to say that Vonnegut is trying to pitch one system above the other, or that he is offering some sort of alternative; however, he is never this absolute. What Vonnegut has created in the new social sphere has taken the middle road, taken two opposing systems and created a hybrid system, incorporating what could be seen as the positive in both, while indicating to the reader that neither is sufficient. The freedom of the open market on the one hand, with the state controlling the means to live on the other hand, providing a stable socialist system of care for the masses. He seems to be considering the possibility of a happy medium between them both, a system that might look after everyone, but that is still falling short of success. The two opposing ideologies are shown to be from the same scale, they interact with similar communication spheres, both take away freedoms from the individual, and neither make individuals feel fulfilled and valued.

Vonnegut had grown up in comfortable surroundings and realized he was "being raised to become bourgeois"[19] when he had gone to work for his uncle and he had been placed higher than most people on the time clock; as well as earning as much as some of the men working there, he had been "embarrassed,"[20] and felt it was cronyism. His early realization of how the system worked, coupled

---

18 Mikhail Bakhtin, "Introduction," *Rabelais and His World*, p. 6.
19 Charles J. Shields, "You Were an Accident 1922–1940," *And So It Goes: Kurt Vonnegut, A Life*, p. 30.
20 Charles J. Shields, "You Were an Accident 1922–1940," *And So It Goes: Kurt Vonnegut, A Life*, p. 30.

with his experiences during the war, had left him questioning what was going on around him. The growing anti-communist feelings of the late 1940s and 1950s in America would have also been evident to him:

> fears of internal communist subversion reached a nearly hysterical pitch. Government loyalty boards investigated millions of federal employees, asking what books and magazines they read, what unions and civic organizations they belonged to, and whether they went to church … libraries pulled books that were considered too leftist … [including] Thoreau's *Civil Disobedience* …[21]

McCarthyism,[22] and the sense of subversion, was creating an atmosphere of intolerance and unease in America. Voicing any doubts or having beliefs perceived to be against the political system could ruin you. Vonnegut later stated in an interview with NPR that "Karl Marx got a bum rap, all he was trying to do was figure out how to take care of a whole lot of people,"[23] Vonnegut also evokes Thoreau[24] directly in the novel as a signpost for standing up for something better: Finnerty explains that "Thoreau was in jail because he wouldn't pay a tax to support the Mexican War. He didn't believe in the war" (PP, 143). Vonnegut is using the novel to research the problems of the current social idioms and trying to see how both might work, and how society might be able to adapt. The carnivalization comes with the "turnabout"[25] of the then current social structure, highlighting how ridiculous it was becoming. Vonnegut was not presenting a remedy for the situation, just trying to highlight the shortfalls that were being created. There is a sense that the two-world model polarized by Capitalism and Communism was inadequate, and there was a need for something new. In creating a satirical narrative, looking at both ideals through the eyeglass of a new order, or new idea, Vonnegut can render them both in need of revision, for further analysis and thought. Each ideology becomes grotesquely ridiculous and inadequate.

---

21 Wendy Hall, *"Anti-Communism in the 1950s,"* The Gilder Lehrman Institute of American History 2009–2019, ap.gilderlehrman.org/history-by-era/fifties/essays/anti-communism-1950s. Accessed August 28, 2022

22 McCarthyism refers to the anti-communist movement of the Republican U.S. Senator Joseph McCarthy of Wisconsin, dated roughly from 1950–1956—many people were accused of communist sympathies and treated unfairly, often without any evidence (see footnote 21).

23 Kurt Vonnegut, "Kurt Vonnegut Judges Modern Society," *Morning Edition*, NPR, Jan 26, 2006, 1:05 seconds, npr.org/templates/story/story.php?storyId=5165342, Accessed August 28, 2022.

24 Henry David Thoreau (1817–1862)—An American author, poet and philosopher, author of *Civil Disobedience* and *Walden*.

25 Mikhail Bakhtin, "Introduction," *Rabelais and His World*, p. 11.

The nature of the text is already proving to be dialogic in nature: There are many connotations within the text that the reader is pushed to consider and assess. One of the early metaphors for the problems that society is facing, and which acts as a foreshadowing of what is to become in the novel, is the incident with the cat. Paul finds a cat by the golf course and decides to bring him to the plant as a mouse-catcher. The plant, or Ilium Works, is where Paul is manager, and considered the "most important, brilliant person in Ilium" (PP, 1). The previous night a "mouse had gnawed through the insulation on a control wire" (PP, 2) affecting several buildings at the plant, and putting them out of commission. This is ironic by itself, that the all-powerful machines, capable of the quickest and productive procedures, can be thwarted by a tiny mouse. It is as if nature itself is fighting back against technology. Vonnegut's use of the mouse is also reminiscent of John Steinbeck's, *Of Mice and Men*,[26] one of the great American novels to question the very nature of the obtainability of the "American Dream." It represents the freedoms of idyllic life fighting against the restraints of society. In this novel, the character of Lennie, a man with learning disabilities, strokes a mouse because of its softness and accidentally kills it. It is a foreshadowing of the tragic death to come later in the novel when Lennie accidentally kills a woman who is nice to him. Society's reaction against Lennie is brutal with their inability to see the death as anything other than murder, turning on what they do not understand. The technology in the novel is representative of everything that is considered good or progressive for society. Vonnegut uses the mouse as a symbolic means to show the reader how vulnerable their society is. The managers and engineers have put all their faith in society and have therefore made all society susceptible as a consequence. It is tragic to think that society is willing to put its faith and future into something so fragile and clearly so fatally flawed, technology that can be prevented from operation by the tiniest of natural creatures. A collective belief system, maybe even founded on good intentions, can end up in bad ways and denying individual people their humanity.

Taking the cat with him, Paul goes to check on Building 58, whose warning light was flashing back at the office. The old part of Building 58 is Paul's pet project and is there to show the reader that Paul is serious about beginning to question the authority of the new order. The building is the original machine shop set up by Edison in 1886, and he has already persuaded "head office" to keep it as historical value. Paul seems to think of it with increasing romanticism:

---

26 John Steinbeck, *Of Mice and Men*, Penguin, 2002, New York.

he often imagined … that he was Edison, standing on the threshold of a solitary brick building on the banks of the Iroquois, with the upstate winter slashing through the broomcorn outside. The rafters still bore the marks of what Edison had done with the lonely brick barn: bolt holes showed where overhead shafts had once carried power to a forest of belts, and the wood-block floor was black with the oil and scarred by the feet of the crude machines the belts had spun. (PP, 7)

The language used evokes a time, long since passed, where man was working within the natural environment, "the lonely brick barn" on the banks of the river, a pioneering spirit of the industrial age. The language denotes previous hard work with "slashing" and "scarred" wood, as Paul imagines being at the forefront of a time where "strength and important mystery" (PP, 8) fueled the inventive spirit. Edison, most famous for his invention of the lightbulb, was also responsible for the invention of the phonograph, another element of the polyphonic nature of Vonnegut's narrative, interlinking with the title *Player Piano*, which is ironic considering the phonograph was one of the technological advancements contributing to its demise. Vonnegut's dialogical narrative plays with the notion of a nostalgic past and technological present. Just how natural and romantic were the past generations when many of the remembered historical scientific figures were responsible for the beginning of our technological advancements now.

The cat, spooked at the sounds of the machines, jumps from Paul's arms into the aisle, "She faced the oncoming sweeper, her needle-like teeth bared … and the sweeper gobbled her up … into its galvanized tin belly" (PP, 12-13). The cat, processed by the machine, is spat out at the end, just in time for the cat to make a desperate bid for escape by climbing up the fence, only to trip the alarms which electrified the wires—she is killed, "dead and smoking, but outside" (PP, 13). The death of the cat by technology, so early in the novel, is symbolic for what is to come later in the narrative. She is representative of the people in the new American society who are forced into an environment that is alien to them and which denies them their liberty. If Paul had left her by the golf course where he found her, she would still be alive. Taking her and forcing her to accompany him into Building 58 led her to her death. It scared her, her freedom was compromised, and she was forced to face up to the dangers she was confronted with. She fought valiantly, facing up to her attacker. Her death, perhaps inevitable as soon as she was taken into the technological environment, feels as though there was little she could do to escape, only to have to face up to what was before her. Her efforts, although ending in death, did mean that she was "but, outside," suggestive that freedom, even though she was dead, was better than to be captive in a hostile environment. The situation feels like a metaphor, a warning, of what is to come in the novel. Vonnegut is careful to influence the reader, manipulating their sense of horror as they imagine the charred and "smoking" body of the cat. The carnivalizing effect leaves the reader uncomfortable, it is a satirical and dark humor, and they are left with a feeling that one cannot stand up to ideology and win. On the other hand, the cat was supposed to be there to destroy the nature of the mouse, to represent the ideology of society in its fight for its beliefs, but its fight is futile. Freedom cannot be taken forever, and humanity will always fight back for its rights as individuals. Humanity must have freedoms to be fulfilled and happy, it is the nature of humanity that cannot be fought against. It may take time, but restriction and subjugation forces humans into action, as we see later in the narrative.

The character of Paul is representative of a type of antihero: He feels uncomfortable with what he sees going on in society, but he is reluctant to stand up fully for what he believes. In many ways he is selfish, he lacks awareness of his wife's needs, and is not prepared to put himself out to save the dignity of others. He lacks the courage and sense of utilitarian morality to stand up against what is wrong until he is forced to by others, until the decisions are taken away from him. He wants to do something, and even prepares for a new life, but teeters on the edge until his choice is gone. This could be a representation for how Vonnegut sees many people in society: they feel uncomfortable with changes that take place, jobs being lost, people being treated unjustly; they are not happy about it, but maybe they do not do enough to stand up and be counted: "Paul wished he had gone to the front, and heard the senseless tumult and thunder, and seen the wounded and dead" (PP. 7). Individuals wish that they could do more, but they struggle with the courage to demand change. It is often easier to be a safe bystander than to be at the front of the charge for freedom.

At the beginning of the novel, the reader gets a sense that Paul is discontent. He appears to have a deep understanding of history, of the mechanics of the new America, and he seems to have invested in the sense that it was better than what went before. Paul understands business and saw humanity, with all its emotional weaknesses as: "'Expensive' ... 'and about as reliable as a putty ruler ... Hangovers, family squabbles, resentments against the boss, debts, the war—every kind of human trouble was likely to show up in a product one way or another'" (PP, 14). He does not question the reliability of the machines, or the fact they are more economical; after all, using humans instead of machines is "expensive" but there is a sense that he acknowledges that something is missing, the "happiness" (PP, 14). The happiness of having to allow workers Christmas vacation is mentioned by Paul amongst the negative aspects of managing a human workforce. He seems to remember with some nostalgia what it would have been like before, in the old days and he smiles to himself at the thought of what that meant. Although he does not openly state something is missing in the new America, the reader can see that he is beginning to question whether something has been lost in the devaluation of human beings, in the mechanization of the spirit. Vacations and personal time are seen as inefficient and inconvenient, but it gives people time with family and friends, a time to unwind and relax, something that is priceless and cannot be measured by metrics.

This notion is encapsulated in the way Paul sees the technology and mechanisms of the machines around him. He has a romantic view of history, of the feeling and need to be in touch with what has come before. It is as though, in creating a world dominated by the machines, by metal, it has lost some of the warmth and feeling Paul senses is needed, by himself, and by people in general. He views Building 58 as something for him, something he does not want other people to defile, "he discouraged and disliked visitors" (PP, 6). His romanticism and need for human contact allow him to see the machines through a nostalgic eyeglass. Even Vonnegut's description of one of the mechanisms as "A thousand little dancers whirled about one another … pirouetting," (PP, 12) evokes the sense of country dancing around a maypole. Paul is nostalgic for a past time when people had contact with one another, when there was real human contact and enjoyment, for festivals. Again, this sense of a need for contact suggests an element of Bakhtin and represents the carnivalesque nature of the two-world society. The need for festival and release for society to remain functioning. The need for nostalgic human contact seems almost primitive, and feels like it belongs with the lower, less controlled, population of society. However, there is an awareness in Paul that it was a basic human need for everyone, to transcend the two worlds:

> The material bodily principle is contained not in the biological individual, not in the bourgeois ego, but in the people, a people who are continually growing and renewed … Manifestations of this life refer not to the isolated biological individual, not to the private, egotistic 'economic man,' but to the collective ancestral body of all the people.[27]

Paul understands that by creating a world where people are replaced by machinery, that a human necessity for contact, for a deeper spiritual yearning, is lost. He

---

27 Mikhail Bakhtin, "Introduction," *Rabelais and His World*, p. 19.

does not seem to be aware what this meaning is, but he is beginning to look for something else, an ancestral contact, a connection to history and what has come before him. He appears so desperate for this contact that even the exaggerated language of the grotesque forms of the machine with its "crazy spinning movement" and "black snake of cable" (PP, 12) can be interpreted as the "pirouetting" dancers. He feels so connected to Edison, and the early inventors, because he feels those are his ancestral connections, he belongs to and affiliates with those men of science who were on the precipice of a new world, a new order of things.

Even the discussion regarding the industrial revolutions that has led society to the point that Paul inhabits, all appear to be pointing in one direction, to "devaluate human thinking" (PP, 15). The narrative states that the first revolution experienced in the society devalued "muscle work" (PP, 15), the second, the revolution leading to the automation of society, devalued "routine work" (PP, 15) or the work of industry and productions, and the third, as Paul predicts, will be that of "the real brainwork" (PP, 15). He states, "I guess the third one's been going on for some time, if you mean thinking machines" (PP, 15). Paul is fully aware of what is taking place, he realizes the route that mankind is taking, but life carries on, it continues the current course. He has a "gulp of whisky" (PP, 15) when he is back in his office alone because he knows that the future does not look good for humanity, and it is overwhelming. As the devaluation of humanity continues, no one, even the managers and engineers, will be safe, and machines will be able to think for themselves.

The obsession that Paul has with the past, and the nostalgia that it holds for him, does not stop at Building 58. He begins to spend more and more time thinking about what it would be like to live a simple existence, something more honest. He needs more contact with something he perceives as "real," and less sterile like the machines. His realization that something integral is being lost in the machine world, that he needs something more, leads him to visit Homestead in secret. The first of these visits in the novel is when Paul takes a trip, in his old Plymouth, to fetch a bottle of Irish Whisky. The old car represents Paul's own history: "he had had the car at the time of the riots" (PP, 23) and the "patina of rust" (PP, 23) it had accumulated over the years added to its appeal as a "harmless antique" (PP, 23). Although Paul tries to tell himself it is "harmless" it is really a testament to his resistance against the machine of society. The car contains many items that Paul has collected and preserved inside over the years, a part of living history or mobile museum. One of these items is a pistol and "having a pistol where some unauthorized person might get it was very much against the law" (PP, 23). The car acts as a satirical device: It is ridiculous to think that Paul, living with the social status and luxury that he does, sneaks out in a car that is rusty with its "headlamp's busted" (PP, 24) in order to collect alcohol, or to see "one of the few persons he had ever felt close to" (PP, 24). He is consistently after a personal connection, and after meaning in his automated life.

The saloon, or bar, that Paul visits when in Homestead is another important representation of human contact and nostalgia. It is typical of a different time that Paul longs for, and he wants to be able to go to a bar, blend in and be unrecognized. It is a place representative of relaxation, vocal opinions, and comradery, a place where you might be able to be yourself. He even muses to himself about an automated bar that he and his friends, Finnerty and Shepherd, came up with in their younger years. They had even been able to set one up as an experiment:

> With coin machines and endless belts doing the serving, with germicidal lamp cleaning the air, with uniform, healthful light, with continuous soft music from a tape recorder, with seats scientifically designed by an anthropologist to give the average man the absolute maximum in comfort (PP, 26).

The bar experiment represents everything that Paul longs for now, a place where machines are there to give human beings the optimum comfort, and where machines are not used against them to make them devoid of contact and value. The machines are there to enhance human life, not detract from human experience. The memory of working with his friends closely is what connects him to the memory, it is the meaningful human contact that he really longs for. He needs to be released from the control of machinery, even if it is for a short time.

The bar episode is another satirical element used by Vonnegut as the information is shared with the reader that this seemingly perfect scenario for a bar completely failed. The human contact and interaction were missing again, automation had failed to reproduce the human element. People preferred the traditional "dust-and-germ trap of a Victorian bar" where there was "bad light," "poor ventilation," and "inefficient," "unsanitary" (PP, 26) conditions. The experiment, scientific in nature, looked after the needs of the human body, but not the soul and mind, the need for human contact and interaction, the need to express individuality. The fact that it was an "anthropologist" that designed the experiment is also significant as this is someone who is meant to understand humans and society across history. The experiment is functional and designed to meet the needs of the human body only, it does not appear to support emotional needs. This is another pointer to the lack of understanding of the human psyche that the new America exhibits, even an educated social anthropologist gets it wrong. Even

Paul, with his reminiscences of the bar experiment, does not fully understand that it is the human contact of his friends that he misses, he is still looking for the machines to enhance human life and has not fully realized that they might need to be turned off to gain what he really desires.

The impact of the influence that Homestead has on Paul, coupled with his increasing disillusion with his mechanical situation, leaves him with the overwhelming need to do something tangible. He feels that he has little control of what is going on, that he himself is expected to act like a machine, to continue forward, to fulfill the expectations required of him because of his birthright. His father, Dr. George Proteus, was the first "National Industrial, Commercial, Communications, Foodstuffs, and Resources Director" (PP, 2), a position that only the President of the United States had power over. The language associated with the system's persuasive nature over Paul and their encouragement for him to follow his father's footsteps always seems to suggest an intoxicating power over him that he finds almost impossible to resist. It makes him feel small, as though he has no choice but to comply; he often felt "dwarfed" (PP, 130), or "resentfully" (PP, 130) unable to disagree. He often feels so intimidated by the establishment that he does not value his own opinion and he uses his wife's thoughts as his own, as protection.

The feelings of expectation and inadequacy lead Paul to act on the need for something tangible. This takes on the form of buying a farmhouse, "just outside the city limits" (PP, 148), the Gottwald House. The real estate manager tries to dissuade Paul from buying the home as he feels it completely unbefitting for someone of Dr. Paul Proteus's station in life, to be buying and living in a house that has no modern mechanization and luxury: "'If you try to force me to sell it, I'll quit'" (PP, 151). The house is completely untouched by modernization and mechanization, even the grandfather clock has "'wooden works'" (PP, 152), and this is appealing to Paul. He sees the house as having a homely and human touch, "'the house breathes *with* you, like good underwear'" (PP, 150) and it "seemed to have twisted and stretched on its foundations until it had found a position of comfort for all of its parts—like a sleeping dog" (PP, 153). The personification of the house is important, it feels as though it can move and adjust itself to you, like an old friend. It is ironic that Paul says he wishes not to be "disturbed by any human beings" (PP, 153) because it is the need for the human touch that he is desperately seeking. He is looking for the "other," something primal that draws him to a homeliness and nostalgia of the house, as if he is looking for a family connection and a shared past.

Haycock, one of the original people to have occupied the house, having lived in it from birth, also represents the nostalgic past that Paul desires. Vonnegut again uses the satirical element to highlight some of the absurdity of the situation. Haycock hates the thought of Paul owning the house: he hates everything that Paul stands for, he is unchanged by the events of the past ten years and is only concerned with remaining at the house until his death. He sees Paul as a fraud, as to him there are only "Three kinds of doctors: dentists, vets, and physicians" (PP, 154), if you are not one of those "'Then you ain't a doctor'" (PP, 154). He lives in a bygone era, his own reality and the reality of the house, a microcosm of what used to be. He puts no value in the new system and talks of his own work on the farm as "out in the barn shoveling *my* thesis" (PP, 155); he is not interested in the pretensions of the current society. Paul sees Haycock as a complication, he was not expecting to have to deal with such an antiquated and difficult man. This could be a suggestion to the reader that Paul is in love with the idea of the past, the romantic notions of living closer to nature, of greater human contact, but is Paul ready for this, does he really understand the current relationships he has, or is he simply running away from the expectations that are put on him by his father's success? He appears to be confused as he interacts with the duality of the social sphere. He is coming to terms with the carnival mask, taking on and enacting the "other," and being attracted to the different life he is performing as a new fixed reality for himself. He wants his carnival costume to remain permanent, yet he does not understand what this really means yet, for him and society.

The name chosen by Vonnegut as Paul's surname, Proteus, brings another dimension to the text and adds to the dialogic nature of the narrative. Proteus is the name of a Greek god who is considered the first-born son of Poseidon, the god of rivers and oceans. Paul is the first son of a very influential and successful man, who could also be considered within his domain as a god. Being the son of a god puts pressure and expectations on him. Paul is representative of a protean sense of change in the novel, he is malleable and at times inconsistent in his attempt to follow his emotions rather than what is expected of him: "Paul realized that his judgement had been pushed into the background by more emotional matters" (PP, 80). Several chapters later he is asserting that "his dissatisfaction with his life was specific" (PP, 134), he is constantly changing the extremes of his viewpoints, and the reader can see his thoughts being influenced by the characters interacting with him, whether that is Anita, Kroner, or later Lasher. The inclusion of Greek mythology is not isolated to Paul and influences some of the other characters important to Vonnegut's development of Paul as a character. This is also important to the sense of the keynote play at the Meadows, discussed later.

The inclusion of Greek mythology is important to the dialogic nature of the text, for what Bakhtin calls the "stylistic uniqueness of the novel"[28] that allows complex and often hidden meanings to be incorporated into the text, to build a realistic interpretation of a cultural theoretical background. The narrative of the new America that Vonnegut has chosen is a parody of our own perceived reality and incorporated into this are the nuances open to the western culture we already have. Bakhtin explains this as:

> the combination of these subordinated, yet still relatively autonomous, unities … into the higher unity of the work as a whole: the style of a novel is to be found in the combination of its styles; the language of a novel is the system of its 'languages.'[29]

Vonnegut incorporates many seemingly autonomous elements into his narrative, he chooses the names of characters and includes elements that appear to build a complex narrative world, full of connotations. A believable society, one which could be plausible if we do not take heed, must be built on a range of cultural signifiers. Paul, although a seemingly straightforward character, has cultural and historical significance associated with him. Human beings are never straightforward, and Vonnegut appears careful to consider this element in the novel. The interchanging of Paul's perceptions in relation to those of the characters around him shows how complex and complicated people can be. It is also important to the historical element in the text, and the yearning that Paul has for a different era, and what he perceives as a less complicated time, where people could live more simple lives. History is incredibly complex, and we often read it in our own context. Paul believes living in a non-mechanical world would be easier, that it would create more human contact, but in reality, he is looking at history as a romantic notion, just as the naturalists during Victorian times would have done: "it offers an almost photographic representation of life and stresses how heredity and environment shape people's lives."[30] The Victorians understood the increasing complexity of a society changing with industrialization, of mechanization, and the responsibilities this placed on humanity. Vonnegut is not offering an alternative to our world, he is not saying that mechanization is wrong, he is simply asking humans to question everything that is placed in front of them as

---

28 Mikhail Bakhtin, "Discourse in the Novel," *The Dialogic Imagination*, p. 262.
29 Mikhail Bakhtin, "Discourse in the Novel," *The Dialogic Imagination*, p. 262.
30 John Peck & Martin Coyle Eds., *How to Study Literature: Literary Terms and Criticism*, New Edition, The Macmillan Press, 1993, London, p. 91.

advancement, an element that Paul must consider as the narrative progresses. What are the consequences of unchecked technological advancements on society?

The dialogic nature of the text is developed even further with the introduction of the "Shah of Bratpuhr, spiritual leader of 6,000,000 members of the Kolhouri sect" (PP, 19). Vonnegut intersperses the novel with the Shah's diplomatic visit to the United States of America to understand how the new American system works. America sees it as an important social imperative to spread the effectiveness of the automation of production, to help develop the undeveloped global world around them. As the Communist Manifesto asserts regarding Capitalism: "by the rapid improvement of all instruments of production … draws all nations, even the most barbarian into civilization."[31] The new America welcomes the diplomatic visit because they see themselves as the model for the rest of the world, they want the Kolhouri Sect to become mechanized in line with their own image. This adds another aspect to the elements that are already resident within the text, and one which Vonnegut uses in order to create a juxtaposition in the narrative. The north side and south side of the river represent a dual-world perspective in Paul's America, but there is also the duality of the new America and the Kolhouri Sect. Both these polarizations act in similar ways within the narrative, as a carnival interaction that highlights the contradictions and inadequacies the new society has built into its foundation.

Building on the ideas presented in the dialogic text, Bakhtin discusses the use of the Chronotope in the *Dialogic Imagination* and it highlights a medium through which Vonnegut's use of time can be assessed: "the spatial and tempo-ral [converges] … classes, estates, religions, nationalities, ages—intersect at one spatial and temporal point."[32] Vonnegut is able to utilize the sense of time within *Player Piano* much more subtly than he does in his later novels like *Slaughterhouse-Five*. The reader is exposed to the "everyday time,"[33] that is, the relative time that Paul resides in, a time in the future that we are not fully aware of. Of course, the novel having been first published over 50 years ago also influences its time space, as we read it from an alternative future from that of the "new" America, the America that Vonnegut himself resided in. We, the reader of "today," get to question what is going on in the novel and can cross-reference with what we know has happened with technology post-World War Two to current times.

---

31 Karl Marx & Frederick Engels, *The Communist Manifesto*, International Publishers, 2016, New York, p. 13.
32 Mikhail Bakhtin, "Forms of Time and Chronotope in the Novel," *The Dialogic Imagination*, p. 243.
33 Mikhail Bakhtin, "Forms of Time and Chronotope in the Novel," *The Dialogic Imagination*, p. 111.

However, although it is important to mention and acknowledge this aspect, it is also important to ascertain that it is not our goal to explore how far Vonnegut was right or wrong in his novel. He is rather warning humanity and keeping them alert to the idea that blindly accepting every technological advancement, without careful and considerate thought, can be particularly damaging to humanity. He saw the advancements and terrible catastrophic death of thousands of innocent civilians as a wake-up call to civilization, an alarm that society must be cautious.

Along with the everyday time, the reader is exposed to the historical inversions, described by Bakhtin as having distinctive features, and this notion within the text incorporates any historical time that comes before the third world war. It is used by Vonnegut to compare, or suggest, a previous historical time of nostalgia, generally by the character of Paul as he tries to negotiate his feelings of discontentment with the current system of the new America. Bakhtin explains the feature as:

> the essence of this inversion is found in the fact that mythological and artistic thinking locates such categories as purpose, ideal, justice, perfection, the harmonious condition of man and society and the like in the past. Myths about paradise, a Golden Age, a heroic age, an ancient truth, as well as the later concepts of a 'state of nature,' of natural, innate rights and so on[34]

The time introduced by the Shah is Folklore time and it is connected to the idea of historical inversion. This is used by Vonnegut as a juxtaposition to the new America, as a counteraction to the advanced technological environment the main characters are living in. There needs to be an alternative that is allowed to question the authority of the new system and can question it with its own authority. The Shah represents the Bakhtinian idea of "Folkloric man,"[35] who does not just represent the folk people, but who "is the great folk." This character must be the "very antithesis of 'a little tsar ruling a great Folk': folkloric man *is* the great folk, great in his own right."[36] In this sense, Vonnegut uses the character of the Shah, sporadically placing chapters dedicated to his visit, to undermine the serious nature of the system Paul is trying to negotiate. The Shah can see through the superficial nature of what he is presented with and is able to highlight the inadequacies of what he sees. It is apparent that Vonnegut is incorporating many elements in the novel to create a text that is complex and reflective of the human

---

34 Mikhail Bakhtin, "Forms of Time and Chronotope in the Novel," *The Dialogic Imagination*, p. 147.
35 Mikhail Bakhtin, "Forms of Time and Chronotope in the Novel," *The Dialogic Imagination*, p. 150.
36 Mikhail Bakhtin, "Forms of Time and Chronotope in the Novel," *The Dialogic Imagination*, p. 150.

condition. The dialogic nature of the text is multifaceted and forces the reader to look further into the narrative to continually question what is happening. The reader is forced to be non-passive and to take an active part in the novel, exactly what Vonnegut appears to be asking of us all, as human beings, to do in society. We must not sit back and passively watch as others in society make all the decisions.

The Shah's ability to speak directly of what he sees is partly due to his lack of English skills, and partly due to his interpreter, his nephew Khashdrahr Miasma, who acts as a go-between, often altering what the Shah says to a more polite version for his American chaperones. Just as Bakhtin sets out, the Shah is "a *realistic fantastic*: in no way does it exceed the limits of the real, here-and-now material world."[37] He is a plausible character who is representative of a more "primitive" people, of a folk class. He emphasizes the heteroglossic nature of the text that, to Bakhtin, is present in all situations, by changing the words that the Americans use to describe elements of their society, often with a much more illuminating and honest effect. For example, when Dr. Ewing J. Halyard, the United States Department of State's official responsible for his tour, explains to the Shah how the Homestead population are "'Citizens, employed by government'" (PP, 20), and having the "same rights as other citizens—free speech, freedom of worship, the right to vote" (PP, 20), the Shah knowingly continues to call them "'*Takaru*'" (PP, 22) translated as Slave. As Halyard continues to explain the way the social structure functions, he explains that in some cases, such as New York, it has proved harder to implement due to the number of skills "difficult or uneconomical to mechanize" (PP, 21) and that higher percentages of people "hadn't [been] liberated … from production" (PP, 21). The Shah responds to the explanation of the Army and Reconstruction and Reclamation Corps as "'*Kuppo!*'" (PP, 21), or Communism. He understands the nature of the social structure that is before him, and although the American government has rebranded social characteristics with a different language, the Shah is forced by his own use of language to break down these barriers to a more simplistic version, and one which sheds light on what is really taking place. This use of heteroglossia by Vonnegut is important as it sheds light not only on what is going on in the everyday time of the text but also on the system that he is trying to reflect. Often something is rebranded to sound better, or to look like something else, less harmful. Vonnegut implores us to look past this, to seek out and question what is in front of us, and call it for what it is,

---

37 Mikhail Bakhtin, "Forms of Time and Chronotope in the Novel," *The Dialogic Imagination*, p. 150.

no matter what the repercussions may be. This also relates to what happens with the keynote play at the Meadows, the Engineers and Managers team building, further on in the text, as discussed later.

When the Shah is introduced to the EPICAC XIV machine it is explained to him that the EPICAC series of machines provided "informed guidance that the reasonable, truth-loving, brilliant, and highly trained core of American genius" (PP, 117) could have provided, if only "they had inspired leadership, boundless resources, and two thousand years" (PP, 117). The "President [of the United States] Jonathan Lynn, born Alfred Planck" (PP, 118) joins them, and Halyard clearly detests the man, preferring to call him just "Planck" and thinking that he had known "smarter Irish setters" (PP, 119). The term "Planck" is another satirical interjection by Vonnegut to render the system laughable, a man born with a silly name, clearly not as smart as he could be, considering the technologically advanced motivations of the society they live in, is the superficial leader of the country. Even the Shah's nephew is surprised to learn that he governs without any connection to their "spiritual destinies?" (PP, 119) Halyard thinks to himself:

> The more Halyard thought about Lynn's fat pay check, the madder he got, because all the gorgeous dummy had to do was read whatever was handed to him on state occasions: be suitably awed and reverent, as he said, for all the ordinary people, stupid people who'd elected him to office … [he] imagined with horror what the country must have been like when, as today, any damn fool little American boy might grow up to be President, but when the President had had to actually run the country! (PP, 120)

Vonnegut makes light of what the President's role is in the new America: it is a superficial role, being at the helm as a front person, effectively a mannequin to look good on state occasions. He suggests that the role of the President in the America at the time of writing the novel is just as scary, possibly suggesting that Presidents are often under-qualified to lead and make decisions, that "stupid people" vote for the wrong reasons, voting in the wrong type of person.

The president declares EPICAC XIV the "greatest individual in history, that the wisest man that ever lived was to EPICAC XIV as a worm was to the wisest man" (PP. 120). The Shah considers the size of the machine, not realizing that the President is using the expression as a metaphor, not as a size comparison. The Shah requests to ask a question, he approaches the machine, and "dropped to his knees" (PP, 121). He speaks to the machine but the "word[s] echoed and died– lonely, lost" (PP, 121). He states "'*Nibo*' 'nothing'" (PP, 122). The men watching the episode are confused, and they all think he has gone mad as he is speaking directly to a machine. Khashdrahr explains that in their culture they believe that one day "a great, all-wise god" (PP, 122) will come to them to answer a specific riddle. The Shah asked the riddle to the machine, but it was unable to answer. The Shah is emotionally exhausted by the turn of events and states the word "*Baku!*" (PP, 123); his nephew explains that he is using the word to describe the machine as a "false god" (PP, 123). The whole narrative episode is used by Vonnegut to highlight the absurdity of how the machine EPICAC XIV is treated. It is treated as an individual, as a human being, who is considered the greatest individual of all time. It is personified to the extreme and is given the status of a god by the important people in society. It is completely absurd that those around the machine seem to worship it as a god, stating that it is essentially all-knowing. The Shah, already proven to be able to see through the smokescreens that society has manufactured, is taken aback by the way they describe and treat the machine. He tests the statements that are made by the parameters within his own environment and culture, and he finds that they are false. The machine is unable to answer a question put to it by another human being, it is unable to think and communicate as a human, it needs to be "given the facts by human beings" (PP, 117).

Having understood more of the different aspects of the new American society, the Shah asks, "if he might see the home of a typical *Takaru*" (PP, 161), now "freely translated, from one culture to another, as '"average man"'" (PP, 161). The average man is described as "statistically average in every respect" (PP, 161) he is so average that the machines can predict the kind of life that he will have, including any arrests and sexual experiences, and that he will die at the age of "76.2 of a heart attack" (PP, 161). The example of an average man in the narrative, known as Edgar R. B. Hagstrohm, is in the middle of a life crisis and is unprepared to have any guests. His wife has found out about his extramarital affair, the second one predicted by the machines. Unfortunately, he is not given any choice about the visit, he is a "slave" to society. This episode gives the reader a deeper insight into the workings of the Homestead lifestyle, and it is here that their ordered life in terms of the "*complete* security package" (PP, 166) is made evident. Halyard explains the workings of the system and determines that Edgar's "standard of living is constantly rising" (PP, 166). He considers the bad old days where people used to be able to spend their earnings on "impulse" (PP, 166) and "illogically" (PP, 166), and tells the story of someone he once knew: "we had a crazy neighbor who blew all his money on an electric organ, while he still had an old-fashioned icebox and kerosene stove in his kitchen!" (PP, 166). The Homesteaders get $30 in wages a week to spend on whatever they like: "his take-home pay—cigarette money, recreation money, small luxury money the machines let him have" (PP, 166) means they have little, or no, autonomy. The little amount that Edgar had was going to be spent on his mistress, his only form of resistance against the structure that controls every aspect of his life, his only freedom of choice. Edgar sympathizes with the man in the story who buys himself the electric organ: "Expensive, impractical, strictly personal—above and beyond the goddamned package" (PP, 166), he envies his freedom to do as he pleases. The language used by Vonnegut suggests that the lives of the "nonofficial ... extrapolitical'[38] members of society are disenfranchised, disaffected, and unhappy.

The Shah believes the Homestead society represents the communist ideology, they have little autonomy and are not allowed to make decisions for themselves. The state holds all the power, and all the money in their lives is controlled. The segregation of the city represents the two ideological systems. The north side of the river is representative of a Capitalist world, where only the chosen few are wealthy and powerful. Their world is based on efficiency, where value is placed on productivity and consumerism and their innate ability to regulate the rest of society. In *The Theory of Capitalist Regulation: The US Experience* (2015), Michel Aglietta states:

> They [theorists] compare existing economic systems according to these norms of absolute efficiency and conclude that capitalism is both the least bad alternative and the only system amenable to advance towards an optimal configuration.[39]

The system developed on the north side is always working toward an "optimal configuration" and cares little for the welfare of the human mind. Productivity is centered only on what is efficient and considers the emotional needs of human beings as no more than economic intrusions. The few people in this world who can continually accumulate money have choices of housing and the autonomy of choice. These are the elite, the leaders of society, and they have all the freedoms that are withheld from the rest of the system. The south side of the river, representative of the communist system, where the majority of folk live, is the controlled zone. These people are seen to be surplus to requirements. Their world is tightly controlled for convenience and efficiency. Their choices are limited, with many, if not all, of their life choices being made by the state. Their houses, and domestic items, are all brought through the pay system and are chosen by the machines.

---

38 Mikhail Bakhtin, "Introduction," *Rabelais and His World*, p. 6.
39 Michel Aglietta, "Introduction: The Need for a Theory of Capitalist Regulation," *The Theory of Capitalist Regulation: The US Experience*, Verso, 2015, New York, p. 10.

They have little choice, little autonomy, and the reader is left with the sense that these people's lives are similar, almost identical to one another. Their physical needs are seen by the system to be met and exceeded, and their need for any mental or emotional well-being is not considered. The use of the Shah as a device in the text enables Vonnegut to illuminate these two sides of the social organization. The reader already has doubts as to the true efficiency of the structure through the character of Paul who appears emotionally unhappy. The Shah, through the heteroglot nature of the text, allows language to play an important role in revealing the underlying issues facing the social structure:

> The author exaggerates, now strongly, now weakly, one or another aspect of the 'common language,' sometimes abruptly exposing its inadequacy to its object and sometimes, on the contrary, becoming one with it, maintaining an almost imperceptible distance, sometimes even directly forcing it to reverberate with his own 'truth.'[40]

The nature of translation and language allows the social ideals incorporated by the new America to be apparent. The reader can recognize how limited the complete organization is, and how the need for economic efficiency has become a restraint on society, rendering many in its care to be unhappy and disillusioned. The power, given to the chosen few by the machines, was forcibly taken from the majority and they have become disconnected. The efficiency of automation has forced all people, both north and south, into having to behave like a machine: "Paul unlocked the box containing the tape recording that controlled them all" (PP, 10).

The character of Finnerty is also important to the representation of society. If the character of Edgar R. B. Hagstrohm is the example of the "average man," and the representative of the disillusionment of the Homestead, then Finnerty could be considered the character representative of the "brilliant man," representative of the disillusionment of the north side of the river.

> 'Finnerty, Edward Francis Finnerty, Ph.D., one-time EC-002.'
> 'There's a collector's item—a double-o-two number!' said Lasher. 'I've known several single-o men, but never a double-o. I guess you're the highest classification I ever had friendly words with. If the pope set up shop in this country, he'd be only one notch up' (PP, 90)

---

40   Mikhail Bakhtin, "Discourse in the Novel," *The Dialogic Imagination*, p. 302.

Finnerty is the character with the highest classification in the novel and has the ability to see through the illusions of the society he has been forced to live within. When the reader is introduced to Finnerty, early in the novel, he is the "mutant, born of poor and stupid parents" (PP, 35) and he confesses to Paul that "he'd never felt he belonged anywhere" (PP, 35). Just as the Shah interjects a sense of questioning into the narrative using translation, Vonnegut uses the character of Finnerty to interject a sense of intellectual wisdom into the text. He is the intellectually superior character able to question the system around him, and the character willing to do something about it. He understands the limitations of mechanization, the machines cannot exist without the continual compliance and maintenance of humans: "'If Checker Charley was out to make chumps out of men, he could damn well fix his own connections…'" (PP, 60).

The effect that Finnerty has on Paul is interesting. Paul looks up to him, admiring his ability to question authority and act on it, something that Paul struggles with. In a way, Paul often comes across as jealous of Finnerty, as he can do the things Paul secretly wishes he could do but is unable to bring himself to do: "there was enchantment in what Finnerty had done, a thing almost as inconceivable and beautifully simple as suicide: he'd quit" (PP, 62). Finnerty is the character able to take on the player piano and redefine it as a human instrument. Paul, when he first goes into the bar, is only able to put "his back was against an old player piano" (PP, 25), but Finnerty is the one willing to try and control it: "Finnerty sat at the player piano, savagely improvising in the brassy, dissonant antique" (PP, 105). Just as the title *Player Piano* is used by Vonnegut to suggest the control that automation of technology has on humanity, a physical player piano, placed in the saloon bar in Homestead, gives the characters the chance to question and take back control. Finnerty can take out his frustrations on the social system by physically playing the machine, it becomes a metaphor for the new America and the willingness to fight against it. The bartender later describes Finnerty as "The piano player" (PP, 270), he is the character willing to take on society and the system, to literally play the piano and challenge its mechanization. The sense of carnivalization becomes the absurdity of the significance that the instrument has. The player piano is always situated in Homestead and is the symbol of resistance, it becomes representative of the struggle against technology.

The character of Shepherd is the opposite of Finnerty. He is the character willing to play the system and enthusiastically engages in all that it has to offer. Shepherd is ruthless and is willing to take any opportunity to get one over on Paul; he is a continual presence within the narrative, not only because he was an old college buddy of Finnerty and Paul, but because he continues to manipulate, or woo, Paul's wife Anita behind the scenes. He sees Paul as an opponent and wants to win everything that he has for himself. Shepherd is comparable to Paul's father, a person that Paul struggles to live up to, and whose legacy he feels pressured by: "'when you see him [Shepherd] at just the right angle, he's the spitting image of your father'" (PP, 64). This is a foreshadowing of what is to happen in the future of the narrative, as Shepherd works on taking over Paul's positions in society. Paul's dead father is surrounded by a sense of "mythology" (PP, 63), his importance, in many people's eyes, is similar to that of God, with a "great omnipresent and omniscient spook" (PP, 63). Shepherd understands the system and wants everything it has to offer, just as Paul's father had when he was alive.

Women are especially important in the novel to reflect the patriarchal nature of the system. Paul's secretary, Doctor Katherine Finch (PP, 106), is as qualified as he is, yet she is only his secretary. She has clearly passed the testing and attended college which is shown by her title. No women hold any important roles in the new society, only the "Grand Old Men—the district managers, the regional managers, the associate vice-presidents and assistant vice-presidents, and vice-presidents" (PP, 189). Although Paul trusts Katherine, saying "'I expected Katherine to watch over things for me...'" (PP, 107) there is a feeling in society that this is not acceptable, women are not seen as trustworthy or reliable: "'You know what Kroner would think of *that*...'" (PP, 107), Paul is told. Bud Calhoun, having made himself redundant by inventing a machine to do his job more efficiently, even believes Katherine's job can be completed by a machine and upsets her by pointing it out forcibly: "He pointed to Katherine. 'This is ridiculous! If policy is iron-clad [the policy of who is allowed into the works and who is not], why not let a machine make the decisions? Policy isn't thinkin' it's a reflex'" (PP, 77). She is visibly shaken and "she was crying" (PP, 78) at the thought of her job becoming redundant, but Paul "slipped into his office" (PP, 78) not wanting to deal with female emotions. There is no standing up for the rights of Katherine at any point in the narrative: She is not seen as important enough, she is another commodity of the social hierarchy, and her emotional reactions are seen as a weakness.

Paul's relationship with Anita is also a classic example to show how women are seen and treated in the social structure. Paul is machine-like, and he treats Anita as something he must endure: "she was what fate had given him to love, and he did his best to love her" (PP, 136). He treats Anita with complete indifference, he tells her to "'Beat it'" (PP, 49), and sees her as little more than a reflection of himself: "her strength and poise were no more than a mirror image of his own importance, and image of power and self-satisfaction the manager of the Ilium

Works could have; if he wanted it" (PP, 33). Robert Tally states "Proteus is, in fact, living a machine-life … in a manner much more machine-like than that of his wife"[41] and this is true. Anita is far from machine-like; she is looking for a closeness that Paul is incapable of giving her. Even though Paul believes Anita acts like a machine because she "had the mechanics of marriage down pat" (PP, 17) and is "disturbingly rational" and "systematic," she only behaves like this because she is reflecting the way she is treated. Ironically, she is indeed a reflection of Paul, but unfortunately for him, not in the way that he believes she is. When he tells her to "beat it" she stays "clenching and unclenching her hands" (PP, 49), she is incredibly aware of how she is being treated, and it is making her unhappy.

Anita gives Paul every opportunity to understand her and the situation, often mentioning Shepherd throughout the novel because of his attention towards her. Paul is indifferent because she holds no value to him. Shepherd on the other hand is interested in what Anita has to say, and values her opinion, "he hasn't got a wife to help him plan, so he came over this afternoon to get my help" (PP, 158). Even when Anita is caught having met Shepherd, and wearing his team shirt, Paul only thinks of working the situation to his own advantage, not concerned for what is happening: "this semblance of wrongdoing could now be turned to advantage" (PP, 249). Anita is "sick of being treated like a machine!" (PP, 249) and asserts that Finnerty was right: "'All you need is something stainless steel, shaped like a woman…'" (PP, 249). The kiss she gives him is to show him what he is losing, it is "stunning" (PP, 251) because he is losing something amazing, it is an attempt to wake him up, and turn on his emotions. Anita is not stupid enough to go with Paul, she knows things will not change and she has her own mind; she likes the comforts that the north side of the city can give her, and she does not want to return to Homestead, telling Paul "'I'm not as dumb as you think'" (PP, 251). Robert Tally suggests that: "Anita, not Paul, was correct in thinking that Paul's plan for a world apart from the machines was like another machine for him, where he hopes to engineer his own mechanical utopia."[42] This could be considered accurate, Paul wants to have a new life in Homestead but still does not fully understand the implications of what this means, and he may not even understand this fully until the close of the novel. He hankers for a pastime of technology, where men made experiments with their hands and behaved like

---

41 Robert Tally, "Misanthropic Humanism," *Kurt Vonnegut and The American Novel: A Postmodern Iconography,* Bloomsbury Publishing, 2013, New York, p. 28.

42 Robert Tally, "Misanthropic Humanism," *Kurt Vonnegut and The American Novel: A Postmodern Iconography,* p. 28.

Edison. Much of his nostalgia is for the scientific mechanical past, not the real primitive past where there are no machines. It is Anita who has the emotional depth to understand this, and to really understand how both Paul and society function in general.

Vonnegut is careful to point out, by means of satire, women's overall importance in the social structure, and he also parodies what he encountered in his own society at that time. He makes light of their situation, often referring to women by their bodily features: "like a television queen with a forty-inch bust" (PP, 39), "'Big tits will get you in anywhere'" (PP, 94), or "bosoms like balloon spinnakers" (PP, 258). The descriptions are funny but carry a serious tone, drawing attention to the derogatory treatment of women. Women are often seen as the homemakers and child givers, and he even describes one woman on the television as "a large earth mother of a woman" (PP, 26), although she is interesting enough to watch occasionally but not to listen to, "her voice shut off by the volume knob" (PP, 26). Women are seen but offer no important options to society. This is further compounded by the segregation that the women encounter, the wives being deposited together while the men get on with the real work: "Mom was Kroner's wife, whom he always brought to social functions, deposited with other wives, and ignored until the affectionate moment when it was time to retrieve her and cart her hundred and eighty pounds home" (PP, 45). Kroner's wife does not even get the dignity of a name in this passage, she is only seen through the function she performs in society, as a Mom-type character, or an "ideal" wife. She is literally deposited like an object and picked up again when it is time to go. This segregation is repeated throughout the novel, it is never questioned and always accepted as the norm. Later in the novel, when Paul and Anita visit Kroner and his wife, Paul is "counting away the seconds before it would be polite to separate the men and women" (PP, 125), and again at the arrival at the Meadows team-building weekend, "'Ladies over here!' ... 'Men will assemble over on the dock'" (PP, 186-187). In *The Second Sex* (1949), Simone de Beauvoir explains the relationship between men and women as:

> History has shown that men have always held all the concrete powers; from patriarchy's earliest times they have deemed it useful to keep women in a state of dependence; their codes were all set up against her; she was thus concretely established as the Other. This condition served males' economic interests; but it also suited their ontological and moral ambitions.[43]

---

43 Simone de Beauvoir, "Chapter One: Myths," *The Second Sex*, Trans. Constance Borde and Sheila Malovany-Chevallier, Vintage, 2011, New York, p. 159.

Vonnegut uses "other" as a carnivalization to highlight the segregation that is being imposed by the new social structure: "this double aspect of the world and of human life existed even at the earliest stages."[44] It is an element that is repeated throughout, the sense of the two-world society separating the powerful from the weaker "other" of society. Vonnegut uses satirical laughter to bring attention to the segregation that takes place on many different levels, the north from the south, the social ideologies, the men from the females, the young and the old, and so on.

Anita struggles to fit into the traditional idea of "woman" in the narrative: She is a strong woman with strong opinions, and "had made the mistake of saying she was interested in guns" (PP, 125) but "Kroner had politely told her that his weren't the kind women liked" (PP, 125). She also knows her own opinions: "Anita was the only one whose contempt for those in Homestead was laced with active hatred" (PP, 174). She fully understands the system, seeing that "'If someone has brains' … 'he can still get to the top. That's the American way'" (PP, 184). Of course, this is the "American way" for males in the narrative and women must be happy to support them in getting to the top. She is prepared to work hard to get what she wants, and she is happy to push her husband forward by giving him the constructive support he needs to get a promotion. This sense of a woman being power hungry is the opposite view of women that Kroner's "ideal" wife, Janice, exemplifies: "[she] smiled sweetly from the living room. She was a fat repository of truisms, adages, and homilies" (PP, 124), the typical mother figure full of wisdom who wanted everyone to "confide in her" (PP, 124). This could be Vonnegut pointing out that unless you are prepared to fulfill your roles in society, things will be made difficult for you. Paul doesn't value Anita, yet she is not prepared to sit back and accept her fate. If Paul is not prepared to get what she wants, she will be forced to get it herself. She will not accompany Paul into his new life because she knows you cannot rally against the machine and expect to survive. She would rather work within the confines of society to fulfill her goals, following him would mean she had an even lesser position in the social structure.

In juxtaposition to the role of women in society are the "great men" who are at the top of their game, the top of the social structure within the city, and the area division they serve. They are representative of the patriarchal structure constructed by the automation of the industry, as a progression from the pre-World War Three values prevalent in our own society on which the narrative is based

---

44 Mikhail Bakhtin, "Introduction," *Rabelais and His World,*. 6.

on. Kroner and Baer are the men next in the hierarchy, above Paul, the men Paul answers to: "Baer embodied ... knowledge and technique of industry; Kroner personified the faith, the near-holiness, the spirit of the complicated venture" (PP, 44). They complement and work so well together that they are "approximately [a] whole man" (PP, 44). They are essentially the "corporate personality" (PP, 63) and are reflective of what is considered successful within the system. For example, the Kroner home is the "ideal" industrialist's home, a physical manifestation of power and success, only accessible by those who are effectively playing, and winning, the game of the industry. It is a reflection of what an industrialist's home may have been like in the late nineteenth century, an "anachronism" (PP, 124) that people paid little attention to but represents a significant statement about perceptions in the narrative, and within the system of the new America. The Kroner house was a "Victorian mansion, perfectly restored and maintained down to the filigree along the eaves, and the iron spikes along the roof peak" (PP, 123), it is the "archprophet of efficiency" (PP, 123). It represents the extraordinary accomplishments of the early American industrialists like John D. Rockefeller, Cornelius Vanderbilt, and Andrew Carnegie, men who people like Kroner wish to associate themselves with. He prefers this type of home to the "wipe-clean-with-a-damp-cloth" (PP, 124) home because it connects him to success on a massive scale. The great American industrialists are the type of man the automated system wishes its leaders to emulate. They want to reproduce and exceed the industrial success previous generations enjoyed, to become the innovators of the mechanization of industry.

Dr. Francis Eldgrin Gelhorne, the National Industrial, Commercial, Communications, Foodstuffs, and Resource Director, is the "Old Man" (PP, 190) character of the narrative. He is at the top of society and therefore seen as the most successful and wise. He is seen to say, "so many memorable things, it was hard for a person to stow them all away in his treasure house of souvenirs" (PP, 193). It is ironic that Gelhorne, being seen as "the last of a race" (PP, 227) by Paul, has "no college degree of any kind, other than bouquets of honorary doctorates" (PP, 227). He is at the top of the social structure, yet he did not get there by the same means as anyone else. Vonnegut is making the system appear farcical: Every other person is classified by his intelligence, while this man's "classification card would have come flying out of the card files like an old Wheaties box top" (PP, 227), and the irony of the situation is not lost on Paul. Even Gelhorne's advice to Paul represents the hypocrisy in the situation:

'Nobody's so damn well educated that you can't learn ninety per cent of what he knows in six weeks. The other ten percent is decoration.' ...

'Show me a specialist, and I'll show you a man who's so scared he's dug a hole for himself to hide in.' ...

'Almost nobody's competent, Paul. It's enough to make you cry to see how bad most people are at their jobs. If you can do a half-assed job at anything, you're a one-eyed man in a kingdom of the blind.' ...

'All right. I got rich, and I told you ninety per cent of what I know about it. The rest is decoration. All right?' (PP, 229)

The satirical nature of the inclusion of the advice to Paul, from Gelhorne, is important to the overall structure of the narrative. The foundations of the society, and the ideology that it promotes, are based on principles from a previous generation. Gelhorne represents the old industrialists of the nineteenth century who made their millions with hard work and persistence. The system is changing and Gelhorne is one of the last of his kind; he does see through the hypocrisy of the system, but he worked hard to get where he is and is happy to play the role of the wise "Old Man." In revealing this information, Vonnegut allows the reader to see even further into the satirical and hypocritical nature of the new American ideology, and this is made even more prominent as the reader encounters the events at the Meadows, the annual team-building event.

The carnival aspect of the narrative is brought to the forefront by the yearly visit to the Meadows. The carnival atmosphere of feasting and games is overt in this sequence in the novel, and Vonnegut uses it to satirize the opulence and extremes in juxtaposition to the situation in Homestead:

> The Meadows was a flat, grassy island in the St. Lawrence, in Chippewa Bay, where the most important men, and the most promising men ('Those whose development within the organization is not yet complete,' said the *Handbook*) in the Eastern and Middle-Western Divisions spent a week each summer in an orgy of morale building—through team athletics, group sings, bonfires and skyrockets, bawdy entertainment, free whisky and cigars; and through plays... (PP, 39)

The Meadows is a satirical device to render the new system even more ridiculous than the reader has already been introduced to. In the traditional sense of the carnival, the lower echelons of society would be able to partake in the event, it being an outlet for them to expel their grievances against society, and for them to become important for a day. The class structures are broken down in the carnival to give people an escape from their lives, whether this was as a member of the ruling class, or as a peasant. The event is reminiscent of the carnivalesque assertions regarding banquet imagery made by Bakhtin:

In the oldest system of images food was related to work. It concluded work and struggle and was their crown of glory. Work triumphed over food. Human labor's encounter with the world and the struggle against it ended in food, in the swallowing of that which had been wrested from the world. As the last victorious stage of work, the image of food often symbolized the entire labor process.[45]

However, at the Meadows, it is an event only for the elite in society, where the culmination of work is seen predominantly for the important people. This is the very reason for the unease building within the society; Bakhtin's "two-world" dynamics have been destroyed leaving the people without a release from their everyday lives. The Homestead people have had all their importance stripped away, even the traditional workings of society have been taken from them: They no longer fulfill the lower jobs in the social structure as these are controlled by the machines. Their meaning is void to such an extent that the elite no longer feel it necessary to allow them time to engage in the carnival atmosphere. The lower class in the south no longer have an official outlet for their frustrations, they do not have anything to look forward to. The Meadows becomes grotesque because it is a closed event that does not incorporate the entirety of the population, only the powerful have meaning in the society of automated industry. The people will be eventually forced to create their own carnival to restore the equilibrium in the social order.

The keynote play at the opening of the Meadows is another satirical device that Vonnegut employs to highlight the hypocrisy that is taking place in society. The play evokes the movements of *"Labor Unionism* … Rugged Individualism, Socialism, free Enterprise, Communism, Fascism' and—" (PP, 212) as once bright stars that have fallen down and have failed. The New American star, the *"image of the Oak, the symbol of the organization"* (PP, 212), is also about to fail, but a young engineer shouts at the old man, the caretaker of the heavens, to leave the star: "There's never been a more brilliant, beautiful star!" (PP, 213). A radical argues that "There's never been a bloodier, blacker one!" (PP, 212). What follows is a mock trial by The Court of Celestial Relations, where The Star of Organization is put under a formal examination for the direct damage it had done to human beings living under its light. A witness, John Averageman, representative of "a million witnesses" (PP, 213) is called to the stand to testify. The prosecution asserts that the standard of living in America has fallen by "eighty per cent" (PP, 214) and that the average man has been forgotten, the "average

---

45 Mikhail Bakhtin, *Rabelais and His World*, p. 281.

man is just nothing any more" (PP, 215). The defense rises to the occasion by pointing out that people have become richer than "the wildest dreams of Caesar or Napoleon or Henry VIII! Or *any* emperor in history!" (PP, 216).

Vonnegut is using this small propaganda play to show how the elite are retained by the indoctrination system. This play is designed for managers and engineers, not the people of Homestead, and is used as a tool of counter-information. Any doubts that might arise in the elite of society can be easily put to rest with this play. It uses the average man's experience in the system and manipulates this experience by the clever use of language. Any manager doubting what is going on in society could easily think of themselves as doing the utilitarian good for the masses. The play is careful to use historical and mythological references to "back up" the claims it is making, the Ancient Greek symbolism adding legitimacy and historical authenticity. The play also suggests that there is still discontentment in the general population, and the reader must remember that the general population is most of the society. The small group of men attending the Meadows are the direct beneficiaries of the system, not the general population as the play is trying to insist. The average man is being forgotten because he does not hold any value to the new automated system, he is surplus to requirements. His need for money, for meaning, has been taken away by the few who hold the power. This play is representative of another aspect of the carnivalesque, where the need for the festival and emotional outlet is denied. It is the top of society, in the case of the Meadows, that can partake in the carnival atmosphere, they are allowing themselves to be reassured and given the opportunity of release. The two-world condition has become disproportionately weighted, with the tiny minority of the social sphere allowed to have everything, and there is, therefore, no way for the lower sphere to find meaning. There is a need for the two sides to interact and engage with one another on an equal level, even though this is temporary and artificial, and if this is denied, the lower sphere is left frustrated and angry. There is a clever juxtaposition in the narrative, "of a continual shifting from top to bottom, from front to rear,"[46] described by Bakhtin. The text appears almost anti-carnival in this respect, but it is required as an element for the carnivalesque aspect in the novel to work. The carnival is the equalizing element in society, it is what keeps the continual shifting from going too far or becoming permanent. The universe appears cyclical as these elements are repeated, as evidenced by the failure of the many fallen stars evoked in the play. There is a need

---

46 Mikhail Bakhtin, "Introduction," *Rabelais and His World*, p. 11.

for the exaggeration of one side to force the continual motion required for the carnival aspect of society. Further examples of this are the American Revolution (1765–1783), or the French Revolution (1789–1799), where one side takes back the power exploited by the opposite.

The mutilation of the oak tree, the physical representation of the Spirit of the Meadows, and the symbol for Organization, is symptomatic of the failures that the system is encountering and refusing to acknowledge. It is also a reflection of how Paul is feeling at the time of his exit from the Meadows: "Doctor Paul Proteus was saying goodbye forever to home" (PP, 237). He recognizes that even though he is not happy within the system, it is hard to let go because it has been his entire life: "no man could live without roots" (PP, 237). The system's need to control and defend what it has built has forced Paul's hand into submission. He is chosen at the Council House to take on the responsibility of pretending to leave, to become a traitor, a "saboteur" (PP, 233), a dirty word for those rallying against the system and threatening to take down the machines. He is to infiltrate the "Ghost Shirt Society," (PP, 230) the presumed resistance against the social order. It is hard to tell, as a reader, whether Gelhorne and the others have manipulated the situation by preempting Paul's resignation. Have they done this on purpose to save face and halt any impact that a senior manager quitting from the organization might cause, or do they genuinely believe in the performance that Paul has been trying to improvise, his continued investment in the system? Judging from the heteroglossic nature of the narrative by means of suggested interpretations, Vonnegut is suggesting that the system cannot be trusted, that it is a carefully controlled and oiled machine ready to outwit even the most intelligent of society. It is a clever and simple maneuver that renders Paul's gesture of quitting useless, he can only repeat the words to himself when everyone leaves: "'I quit, I quit, I quit,' he said. 'Do you hear me? I quit!'" (PP, 231). There is an awareness in the novel that you are always being watched by the system and that nothing passes by them. Kroner always implies that he knows everything, and this feeling is supported by the continual presence of the loudspeaker at the Meadows constantly telling people what to do, or what they should be thinking: "'No rough-housing indoors!' said the loudspeaker sharply. "'You know the rules. No roughhousing indoors. Save your ginger for the playing field. After registration, report to your tents, get to know your buddies, and be back for lunch in fifteen minutes'" (PP, 190). The north side of the river is therefore not as free as the text suggests at the beginning of the novel, but highly controlled and rule-driven, just as Homestead is strictly ordered.

The use of mirrors at the Meadows event is also interesting in the narrative. They represent another form of mind control, manipulation and propaganda. The mirrors can be found all over the event: "He faced his own image in a mirror framed by fluorescent lamps. Over the mirror was the legend, **THE BEST MAN IN THE WORLD FOR THE BEST JOB IN THE WORLD**. The island was covered with such booby traps"[47] (PP, 221). The managers and engineers must believe that they are the best at what they do, they must invest themselves in the system for the system to remain in control. The manipulation, or even brainwashing, of the managers and engineers at the Meadows calls into question the sense of camaraderie and friendship within the novel. Paul does not seem to have any real friends that he can confide in as the system has been constructed to promote competition and treacherous behavior. Shepherd is a fine example of this, he is supposedly one of Paul's old college friends, "When Paul, Finnerty, and Shepherd had graduated from college … they had felt sheepish about not going to fight" (PP, 6). There is a suggestion that Paul was closer to Shepherd in the old days, enough to know his feelings about personal matters. The narrative implies that the system works against this, that friendships are more about a necessity of business rather than about having real friends. Uniquely, the character of Ed Harrison, who Paul happens to sit beside on the first day, is the only person who is prepared to stick with Paul:

> Harrison had apparently taken a liking to Paul, and now, with no personal reasons for turning against Paul, he was sticking with him as a friend. This was integrity, all right, and a rare variety, because it often amounted, as it might amount now, to career suicide. (PP, 236)

Harrison is willing to stick by Paul even though he had only just met him at the beginning of the event, suggesting that not everyone has been manipulated by the system and that some human characteristics could not be changed. He is referred to as having "integrity," a characteristic the new American system did not promote in terms of friendships.

The better virtues of humanity are reflected in the inclusion of the natural world, first by Thoreau, who embodies the connotations of the natural lifestyle of Walden, but also by the inclusion of elements of the Indigenous American Tradition. Vonnegut is careful to include the tradition as a satirical device to highlight the deficiencies of the current system. In the instance of the mystical

---

47 Emphasis in original text.

spirit of the Meadows Island, an actor is hired to play the role of an indigenous American person:

> 'My people were brave people,' said the Indian. 'My people were proud and honest people. My people worked hard, played hard, fought hard, until it was time to go to the Happy Hunting Ground' …
>
> 'Now our braves are gone, our strong young men—gone from this island, which belonged to my people, lo, these many moons ago' … 'Now other young men come. But the spirit of my people lives on, the Spirit of the Meadows. It is everywhere: in the wind through the pines, in the lapping of the great blue water, in the whir of an eagle wing, in the growl of summer thunder…' (PP, 222)

The assumption is that because the "Indian" is clearly an actor, the history is obviously fake and put on to inspire a magical atmosphere at the Meadows events: the "same actor had been hired for years … he had become such a regular at the Meadows" (PP, 222). The men are taken aback to find that there really may have been indigenous Americans on the island: "'so there really *were* Indians on this Island'" (PP, 224) is Harrison's response to an old arrowhead being found. Berringer replies "'You deaf, dumb, and blind? Whaddya think they have been trying to tell you for the past half-hour?'" (PP, 224). The strict world of automation does not seem compatible with the naturally harmonious and spiritual world of the indigenous American traditions. It seems ridiculous that the leaders of the New America would try to evoke this sense of ancestral connection considering that their whole ethos is to make human beings more and more redundant. They are taking humanity further away from a "natural" life and replacing it with automation, and there seems little room for working with nature. The two are contradictions and reflect the further complicated nature of how the elite see themselves and how they see the rest of humanity. They require a spiritual connection that they are denying to everyone else. It is also a spiritual connection that does not belong to them and is an appropriation of indigenous culture. The men at the Meadows all appear to have stronger cultural connections to European colonialism than a native ancestry. They are evoking an indigenous culture to create a mythical and ancient connection that they want their managers and engineers to have with their own society. The hiring of a fake actor to play the role shows how manipulated the spiritual connection really is, and how manufactured and mechanical the leaders of the society see the emotional and spiritual health of humanity. Their only interest in the mental and emotional well-being of individuals is in connection with their efficiency and reliability.

The motif of the "Indian" is further evoked later in the novel when Paul is being encouraged to join The Ghost Shirt Society, this time as a form of resistance to the government:

'The Ghost Dance ...'

'The white man had broken promise after promise to the Indians, killed off most of the game, taken most of the Indians' land, and handed the Indians bad beatings every time they'd offered any resistance ...'

'With the game and land and ability to defend themselves gone ... the Indians found out that all the things they used to take pride in doing, all the things that had made them feel important, all the things that used to gain them prestige, all the ways in which they used to justify their existence—they found that all those things were going or gone ...' (PP, 288)

The Indigenous American condition since the Europeans landed on the continent could be considered one of indignity. Their treatment is reflected in the way Vonnegut presents most of the society in the novel, those now living in Homestead. Those living south of the river are kept away from the elite of society, their freedoms and land taken from them, and they are only allowed to live in designated areas away from eyesight, just as indigenous people had been treated and moved to reservations. There is a sense of a missing duty of care that is evident in the novel, that those with the social power do not seem to show care and empathy for the lives of others, of those they consider less fortunate or less powerful them themselves. The people living in the south, the bulk of society, have nothing that gives them worth or makes them feel fulfilled, just as the indigenous Americans lost "all the things they used to take pride in doing." Lasher and Finnerty evoke this history because they are trying to convince Paul of the incredible injustices being done to the people. The metaphor used is a powerful one, and one of significance, as an entire group of people were considered problematic to a new system and treated accordingly.

Vonnegut uses this history because he wants the reader to be aware that they need to approach what they are being told with care. There is a carnivalization at play here, and he is challenging our perspectives to see the flaws in both the north and south sides of the river; they both use the Indigenous American narrative to promote their own ends. The heteroglot nature of the text allows language to be manipulated in different ways. Vonnegut is only interested in the human element, not the furthering of any movement or structure interested in the control of freedoms. This idea is reflected in one of Vonnegut's graduation speeches where he discusses the Ghost Dance and what their leadership has in common with the cubist movement, and how the organizational model was also effective for Adolf Hitler. Effectively, Vonnegut describes the elements required to create a large group in society that can control and dominate the public in an almost mesmerizing way. The elements included "A Charismatic, gifted leader who described cultural changes which should be made," "respected citizens who testified that this leader was not a lunatic …," and a spokesperson who was able to convince the public why the leader "was so wonderful."[48] People must be very careful about the information they are given and be aware of the ideas and ideals that are fed to them, often repetitively, by those that have vested interests. The system of the Automation of Industry and the Ghost Shirt Society both have their own agendas, both self-serving in their own ways. The information they portray is presented in such a way as to support their agendas, and it might not necessarily be the whole picture. In many ways the perceptions of people are controlled and manipulated by the outcome needed to be achieved. Vonnegut states further on the graduation speech, "let's stop giving corporations and newfangled contraptions what they need, and get back to giving human beings what we need."[49] The information assimilated by people is often agenda-led, if we are to progress as a cultural society, we need to look at what is best for humanity, not engage with what is best for the corporate bottom line.

The Ghost Shirt Society is the culmination of what has been taking place throughout the text from early in the novel. The element of the carnival has been an ever-present, yet subtle, intervention that has been running throughout the narrative: "from the direction of Edison Park, came faint band music" (PP, 84). The reader is aware that there is something taking place although the narrative does not explicitly reference what it is. At first, the parade is a suggestion of music in the background, of "where everyone might be" (PP, 84), and there is no real explanation of what might be going on, just that there are many people involved. The mention of Edison Park is also important in the text, the suggestion that the music could be linked to the idea of electricity and technology by the evocation of "Edison." Perhaps a suggestion of the energy that is growing in society, that people are converging, and something is building or coming to ahead. Also, perhaps

48 Kurt Vonnegut, "What the Ghost Dance of the Native Americans and the French Painters Who Led the Cubist Movement Have in Common," *If This Isn't Nice, What Is? The Graduation Speeches*, Kindle Edition, Ed. Dan Wakefield, Seven Stories Press, 2014, New York, p. 92.

49 Kurt Vonnegut, "What the Ghost Dance of the Native Americans and the French Painters Who Led the Cubist Movement Have in Common," *If This Isn't Nice, What Is? Advice for the Young: The Graduation Speeches*, p. 95.

an allusion to the feelings that Paul has in relation to the nostalgic past, when life and experience were organic and not dictated by machines.

As the narrative progresses, the interruption of music and the idea of the parade grows: "The parade turned a corner, the whistle blew again, and the music stopped. Down the street, another whistle shrilled, and the whole business began again as a company of kilted bagpipers swung into view" (PP, 87). This is suggestive of the disenchantment with the current "technological" establishment gradually building among the citizens. This acts as a presentation of Paul's own feelings towards society, and his increasing feelings of dissatisfaction with his life. This is reflective of Paul's mental and emotional state, the text becoming a kind of stream of consciousness, the element of parade translating to a climactic carnival state. The carnival is represented by the element of costume and parade, the nature of The Ghost Shirt Society as a catalyst, ending with the revolution of the carnival atmosphere, the turnabout taking place in society. The resistance wants to take full advantage of the disillusionment facing the technological culture and have orchestrated a situation to compound Paul's disenfranchised state. His feelings have been growing through the text and through manipulation, and it has reached a point where any choices he may have had have been taken away from him. This is another ironic point in the text, he is another cog in another machine, "there was no middle ground for him" (PP, 306), and there is a sense that just like Gelhorne may have been taking advantage of a situation by turning it into something positive for the "system," the same could be happening with Finnerty and Lasher, having influenced Paul's personal disillusionment with the system for their own ends: "Paul coughed politely. 'Uh, you want me to sign it [the bureaucrat warning letter]?' Von Neuwmann looked surprised. 'Heavens, they were signed and mailed out hours ago, while you were asleep'" (PP, 303). He has little control over what is taking place, he has not even agreed to take part in the society when the letter addressing the officials of the government structure, proposing changes to society, is signed and distributed on his behalf. He was asleep. Already satirical, it is enhanced even further when Paul thanks the professor for doing this on his behalf when he had absolutely nothing to do with it. He has little choice but to go along with the illusion that he is the leader of the resistance, "HISTORY, PERSONIFIED AT this point in the life of Doctor Paul Proteus" (PP, 292),[50] Paul literally becomes history, he is representative of the coming revolution.

---

50 Emphasis in original text.

The character of Reverend James J. Lasher, the chaplain from the Reconstruction and Reclamation Corps (PP, 89), introduced to Paul at the Homestead saloon, is one of the main characters in charge of the revolution. He sees society as:

'For generations they've been built up to worship competition and the market, productivity and economic usefulness, and the envy of their fellow men—and boom! it's all yanked out from under them. They can't participate, can't be useful anymore. Their whole culture's been shot to hell. My glass is empty.' (PP, 90-91)

It is these beliefs in the worship of false gods that drives him to become a part of the revolution. He tells Paul that when you watch an ad about the new American system, "you'd think the managers and engineers had given America everything: forests, rivers, minerals, mountains, oil—the works" (PP, 91). The people have had all their importance taken away from them, spiritual and self, and they no longer have anything to believe in, what they have left "isn't enough" (PP, 91). The Ghost Shirt Society calls for the everyday people to invert the social structures to take back their cultural power, "'The main business of humanity is to do a good job of being human beings'" (PP, 315). This takes the form of the carnival atmosphere because Vonnegut uses the elements of parade and costume for the revolution to take place. They contact "every big social organization" (PP, 298) to tell them "country men are marching through the streets" (PP, 298) to disable the machines and take back society. The reality of this, and the culmination of the sense of parade and costume continued throughout the text, is the carnival and holiday atmosphere: "Men in every conceivable type of uniform wandered about the fortifications in a holiday spirit" (PP, 324).

In the essence of the carnivalesque, Vonnegut has been able to enact a Bakhtinian exchange in the text to turnabout the balance of power. It is ironic that this has been able to happen, as Dr. Halyard, the representative of the American government, has discounted any interpretation that anything damaging to the system could possibly ever happen, even while it is happening, "'Just some people having a little fun dressing up' ... 'All make-believe.'" (PP, 321). It appears just like a carnival; people are dressed up and they have painted faces in bright colors, yet this is something that may remain permanent since the balance in society has already been disrupted by the managers and engineers having no respect for the everyday person. The carnival people of Homestead represent the lower classes, the disenfranchised which have no real standing in society. Here they are dressed up and practicing the elements of the carnivalesque, their facial paint representing masks to give them the authority of equality. Vonnegut takes this a step further by having them seize the power and to bring down the machinery that is binding them to the lives they have been forced to lead. Even after the revolution has taken place Vonnegut describes the scene as though it were the night after a great party: "Bodies lay everywhere, in grotesque attitudes of violent death, but manifesting the miracle of life in a snore, a mutter, the flight of a bubble from the lips" (PP, 335).

Vonnegut is creating a "turnabout" to emphasize the way in which machines have started to take over humanity's ability to function independently. Workers are only ever employed by the government when a man "cannot support himself by doing a job better than a machine" (PP, 20). Machinery has taken over humanity and in the "turnabout" humanity fights back to destroy their own creations. The function of the carnival atmosphere is the only element able to allow this to happen, it empowers the people, creating a sense of equality and confidence, giving the people the strength needed to succeed. In her foreword to *Rabelais and His World*, Krystyna Pomorska states:

> One of the essential aspects of this relation [man's relation to man] is the 'unmasking' and disclosing of the unvarnished truth under the veil of false claims and arbitrary ranks. Now, the role of dialogue—both historically and functionally, in language as a system as well as in the novel structure—is exactly the same.[51]

Vonnegut uses the carnivalesque aspect of costume and parade in the text to create an "unmasking" of the false inequalities. The value placed on education, and the titled positions it has created, therefore become redundant and arbitrary, allowing the characters release from that system. The text is dialogic, and richly complex, to incorporate a complete turnabout of all social structure, highlighting Vonnegut's need for the reader to consider polarizing aspects in society. He does not offer an alternative, simply a rendering of what is already there as transparent. The aspect of the parade represents the converging elements in the dialogic narrative, the point where Paul, the Shah with his folk response, and all the juxtaposing elements in the text meet to form the revolution. The revolution is the bustling carnival, allowing the tensions and frustrations to be worked out and pacified. Just as the death of the cat at the beginning of the novel represents the reality of the social structure, the revolution feels doomed to failure, the folk element in society cannot win. The carnival forms the release of tensions, not the remedy.

---

51 Krystyna Pomorska, "Foreword," *Rabelais and His World*, p. x.

Vonnegut, concentrating on the satirical nature of the revolution, has "the people" clambering for a drink from the drinks machine in the aftermath of the violence:

> Paul and Finnerty left the car to examine the mystery, and saw that at the center of attention was an Orange-O machine. Orange-O, Paul recalled, was something of a *cause célèbre*, for no one in the whole country, apparently, could stomach the stuff—no one save Doctor Francis Eldgrin Gelbourne ...
> But now the excretor of the blended wood pulp, dye, water, and orange-type flavoring was as popular as a nymphomaniac at an American Legion convention. (PP, 337)

Vonnegut emphasizes the "continual shifting from top to bottom" that Bakhtin mentions. Here, humanity has overthrown the machines and made a stand for independence, only to be dependent on them once more. There appears a "coexistence" needed for humanity, the need for the two-world condition for humans to function, the need for an opposite as a realization of the other. It is not necessarily *"misanthropic humanism,"*[52] or "the human need for utopia" being equaled by an "all-too-human nature that prevents utopia's realization," as Robert Tally ascertains. It is the "balance of nature,"[53] the balancing of life on the edge of chaos, that allows for shifting cycles to take place in society. In essence, the need for a duality that is uncontrollable by humankind, and not misplaced misanthropy.

The Automation of Industry has such an impact on the human beings subjected to its implementation that the reader cannot help but acknowledge the warning that Vonnegut is prophesying to humanity. Much of the text is satirical in nature, it is ironic and funny, often relying on the carnivalesque nature of the narrative to highlight the laughable elements apparent in society. The reader can laugh at the errors the perfect machines make, "the clerical oversight of this deficiency" (PP, 209) in relation to a blunder in an education certificate. However, it is hard to accept the grotesque laughter associated with the death of a young man: "'... There's no need to talk to him now. My boy's all set' ... 'he hanged himself this morning in the kitchen' ... 'my son couldn't find any good reason for being alive, so he quit it this morning—with an ironing cord'" (PP, 88). It is shocking and hideous, yet inevitable, that the mechanization of industry has

---

52 Robert Tally, "Misanthropic Humanism," *Kurt Vonnegut and The American Novel: A Postmodern Iconography,*. p. 29.

53 Elisa Beninca, Bill Ballantine, Stephen P. Ellner, & Jef Huisman, "Species Fluctuations Sustained by a Cyclic Succession at the Edge of Chaos," *PNAS*, Vol. 112, no. 20, May 19, 2015, pp. 6389–6394.

rendered so many people's lives disenfranchised and meaningless. Without the belief in a future, humanity is reduced to nothing, people see little value in themselves. The system encourages this approach, if you do not make the grade, you become redundant and surplus to requirements.

The revolution seems as though it was destined to fail, the Indigenous American metaphor used so proudly by The Ghost Shirt Society is rendered powerless, "'So they were killed or gave up trying to be good Indians...'" (PP, 333). The men Finnerty, Lasher, Paul, and Neumann each resign themselves to the reality of post-revolution epiphany: "'like the Indians' massacre of Custer ... One isolated victory" (PP, 336). Even Paul, whose fervent plans to live a romanticized life at the farmhouse, has been realized as inadequate, and he finds the life not as fulfilling as he thought: "the charming little cottage he'd taken as a symbol of the good life ... [was] irrelevant" (PP, 259). The carnival atmosphere takes on the "continual shifting from top to bottom" as Vonnegut senses the need for some technology that eases human life, balanced with some meaning and accomplishment. The men represent the realization of a world that is forever in fluctuation; "'Nothing ever is, nothing ever will be...'" (PP, 341), all the men are resigned to the "fascinating experiment" (PP, 340), and they toast "'To the record'" (PP, 340). Vonnegut is aware that humanity has the potential to do great good in the world with technological advancement, this is by no means an anti-technology novel. Vonnegut appears to understand that you can never go back in history, never undo what has become before, but what you can do is learn and not make the same mistakes. His novels are about the representation of society, a society that at the time of *Player Piano's* publication, had been through two world wars, and some of the most advanced and expeditious technological changes in all history. He witnessed many of these changes and realized, as a humanist, or a person interested in individual human beings, that these changes were constantly on the edge of chaos. They had the ability to do both good and bad on a massive scale. He does not offer an alternative to what is already there because he does not know all the answers, he just wants every one of us to keep vigilant to the social changes and political narratives we subscribe to. Humanity is at the forefront of everything Vonnegut adheres to.

2

Religion: *Cat's Cradle*

"How do Humanists feel about Jesus? I say of Jesus, as all humanists do, 'If what he said is good, and so much of it is absolutely beautiful, what does it matter if he was God or not?'"[1]

*

Cat's Cradle, the fourth novel published by Kurt Vonnegut, and for which he eventually received his master's degree, is a narrative that closely considers how religion contributes to the ideological thinking of society.[2] It is one of Vonnegut's most powerful books in terms of sociological and political experimentation and highlights the consequences and contradictions created by fundamentalist opinions. It not only explores religion in the traditional sense, the belief in something divinely "other" as a cultural system for behavior and practices, but also in terms of science, and how both can influence social and political organization. The narrative explores how modern culture has progressed to rely heavily on the belief

---

1 Kurt Vonnegut, "Do You Know What a Humanist Is?" *A Man Without a Country*, p. 80.
2 Vonnegut submitted three attempts to the University of Chicago for a master's degree before submitting *Cat's Cradle* as a thesis: the first thesis was turned down, the second one was accepted but he did not finish it, and the third was also turned down. Charles J. Shields, "Goodbye and Goodbye and Goodbye, 1969–1971," *And So It Goes: Kurt Vonnegut, A Life*, p. 276.

that science has all the answers, and that it is always a positive and progressive force, to the extent that it has become a type of new religion.

The juxtaposing relationship between science and religion is an element that Vonnegut is compelled to investigate in the novel and is representative of the cultural shift that was beginning to take place within the period it was written (1963). This juxtaposed relationship has become almost symbiotic in today's modern America as political forces tussle to gain an upper hand, often by placing religion and science in an opposing relationship, a future Vonnegut was concerned had the possibility of devastating consequences. It is also a relationship that emphasizes how fundamental beliefs, irrespective of their opposing natures, behave in similar ways. Any views taken to the extreme without the lens of objectivity and interaction with differing views can only end in a closed and basal mindset, suspicious of any "other." An America socially and culturally divided by fundamental opinions and beliefs, irrespective of where those beliefs sit on the political and religious spectrum, could only end to a devastating outcome, one which could affect all humanity. Vonnegut believed in America and its ability to be the guidepost for freedom and democracy, but he understood there were dangers along the way.

While working for General Electric after the Second World War, Vonnegut had encountered a story of when the writer, H. G. Wells, visited the Schenectady plant. Irving Langmuir, the head scientist at the plant had, "proposed an idea to Wells for a story about a form of water that solidified at room temperature. Wells, the most famous science fiction writer of the day, expressed interest, but … a scientific conundrum didn't interest him."[3] The idea did however fascinate Vonnegut and was later developed into the novel *Cat's Cradle*. The scientific advancements Vonnegut witnessed during the Second World War, particularly the creation and use of the first atomic bomb, left him with an ethical dilemma over how to protect human beings in a world with changing values and beliefs. He had seen a world unstable because of ideological theory put into practice and how those ideas, when taken to the fundamental extreme, had nearly ripped human civilization apart.

The interaction between traditional ideals and progressive scientific ideas in the novel allows the text to become a site of carnivalization where Vonnegut emphasizes that neither side should be considered fundamentally absolute: "One of the essential aspects of this relation is the 'unmasking' and disclosing of the

---

3 Charles J. Shields, "Cooped Up with All the Kids, 1958–1965," *And So It Goes: Kurt Vonnegut, A Life*, p. 176.

unvarnished truth."[4] There can be inherent good and bad in both traditional beliefs and scientific advancements, and that human beings must consider carefully the consequences of their beliefs, particularly if they are beliefs that cannot be questioned or scrutinized by outside sources. Vonnegut uses satire throughout the text to stress the ridiculous elements of our own belief systems and encourages the reader to acknowledge and expose their own dogmatic opinions. Satire and humor were the way for Vonnegut to break through the barrier of deep-rooted and sentimental beliefs and opinions, to communicate an awareness that our own beliefs might just be as subjective as those we consider extreme or fundamentalist.

Vonnegut understood that life is difficult and that bad things happen, and he asserts that the only way it is possible to come to terms with that, is to make fun of the bad. He seeks to emphasize how the bad things happen in the first place, and how easily they might be avoided if we see them differently, with different views, from a different belief or opinion. The reader can see themselves in the fun without feeling threatened in order to consider an alternative perspective. Vonnegut considered the novel *Cat's Cradle* to be a sequence of jokes that also had the capacity to protect. The reader can see the consequences of the fundamental elements of belief on human society from a safe distance, they can acknowledge it but are protected by the humor:

> It's damn Hard to make jokes work. In *Cat's Cradle*, for instance, there are these very short chapters. Each one represents one day's work, and each one is a joke … a joke is like building a mousetrap from scratch. You have to work pretty hard to make the thing snap when it is supposed to snap … Humor is a way of holding off how awful life can be, to protect yourself.[5]

Cat's Cradle is a funny tract that evokes the biblical sense of the parable, and it highlights the serious nature of our personal beliefs and those of society and culture in general. What we believe has consequences, and this is ever important in a world where social media and the internet allow individuals to readily disseminate their ideas freely, without thought for evidence-based research and review.

The novel's title, *Cat's Cradle*, is named after a string game traditionally played by children and is a metaphor that represents the novel as a microcosm of society at large. There appears to be no fixed historical account of where the game originated from as many cultures appear to have a similar game, each with

---

4 Krystyna Pomorska, "Foreword," *Rabelais and His World*, p. x.

5 Kurt Vonnegut, "I Used to Know the Owner and Manager of an Automobile Dealership," *A Man Without a Country*, pp. 128–129.

their own origin story and symbolic meaning. The game consists of one string that is joined to form a circle, and which is then manipulated by the hands to form physical patterns. It is possible to play the game both as a group or individually. With one string, you can create something that passes time and fulfills the need to experiment and create. Each manipulation of the string can be "seen" as something "other," something resembling an article or belief from everyday life. For example, one manipulation appears like a baby's cradle, which could also be an indication of where the title name originated from. From this, the game can also be associated with the nursery rhyme "Rock-a-bye Baby," and it is possible to tell the story of the nursery rhyme with the use of the string's physical representations. The game certainly has many layers of meaning and representations of the cultures that we live in, and in this respect, the game can be considered a collective metaphor for the differing strands of the narrative that come together within the text. These elements within the narrative, although seemingly separate, come together as one, representative of human society. It seems complicated and dysfunctional but is in fact one string that moves in the right sequence, never becoming tangled and broken. Although there are many representations and meanings that a person can read into the differing physical manifestations, they are all a part of the same string and overall structure. The string becomes the illustration of humankind on earth; it might seem diverse, disconnected, and dysfunctional, but it is all a part of humanity. The different interpretations of the string's physical manifestations are the ways in which humans place imaginary meaning on the world they encounter.

The game is not only used as the title of the novel but is also referred to early in the narrative when Newt replies to Jonah about the day the atomic bomb was dropped. His father, one of the scientists responsible for the technology, is at home when it is happening, and uncharacteristically tries to play a game with his youngest child:

> 'Making that cat's cradle was the closest I ever saw my father come to playing what anybody else would call a game. He had no use at all for tricks and games and rules that other people made up ...
>
> 'He must have surprised himself when he made a cat's cradle out of string ... He all of a sudden came out of his study and did something he'd never done before. He tried to play with me.[6]

6 Kurt Vonnegut, *Cat's Cradle*, Dial Press, 2010, USA, pp. 11–12.

It is ironic that this man, who is responsible for a weapon capable of such an atrocity, can be at home trying to play a game of cat's cradle with his child, a child he rarely engages with, when so many people, including children, are being killed by his creation. His work is what normally maintains his concentration and energy, but when that work is being deployed, he is using his child as a distraction. In a sense, the game becomes symbolic of something meaningless, a way of passing the time. There is, in reality, no cat or any cradle, but imagination; we have images of what we believe the strings look like but in reality, they are just strings: "A cat's cradle is nothing but a bunch of X's between somebody's hands, and little kids look and look and look at all those X's … *'No damn cat, and no damn cradle'*" (CC, 165-166). The game is symbolic of human life and symbolic of what the reader encounters in the narrative, it is representative "of the meaninglessness of it all!" (CC, 169). Vonnegut understands the importance of humans' need to give their lives meaning, and how they impose signs and representations to elements in society; they need to have a feeling of purpose. He understands that much of the meaning that we impose on ourselves is arbitrary, it is superfluous to living, but it gives us the comfort to carry on, and it gives us some hope for the future. The symbolism of the cat's cradle is repeated throughout the text, even when Newt explains to Jonah that his sister's marriage is not quite what she told him it was: "'Her husband is mean as hell to her' … Little Newt held his hands six inches apart and he spread his fingers. 'See the cat? See the cradle?'" (CC, 179). There is clearly a separation of what we tell ourselves, or how we want people to perceive us, and how the physical world can be perceived. Vonnegut is acutely aware that representation in society mirrors how human beings work on the personal level, it fulfills their needs. We apply all sorts of meaning and ideology within our different cultures to our social structures. In actuality, the ideals that we impose on living in the world have little to do with the physicality of living day-to-day, and they are there to give our mental and emotional existence meaning. This existence of the physical world together with a perceived intellectual world is the typical characteristic of the carnival: "This temporary suspension, both ideal and real, of hierarchical rank created during carnival time [creates] a special type of communication impossible in everyday life."[7] The imposition of a fixed defining cultural structure on a world that has no fixed defining social mechanism creates a duality that can be exposed with satirical scrutiny. This perception allows Vonnegut the luxury of incorporating the

---

7 Mikhail Bakhtin, "Introduction," *Rabelais and His World*, p. 10.

religious element in the text; it no longer becomes relevant whether the religion is based on truth because it is about the meaning that it brings to human lives. The cat's cradle becomes symbolic, not only as a representation of the meaninglessness of society but also of the hope humanity can afford itself with those imaginative structures.

The opening preface to the novel includes the very first line: "Nothing in this book is true" (CC, ii) and sets the tone for the rest of the narrative. It is accompanied by a verse from the fictitious book of Bokonon that encourages you to live by the "*harmless untruths*" (CC, ii) that make you "brave and kind and healthy and happy" (CC, ii). Already the reader is encouraged to question whether something untruthful can really make you brave, kind, healthy, and happy. They are forced to begin considering what can be constituted as harmless and whether there is a difference between an untruth and a lie. Language becomes an important part of how we view our own beliefs. The reader is aware from the very first line of the text that "nothing" is true, which allows an element of reader awareness in the narrative. The novel is dialogic in nature from the outset and allows the reader a sense of space to consider their own beliefs and values: "The living utterance, having taken meaning and shape at a particular historical moment in a socially specific environment, cannot fail to brush up against thousands of living dialogic threads, woven by socio-ideological consciousness."[8] The idea of "lies and untruths" is also repeated in the opening segments of the novel by the mentioning of "the bittersweet lies of Bokonon" (CC, 2), and emphasized by the use of the first sentence of *The Books of Bokonon*, "'All of the true things I am about to tell you are shameless lies'" (CC, 5). The reader can be in no doubt that the religion they will be encountering within the text is nothing short of fictional. In a sense, the novel mirrors what takes place in Jonah's "factual" (CC, 1) account of the day the world ended, and the fictitious book of Bokonon. They are each representative of the fictions we tell ourselves, and the fictions established in society. In this way Vonnegut is weaving a narrative that is intricate and complex. The element of metafiction is established early on in the novel: a writer in the process of writing a fictional narrative (*Cat's Cradle*), about another fictional narrative (*The Day the World Ended*), incorporating another fictional text (The Book of Bokonon), which are all representative of the fabrications we tell ourselves in society. Vonnegut is inviting the reader to acknowledge that the religion of Bokonon is a fake, founded on the views and sayings of a fictional human being, and to

---

8 Mikhail Bakhtin, "Discourse in the Novel," *The Dialogic Imagination*, p. 276.

consider what they are being told by the narrator of the text is also a fictitious construct. There is never any pretense of Bokononism's validity as a religion based on anything other than complete made-up nonsense.

The confession of "harmless untruths" (CC, ii) and lies so early in the novel implies that religion is a device used by human beings to make them feel better about the world they live in. We can live by "harmless untruths" that make us feel better about ourselves and the culture we live in as it gives us meaning. This suggests a shared human experience in the narrative, experiences of what it is to be a human being living in the physical world, that allows religious faith and belief to be presented as truth. It is hard to disagree with this shared experience and concur with what Bokonon is stating. For example, in the physical world we all know that every human will be born and eventually die, this experience is universal to humanity. It is in this way that small references to Bokonon's words appear in the narrative, of which the reader cannot help but see truths in even though they know it to be fiction: "'Maturity,' Bokonon tells us, 'is a bitter disappointment for which no remedy exists, unless laughter can be said to remedy anything'" (CC, 198), or "'what an ugly city every city is!'" (CC, 27). No human can help growing old, even though much of the media environment is engaged in the representation of the fallacy that it might just be obtainable, and many humans might argue that human cities are in fact very ugly in comparison to what they see in nature. To some extent this renders the reader as an accomplice to the untruths in the narrative and puts them in a difficult situation. Even though they are fully aware of the flimsy foundations Bokononism is founded on, they cannot help but agree with some of its teachings, or at least see the possibilities in some of its verses. Vonnegut satirically offers the idea that many accepted religious facts have no empirical evidence attached, and that religion can offer shared truths for humanity, although not necessarily created from truth. He exploits what Bakhtin calls the "peculiar logic of the "inside out,""[9] he manipulates the reader to experience how religion can become accepted truth even though it can also be considered untruthful.

It is evident from the outset of the novel, and by the implication of untruths and lies in religion, that Vonnegut is writing the text from the perspective of American culture and its relationship to Christianity. It suggests the difficult relationship Vonnegut had with religion, not necessarily just Christianity, but the belief in something that could not be proved, or aspects he felt had been

---

9 Mikhail Bakhtin, "Introduction," *Rabelais and His World*, p. 11.

disproved by science. Christianity happened to be the religion that was closest to him, within his personal environment:

> Towards the end of our marriage, it was mainly religion in a broad sense that Jane and I fought about. She came to devote herself more and more to making alliances with the supernatural in her need to increase her strength and understanding— and happiness and health. This was painful to me. She could not understand and cannot understand why that should have been painful to me, or why it should be any of my business at all.[10]

After the experiences Vonnegut had throughout his life and his acceptance of humanist values, that is that human beings could find their own strength and understanding within humankind, he found it painful that his wife could turn to religion for the answers. Putting faith in something that could not be tested or scrutinized seemed to wound Vonnegut, belief in humankind should have been where you made your alliances.

At the beginning of the novel Jonah refers to Christianity and to the fact that "I was a Christian then" (CC, 1), and later recounts one of the autobiographical passages from the Book of Bokonon where Bokonon explains his encounter with an "Episcopalian lady in Newport, Rhode Island" (CC, 4) who he said "believed that God liked people in sailboats much better than He liked people in motorboats" (CC, 4-5). Vonnegut is suggesting here that the lady believed God preferred people with money. He uses the location of Newport, Rhode Island, an early colonial settlement, renowned for its mansions and yachting community, as an example of wealth and privilege. The inclusion by Vonnegut is suggestive of how he saw the Christian community in America as exclusive. There appears an elitist undertone that contradicts what Christianity was meant to represent: "The lady claimed to understand God and His Ways of Working perfectly. She could not understand why anyone should be puzzled about what had been or about what was going to be" (CC, 4). The lady thought she understood everything about human existence from her privileged position in a life of money and status, and she appears to have had no understanding of what life might really be like, or how hard it could be because she could not understand "why anyone should be puzzled." The inclusion of this passage shows that Vonnegut aimed to scrutinize Christianity and explore who and why people felt the need to follow any religion at all. This passage suggests a double standard in the establishment of religion and

---

10 Kurt Vonnegut, "Religion," *Palm Sunday: An Autobiographical Collage*, p. 175.

society, and this ambiguous relationship of untruth and perceived truth is what Vonnegut aimed to unveil.

The satirical referencing of Christianity continues throughout the text highlighting the corrupt double standards that Vonnegut saw religion producing in social culture. Later in the novel, Hazel Crosby whispers to her husband that she is glad San Lorenzo is a Christian country, as if this gives her some protection in a country that carries out the death penalty for worshipping the false religion by hanging people on a hook: "'I'm sure glad it's a Christian country' ... 'or I'd be a little scared'" (CC, 137). When Papa, the dictator of San Lorenzo, is dying Jonah asks the Christian minister what sect of Christianity he is from and,

> He said he had had to feel his way along with Christianity, since Catholicism and Protestantism had been outlawed along with Bokononism.
> 'So, if I am going to be a Christian under those conditions, I have to make up a lot of new stuff.' (CC, 215)

Even the supposed Christian minister in the novel brings "a brass dinner bell and a hatbox with holes drilled in it, and a Bible, and a butcher knife" (CC, 214) to Papa's sickbed because he must make up content in order to "MAKE RELIGION LIVE!" (CC, 215),[11] ironic since he is visiting someone who is dying, do you need to make religion live in the presence of a dying man?

Vonnegut carnivalizes religion to the extent that the reader can see the traditions and beliefs presented as fact, are elements aimed at making religion all imposing and believable to human beings. The Christian minister brings the bell, the hatbox with the live chicken inside, the bible, and the knife along because they act as props for what people think religious rituals should look like and it gives them comfort. He wants to make religion believable, to make it "live!" Even Papa does not really buy into the spectacle: "'I am a member of the Bokononist faith' ... 'Get out you stinking Christian'" (CC, 218). Bokonon also understands the need to make religion live for it to be believed: "'It was his own idea. He asked McCabe to outlaw him and his religion, too, in order to give the religious life of the people more zest, more tang'" (CC, 173). Vonnegut understands that human beings need to have some meaning in their lives which is why they have a tendency towards religion. For him, Christianity as presented as fact is a misrepresentation of what religion is. It cannot be proven by the scientific method, so therefore there is no evidence to support it. Human beings should be alert that

11 Emphasis in original text.

religion is there as a means of comfort for a life that has no answers. They should also be alert to the fact that in being presented as "truth," religion has the power to manipulate and influence people's behaviors. The traditions and rituals, as shown by both the Christian minister and Bokonon in the novel, are there to help human beings invest in the belief of the religion. Rituals and traditions are an interactive way for religion to embrace its followers. The interplay of Vonnegut's desire of evidence-based knowledge and its interaction with religion is another dialogical thread in the novel, and it is the fundamental element of religious and scientific dialog. How could a faith-based system ever produce scientifically rigorous evidence for its credibility, one of the eternal philosophical questions facing humanity.

The idea that humans need to find a belief in something, even though it might be founded on a lie or untruth, is an element that is repeated throughout the novel and is present in many of Vonnegut's narratives. For example, the need for the Christian minister in *Cat's Cradle* to make something up for the religion to give comfort and to be believable is an idea repeated in Vonnegut's later carnivalesque novel, *Slapstick*. The two children, Wilbur and Eliza, the main characters in the novel, reveal their true intelligence together, when it was previously thought that they had no intellectual capability whatsoever. The immediate reaction of the adults, the human beings, around them is one of shock and horror, and they find it difficult to accept and come to terms with what they thought was the truth is in fact an illusion. The children do not fit into the "ideal" of what is considered normal, and they realize that they will need to pretend once more that they have no intellectual capacity in order for people to feel secure and comfortable again, "Our genius did not fail us. It allowed us to understand the truth of the situation ... It told us that all we had to do to make everything all right again was to return to idiocy."[12] Although they try to recreate the illusion again by pretending to be idiots once more, their plan fails. The adult society around them will not allow it so they are separated and treated badly. Society does not seem to be able to comprehend fact when it does not support their comfortable illusion, and they are suspicious of what the "other" means. Just as the Christian minister is forced to create an illusion in *Cat's Cradle* with his made-up rituals and religious relics, he realizes that the illusions give people comfort and something to believe. This is a problematic and contradictory element in Vonnegut's narratives, he wants people to question and search for illusions of "truth" in society, but he

---

12 Vonnegut, Kurt. *Slapstick*, Dial Press, 2010, USA, p. 85.

simultaneously suggests that they might find it impossible because it is too comfortable and unsafe to continue the participation. The human brain might not be able to cope with the reality of what is behind the illusion.

As the interaction of religious ideas continues throughout the novel, Bokononism has one important aspect that Vonnegut insinuates is missing from Christianity. Bokononism is truthful about its untruth and lies, whereas Christianity is always presented as fact. In his book *Sanity Plea* (1994), Lawrence Broer refers to the novel's religious element, saying: "only a cynical religion like 'Bokononism' will serve to make existence tolerable."[13] Many religions offer some type of "idea" of how the world can be "righted," but Vonnegut does not offer this, his religion is created by a human man and can therefore only act within human limitations. It is cynical because it is based on the truth of lies, there are no pretenses with Bokononism, just the cynical truth. It takes the bitter side of life and makes it funny; it offers the readers relief from society by laughing at what is revealed as ridiculous. Vonnegut carnivalizes socially accepted ideals to allow the shift needed in perception by the reader. They are allowed to see society from a different viewpoint, from the many viewpoints of the characters as the narrative progresses, which facilitates the heteroglot nature representative of wider society. Being a human being is hard and not always that great, and Bokononism allows the reader to see life for what it is, without the pretenses and from a different vantage point.

Bokononism is referred to from the beginning when John, or Jonah as he asks to be referred to, the protagonist of the novel, explains that he is writing a book, called "*The Day the World Ended*" (CC, 1), a "factual" (CC, 1) book regarding "what important Americans had done on the day when the first atomic bomb was dropped" (CC, 1). The importance of the idea, of the fictitious "factual" (CC, 1) book, is a clever carnivalization by Vonnegut to show what he is setting out to achieve. Vonnegut is also writing a book, a fictional book laced with factual references, which also transpires to be a story about how the world ended, or how the world is changed beyond our wildest predictions. There is also the sense here of the book as a parody of the bible, recreating the early story of the world together with the life and teachings of Bokonon. Alternatively, it could be considered a form of a fictional history book, taking an ironic view of what could happen if humanity does not think about their actions on Earth. Jonah states that he does not "intend that this book be a tract on behalf of Bokononism," (CC, 5),

---

13 Lawrence R. Broer, "*Cat's Cradle*: Jonah and the Whale," *Sanity Plea: Schizophrenia in the Novels of Kurt Vonnegut*, University of Alabama Press, 1994, Tuscaloosa, AL, p. 57.

but he would like it to act as a "warning" (CC, 5). Vonnegut wants the reader to understand the limitations that restrict humanity's thoughts, to begin to question the decisions and actions they take and how this could affect the whole. Simple actions, actions that may work within the general "truths" of society and religion, could potentially be the very cause of Earth's demise. Just as the "Episcopalian lady in Newport, Rhode Island" (CC, 4) did not seem to comprehend that there could be a different interpretation from her religious beliefs, from that of her own comfortable position. The reader needs to examine if they are in the same situation and understand that all human beings need to consider other perspectives different from their own, it is imperative for their survival as a collective group.

The novel could be considered Jonah's personal account of his conversion to Bokononism and his spiritual journey into the untruths of a religious institution. The Book of Bokonon and its teachings are a concurrent motif throughout the whole of the novel, culminating in the meeting and the final written words of Bokonon as an ending. Exposed in the text are the ideas and teachings of the Bokonon religion by the narration of Jonah, often the ideas are expressed together with his Christian views at the time of a described event. His meditations have a retrospective outlook; had he known the teachings of Bokonon at the time he may have acted and thought differently: "I would have been a Bokononist then, if there had been anyone to teach me the bittersweet lies of Bokonon" (CC, 2). The basic beliefs of Bokononism are given by Jonah over the course of the novel and are made up of some of the following terms. A "Karass" is how Bokononists believe "humanity is organized into teams" (CC, 2); these teams supersede all society's boundaries, and you can be connected to someone for what seems like no logical reason. The "tendrils of my life" (CC, 6), or "Sinookas," are the ways in which your life entangles with those of your Karass, how they become a part of your life. A "Wampeter" is the pivot of a Karass, and can be anything from "a tree, a rock, an animal, an idea, a book, a melody, the Holy Grail" (CC, 52), these are spiritual orbits, and the "*Karass* revolve about it in the majestic chaos of a spiral of nebula" (CC, 52). There are special types of Karass called a "Dupress," which consist of only two people and can never be "invaded, not even by children born of such a union" (CC, 86), and its members always die close together. A false Karass can exist, called a "Granfalloon," and is described as "a seeming team that was meaningless in terms of the way God gets things done" (CC, 91) and examples of these are given as "the Communist party, the Daughters of the American Revolution, the General Electric Company, the International Order of Odd Fellows—and any nation, anytime, anywhere" (CC, 92) A person can have a "Vin-Dit," or "personal shove in the direction of Bokononism, in the direction of believing that God Almighty knew all about me, after all, that God Almighty had some pretty elaborate plans for me" (CC, 69). A person can act as a "wrang-wrang" and this is someone that "steers people away from a line of speculation by reducing that line, with the example of the *wrang-wrang's* own life, to an absurdity" (CC, 78). For example, this might be a communist or a nihilist, etc., and their behavior makes you realize you could never live like that, and they turn you to the path of Bokononism.

The naming choices that Vonnegut makes in relation to Bokononism such as Sinookas or Wampeter, and the belief system, are chosen for comical value and their arbitrary nature. This could suggest a feeling in the novel that on closer inspection, some choices made by early religious leaders might also seem arbitrary. Vonnegut purposely chooses fictional names for their strange clown-like sounds, and he uses the unusual words as a literary highlighting technique to encourage closer scrutiny of the validity of the origin of religious ideas. They are strange-sounding names that feel unbelievable and make-believe, and the reader cannot mistake them for anything other than fictional. The explanations and definitions of the religious language Vonnegut chooses are expressed to make the reader forced to think philosophically about their connections. Although there is clear understanding that they are lies, Vonnegut often makes them seem highly plausible, and we are encouraged to draw parallels to think about the beliefs of society at large.

Vonnegut uses Bokononism to emphasize how human beings could eventually get to a point where the destruction of the world is inevitable, because humanity seems to have such difficulty in understanding their own fundamental beliefs. Vonnegut uses dark humor that parodies the creation and release of the first atomic bomb, and the ultimate destruction of civilization. He uses satire as an invitation for the reader to question how and why a weapon of such magnitude could ever be used. Bokononism becomes the carnival mask that allows the reader to seek fundamental answers to questions regarding the nature of humanity, and why they can appear indifferent to human suffering. In the very short, fourteenth book of Bokonon, the title is stated as, "'What Can a Thoughtful Man Hope for Mankind on Earth, Given the Experience of the Past Million Years?'" (CC, 245), and the answer is beautiful in its simplicity, "'Nothing'" (CC, 245). The carnivalization of religion allows Vonnegut to point out the intrinsic self-destructive nature of humankind, and at the same time signals to the reader that there must be more than one outcome for their future. The title of the fictitious book, "a factual book," suggests that there was no complete ending for the world, that someone has been able to write down what happened, therefore the day the world ended cannot be an all-encompassing end. Vonnegut is suggesting that it is never too late to change, to seek a new ending, a new beginning. The use of ironic interplay with the reader is also strong with this title considering the book is written based on the lies of Bokonon, a suggestion that there can be no "factual" when it comes to spirituality as it is based on faith alone. Jonah says, "Anyone unable to understand how a useful religion can be founded on lies will not understand this book either. So be it" (CC, 5-6). It is useful to see the world through the lens of Vonnegut's make-believe religion; it highlights the inadequacies of our own society and the foundations of our own religious beliefs; it gives us the ability to question everything we are taught as fact.

In his critical companion, Marvin (2002) says that in the novel *Cat's Cradle*, "Vonnegut creates a new religion with a full set of scriptures and rituals, and he shows how it brings a sense of meaning and purpose to the lives of people who have found no consolation in other religions."[14] The sense of usefulness is evident here, Vonnegut stresses that religion is useful in the comfort and predictability, or structure that it can give people. It may not be strictly "truthful" but there is a sense that it can bring enough meaning into a person's life that they can cope with the unpredictability that human life can bring. Bokonon understands the true workings of society, the lies that are told, and how humans behave. Vonnegut invites us to do the same as Bokonon, following in his example, ironically much the same as how a prophet may live his life to be an example for his disciples. People need to understand the world they are living in to achieve true liberation. If belief is founded on dogmatic "truth" it can render humanity incapable of rational thought and capable of committing terrible acts. In showing Bokononism to be based on lies, there becomes a different dynamic. On one hand, yes, there is use in religion to give people comfort and cohesion, but on the other hand, society should not be able to use it as an excuse. Bokonon is always careful to point out his lies, making it impossible for them to be used as platforms for the validity of human actions. As a carnival masque, the characterization of Bokonon can be seen as a continual Bakhtinian turnabout, and the reader can see that through the cynical nature it projects. Bokononism can also exemplify how humans have the capacity to stand by and watch, indifferently, in extreme situations. Vonnegut is consistently pushing the reader to value the existence of other human beings, often through the medium of Jonah's cynical voice. The reader can see that Vonnegut is concerned about humans supporting and valuing

---

14 Thomas F. Marvin, *Kurt Vonnegut: A Critical Companion*, Greenwood Press, 2002, Westport, CT, pp. 77–78.

other humans, and this is a thread that we can see through all his novels and short stories. His experiences during war, which he uses extensively in his novel *Slaughterhouse-Five*, allowed Vonnegut to understand that humans are capable of terrible things if given the right circumstances. Bokononism takes the right circumstances away, as there can be no good excuse if they are based on untruths.

Together with the continual presence of religion in the text are the observations made about the social ideologies overtly present at the time Vonnegut wrote the narrative. Having been written in the years following the Second World War, the text is preoccupied with the struggle between the communist ideals and the existence of dictatorship as a form of government, being at odds with the American dream of freedom and individualism.[15] This is also a strong element that is present in contemporary America as individuals struggle to make sense of how to deal with a changing world in terms of climate change, pandemic, and continued conflicts. What is the best way for human beings to react to an uncertain world and adapt to create structures that can stand up to the challenges? Vonnegut's postwar novel exposes the limitations that he saw in the differing political choices of the time. Vonnegut appears to question how any society can claim to have the "true" form of government considering that life is meaningless and there are no fixed ideals. He points out the flaws in all fundamentalist ideas, as many ideologies can become a form of religion to those that buy into its principles, to the extent they are willing to impose their ideals on others: "'Our politicians like to say that we have religion and the Communist countries don't. I think it is just the other way around. Those countries have a religion called Communism, and the Free World is where sustaining religions are in very short supply."[16] It is pointed out in the text that: "Americans couldn't imagine what it was like to be something else, to be something else and proud of it" (CC, 97), and this suggests that even the ideals of "freedom" can be destructive. America, the purported land of freedom, cannot comprehend the possibility that there might be another way of life just as valid, that "freedom" only extends to something that mimics itself. Vonnegut appears critical of what America and its foreign policy have become: "'The highest possible form of treason' ... 'is to say that Americans aren't loved wherever they go, whatever they do ...'" (CC, 98). Ideology becomes fundamentalist when it dictates what people should think and

---

15 By the time of *Cat's Cradle's* publication in 1963, Vonnegut had observed America's policy of containment in relation to Communism with The Korean War (1950–1953), The Vietnam War (1954–1975) and The Bay of Pigs (1961), a CIA backed group of exiled Cubans opposed to Fidel Castro dictatorship, together with The Cuban missile crisis (1962).

16 Kurt Vonnegut, in "Religion," *Palm Sunday: An Autobiographical Collage*, p. 180.

believe about themselves, when its ideas are forced upon others, and it cannot interact with other cultures and ideologies without trying to replicate itself in that society. Just as dictatorships are considered abhorrent, so too is an American culture that dictates how others should live. Society must be aware of itself to the point that it can regulate and protect itself against fundamentalism. If ideas and beliefs become extreme, and balance is lost, theorizing and metaphorical language become action, and freedom becomes impossible.

The novel not only looks carefully at society within the religious context and at social ideology, but it also suggests that we look at ideas presented to us through history, literature, and myth. As readers, people are often caught up in the stories presented by literature and the feeling of "reality" within the boundary of literary time. Embedded within the novel are several references to biblical and historical figures we know little about, along with characters from literary history. In this sense, Vonnegut is again carnivalizing our view of our own culture, whether it is religious and biblical, historical, or literary. He is bringing together cultural references, ones that we often accept as "truth," even though they are founded on little more than imagination. In considering religion and the "truths" that it teaches us as absolute in society, we must also consider what other beliefs we have, that we do not necessarily question. Our entire belief systems must be deconstructed and assessed for us to comprehend how belief imposes restrictions on our lives. Vonnegut, just as Bakhtin states Rabelais set out to do, intends to show the reader more meaning about their own world: "Rabelais did not implicitly believe in what his time 'said and imagined about itself'; he strove to disclose its true meaning for the people."[17] Vonnegut does this in two ways in the novel; he uses the names of characters as allegorical representations, and he directly references historical figures whose lives we think we know, but have little factual evidence for. This also incorporates the historical events and time periods those historical figures are representations of. Just as the fictional names associated with Bokononism give reference to the comical nature of belief having no basis in fact, the names that Vonnegut has chosen for his characters, along with the types of characters he has included, also have relevant importance to the carnivalization in the novel. These characters are often used in discussions with Jonah as devices to draw attention to religious arguments or connotations. They are in the text to carnivalize the accepted norms in society, to turn them upside down to reveal the underlying alternative.

---

17 Mikhail Bakhtin, "Rabelais' Images and His Time," *Rabelais and His World*, p. 439.

This idea of using literary and historical signifiers in the narrative relates closely to Bakhtin's ideas on the Chronotope and shows how Vonnegut is manipulating the text in order to reveal to the readers how their beliefs are formed. They are reading the narrative from a unique perspective, loaded with preconceived ideas and beliefs:

> These generic forms, at first productive, were then reinforced by tradition; in their subsequent development they continued stubbornly to exist, up to and beyond the point at which they had lost any meaning that was productive in actuality or adequate to later historical situations.[18]

The ideas present in the novel suggest Vonnegut is influencing how we see past times and the relationship that we have with historical individuals. The reader has been taught a "version" of history that they once thought was "truth," but they are now forced to question whether it is productive or holds value. It encourages the reader to be suspicious of absolutes, and the ideas taught by their accepted culture now become inadequate. The number of Vonnegut's choices of historical reference points within the text allows the reader to glimpse the magnitude of how complex and interwoven lies and elements of fact are within society. The literary world that Vonnegut creates in the novel mirrors the difficulty in accessing and understanding how religion and science really influence the mechanics of society. If everything our culture is based on is historical untruths and subjective perception, how can human beings navigate the world on a larger scale?

The first deliberate literary name that Vonnegut chooses is the name of Jonah. The protagonist in the novel asks to be called Jonah from the very beginning, and in considering the role of the character in the novel, it would be hard to deny the parallels to the biblical reference to the Hebrew Scriptures, *The Book of Jonah* in the Old Testament. Jonah repeatedly refuses to prophesy the will of God to the city of Nineveh; he tries to sail away but is thrown overboard for endangering the life of the crew, only to be swallowed by a fish. When he repents to accept his role given by God, it becomes clear that he did not accept his role because he did not want God to forgive the Ninevites. When God does forgive them, Jonah becomes resentful and angry. God says "And should not I pity Nineveh, that great city, in which there are more than 120,000 persons who do not know their right hand from their left" (Jonah:4:11).[19] The biblical book lists no author, and "because it

---

18 Mikhail Bakhtin, "Forms of Time and Chronotope in the Novel," *The Dialogic Imagination*, p. 85.
19 *Holy Bible*, English Standard Version (ESV), Good News Publishers, 2007, Wheaton, IL, p. 1016, Jonah 4:11.

tells of a fish swallowing a man, many have dismissed the book of Jonah as fiction."[20] It is interesting that Vonnegut decides to emphasize this particular text from the bible, as it is a story that has often been considered fictional. It may have been chosen as representative of the historical stories present in a culture that are presented as fact, the Bible being considered the factual word of God, yet the story being considered fiction by some. The suggestion in the novel here is that Jonah, or John, does not actively want the world to be saved from Ice-9. He certainly appears passive in the story, never acting out in a proactive way, but appears almost like a simple observer. He certainly makes judgments and comments, and is surprised at the reactions of the other characters in the novel, but how far does he go to change their minds? The reader could think he should actively and aggressively challenge many of the characters in the narrative, considering their often-destructive implications, but he chooses not to. He calls himself "bristly, diseased, [and] cynical," (CC, 27) stating that "I thought the worst of everyone" (CC, 27). Jonah's reaction suggests that Vonnegut was reflecting on how he saw many people in the modern world beginning to feel, and that they had learned to expect the worst society has to offer because they had seen too much destruction during the world wars. They had witnessed the capacity for human beings to create such destruction and devastation throughout the world community. Perhaps with these feelings, Jonah, like his biblical counterpart, thought it better for the world to be destroyed. He thought he would never find any good in humanity: "Somewhat like the biblical Jonah, who disobeys, then grudgingly accepts, then questions God's orders, demanding that God justify his actions and explain his apparent inconsistencies, the 'Jonah' of *Cat's Cradle* seeks answers and 'moral clarity.'"[21]

It is also prudent to acknowledge in relation to Jonah, that links have been made between the character of Jonah in the bible and the modern cultural reference to the story of Pinocchio. Both characters of Jonah and Pinocchio embark on a spiritual journey of learning and redemption, and both are swallowed by a Whale. The character of Pinocchio obviously has the connotations attached to lies and his need to understand how these affect himself and other people. Perhaps Vonnegut might be suggesting the same connotations for Jonah and humanity in general, especially in connection to belief, both in terms of religion and science. There needs to be an acknowledgment of the inconsistencies that are told and

---

20 *Holy Bible*, "Introduction" to the Book of Jonah, English Standard Version (ESV), p. 1014.

21 Robert Tally, "The Dialectic of American Enlightenment," *Kurt Vonnegut and The American Novel: A Postmodern Iconography*, p. 56.

how these relate to our behaviors and choices in society. This again evidences the dialogic and multilayered narrative that Vonnegut has created. There are many parallels and connections we can make to show the interconnectedness of the text, and this mirrors how complicated and how abundantly messy navigating life as a human can be, something Vonnegut was obviously acutely aware of.

Vonnegut also references Herman Melville's *Moby Dick*, another fiction based on the observations of a passive character. The opening words of the novel, "Call me Ishmael,"[22] being among the most famous in literary history, is replicated by Vonnegut at the beginning of *Cat's Cradle*: "Call me Jonah. My parents did, or nearly did. They called me John" (CC, 1). *Moby Dick* charts the story of Ishmael's experiences on the ship *Pequod* at the hands of a tyrannical man, Captain Ahab, and he is to be its only surviving crew member. The story is narrated from Ishmael's perspective, just as Jonah narrates about the day the world ended. The character of Ishmael is symbolic of the idea of exile from society, as he alludes to feelings of alienation from society as his reasoning for joining the ship's crew: "having little or no money in my purse, and nothing particular to interest me on shore, I thought I would sail about a little and see the watery part of the world."[23] The ship is captained by a tyrannical man willing to sacrifice the lives of the crew in order to fulfill his own sense of revenge. This is a possible reflection of the greater society Vonnegut contemplates in his near future, the crew, or people in society, being at the mercy of tyrannical leaders who care little for their well-being or that of a greater social future.

The reader also encounters a further biblical reference here, Ishmael being the son of Abraham from the Book of Genesis. Sarah gives her female servant, Hagar, to Abraham when she is unable to produce children, allowing him to bear a child with her, Ishmael. When Sarah finally produces her own son, Isaac, she insists that Abraham exile both Hagar and Ishmael into the desert through fear that Ishmael will be a bad influence on Isaac: "Cast out this slave woman with her son, for the son of this slave woman shall not be heir with my son Isaac."[24] From the beginning, there are two very strong biblical references that Vonnegut has used together, further supporting the idea that he is willing people to consider closely and to evaluate the cultural references he is signposting. His choices of biblical characters have issues with the society they are placed in, both in a sense being exiled from what they understand as accepted. One is cast into the desert

22 Herman Melville, *Moby Dick*, Oxford University Press, 1998, Oxford UK, p. 1.
23 Herman Melville, *Moby Dick*, p. 1.
24 *Holy Bible*, English Standard Version (ESV), Genesis: 21:10, p. 18.

because of his parentage, and the other tries to run away from his responsibilities in order to cause the destruction of society. Both characters have no control over what happens to them, they are chosen by what feels like random decisions, one of birth and one by God. The reader has no idea of whether these stories are literally true or whether they are metaphorical stories. They are relevant to the narrative of the end of the world because they highlight the need for the reader to question the motivation behind society and that of the characters. Jonah is the pivotal character in the novel, the Wampeter that Vonnegut chooses. Vonnegut is playful, creating a fictional character steeped in both biblical and literary heritage. Jonah is a character that undergoes a religious pilgrimage to Armageddon fully aware that his whole belief system is based on the lies that one human being fabricates. The character is both ironic and cynical; the satirical effect forces the reader to consider the construction of religion and belief in society as it is steeped in so much symbolism.

Jonah's cynical social commentary throughout the narrative is enabled because of his roles as researcher and writer. Situations he encounters are seen at a distance allowing him to have the retrospective power of a historian. He seeks to accumulate the facts, but also the motivations and feelings of the characters employed in the events. This function allows Vonnegut to engage a strong satirical voice, pointing out the humorous nature of what he uncovers. The double standards are illuminated in both a personal and social context here and as Bakhtin points out, "laughter has a deep philosophical meaning, it is one of the essential forms of truth concerning the world as a whole, concerning history and man."[25] Although Jonah possesses a strong sense of awareness in the comments he makes, he never seems able to change perspectives. His character performs the role of a narrator, but when he is given the power to change something, he is unable to: "I pondered asking him [Bokonon] to join my government … But then I understood that a millennium would have to offer something more than a holy man in a position of power" (CC, 226). He is trapped in his social sphere, aware of its existence, yet powerless to make changes because of what might happen: "So good and evil had to remain separate; good in the jungle, and evil in the palace. Whatever entertainment there was in that was about all we had to give to the people" (CC, 226). Jonah's character is a complicated and clever device deployed by Vonnegut to act as an anchor for the dialogic communication taking place in the

---

25   Mikhail Bakhtin, "Rabelais in the History of Laughter," *Rabelais and His World*, p. 66.

novel. Everything in the text rotates around him and his quest for understanding and "truth," something that Vonnegut clearly suggests is impossible.

The other key element in the novel and in direct relation to religion is the progression of science and scientific research, and how they relate to belief. On the one hand, Vonnegut appears to be questioning the validation of religion, but on the other hand, he appears to be questioning the ethics of scientific research, and how far this should go or what it is used for. There is an interaction between the two ideas, indicating that Vonnegut is considering the two to be strongly interwoven, and both being important issues in society in general. Jonah appears to have been on a spiritual journey that leads him to explore and research how scientific and technological advancements allow for the end of the world. It appears both prophecy and retrospection as his research leads him to the very end of the world. It is as though Vonnegut wants us to see clues for how the end will turn out so that we can change and correct its course. The text is purposefully clever and complicated, to allow the reader the space to engage in the carnivalization process. Religion and Science, although often separated and seen apart, are interconnected and a part of the same spectrum. Belief or faith in scientific exploration is exactly the process of religious exploration. Extreme opinion and belief in both can act in very similar ways, and with similar outcomes.

The complex and multifaceted nature of the narrative in terms of religion juxtaposed with the equally complicated elements of scientific exploration and belief allow the narrative to enact the carnival atmosphere. The research facility in the narrative, The Research Laboratory of the General Forge and Foundry Company, introduces several characters with symbolic importance, and who introduce the element of science as a juxtaposition to religion. These characters are pivoted to Jonah for the reader to connect the synergetic nature of the relationship of science to religion. There is a mutual connection between them both in Vonnegut's modern American society, seemingly opposite, but mutually reliant on one another. They both express dogmatic approaches in their fundamental beliefs, not open to interaction from outside inquiry. The characters that highlight Vonnegut's carnival interaction are Dr. Breed, his secretary Miss Faust, Dr. Felix Hoenikker, the creator of Ice-9, and Knowles the elevator operator.

The supporting staff of the scientists at the research laboratory are some of the most interesting, and they expose how fixed and rudimentary the scientific community is viewed by Vonnegut. The introduction of Miss Faust allows the reader to encounter how the scientists function behind the scenes, in a sense she is a gatekeeper to their views, allowing Jonah to see their interactions. The name Faust is synonymous with the old German tale of a man who supposedly sold his soul to the devil. The idea of Faustus is a representation that is commonly used in literature after Christopher Marlowe's use in his play *The Tragical History of Dr. Faustus* (1588-1593). Although Vonnegut does not appear to be suggesting Miss Faust is making packs with the devil directly, she does have some interesting conversations with Jonah and reports to him the conversations she has been party to with both Dr. Hoenikker and Dr. Breed. The scientific men have the capability to bring about the downfall of humanity by pursuing scientific avenues they consider "truth," regardless of what they might cost to wider humanity, just as Dr. Hoenikker eventually does with Ice-9. She is described as a "merry, desiccated old lady" (CC, 37) who upholds the traditions of the office, but is aware of the contradictions that the scientific community is engaged in:

> 'Dr. Hoenikker had all those things in his life [intimate things, family things, love things], the way every living person has to, but they weren't the main things to him' ...
> 'Dr. Breed keeps telling me the main thing with Dr. Hoenikker was truth' ...
> 'I don't know if I agree or not. I just have trouble understanding how truth, all by itself, could be enough for a person.' (CC, 54)

Miss Faust questions the scientific idea of "truth" and appears to have an awareness that there is a human need for more, for a spiritual understanding of life, for a need for something to make the human experience bearable. Through Jonah, Vonnegut suggests that "Miss Faust was ripe for Bokononism," (CC, 54) suggesting that she can see through the illusion and accept the notion of useful lies, as she does not see how "truth" can be enough. Maybe Vonnegut is suggesting that she is selling out her understanding by continuing to work at the laboratory when she knows there is more than the "truth" they are pursuing scientifically. She is also allowing herself to be fully immersed in the "truth" of religion, so in another sense, she is not engaging with the ideas of "truth" not being enough. Vonnegut suggests she holds the ability to question but she chooses to wholeheartedly believe that "'God really is love, you know ... no matter what Dr. Hoenikker said,'" (CC, 55). She does not want to question or challenge the traditions of the office, even though it is obvious she does not agree with everything the scientists believe, perhaps showing how some people in society can see through the illusions of "truth" presented by culture, but do not want to misplace the comfortable aspect of conformity. If she did make a pact with the devil, it was to support Dr. Hoenikker even though she must have known it was at a dangerous cost and could eventually harm humanity, he in effect becomes the devil. Although there is no definitive account, the mythical Faust is reported to be a scholar and in turn possesses the ability of intellectual analysis and evaluation. He becomes disillusioned with idealism and with his faith, which leads him to make the pact with the opposing force, the devil. On the other hand, if Miss Faust were to turn to Bokononism, she too might be selling out and giving up on her own ideals, showing that the relationship with science and religion for individuals is clearly a complicated one. Vonnegut seems to be suggesting she can think critically, but it may be her staunch religious beliefs that render her a Faustian character. She is selling out by working for people who she does not believe align with her ideals. She is siding with the devil because she is scared to accept the possibility that there is something else, that the religious "truth" she so dogmatically believes may not be quite the absolute truth she thinks it is. The idea of truth is manipulated by Vonnegut here in the narrative because there are many versions that interact with each other. Every character seems to believe they have the "truth" and do not consider that their "truth" is impossible because there is no absolute truth. Each of the characters seem to evade any real interaction with each other in terms of discussion and understanding, although they all seem to hold strong beliefs or opinions, they do not challenge each other. In order to keep fundamental approaches, there needs to be no interaction with those outside the capsule of fixed ideas.

The other important staff member is the character of Lyman Enders Knowles, or just Knowles, who is also important in considering where society places its value. He is described as "a small and ancient negro" (CC, 58), who "was insane" (CC, 58). He is another example of Vonnegut's clever use of characterization for supporting characters that appear in the novel. They are generally introduced in passing and interject a level of resistance in the novel, normally by a quick conversation, thereby giving the reader philosophical questions to ponder. They are often introduced under the guise of lunacy, or "otherness":

> 'This here's a *re*-search laboratory. *Re*-search means *look again*, don't it? Means they're looking for something they found once and it got away somehow, and now they got to *re*-search for it? How come they got to build a building like this, with mayonnaise elevators and all, and fill it with all these crazy people? What is it they're trying to find again? Who lost what?' Yes, yes! (CC, 59)

Vonnegut gives the mad elevator operator the surname of Knowles, which could literally mean knowledge. He suggests, when referring to the scientists as "crazy people," that they are carrying out something insane and ridiculous.

In considering what Dr. Felix Hoenikker creates, one might believe that he sees something that everyone else does not. He is branded as "insane," yet he is the character that blatantly calls the scientists crazy for researching things that have been forgotten. While Dr. Breed represents the growing social views on scientific research, the "insane" character is overlooked and ignored, and rendered comical. Those around him see little value in the points that he makes, the points that society is trying to cover up or ignore. Vonnegut uses the carnivalesque to create literary carnival masks for the characters, allowing each character to represent a facet of society. Knowles is the character overlooked in the social structure of the narrative. He is given a voice in the text to force the reader to question whether the knowledge that the scientists are working on is really of great importance, or just extremely damaging as Ice-9 proves to be. It would be hard to ignore the fact that Knowles is also African American, he appears marginalized and treated without worth, referred to as a "negro." Here, Vonnegut shows how society can treat marginalized groups, even though it could be argued that Knowles is one of the most insightful and knowledgeable characters in the novel, he is ignored and ridiculed. He is outside the established norm of the accepted discourse of society. Again, Vonnegut suggests that all individual human beings should be valued and included in society, everyone being allowed to contribute to the overall cultural dialogue and wellbeing of society. By marginalizing individuals and groups, you isolate culture from knowledge and growth, keeping it stunted and unable to progress in a positive way. Knowles understands the dangers of the research laboratory, but no one is prepared to heed his warning.

The scientists represent the fundamental beliefs of the scientific community, and Vonnegut is careful to show the reader that they too, can be hostile and dismissive of the sense of "other." Dr. Breed is an interesting character and Vonnegut has been careful with his symbolic name choice: "Breed was a pink old man, very prosperous, beautifully dressed. His manner was civilized, optimistic, capable, serene" (CC, 27). His views represent the scientific views of society, and he is genuinely taken aback when Jonah implies that "the creators of the atomic bomb had been criminal accessories to murder most foul," (CC, 39). Breed is representative of someone who is considered civilized, he is wealthy and well dressed, and really does appear to be the archetype of a successful human being in society, he is well-bred. Unfortunately, Breed does not possess the capacity to value others' opinions or the insight to see the destructive nature of his own. He accuses Jonah of asking questions "aimed at getting me to admit that scientists are heartless, conscienceless, narrow boobies, indifferent to the fate of the rest of the human race, or maybe not really members of the human race at all" (CC, 39). He goes on to announce that "New knowledge is the most valuable commodity on earth. The more truth we have to work with, the richer we become" (CC, 41). The irony here is that this is exactly the opposite of what Breed and Felix Hoenikker achieved for humanity. They may be richer in the monetary sense, but how "richer" does the world really become? Science becomes a commodity of a capitalist society, pursuing new knowledge for monetary gains, and not the enrichment of humanity and their future stability. Dr. Breed is the representation of the corporate scientific community that places value on the monetary benefits of scientific and technological advancement. This element eliminates the basic principles that advancements should enhance human life and make it more manageable. This scientific laboratory creates the complete opposite in the near annihilation of the human race, making the lives of those left behind difficult and dangerous, and a place with money has no value, cynically ironic and frighteningly imaginable.

In searching for scientific truth, the scientists render the world useless and destroyed. Jonah states had he been a Bokononist at that point it "would have made me howl" (CC, 41) as "Dr. Breed sees science as "the very antithesis of magic" (CC, 36), a view that could be "breeding" throughout humanity. There is a continuous carnival turning around with the interaction between the characters at this point, Vonnegut stressing the juxtaposition of science and religion working against each other. He does not suggest either is worse than the other, but that there needs to be a balance between scientific truth and religion that gives people hope. Vonnegut is seeking to: "permit the combination of a variety of different elements ... to liberate from the prevailing point of view of the world, from conventions and established truths ... to realize the relative nature of all that exists, and to enter a completely new order of things."[26] He stresses the need for analysis and evaluation of the current social structure and of the conventions that civilization follows. He requires people to seek a "complete new order," one that does not value too much power in one place, a balanced society that values the human being first. He does not want to destroy science or spirituality, but to "realize the relative nature of all that exists," to consider humanity, and what is best for human beings to thrive in safety.

Like Breed, the character of Felix Hoenikker, the creator of Ice-9, is also used by Vonnegut to carnivalize the reality of science and weapons of mass destruction. Jonah strives to understand what happened at the family home of Hoenikker when the atomic bomb, called "Little Boy," was dropped on Hiroshima by a

---

26 Mikhail Bakhtin, "Introduction," *Rabelais and His World*, p. 34.

Boeing B-29 bomber on August 6, 1945, and what President Truman announced as having, "added a new and revolutionary increase in destruction."[27] What he discovers could be considered very disturbing to the reader: "He was playing with a loop of string. Father was staying home from the laboratory in his pajamas all day that day" (CC, 8-9). Seen from the child's perspective, it can strike the reader as being very straightforward and innocent, the remembrance of a game and his father wearing his pajamas. The child is completely unaware of what is going on in the world at that very moment, he is innocent of the suffering. His father is at home from work and is simply sitting in his study smoking a cigar. There seems nothing particularly alarming, just a simple domestic scene, yet there is everything wrong with the situation. The scene is used as dark satire to expose what is happening with the attitudes in the world at large. It is disturbing that the tranquility of this scene is twinned with a simultaneous scene that is incomprehensibly horrific and destructive. The man who was fundamental in enabling the horrific destruction is sitting at home in his pajamas, seeming very happy and content, his "truth" playing out in the lives of so many individuals. What has gone wrong in a world where thousands of people can die and another group of people can be at home with their creature comforts, oblivious to what is taking place? A further satirical blade is added considering the name Felix "means 'happy' and Hoenikker certainly is happy as he enjoys an endless childhood of discovery and wonder, but his happiness is paid for by a vast amount of human misery."[28]

Continuing with the dialogical narrative style, Vonnegut employs not just mythical and biblical references together with allegorical characters (names), but he also incorporates historical events and allusions to historical people that are stitched into the narrative to underscore the relationship between religion and science. The character of Felix Hoenikker is based on historical events, as Vonnegut stated he "was a caricature of Dr. Irving Langmuir, the star of G.E. Research laboratory ... Langmuir was wonderfully absent-minded. He wondered out loud one time whether, when turtles pulled in their heads, their spines buckled or contracted."[29] The "Manhattan Project" (CC, 16) was a real research project established by President Roosevelt and Winston Churchill to research

27 Jack Bell, "Senators May Ask Setup of World Security Council," *The Independent-Record*, Vol. 11, no. 257, 6 August 1945, Helena Montana, p. 1.

28 Thomas F. Marvin, "Cat's Cradle," *Kurt Vonnegut: A Critical Companion*, p. 84.

29 David Hayman, David Michaelis, George Plimpton, & Richard Rhodes, "Kurt Vonnegut: The Art of Fiction LXIV," *Conversations with Kurt Vonnegut*, William Rodney Allen, Ed., The University Press of Mississippi, 1988, Jackson, MS, p. 182.

and develop the creation of the atomic bomb. Hoenikker is also clearly representative of the "father of the atomic bomb," Dr. Robert Oppenheimer, who stated at the initial testing of the atomic bomb that, "we knew the world would not be the same."[30] The headline of *The Independent-Record*, on Monday, August 6, 1945, said: "New, Destructive Atomic Bomb Dropped on Japan. Truman Tells of Great Scientific Gain: Missile Using Pent-up Power of Universe Is Answer to Peace Bid Refusal.'"[31] Vonnegut's objective was to highlight the realities and extreme dangers that the atomic bomb possessed, and to point out where it could lead humanity; he did not see it as a potential pacemaker. The creator of the atomic bomb in the narrative is the creator of Ice-9, the very weapon that freezes and kills the majority of Earth's inhabitants: "[a] bittersweet satire occurs in *Cat's Cradle*"[32] as it "envisages an icy apocalypse of the post-holocaust world which, in Robert Frost's well-known words, "for destruction ice ... would suffice.'"[33] Although science has the capacity to accomplish great things for humanity, Vonnegut recognized the ability of science to damage it beyond recognition. It might not be an action done on purpose, but the great potential that science will destroy humanity, if pursued for the wrong reasons, must be acknowledged. Science and technology must always be treated with great responsibility.

The characterization of Bokonon is also an interesting one, and one that is mixed with factual historical information, and to the extent that it feels almost like an ancient Greek drama. Bokonon's real name is Lionel Boyd Johnson, and he was born to a wealthy family as his grandfather had supposedly found buried pirate treasure, "presumably a treasure of Blackbeard, of Edward Teach" (CC, 103). He was interested in both education and the ritual of religion, but seems to have led a free, young man's life. His education was put on hold when he enlisted in the First World War, where "he was gassed in the second Battle of Ypres" (CC, 105). He appears to have set sail for home, captured by a German submarine (U-99), and was then captured by the British destroyer, the Raven. The Raven was then damaged, and he was stranded on an island in Cape Verde Islands. He joined a fishing vessel that got blown off course to Newport, Rhode Island where "he worked as a gardener and carpenter on the famous Rumfoord Estate"

---

30 *The Decision to Drop the Bomb*, dir. Fred Freed & Wilmette III, *Films Inc.*, 1965, *Internet Archive*, Film supplied by PeriscopeFilm.com, https://archive.org/details/90984-the-decision-to-drop-the-bomb-vwr, Accessed August 28, 2022.

31 *The Independent-Record*, Vol. 11, no. 257, 6 August 1945, Helena Montana, p. 1.

32 Donald E. Morse, from Chapter 3: "No Reviews and Out of Print," *The Novels of Kurt Vonnegut: Imagining Being an American*, Praeger Publishers, 2003, Westport, CT, p. 58.

33 Donald E. Morse, from Chapter 3: "No Reviews and Out of Print," *The Novels of Kurt Vonnegut: Imagining Being an American*, p. 58.

(CC, 106). After the war, the young Rumfoord proposed a sailing trip around the world, which Bokonon joined as the first mate. He saw many wonders of the world, and was again stranded, but this time in India where he became a follower of Mohandas K. Gandhi. He was arrested, jailed, and he then tried to return home on the *Lady's Slipper II*. He sailed the Caribbean, sought shelter from a hurricane in Haiti, and was offered a large sum of cash to transport a Marine deserter to Miami. He was shipwrecked by a gale on the rocks of San Lorenzo where he "resolved to let the adventure run its full course" (CC, 107). As he emerged from the water, naked, it was like a "rebirth for him" (CC, 107). He came by the name Bokonon because "'Bokonon' was the pronunciation given the name Johnson in the island's English dialect" (CC, 108).

The life of Bokonon is portrayed as fantastical. The reader cannot help but laugh in places, as it appears a history of epic proportions, with twists and turns, incredibly bad luck, together with incredibly good luck. What is clear is that Vonnegut has mingled fiction with elements of historical fact. The amount of detail in the account gives the story an air of truth. It feels plausible because the reader can understand and recognize some of the points of historical interest. It is easy to imagine Bokonon in the situations described in the novel from pictures they may have encountered in school history lessons. He also uses historical people as points of reference, giving the story more credence. This is a cunning move by Vonnegut, as it places the reader in an awkward situation, and it is as if Vonnegut is using Bokonon as the personification of religion in the text. We know that Bokonon is a fictional character, a creation of the writer's mind, yet there is a carnivalization in the way that he is being used. On one hand, the fictional character is just that, fictional, but on the other hand, he incorporates historical reality. It is based on real events that happened. It forces the reader to evaluate, just as the "useful" religion forces us to look closely at our own religious ideas. We are forced into a realization that although some truths are there, it is a work of imagination, based on lies. It feels real yet the reader knows it is not. Even the commanding use of the figure of Edward Teach, or Blackbeard as he came to be known, gives the appearance of knowledge, of truth, yet history reveals we know very little about his life. We can only surmise what day-to-day lives may have been like for historical people, and in this way, they are just like literary characters in historical fiction. We accept truths on many levels of society, in many facets of our world, yet Vonnegut is saying, ask questions and do not just accept what you are told. There may be personal truths, yet they can be mixed with lies, and the word truth can embody something which is useful, is good for humanity, even if it is not founded in a complete "truth." All facets appear to be related and linked together, just as people are in any social structure, and just as the string of the cat's cradle game.

Vonnegut incorporates the role of the carnival, to confuse the identity of characters, to turnabout fact and fiction, and to expose society in satirical laughter that exposes its flaws. In many ways Vonnegut is mirroring what happens in society, there are so many versions of the truth that it is hard to distinguish what to believe. As society progresses, especially with today's social media, there are so many differing ideas of truth that it seems impossible for people to relate to one another. Vonnegut was able to see a future where science and religion could confuse humanity and become a source of suspicion. Each group finds it difficult to find common ground to see value in the other. He wanted his readers to see that there is no absolute truth, but to believe in each other and humanity, regardless of differing views and opinions. This is an element of Vonnegut's work that is important to modern America today, as we see an increased polarization of ideas and values important to contemporary culture creating divides and suspicion of each other. Vonnegut implores humanity to work towards creating understanding and communication across political divides, his experience suggesting that this is the only way forward to ensure a successful human future.

As Jonah struggles to transverse his way through the complexities of society, he takes the reader on a horrifying journey of revelation. In the narrative sequence when Papa turns the Ice-9 on himself, and just before he condemns the world to the apocalyptic end, he says "'Now I will destroy the whole world'" (CC, 238). Vonnegut stresses that it would just take one person, whether through mental illness or selfish political ambition, to make a decision that would change the course of human history. It would only need the intellectual apparatus and capability to create such a weapon, and then one person, selfish or stupid enough such as Papa, to use it: "'What hope can there be for mankind,' I thought, 'when there are such men as Felix Hoenikker to give such playthings as *ice-nine* to such short-sighted children as almost all men and women are?'" (CC, 245). Vonnegut underscores the fact that if these types of weapons were not invented and created in the first place, then there would be no potential for their use. Again, this assertion is full of complexity because it refers to both our current social world order, and to the metafictional element within the text. Vonnegut presents the question of why would God give his "short-sighted children as men and women are" (CC, 245) the mean of destroying themselves? He questions the motivations of what is behind the ideas of freedom and of accepted "truth." It makes little sense for humans to allow weapons of mass destruction to be made, to produce something that could cause total global devastation and complete annihilation of themselves. It makes even less sense for God to allow humanity to continue with the project, allowing the creation of the technology to destroy totally. Vonnegut's experiences of war enabled him to see the futility in killing each other and he could find no sense in the action, on any level.

Considering the historical figures that Vonnegut has evoked in the text, we find they are generally figures that fight against the accepted social control, often becoming exiled, such as Ismael or Edward Teach. They are the people willing to stand up for their freedoms regardless of what it costs them. Later in the novel, Vonnegut evokes figures associated with social control, in chapter 102: "Enemies of Freedom" (CC, 227), Dr. Vox Humana, the Christian minister, has created a target practice area with cardboard cut-out caricatures. After he had "prayed for guidance from Above" (CC, 229) he created them in the form of "old Joe Stalin," "old Fidel Castro's," "old Hitler," "old Mussolini," "old Karl Marx," "old Kaiser Bill" "old Mao" (CC 229-230). This is ironic considering that the New Testament within the Bible preaches pacifism and detachment from involvement in worldly politics. Here we see them used as target practice as society metaphorically takes shots at figures who seek to control the individual. Dr. Vox Humana, whose name is also the name of an organ reed stop, embodies the voice of God on earth, ironically another form of social control. Vonnegut is evoking people that he considered to be against freedom: "'they got practically every enemy that freedom ever had out there.'" (CC, 230), and this can be linked to the earlier suggestion of the meaningless teams, or Granfalloons, of "the Communist party, the Daughters of the American Revolution, the General Electric Company, the International Order of Odd Fellows—and any nation, anytime, anywhere" (CC, 92). The groups can be thought suggestive that Vonnegut believed that named groups for human individuals do not hold meaning or importance. The forming of these groups might segregate humanity in different ways rather than bringing them together. Some of the groups might also be thought to teach "truth" when there is none. We must concentrate our efforts, not picking on individual groups for destruction, but working together as humans, a united humanity.

In summing up the novel *Cat's Cradle* Donald E. Morse states that, "Vonnegut's invention works overtime as he combines a satire on modern 'feel good' American religion and with another on a banana republic's military dictatorship."[34] The two elements of wider society are brought together to exemplify the weak points of both ideals, and of how ideas seemingly in opposition

---

34 Donald E. Morse, from Chapter 3: "No Reviews and Out of Print," *The Novels of Kurt Vonnegut: Imagining Being an American*, p. 60.

can inadvertently have similar outcomes. Vonnegut reflects on the social ideologies that were in conflict at the time the novel was written, ideas Vonnegut was exposed to first-hand. He witnessed right-wing fascist dictatorship with Nazism, the fight against communist ideas, and closer to home, both Christian fundamentalism and capitalist extremes. The appearance here is that Vonnegut is drawing attention to the fact that each differing idea present in society can act in similar ways if they are taken to the extremes. Each has the capacity to kill individual human beings in the narrative, and every individual human was worth fighting for. Once an ideology is taken to extremes it has the capability to become dangerous. Morse goes on to suggest Vonnegut "then laces the brew with caricatures of what it means negatively to imagine being American in his portraits of American greed, backslapping-good fellowship, and shortsightedness."[35] He suggests that the Granfalloons of the world, such as individual nations, can be breeding grounds for hypocrisy, just as religion may be considered by some to be founded on "untruths", so too can social structures. To Morse "the result is a truly fantastic satire- bittersweet and cutting" and this is the very reaction that Vonnegut is striving for. He needs humanity to recognize just what the stakes are. It is a bittersweet realization to acknowledge that your own society, although painting itself as "free," is in truth based on corruption and lies, a realization that the narrative suggests could be present in all ideology.

Science in the novel, is the fundamentalist belief that allows the end of the world to take place in the text, the "new" religion of the modern age that has been allowed free reign to do as it pleases: "Pure research men work on what fascinates them, not on what fascinates other people" (CC, 49). It is the one thing that Papa recognizes as being the most powerful ideology: "'you—Franklin Hoenikker—you will be the next President of San Lorenzo. Science—you have science. Science is the strongest thing there is" (CC, 146). Science and the capabilities it possesses allows those in control to do whatever they wish, and if unchecked has the potential to destroy humanity. Dr. Breed sees science as: "'men are paid to increase knowledge, to work towards no end but that ... New knowledge is the most valuable commodity on earth. The more truth we have to work with, the richer we become'" (CC, 41) He views science as a type of religion because he thinks that men should only be focusing on research and finding out new knowledge. He sees it as the fundamental foundation of a good society, that research should be at the core of cultural belief regardless of the human cost. The scientists in the novel

---

35 Donald E. Morse, from Chapter 3: "No Reviews and Out of Print," *The Novels of Kurt Vonnegut: Imagining Being an American*, p. 60.

are "blinded by their own faith in science as 'magic that *works*' and in science as an ideology higher than respecting the dignity of any human."[36]

Dr. Breed suggests early in the narrative that belief in superstition is a flaw of society, that belief in such things is "brackish" and "medieval" (CC, 36). This is symbolic of what Vonnegut sees as problematic for society and not only in the religious context. Vonnegut allows Dr. Breed to make sweeping comments about "magic," or the ideas of religion during the Christmas period, an important spiritual holiday, because it highlights the belief in elements like Father Christmas, that we know to be untrue. Although ironic, he says of science that "'we don't *want* to mystify. At least give us credit for that'" (CC, 36). Vonnegut carnivalizes what he sees as a misrepresentation in terms of how science is viewed in society. Science is viewed as an absolute that does not mislead. However, Vonnegut seeks to question its motivations and place in modern society, just as he drives the reader to question religion, science does not always have altruistic intentions, especially when money is involved.

Later in the novel, Jonah tells us that: "It was the belief of Bokonon that good societies could be built only by pitting good against evil, and by keeping the tension between the two high at all times" (CC, 102). Vonnegut strives to disrupt the social conventions typically associated with today's western civilization. Although he does not condemn any facet of its composition, his suggestion is a society of restraint, of balance, that neither religion nor science can have absolute power. By Bokonon's suggestion that "pitting good against evil" must be always kept in society, there is a carnivalesque element to the discussion. The "two-world condition"[37] described by Bakhtin is required to maintain an equilibrium in the world, and a society that is protected from damaging extremes. Allowing one to gain more control would be catastrophic, as we can see from historic examples such as the religious Crusades, or the scientific and technological advancements made during the world wars to enable more efficient mass killing. Without the constant restraint of an opposite, unlimited influence and power can lead to the mass destruction of human individuals. The key to decoding Vonnegut appears to be his belief in humanity, and his consistent struggle against anything that causes them harm. If social forces are kept in check, regardless of what beliefs and views they hold or where they are on the political spectrum, and that absolute

---

36 Paul L. Thomas, ""No Damn Cat, and No Damn Cradle": The Fundamental Flaws in Fundamentalism according to Vonnegut," *New Critical Essays on Kurt Vonnegut. Ed. David Simmons*, Palgrave Macmillan, 2009, New York, p. 43.

37 Mikhail Bakhtin, "Introduction," *Rabelais and His World*,. 6.

truth is not allowed to divide humanity, then the outcome prophesied by the deployment of Ice-9 in the novel can be avoided.

The "two-world" element is another dialogic thread in the novel that is woven into the narrative at multiple points. A good example of this is the introduction of the weightlifting theory of Charles Atlas who proposed that muscles could be built by *"pitting opposing muscle groups in tension against each other"*[38] This is used as a comical metaphor, again heightening the element of carnival laughter in the narrative. He writes into the history of Bokononism to comically emphasize how simple life can be. The real Charles Atlas was a bodybuilding pioneer of the 1920s. He created a business based on the name "Atlas" and that was famous for its aggressive advertising campaign. This is ironic in three ways: firstly, he simply suggests that to create something good, one element must be pitted against the other: the two-world condition. Secondly, he is using an example of a commercial enterprise that rests on the premise that if you can make something popular enough, people will follow it. This is an encapsulation of the American Dream, the idealistic utopian foundation of freedom promised by the Granfalloon, America. The premise for a commercial enterprise did not necessarily need to be based on fact or "truth." It is also a notion that can be seen to be employed by Bokonon, to outlaw Bokononism makes it become more desirable and propel its popularity. Thirdly, by exploiting Greek mythology he allows this minor character the status of holding the world upon his shoulders. It is ironic; it seems ridiculous, that this muscle-building man, of whom the social stereotype is of stupidity or dumbness, can be the balance and foundation of the world. Bokononism promotes ideas of equality and no absolute power, yet these two foundational points incorporated by Charles Atlas exploit the ideals of the current system, both historically and socially. The dual notion of the world is represented by Vonnegut at different levels of society as an example of how simplistic and interconnected the notion can be considered. If the elements are held in check by one another, it creates balance, and it does not even matter if an element is founded on an untruth.

The two-world condition impedes Jonah from making any change to society when he becomes president because he cannot have Bokonon in his government. The change would create imbalance and Bokononism promotes balance. It could never work because the social ideology of dictatorship would be completely disrupted. In a sense, San Lorenzo takes on the role of carnival, it allows the characters to interact and change their roles, just as the carnival mask, but it

---

38 Marc Leeds, *The Vonnegut Encyclopedia*, Revised Edition, Delacorte Press, 2016, New York, p. 27.

does not allow permanent change. The laughter created by Vonnegut's figurative world is symbolic of his reaction to the culture surrounding him. The basis of Bokononism, founded on the advertising principles of capitalism, yet promoting the balance of bodybuilding, of tension, is a carnival turnabout that cannot be permanent. Bakhtin said: "Laughter created no dogmas and could not become authoritarian; it did not convey fear but a feeling of strength ... it was related to the future of things to come and was to clear the way for them."[39] Vonnegut is not trying to change things instantaneously or setting out to destroy the world we currently function in. He alerts the reader to the ridiculous elements, the aspects that do not benefit humanity in order that we can change them for the future. Realization and acceptance are required before change can take place in any society. Vonnegut understood the complexity of the interactions within human culture, and how these points of human contact can often cause confusion and contradictory elements. Human beings want things to progress and develop in society for the better, but if changes are made, do they become the fundamental points of reference? Human civilization is contradictory and complex, creating balance and positive outcomes in a world with no absolutes is enigmatic.

An interesting aspect that is further exposed, is the role that education holds in society. The traditional "truths" of our culture, already discussed, those stemming from religion, literature, myth, and history, are all taught through education. In this we can see that unless balanced, education is not always a positive thing. Bakhtin discusses how in medieval times it was often the educated in society that held power, and educational material was generally used by government, including religious authority, to bring "students to repentance."[40] Via this categorization, education is transformed into a weapon of control: "As a spokesperson of power, seriousness terrorized, demanded, and forbade ... it therefore inspired the people with distrust."[41] People demanded the need for laughter and carnival release, it was a requirement and was the form of resistance and freedom. Laughter was a thing to be trusted and believed, it did not follow traditional social protocols. To some extent, Vonnegut suggests that society no longer has this allowance; it no longer questions and distrusts. Education is often taught as truth and the expected norms of society are not questioned. Vonnegut offers the reader the laughter that Bakhtin values, the ability to laugh and see through the lies we tell ourselves. Bokonon says of education: "'Beware of the man who works

39 Mikhail Bakhtin, "Rabelais in the History of Laughter," *Rabelais and His World*, p. 95.
40 Mikhail Bakhtin, "Rabelais in the History of Laughter," *Rabelais and His World*, p. 95.
41 Mikhail Bakhtin, "Rabelais in the History of Laughter," *Rabelais and His World*, p. 94.

hard to learn something, learns it, and finds himself no wiser than before' … 'He is full of murderous resentment of people who are ignorant without having come by their ignorance the hard way'" (CC, 281). Just as Bokonon teaches that Granfalloons are a false Karass, we see here a pattern that teaches us that "absolute" notions are imposters and cannot be trusted. We can consider the pressures put on the individuals in society as misleading forces, ones that control and evade reality, and humanity is just as ignorant as it has always been.

In the process of highlighting the inadequate nature of our current social system, Vonnegut often alludes to how it needs to be changed, although never purporting his views as superior or absolute. In an article written for *In These Times* Vonnegut writes that: "power corrupts us, and absolute power corrupts absolutely. Human beings are chimpanzees who get crazy drunk on power … our leaders are power-drunk chimpanzees."[42] He realizes the shortcomings of the world that he lives in, he realizes that the politics of a nation has little to do with humanity but more to do with power, and he sees absolutes as crazy and corrupting. To draw attention to how universal the human experience can be, he satirizes normal situations in the narrative to generate laughter to emphasize the point. For example, it is universal that all human beings will age over time and eventually die, which really does render absolutes as impossible as nothing is fixed and infinite.

In the novel, when Jonah visits the cemetery to see the memorials to the Hoenikkers' he muses that he might take a photograph and use it as the "jacket for *The Day the World Ended*" (CC, 60). However, when he sees it, it appears as "an alabaster phallus twenty feet high and three feet thick" (CC, 61). The imagery here is startlingly humorous, especially considering that it is the memorial of the mother, the memorial of the father being a simple "marble cube forty centimeters on each side" (CC, 62). The suggestion here could be the importance of gender in the roles of society, a huge statue for the mother in relation to the father's, rendering his life and achievements impotent and small in comparison. This could also be another indication of how Vonnegut viewed the scientific advancement of the atom bomb, or of a scientific weapon capable of similar volumes of mass destruction. The inventor, in this case, getting an insignificant memorial parodies his perceived importance in the scientific community. In this same sequence, we are reminded by Vonnegut of how interconnected a small society and the world is, "'It's a small world' … 'When you put it in a cemetery'" (CC, 64). No matter

---

42   Vonnegut, Kurt, "Cold Turkey," *In These Times*, May 10, 2004, inthesetimes.com/article/cold-turkey, Accessed August 28, 2022.

how important and great we think our lives are, no matter who we are, or what our social importance is, we all end up the same way: as a memorial. Vonnegut understands the human condition, and he is attempting to get the reader to look at it on an individual human level. Again, absolutes are impossible as nothing is fixed and infinite.

A few chapters on from the graveyard sequence, Jonah has a spiritual epiphany when he comprehends his family connection to the angel statue: "I had a Bokononist vision of the unity in every second of all time and all wandering mankind, all wandering womankind, all wandering children" (CC, 73). Jonah's epiphany is a realization, not just in the personal sense, but also in a worldly spiritual sense. It seems ridiculous that he should come across such a thing, randomly in a store, but it is a human experience that little coincidences happen all the time. Jonah connects all of humanity together, all people united in the act of being human, connections that link the past, present, and future generations. In creating this link Vonnegut stresses the importance of human beings as one species, as a collective with shared experiences. He wants the reader to also make the connection, to look at humanity as a collective, and not just in terms of the political party or religion that may be popular. This sense of connection suggested by the text also mimics the Bakhtinian dialogic nature of the narrative, there are so many connections and strands in the novel that it is impossible to establish any definitive meaning that Vonnegut suggests we accept. Life and the novel represent one another, another two-world element to the overall narrative symphony, contradictory and complex.

This ideal is carried throughout the novel and is one which is explicit in the choice of chapter titles Vonnegut chooses when Jonah is writing his book after the Ice-9 has been unleashed on the world; chapter 122: "The Swiss Family Robinson" (CC, 275), and chapter 123: "Of Mice and Men" (CC, 276). He evokes the novel, *Swiss Family Robinson* (1812),[43] by Johann David Wyss, a novel of cooperation, to highlight a sense of family values, belief in self-reliance, and use of the natural world. The novel of John Steinbeck, *Of Mice and Men* (1937),[44] is also evoked as the novel that charts the "American Dream," and embodies the individual's quest for a better life with more meaning. Again, Vonnegut teases the reader with the two novels, one novel ending with a family living happily outside human society, and the other novel ending in disaster, having society turn against what they do not understand. There is an interaction between the manifestation

---

43 Johann David Wyss, *The Swiss Family Robinson*, Bantam Dell, 2008, New York.
44 John Steinbeck, *Of Mice and Men*, Penguin, 2002, New York.

of control and how to oppose it, a need to balance the forces present in human society. The successful family must be taken away from society in order to be successful, and the character who does not fit in with the norms of society is unsuccessful and killed. What Vonnegut seems to openly suggest is always the idea that if you have one force in control, with complete power, it ends up corrupting itself and human society. Humanity needs to think smaller, on a more personal level, one human being looking after the human beings they come into contact with, in order to succeed long term.

The use of literary texts as social markers by Vonnegut continues to give the overall narrative a sense of authority and knowledge. Again, it also adds to the sense of a complex narrative that mimics the views and differences in society, with so many cultural references in one place. Even though they are fictional, our society uses the texts as reflections of the society in which they were written. Vonnegut is imploring the reader to do the same with his narrative, to look deeper and make connections with the social arrangements they are reading from. The text is a heteroglot composition that uses the chronotype and time to add an element to the text which allows Vonnegut to draw examples and knowledge from across history: "the literary artistic chronotope, spatial and temporal indicators are fused into one carefully thought-out, concrete whole."[45] Vonnegut understands that we can learn from the mistakes and the ideas of the past if we are willing to accept the lessons that it has to offer. By using the historical and other literary references in the narrative the reader's sense of authority from the text is stronger. Vonnegut can incorporate so much more in terms of value in the text when he brings together examples that the reader can learn from. The novel is a carnivalization of the society Vonnegut is writing from, and a carnivalization of the world in which we find ourselves today. The historical and literary signposts allow the text to become a carnivalization of our own social culture.

In the penultimate chapter of the novel, Jonah mentions the seventh book of Bokonon, "which he [Bokonon] called 'Bokonon's Republic'" (CC, 284). Jonah contemplates for a moment what could have been achieved in society but realizes Bokonon had already addressed it in the seventh chapter, a book about Utopias: "The hand that stocks the drug stores rules the world. Let us start our republic with a chain of drug stores, a chain of grocery stores, a chain of gas chambers, and a national game. After that, we can write our Constitution" (CC, 285). There is a direct satirical taunt at the current western system of capitalism

---

45   Mikhail Bakhtin, "Forms of Time and Chronotope in the Novel," *The Dialogic Imagination*, p. 84.

here, and an attempt to extricate the meaning behind the value placed on certain areas, the value being the potential for vast sums of money. Vonnegut suggests that it is not the people, or the government they believe democratically elected to power, that runs a country, it is the corporations ruling from the shadows. A political party is a Granfalloon, it is the corporations behind the drug stores, the grocery stores, and the power suppliers that control the power of society because it is those entities that monopolize the monetary system. The inclusion of this taunt at capitalism from the perspective of the Bokonon religion, emphasizes a sense of an inevitability that everyday working people do not feel that they hold the power to change the system. Bokononism allows for a utopia that is based on the power of drug companies because it is a lie. There can be no real utopia when the main function of society is to generate large quantities of money. In recognizing how society really functions, as opposed to what people are led to believe, Vonnegut is again suggesting to the reader that something can be done, that in the acknowledgment there is power. The structures of society must be addressed, and society must assess what its principal aim is, to generate more and more money or to ensure the safety and future of humanity. The reader must embrace the carnival state for us to allow the inversion of our social perceptions, we must enact the carnival state for us to see our reality for what it is, founded on lies.

Vonnegut suggests that we need to control technology, to harness and supervise its progression and not give its power to individual corporations so that it does not progress to such an extent where it can harm humanity. In this sense, Vonnegut is suggesting that the accumulation of money has become like a religion, that we have allowed it to dictate our cultural rituals and practices. It could be argued that the massive tech companies of today have already had an impact on our rituals and practices by monitoring our every interaction and movement, through surveillance technology. The future that Vonnegut dreaded and warned of when writing *Cat's Cradle* might already be upon us.

To Vonnegut there is always a suggestion of hope, "As it happened – 'As it was *supposed* to happen,' Bokonon would say" (CC, 84), which tells us that we have something very important to learn. It becomes easy to forget the simple premise that Bokononism is founded upon blatant lies. If Bokonon is stating that something is supposed to happen that way, it tells us that we can change it. There is no fixed or definite way. Again, the carnival nature of the text is exposed, Vonnegut is pleading with us to acknowledge that everything Bokonon says, although it has its validity, is a complete misdirection. We do not have to put up with the fixed way society is, we can change things for the better and have balance. At Papa Monzano's death he says: "He (Bokonon) teaches the people lies and lies and lies. Kill him and teach people truth … I am a member of the Bokononist faith, 'Papa' wheezed. "'Get out, you stinking Christian'" (CC, 218). There is an ironic use of what truth and lies mean or stand for. Papa is right in his death speech, Bokonon does teach lies, not only of his religion, but he exposes the lies of society. His religion is based on the lies that society perpetuates and his aim is to expose them. Although the reader can see the lies that he bases his religion on, he is still a wise man, he can see past the "truths" told to us, and he effectively becomes the man he claims to be.

The closing sequence of the novel is given to Bokonon, dressed in a "white bedspread with blue tufts" (CC, 286); he looks comical, creating a laughter that exposes the reality of the situation, it is coupled with the words, "I would write a history of human stupidity … make a statue of myself, lying on my back, grinning horribly, and thumbing my nose at You Know Who" (CC, 287). Bokonon understands human nature, he has exposed the lies and is happy to create a silly face at God. He is humorous, the situation is funny, and the last gesture of the novel is to pull a face, one that suggests a lack of respect. Vonnegut creates the humor for satirical effect, he emphasizes our need to accept our flaws and to look deeper underneath the surface of society. To achieve the carnival atmosphere is the only way to acknowledge this, to experience the shifting of form, from one experience to another. It is not clear here whether Bokonon is talking of himself, or whether he is giving the advice to Jonah to carry out, as after all, it is Jonah who recounts his "dream of climbing Mount McCabe with some magnificent symbol and planting it there" (CC, 285). Jonah's own life could be that very symbol he has been considering without realizing it. In taking his own life in the manner suggested by Bokonon he could be opting out of the struggle of what it is to be human, he could be taking back the power in his eternal statuesque "thumbing my nose" at God.

In *Kurt Vonnegut and the American Novel*, Robert Tally suggests that "Vonnegut sees most people as fundamentally flawed, petty, avaricious, and prone to acts of almost incredible cruelty. Yet, for all that, Vonnegut also cannot abandon humanity; he marvels at human absurdity, noting sadly or just curiously man's absurd perseverance."[46] Vonnegut does not dislike humanity; in fact, his novels display the opposite of the "'misanthropic humanism,'"[47] Tally suggests.

---

46 Robert Tally, "The Dialectic of American Enlightenment," *Kurt Vonnegut and The American Novel: A Postmodern Iconography*, p. 55.
47 Robert Tally, "The Dialectic of American Enlightenment," *Kurt Vonnegut and The American Novel: A Postmodern Iconography*, p. 55.

Instead, Vonnegut displays a deep affection for Humankind and is preoccupied with trying to negotiate a world that has little meaning or understanding for them. It is hard being a human being, after all Vonnegut was a human being too, and he witnessed first-hand some of the most deplorable collective human behavior. It is this large collective behavior that Vonnegut was suggesting is at the root of the problem, and the suggestion that social ideology, when left unchecked, can lead to damaging fundamentalism. Individually human beings, unless mentally ill or criminally insane, will generally work towards their basic needs and comfort, but by working in much larger groups the mentality changes and people can become swept up with a herd mentality. Vonnegut promotes "faith in the human, [and] in the potential humanity in all humans. "[48] He believes in individual human kindness and in the good they are capable of achieving. The only way for individuals to achieve this is a vigilant awareness of the dangers social pressures can cause. To Vonnegut, human beings are inherently good, and not inherently bad, but it is the social restraints they are forced to live within that makes them do stupid things. Vonnegut considered himself a Humanist: "We humanists try to behave as decently, as fairly, and as honorably without any expectation of rewards or punishments in an afterlife ... We humanists serve as best we can the only abstraction with which we have any real familiarity, which is our community."[49] Vonnegut understands the dangers of fundamentalism in society and implores the reader, through the satirical nature of his narrative, to become aware of the issues these dangers pose to society. The carnivalization of modern society in the text allows us to become aware, but also affords us the time we need to change the outcome. Changing our interaction with society, with the ideas it perpetuates, may enable us to save it before it is beyond hope. Vonnegut had hope, he needs the reader to invest in that hope too.

Vonnegut writes novels to create laughter that empowers the reader with the carnival costume they need in order to take part in the social catharsis. They are his metaphors for what he sees in the world around him. His reader is there to learn, but just as he suggests in the novel, he is not there to give answers. He uses satire to show the reader how ridiculous the world can become, and how far it can go if we do not acknowledge that humanity is important enough to save. The narrative suggests that humanity is connected at all levels and that the lies we tell ourselves could endanger all of us. Jerome Klinkowitz comments that:

---

48 Paul L. Thomas, "'No Damn Cat, and No Damn Cradle': The Fundamental Flaws in Fundamentalism according to Vonnegut," *New Critical Essays on Kurt Vonnegut*, p. 42.

49 Kurt Vonnegut, "Do You Know What a Humanist Is?" *A Man Without a Country*, pp. 79–80.

> If made out too much like real life, novels can be mistaken for messages; we need to be reminded they are metaphors. Otherwise reading the words of fiction becomes as ridiculously misdirected as trying to sound out meaningful words from the brand names on delivery trucks.[50]

Vonnegut is here to give us the apparatus of the carnival but to never give us the absolutes because it is impossible, he does not want to misdirect us when we have all been so misdirected already.

Cat's Cradle is therefore a novel able to penetrate the fundamental beliefs of human cultural convictions, the beliefs deeply embedded in our cultural practices. Vonnegut is not reserved about exposing what he finds there; instead, he sets out to expose any illusions, to enable the reader to make an authoritative decision on the usefulness they pose. It encourages the reader to consider their long-held beliefs, to consider their validity, and any apparent alternatives. The novel creates satirical laughter that exposes the foundations of human society and acknowledges the human condition as naive and in a sense childlike. If the end of the world takes place there will be no need for the material wealth that is valuable today. Money and the economy, so important now, will no longer be relevant. In the cold and frozen world of *Cat's Cradle*, with the majority of the world's inhabitants dead, there will be no need for money, and no desperate need for food because it is frozen "until … ready to thaw and cook" (CC, 276). The narrative is one of Vonnegut's most effective as it navigates the imaginative structures of our social sphere. It is grotesque in its choice of thematic confrontation to concentrate on belief systems held important to many, and in its use of catastrophic mass destruction. It carnivalizes accepted perceptions just as J. G. Ballard's novel, *Crash* (1973),[51] carnivalizes the traditionally accepted perceptions connected to auto accidents. Its aim is to shock the reader with grotesque suggestions and expose the views the reader has never questioned or even considered questioning previously. Vonnegut wants his reader to notice their fixed perceptions, the subconscious acceptance they were unaware of, and he does it in the hope that more awareness will encourage positive change. Not only does he want us to realize the destruction that scientific progression can cause if placed in the wrong hands, but he also asks the reader to question, to act with caution, in accepting the very ideas and "truths" our society is perpetuating in the human mind. Vonnegut does not state that it is inevitable that we destroy humanity; he

---

50 Jerome Klinkowitz, *Kurt Vonnegut*, Methuen, 1983, New York, p. 73.
51 J. G. Ballard, *Crash*, Vintage, 2004, London.

is suggesting what could happen if we do not have the capacity to evaluate our own beliefs. His vision is a humanist one and it includes a humanity that acts with responsibility. Vonnegut is asking us, as human individuals, to act with responsibility, to evaluate ourselves and act for the good of us all. He offers us no definite way of making society better, he only signposts what we might want to consider. The "Cat's Cradle" is just an imaginary game, one that can be played by anybody, and we can all affect the strings. Vonnegut believes in humanity and that faith can go a long way:

> 'There is a willingness to do whatever we need to do in order to have life on the planet go on for a long, long time. I didn't used to think that. And that willingness has to be a religious enthusiasm, since it celebrates life, since it calls for meaningful sacrifices.
>
> 'This is bad news for business, as we know it now. It should be thrilling news for persons who love to teach and lead. And thank God we have solid information in place of superstition! Thank God we are beginning to dream of human communities which are designed to harmonize with what human beings really need and are.
>
> And now you have just heard an atheist thank God not once, but twice.[52]

If human beings can cultivate a deep faith in one another, they can work together for a better future. They will be able to fulfil their basic need for "communities … designed to harmonize with what human beings really need and are," rather than struggling in societies fragmented by money and greed. Human beings need other human beings, and if we can engage in this with a "religious enthusiasm," humanity will have every chance in the future, whatever our individual beliefs.

---

52 Kurt Vonnegut, "Religion," *Palm Sunday: An Autobiographical Collage*, p. 191.

3

War: *Slaughterhouse-Five*

"In case you haven't noticed, we also dehumanized our own soldiers, not because of their religion or race, but because of their low social class."[1]

*

Slaughterhouse-Five is one of the most recognized of Vonnegut's novels and is widely considered to be the most successful. The novel expresses his cathartic narrative in response to the horror of his experiences in the firebombing of Dresden during his incarceration as a prisoner of war in Germany, during World War Two. It was no secret that Vonnegut deplored war and openly spoke against it. What he observed as a serviceman always remained with him; he was a humanist with a deep concern for the well-being of Earth's inhabitants. As a witness of war, his experiences of the mass killing of innocent men, women, and children had shown him how nonsensical acts of war are: "**Killing industrial** quantities of defenseless human families, whether by old-fashioned apparatus or by newfangled contraptions from universities, in the expectation of gaining military or diplomatic advantage thereby, may not be such a hot idea after all."[2] Vonnegut understood

1 Kurt Vonnegut, "Do You Know What a Humanist Is?" *A Man Without a Country*, p. 87.
2 Kurt Vonnegut, "I Turned Eighty-Two on November 11," *A Man Without a Country*, p. 74—emphasis in original text.

that the ideals of war differed greatly from the reality of the experience. It did not matter by what means mass quantities of human beings were killed, the fact that so many were killed needlessly was at the core of his personal message.

The first chapter of *Slaughterhouse-Five* functions as a prologue to the rest of the novel by introducing the reader to the ideas presented in the overall narrative: "ALL THIS HAPPENED, more or less. The war parts, anyway, are pretty much true ... I've changed all the names."[3] The narrator states from the first line of the chapter that everything in the novel is "more or less" true and, therefore, suggests that the novel has already been decided and written. The act of Vonnegut writing the story from the perspective of retrospect, regardless of the "more or less," means this is now the accepted version, and it is this element that allows the carnivalization to take place in the novel. Vonnegut's experiences, and retrospective thoughts on those experiences, allow a narrative that manipulates the sense of normality to a point where there can be no "normal." The act of war renders all that is considered normal and safe impossible, that any sense of belonging and continuity are illusions of society. The novel is Vonnegut's own sense of reality, carnivalizing past, present, and future. The "normal" everyday perceptions of the individual succumb to the turnabout that Bakhtin suggests in *Rabelais and His World*,[4] that "liberate from the prevailing point of view of the world."[5] The carnival life allows the ideals of war to be exposed as a fabrication of those in power to misuse individuals. The "more or less" becomes the multitude of experience, or the differences in individual experience. The narrative allows the space for personal interpretation as there is no absolute truth in human subjectivity. Vonnegut maintains that the factual events are there, although there may be changes to how they can be comprehended. The novel is distinctly dialogic in nature which legitimately allows Vonnegut to experiment with perceptions from its outset. There is not one absolute experience or outcome of war that can support the killing of "industrial quantities of defenseless human families."[6] The acknowledgment by the narrator that "There would always be wars" is in response to Harrison Starr's question, "'Why don't you write an anti-glacier book instead?'" (SF, 4). The acknowledgment displays an awareness of the nature of humankind. Stopping humanity from going to war is equal to stopping a natural phenomenon, it is in its nature to exist, and near impossible to stop. Vonnegut

3 Kurt Vonnegut, *Slaughterhouse-Five*, Dial Press, 2009, New York, p. 1—emphasis in original text.
4 Mikhail Bakhtin, "Introduction," *Rabelais and His World*,. 11.
5 Mikhail Bakhtin, "Introduction," *Rabelais and His World*, p. 34.
6 Kurt Vonnegut, "I Turned Eighty-Two on November 11," *A Man Without a Country*, p. 74.

does not want the reader to change historical events, it is impossible to change history, but he wants the perception of what war means to change, to stop so many defenseless human beings from being slaughtered for pointless reasons.

In this way, the reader becomes a witness to Vonnegut's historical perception, rather than an accessory to the accepted historical narrative. Vonnegut is not offering a way to change society, but simply an unveiling of awareness through language. The reader expects the traditionally acceptable and "ideal," account of a war experience; they are not expecting aliens and time travel. This alternative sense of reality becomes Vonnegut's device to carnivalize accepted experience, as he takes the expected and exposes its shortcomings. Vonnegut's suggestion that "ALL THIS HAPPENED" (SF, 1), and the nature of its content being predominantly the experience of war, implies a dramatically tragic element to human life. Harrison Starr's insinuation that it is all impossible to change, and hence almost fated to happen again and again, implies a similar idea to that of traditional Greek tragedy. The idea that events are fated by the gods to unfold exactly as they are supposed to, regardless of the pain and suffering endured by human beings: "Tragedy is a kind of protest; it is a cry of terror or complaint or rage or anguish to and against whoever or whatever is responsible for 'this harsh rack', for suffering, for death."[7] Vonnegut, however, does not believe in gods, he is a humanist and the "more or less" is a hint at what is to come. On one hand, he acknowledges historical events cannot be changed, even to some extent that humans may even repeat the mistakes they have already made. On the other hand, there is a sense that we can acknowledge how we are witness to the events, and the "more or less" (SF, 1) could indicate that there can be a change in how people perceive social narratives. The events remain the same, yet there is a change in collective understanding. Our perceptions can be altered, and by carnivalizing war and his own experiences, Vonnegut allows the reader to change what has happened in the past, by perception alone. Therefore, people have the power to change the events of the future: the "industrial quantities of defenseless human families" can be saved.

Although one of Vonnegut's leading motivations, the need for the novel to examine and analyze the perceptions held by people regarding their own historical and cultural attitudes to war, it did not make it any easier for him to explore his own memories. He understood the official sterilized version, but to reflect the truth of what happened he needed to consolidate his personal version of history.

---

7   J. A. Cuddon, *Penguin Dictionary of Literary Terms and Literary Theory*, Third Edition, Penguin, 1991, London, p. 985.

The indication within the novel suggests how hard and complex this process was for the narrator, reflecting Vonnegut's own experience:

> I would hate to tell you what this lousy little book cost me in money and anxiety and time … I thought it would be easy for me to write about the destruction of Dresden, since all I would have to do is report what I had seen. (SF, 2)

This is not just a "lousy little book" otherwise it would have been much more straightforward to tell the story. As Charles J. Shields documented in Vonnegut's biography, *And So It Goes: Kurt Vonnegut, A Life*, Vonnegut did not know how to write about his experiences: "As Knox said, 'he didn't know how to approach it.'"[8] The process of writing to express personal trauma was difficult, how do you begin to write a story which you may only remember as fragments of horrible moments? The connotations of "lousy" suggest that Vonnegut questioned the importance of his own beliefs: If every human being is valuable, how can his perspective be worthy of writing? Vonnegut's reference to lousy again reflects the difficulty of finding the words and expressions to do deserved justice to the deeply complex material.

The act of remembering and memory are also important elements within the novel. The narrator's apparent struggle with remembering reflects Vonnegut's own writing experience, "how useless the Dresden part of my memory has been" (SF, 3). The narrator's confession at finding the book difficult to write is an indicator of how Vonnegut's experiences affected him. The suggestion of a loss of memory points to a psychological need to forget painful experiences, such as the symptoms of Post-Traumatic Stress Disorder. The friend in the novel, Bernard V. O'Hare, is reluctant, he is "unenthusiastic" (SF, 5) and "He said he couldn't remember much" (SF, 5-6), and the impression is given that some people would rather forget and not talk about their memories. These experiences are absolutes for the people involved and the emotional sacrifices they have to make in remembering them can be costly. Possibly, the mind gives up remembering to save you from the horror because it is so difficult to piece together a coherent picture, too painful to comprehend the reality of your experience. In Vonnegut's own words: "there was a complete blank where the bombing of Dresden took place, because I don't remember … There was a complete forgetting of what it was

---

8 Charles J. Shields, "A Community of Writers, 1965–1967," *And So It Goes: Kurt Vonnegut, A Life*, p. 190. Knox refers to Knox Burger, a fellow Cornell alumnus, and an editor who was responsible for publishing Vonnegut's first short story (Also see Vonnegut's letter to Knox dated June 1949, "The Forties," in *Kurt Vonnegut Letters*, pp. 25–26).

like."[9] The language Vonnegut uses here is important because of his use of the word "complete." It is as though the event was so absolute for those witnesses involved, that they simply forgot it, either by choice or from involuntary psychological protection. This is echoed by the discussion of where the climax of the story should take place. If a person cannot remember everything that they have encountered, or if each person's experience of war is different, with individuals encountering a variety of disturbing events, how can a writer possibly be able to prioritize? Where does the writer begin?

Vonnegut's dilemma of a writer having to express the complexity of the reality experienced by the individuals that were witness to events firsthand was a particularly heavy burden. It also demonstrates how deeply connected Vonnegut was to the value and importance that every individual has in society. He wanted to do the events, the individual experiences, and those readers learning from his language a complete justice, reflecting the complex nature that the human experience really is. He wanted to show the humanity in the historical events to influence how society might move forward with decisions of conflict in the future. Vonnegut's own experience and disjointed memories did not make the act of writing easy. If you come to understand and accept that the human condition is one that incorporates war, and those experiences are often horrifically brutal, how do you begin to write about them? Which event do you choose to write about first, or whose death from the many you have witnessed do you include? Does one individual's life outweigh the value of another? With so many questions to answer and the burden of getting it right to also reflect your own personal experiences, it is understandable that Vonnegut struggled with writing the novel. Vonnegut's own words, "I don't remember,"[10] also suggest that he too is in a similar situation to the reader, he does not yet know the whole story. The act of writing and remembering is also a journey for him, one which could reveal perceptions painful to exercise, and the act of writing allows him to release forgotten memory.

The choice of the execution of Edgar Derby as the climax of the novel by the narrator is an example of how the reader should perceive war, and further reflects the complexity of remembering. This story is chosen, out of the many events witnessed, and prioritized, because it represents the futility of the war experience.

---

9 William Rodney Allen Ed., "Playboy Interview: David Standish 1973," *Conversations with Kurt Vonnegut,*. 94.

10 William Rodney Allen Ed., "Playboy Interview: David Standish 1973," *Conversations with Kurt Vonnegut,* p. 94.

There are so many deaths and for what reason? Edgar Derby survived the horror of the war, he survived being a prisoner of war, and he survived the mass destruction of the firebombing of Dresden, yet he is killed for picking a teapot out of the rubble, accused of looting:

> 'I think the climax of the book will be the execution of poor old Edgar Derby,' I said. 'The irony is so great. A whole city gets burned down, and thousands and thousands of people are killed. And this one American foot soldier is arrested in the ruins for taking a teapot. And he's given a regular trial, and then he's shot by a firing squad.' (SF, 6)

The event allows Vonnegut to show the reader that the events in the novel may seem at times ridiculous but absurd things really do happen in everyday life, especially during war. The narrator in the novel remembers the stupidity of the situation: the man that experiences the horrors of the firebombing, who survives and is then put to death for an insignificant impulsive act, but he does not remember some of the horrors he faced himself. He remembers the absurdity of the formal motions of a trial when all around them was complete and utter destruction, as if, in some way, stealing a teapot might make the man responsible for the leveling and desolation of Dresden itself. Vonnegut himself appears to remember individual horrors, but the bigger fixed point of the actual bombing of Dresden eludes him. He possesses the partial truth but must still uncover a complete understanding. Vonnegut uses his knowledge to carnivalize and enlighten the rest of us, but also to flesh out the reality for his own mind. *Slaughterhouse-Five* is not written as a traditional anti-war tract, although it can be considered as such, but it should be considered more an anti-illusion novel. Vonnegut wants the reader to come to their own conclusions about war by looking past the ideology society teaches us. Vonnegut seeks to carnivalize our perceptions of war and how history remembers it from a distance. He seeks truth and possibly the need for redemption; he cannot remember the whole course of events, the events where an estimated "135,000 people died,"[11] but he seeks to be their witness.

---

11 Foreword by Air Marshall Sir Robert Saundby: David Irving, *The Destruction of Dresden*, Ballantine Books, 1963, New York p. 9. (See SF, 239)
The use of David Irving's book may be considered controversial here as he is an historian generally discredited for his comments relating to Holocaust denial. However, I have decided to reference the book as it was directly used and referred to by Vonnegut in *Slaughterhouse-Five*. *The Destruction of Dresden* was published six years before Vonnegut's publication date and was obviously a text he read and considered.

The need for a fictional novel, as opposed to a factual first-hand account of his experiences, suggests that Vonnegut needs to be removed from events, or needs to step back to filter his experiences in order to cope with them. The narrator in the story is never named; he seems believable, often unreliable, and he does not remember many of the events of the firebombing itself. The reader cannot help but assume that the character is based on Vonnegut and much of what is spoken comes from his own thoughts and opinions, but this is problematic. Vonnegut has never held back regarding his opinions on war and his own experiences, but the novel is a fiction. It is a metaphor based on the real experiences of an individual, and the need to tell the reader what has been learned from those experiences. Vonnegut incorporates many factual events and experiences in the novel, but the use of fiction allows him the freedom to express how the events were experienced, how they felt, and how they are remembered. In this way, the narrative can be considered a carnival mask that allows Vonnegut to cut through the ideals of society.

Vonnegut's use of time travel is a good example of how a pure, factual account could not work. To the best of our knowledge time travel is not yet considered factual. His use of an "alien other" in the novel is important in this way because he can use characters and events that otherwise may be impossible in a "real"-life situation. He can carnivalize, to create a "place for working out, in a concretely sensuous, half-real and half-play-acted form"[12] without the constraints of essentialist reality. The experiences of a person are individual and trying to focus on explaining how they felt is difficult. The use of carnivalization, or manipulation of accepted conventions of culture and science, ensures "behavior, gesture, and discourse of a person are freed from the authority."[13] Essentially, Vonnegut is free from all restraints in fiction, he can explore as he pleases without the restraints of autobiographical norms. The reader must consider other possibilities, must consider the implausible as plausible. Their imagination is free to consider the possibilities because they are challenged by Vonnegut to accept their own experiences as individual to them. The reader's own perceptions are contaminated by the prejudices they have been conditioned to hold by their environment. They must challenge themselves to the dialogic nature of humanity:

For Vonnegut to describe his feelings of shock and confusion as a young army private - feelings that later look shape as nightmares—the truth was useless ...

---

12 Mikhail Bakhtin, "Characteristics of Genre," *Problems of Dostoevsky's Poetics*, p. 123.
13 Mikhail Bakhtin, "Characteristics of Genre," *Problems of Dostoevsky's Poetics*, p. 123.

What he needed to communicate was the delirium created by his sense of chaos … *Slaughterhouse-Five* could take any turn, any theme he wished.[14]

The unnamed narrator of the novel discusses the difficulties in his twenty-three-year pilgrimage to exorcise his personal ghosts through writing, and he also mentions several other bodies of work in connection with the war. The fact that Vonnegut's own novel has taken so long to write, without a need to give up his struggle, suggests how important the act of writing and reading is to him in order to organize and comprehend the magnitude of a wider understanding of the events: "'Two decades' worth of false starts, slow-to-come realizations, and revisions had gone into it, and all the while the story—as well as he knew it—had resisted his efforts like granite."[15] A personal catharsis is taking place: the questioning of memory, or historical discourses, and the need to come to some understanding of why humanity behaves the way it does. It is a twenty-three-year struggle to find enough words to piece memories back together, to have a narrative that he feels adequately does justice to his experiences of war, but also to the wider experiences of other individuals.

The main character, Billy Pilgrim, embodies the autobiographical nature of the text and represents a satire of traditional western cultural ideals. The novel considers traditional perceptions of war and inverts these to allow a more balanced viewpoint. War can no longer be about handsome brave heroes and gallant battlefield victory, but it becomes about the destruction of the human being, both physically and mentally. In effect, war represents a people turning on themselves and an act of dismantling. Vonnegut's act of writing the novel appears to be deeply troubling and uncomfortable for him. He lived through the catastrophic event, and in writing it, there seems to be an apparent struggle within himself that he is trying to come to terms with. There is a delicate process of remembering, researching, and maintaining psychological well-being. At times the physicality of putting something into words can seem like a catalyst for solidification, making it impossible for a person to evade or ignore. It is there as a solid form in front of you, your reality recorded forever. Even though Vonnegut professed to be more affected by the experience of extreme and prolonged hunger—"I'd paid my dues—being as hungry as I was for as long as I was in prison camp,"[16]—the very fact that he had forgotten the events of the Dresden firebombing suggests he was

14   Charles J. Shields, "The Big Ka-Boom, 1967–1969," *And So It Goes: Kurt Vonnegut, A Life*, p. 232.
15   Charles J. Shields, "The Big Ka-Boom, 1967–1969," *And So It Goes: Kurt Vonnegut*, p. 243.
16   William Rodney Allen Ed., "Playboy Interview: David Standish 1973," *Conversations with Kurt Vonnegut*, p. 94.

more affected than he realized or cared to publicly admit. He articulates the absolute trauma of his individual war experience through dark humor and laughter, compounding just how physically, mentally, and emotionally debilitating it was.

The use of historical discourse is an aspect that Vonnegut manipulates very well within this first chapter. The referencing of books relating to history or war is used throughout the novel, and this is important to the mechanics of the novel in two ways. Firstly, it shows evidence that Vonnegut has himself researched the narratives that have been established regarding the firebombing of Dresden, and those associated with the war. It invites the reader to seek out the texts to educate themselves about the differing narratives. The novel feels as though it may have more significance as it has been researched and referenced. Secondly, by introducing the differing historical discourses Vonnegut is again extending an invitation to question the differing narratives associated with the events. His question is not relating to the ability to change events, but he is asking us to question our perceptions. The references are used as points to carnivalize and challenge conventions offered by traditional historical discourses. He also uses some texts, almost forgotten, or now considered outdated, to offer an alternative to current thinking. In his essay, "The Otherness of History in Rabelais' Carnival and Juvenal's Satires, Or Why Bakhtin Got It Right In The First Place," Paul Allen Miller states that Bakhtin's carnivalesque inversion can be considered "an ironic decrowning of authoritative discourse."[17] Vonnegut seeks to do just that, to decrown the accepted version that powers in society have established for the masses and seek out the differing perspectives from the experiences of those that have fought and lived through the war. He is preoccupied with why humans act the way they do, what is it about their psychology that allows them to continue to make destructive and violent decisions.

The referencing of supportive texts also reinforces Bakhtin's ideas of the chronotope, and the heteroglot nature of the narrative. The historical texts offer differing opinions on what war means for human beings, and the different perspectives that events can have. There is also a realization that texts can be manipulated, and subtlety misrepresented to enforce ideological perspectives. The narrative is multi-voiced in this respect, and the reader is empowered to formulate their own perception and reaction to the text:

---

17 Paul Allen Miller, "'The Otherness of History in Rabelais' Carnival and Juvenal's Satires, Or Why Bakhtin Got It Right the First Time," Eds. Peter I. Barta, Paul Allen Miller, Charles Platter, & David Shepherd, *Carnivalizing Difference: Bakhtin and The Other*, Routledge, 2001, London, p. 141.

all socially significant world views have the capacity to exploit the intentional possibilities of language through the medium of their specific concrete instancing. Various tendencies ... circles, journals, particular newspapers ... individual persons are all capable of stratifying language, in proportion to their social significance, they are capable of attracting its words and forms into their orbit by means of their own characteristic intentions and accents[18]

The inclusion of so many alternative readings of just one war enables Vonnegut to stress the individual nature of perception, that people develop their own interpretation by means of bringing those ideals "into their own orbit" subject to their own "intentions and accents." The historical chronotopes add a multilayered and complex nature to the overall text, emphasizing both the intricacy of human life and the "carefully, thought-out, concrete whole"[19] needed for the text to be considered with any authority.

The first discourse he mentions at length is *Extraordinary Popular Delusions and the Madness of Crowds*, by Charles Mackay (1841), an interesting choice and one which can be considered to sum up the need for the narrative of *Slaughterhouse-Five* in the first place. It is a historical text attempting to explore and explain why instances of mass mania happen, looking at several events from the tulip mania of the early seventeenth century to the witch trials of the sixteenth and seventeenth centuries. All the events taking place appear to have no real foundation in truth, apart from the fact that once a notion became a part of the social conscience, as more and more people bought into the idea, the idea spun out of control, in many cases leading to financial ruin, violence, or death. Charles Mackay wrote, "Men ... think in herds; it will be seen that they go mad in herds, while they only recover their senses slowly, and one by one."[20] The book is mentioned in relation to the Children's Crusade,[21] a reference to a supposed Christian Crusade attempted by young people to convert Muslims to Christianity in the Holy Land. Although little concrete evidence exists, the crusade is rumored to have been initiated by monks willing to sell the children into slavery for money. The crusade was supposedly made up of thousands of children or young people, but they never made their destination of Jerusalem, as the ships they sailed on were either taken to North Africa to engage with the slave trade or they were drowned in

---

18 Mikhail Bakhtin, "Discourse in the Novel," *The Dialogic Imagination*, p. 290.
19 Mikhail Bakhtin, "Forms of Time and of the Chronotope in the Novel," *The Dialogic Imagination*, p. 84.
20 Charles Mackay, "Preface," *Extraordinary Popular Delusions and the Madness of Crowds*, Kindle Edition, CreateSpace Independent Publishing Platform, 2011, London, Loc 75.
21 Dickson, Gary. "Children's Crusade." *Encyclopedia Britannica*, March 18, 2018, https://www.britannica.com/event/Childrens-Crusade. Accessed August 28, 2022

shipwrecks. Interestingly, the "Children's Crusade" is also the name given to a civil rights demonstration by young people in Birmingham, Alabama, in 1963, when children were "blasted by high-pressure fire hoses, being clubbed by police officers, and being attacked by police dogs."[22] This is interesting in relation to the dialogic interactions in the text, as many references and historical points can converge to highlight the issues Vonnegut is making. As history progresses, what other events might take on the name of the "Children's Crusade" and add to the multi-voiced nature of the narrative over time? Often the names chosen for events have symbolic meaning, and in these two cases, parallels are drawn between the ways in which the powerful in society further their own interests at the expense of children and young adults.

O'Hare's wife links the soldiers in the war to the Children's Crusade by referring to them as being "just *babies* then!" (SF, 18). She highlights the point that the men were only teenagers when they went to war, they were still only children. She is angry regarding the notion of even writing a book, concerned that the men are thinking in terms of the stereotypical romanticized hero often played by actors in films like Frank Sinatra or John Wayne. They are the stereotypes idolized and admired by young people who are taken in by the grandeur of the roles. She understands the nature of what war is really like, and how the young men were not old enough to fully comprehend the magnitude of what would happen to them, they should never have been swept up in war's destructive nature. The herd-like mentality allows society to engage individuals in the mechanics of war because they are seduced by the romanticized version of what it will be like, they believe the war propaganda. Vonnegut uses the texts to question the motivations for such destructive wars: What is the need, and what does it ultimately achieve? First-hand experience is a powerful motivational tool for a deep understanding of why something has happened and how we might be able to stop it from happening again. Vonnegut is exploring and looking for an explanation. What makes large groups of people, whole nations, act in the way they do?

It is an important point to note that Vonnegut quotes directly from MacKay in chapter one of the novel. His choice of quote is important for its symbolism in relation to his own novel and the creation of his narrative as a metaphorical representation:

---

22 "The Children's Crusade," National Museum of African American History & Culture, The Smithsonian, https://nmaahc.si.edu/blog/childrens-crusade. Accessed August 28, 2022

History in her solemn page informs us, that the Crusaders were but ignorant and savage men, that their motives were those of bigotry unmitigated, and that their pathway was one of blood and tears. Romance, on the other hand, dilates upon their piety and heroism, and portrays, in her most glowing and impassioned hues, their virtue and magnanimity, the imperishable honor they acquired for themselves, and the great services they rendered for Christianity.[23]

The quote embodies the essence of how Vonnegut sees the polarizing views of his own war. His intention is to show the reader how different readings can be extrapolated from one event. There is a juxtaposition of ideas and perceptions created from a single historical point, and the fact that Vonnegut chooses to quote this directly shows how important he sees those opposing perceptions within his own novel. The two viewpoints of History and Romance are opposites, they are both looking at the same violent episode in history, yet both accept the event in absolute terms. On one side you have "ignorant and savage men" and on the other side "piety and heroism," both being the embodiment of the cultural acceptance of stereotypical notions of war. War is seen as absolutes, either one thing or other, a reflection of how society functions, with an inability to assess objectively. Vonnegut understands this and seeks to educate himself with all the discourses available for his own experience of war.

The notion of stereotype is important in the novel as it alludes to the idea of the carnival, and the carnival costume or mask. In the theatre of war, soldiers exchange their normal clothes for a uniform, and this could be perceived as the wearing of a costume. In adopting the costume and participating in the carnival of war, the ideals of war are turned about. This could be seen as a great unmasking of the "reality" of what it is to engage in war and its outcomes. The stereotypes and ideals of war are lost in connection to what the experience really is. The romanticized notion of the great hero is completely different from the disturbing acts necessary by soldiers during the physicality of war. The war costume allows the unmasking of the flaws in society and how those stereotypes are no longer relevant or seen as valid. O'Hare's wife understands that the heroic illusions society portrays of war, along with the stereotypes, are needed to evoke the mass hysteria required for society to engage in war, but it is all nonsense. The whole war narrative within a culture is an illusion that is created for societies to participate in war, constructed narratives to control perceptions. The notion of

---

23 Kurt Vonnegut, *Slaughterhouse-Five*, p. 20: Taken from Charles Mackay, *Extraordinary Popular Delusions and the Madness of Crowds* (1841).

carnival costume is something that takes place throughout the novel, and it is a device used by Vonnegut repeatedly to draw out the absurdity and illusions of the war experience, which are often in contradiction to the ideals held by society.

MacKay is followed directly by the mention and direct quotation, of *Dresden, History, Stage and Gallery* by Mary Endell (1908), a publication written as an account of how Dresden had come to look architecturally at the time it was written. Vonnegut quotes, *"In 1760, Dresden underwent siege by Prussians ... The devastation of Dresden was boundless."*[24] This is ironic, as it is placed in the opening chapter of the novel and supports the MacKay quote beautifully. Vonnegut is undermining social and cultural discourse by highlighting the fact that at the time, in 1908, it was believed that Dresden had undergone its worst damage during the Prussian siege in 1760; however, this was nothing to what it would experience during the firebombing of World War Two. Endell was right at the time of writing the text and could have no idea of what would happen to the future Dresden. Both MacKay's and Endell's references at this point identify clearly that Vonnegut's desire is to highlight the problems people face when trying to piece together an event. Vonnegut seeks to carnivalize the events described from the beginning, and to problematize our perceptions; in Bakhtin's words, "a world dominated by heteroglossia. Everything means, is understood, as a part of a greater whole."[25] Vonnegut realizes that individuals in society understand war from stereotypes and ideals, they accept absolute truths in the discourses presented to them. Vonnegut sees the "constant interaction between meanings, all of which have potential of conditioning others,"[26] and he carnivalizes from the outset to create reader awareness in the act of reading. It is also important to note here that there is a sense that nothing has changed throughout history; war is the same mistake that humans keep making. There is an idealism and essentialism that have become repetitive, the accepted norms that enable war to continue. No understanding of our society and culture can take place without the beginning of a realization that there is an initial problem with the accepted normal. Carnivalization is Vonnegut's means of highlighting this, he is lobbying for realization through his narrative, and what we do with that realization is for us to decide.

---

24 Kurt Vonnegut, *Slaughterhouse-Five*, p. 22: taken from Mary Endell, *Dresden, History, Stage and Gallery*, 1908.
25 Mikhail Bakhtin, "Glossary," *The Dialogic Imagination*, p. 426.
26 Mikhail Bakhtin, "Glossary," *The Dialogic Imagination*, p. 426.

The inclusion of historical discourses does not stop here, as Vonnegut weaves a narrative that subtly introduces texts throughout the novel. He creates an environment that is dialogic, where the narrative is teeming with different perspectives, all of which he is inviting the reader to explore. In a sense, the "Dialogic relationships exist among all elements of novelistic structure ...,"[27] as Vonnegut creates a complex structure in the novel, one which is representative of society. We cannot hope to fully understand society and its functions in terms of absolutes. Many of the discourses introduced in the novel are used in juxtaposition to challenge contemporary socially accepted narratives. MacKay considers the mass group effect and society's capacity for participation in catastrophic events, simply due to pack mentality. Other viewpoints are also offered on the events that took place during World War Two, a good example being *The Execution of Private Slovik* by William Bradford Huie. This text charts the history of a young man, Eddie Slovik, the "only American soldier since 1864 to be shot for desertion."[28] The narrative is appallingly sad and incredible, but it is an example of how Vonnegut carnivalizes the traditionally accepted illusions presented as absolute in society. During World War Two, of the estimated 10,000,000 men signed into the US Army, 2,864 were tried by general court martial for the offense of desertion, 49 men were approved for the death sentence, but only one was executed by firing squad, and that was Private Slovik.[29]

The experience of Eddie Slovik is one which appears important to Vonnegut, and it represents one of the important individual experiences of the war that he sought to include in the text. It is representative of how the ideals of war do not translate to the reality of the personal experience. Eddie Slovik could be considered the "stereotypical" product of a poor and abusive family. He was in prison from a young age but managed to "make good" when he met and married his wife, Antoinette. He was exempt from military duty due to medical reasons but when these rules were relaxed, on November 7, 1943, he received notice that the army was considering his reclassification. On January 24, 1944, he left for Fort Sheridan, Illinois, to begin training. Eddie Slovik spent 372 days in the US Army before being executed. He found army life exceptionally hard and found it even more difficult being away from his wife, the one thing he felt was good in his life. On August 7, 1944, Eddie sailed from New York to Scotland, traveled by train

---

27 Mikhail Bakhtin, "Dostoevsky's Polyphonic Novel," *Problems of Dostoevsky's Poetics*, p. 40.
28 William Bradford Huie, *The Execution of Private Slovik*, The New American Library, 1954, New York, p. 3.
29 William Bradford Huie, *The Execution of Private Slovik*, p. 11.

to Portsmouth, England, and was then shipped from there to Omaha Beach on August 20th. Five days later he was among a group of twelve men, assigned as replacements to G-Company, 109th Infantry. Somehow, Slovik and another man in the outfit, Tankey, never joined the company. According to Tankey, they had been fired upon and had all been split up when ducking for cover, it was dark and they lost each other, and their way. They later managed to stay with the Canadian 13th Provost Corps, traveling with them for about six weeks. On October 8th, both men finally joined their original company, at which point Slovik, feeling unable to fight, handed himself over to the authorities. It was considered that he had deserted twice, once for getting lost and never joining his Company and second for refusing the duties assigned to a soldier. Eddie Slovik was executed on January 31, 1945.

Eddie Slovik came from an extremely troubled background and was not emotionally, or mentally, fit to be entrenched in the experience of war. He was seen as an ex-criminal and was dehumanized for the experiences he was forced to participate in. He believed he was not being executed for desertion, as no other soldier convicted had been executed, but for the thievery he had committed as a child. He believed his prison record had been the deciding factor, and he was being made an example of: "Did *they* shoot Eddie Slovik for the crime of deserting the United States Army, or did they shoot him, as he insisted, 'for bread I stole when I was twelve years old.'"[30] At face value, this appears to be a simple case of a man "not" seen to be at the post he was assigned to. However, Eddie was still working, only with a different unit, he had simply been left behind because he was too scared to come out from a hiding position he had found. No understanding was offered to him, regardless of the individual human life at stake. An example was needed and an ex-con with no value to society was the one chosen. The decision was made irrespective of the facts of Eddie Slovik's life. The assumptions made about Slovik support the essentialist norms of culture never being questioned. It appears that no one offered Eddie Slovik the respect of the individual or questioned the situation. This is a carnivalizing narrative within the text that highlights the way in which human beings are used to propagate the illusions perpetuated by society. Slovik is used by a culture to enforce the idea of a deserter and the consequences of what could happen if you choose that path. He is considered as someone with little importance, and even though he did not carry out the crimes alleged, society considered him a useful scapegoat. He is

---

30 William Bradford Huie, *The Execution of Private Slovik*, p. 109.

used to reinforce the ideas of how someone from a poor background is expected to behave. Society has already brought into those elements of the stereotype, so no one ever thinks to question the situation. Stereotypes can become so absolute and fixed that the illusion purposefully enforced is never challenged. Society can treat human beings as they see fit by manipulation of perceptions, without any need for coercion.

Vonnegut carnivalizes the traditionally perceived notions of reality, he employs the turnabout of the carnival to reflect the complicated nature of discourse and how our perceptions can have a dramatic effect on our reaction to events. The truth is complex and often subjective. Vonnegut's depth of writing challenges the reader and transfers responsibility to them. His writing becomes the vehicle for the reader to question their own sense of reading awareness. He presents a rich text which is ever-changing, making suggestions, yet never really making any suggestions. In his essay "Interpreting the Variorum," Stanley E. Fish refers to "interpretive strategies not for reading … but for writing texts … these strategies exist prior to the act of reading and therefore determine the shape of what is read rather than, as is usually assumed, the other way around."[31] Vonnegut employs historical discourses, introducing the reader to differing versions of an event. It is intentional that Vonnegut presents the information only and does not comment or pass judgment on how the texts should be read, it is the reader's responsibility for interpretation. The inclusion of narratives such as Slovik's shows how events can be extremely complicated. We often see the polished presentation without exploring the complexity of the differing perspectives, and Vonnegut implores us to become more aware.

The Bible is another text chosen in the narrative that encourages individual awareness and questions the values our society conditions us to accept. The narrator states "I looked through the Gideon Bible in my motel room for tales of great destruction" (SF, 27). The state of war is consistently reoccurring throughout history and the narrative refers to the destruction of Sodom and Gomorrah as: "Those were vile people in both those cities, as is well known. The world was better off without them" (SF, 27-28). Vonnegut uses irony, in suggesting that we are expected to blindly accept that the people in these historical cities were wholly evil, with no redeeming features. This belief, if absolute, holds that there can be no exception, just as Eddie Slovik is treated as an absolute ex-convict. There appears a dehumanization, with no awareness of individual value. Religious

---

31 Stanley E. Fish, "Interpreting the *Variorum*," *Reader Response Criticism*. Ed. Jane p. Tompkins, The John Hopkins University Press, 1980, Baltimore, MD, p. 182.

indoctrination expects us not to question, as questioning raises too many flaws in the system. Lot's wife is commended for looking back by Vonnegut: "[she] was told not to look back where all those people and their homes had been" (SF, 28). She must not question, she must not consider them as individuals with differing personalities, experiences, and families. She should not question the order she was being conditioned to accept: "But she *did* look back, and I love her for that, because it was so human" (SF, 28). There is a sense in the text that she was the one in the right, she dared to care for those being killed. Lot's wife saw them as individuals and could not control her need to be their witness, to see their destruction with her own eyes. Essentially, Vonnegut postulates that humanity is in fact a species that naturally cares and questions. It is society that conditions people to disregard human instinct to preserve life and individual value. The confines of culture force humanity into absolutes, forcing people to accept and become immune to the death and destruction created by war across the globe. Lot's wife dared to question traditional authority.

The books that Vonnegut refers to all have in common their ability to question our perceptions of war and the discourses we accept as truth. Each discourse gives the reader another perspective on war and the effects that it can have on humanity. Vonnegut seeks to give us "all" the perspectives he can and seeks to problematize what we know as absolutes so that we are forced to consider all the alternatives. Toward the end of the novel, he mentions the historical account of what happened in Dresden written by the British military historian David Irving, *The Destruction of Dresden*[32] (SF, 238-240). Again, he quotes directly from the text, in this instance using a quotation from the introduction by General Eaker:

> *I deeply regret that British and U.S. bombers killed 135,000 people in the attack on Dresden, but I remember who started the last war and I regret even more the loss of more than 5,000,000 Allied lives in the necessary effort to completely defeat and utterly destroy nazism.*[33]

In including this quotation in the narrative, Vonnegut could be suggesting that General Eaker fails to see people as individuals, they are merely a numbers game in the war to destroy an ideology. However, each one of those vast numbers killed was an individual person, with a life, a family, memories, and a future, it really does not matter who killed who when the war is over, just the sheer number

---

32 David Irving, *The Destruction of Dresden*, Ballantine Books, 1963, New York.
33 Kurt Vonnegut, *Slaughterhouse-Five*, p. 239: taken from David Irving's, *The Destruction of Dresden*, p. 8. Vonnegut uses an undercase "n" for Nazism, the original Irving text is written with a capital "N."

of individual lives having been lost. Vonnegut continues the ideas suggested by General Eaker's lack of sympathy for the dead with the character of Professor Rumfoord, an official Air force Historian, who near the end of the novel fails to see Billy Pilgrim as an individual suffering from the effects of war. This is a further carnivalization in the text to suggest that the narratives of events, particularly how they are seen and read by historians, do not always match up to the experiences of being a part of living history and individual experience. When we read historical accounts from the safety of our classrooms, it does not do the experience justice. In effect, historians perpetuate the myths and stereotypes created by culture, they become so preoccupied with the numbers or events, that they forget the individuals and their experiences.

The placement of the *Destruction of Dresden* quote in the novel follows the account of the atomic bomb dropped on Hiroshima on August 6, 1945, where Vonnegut quotes Truman's statement: *"we are now prepared to obliterate more rapidly and completely"* (SF, 238). So many people were killed during World War Two, and it mattered little what side you were on, the deaths were just as horrific and violent, each side committing equally hideous acts of large-scale death and destruction. So many people died in the deployment of the atomic bombs, and there had been so many deaths throughout the war trying to eradicate an ideology, that itself had systematically tortured and killed innocent individuals not seen as "real" people. Being able to "obliterate more rapidly and completely" does not feel like something to be particularly proud of, especially since many of those killed by the new technology were in fact civilian human beings. Vonnegut problematizes war, it becomes a great destructive force, rendering all those obligated to partake in it as victims. Terrible crimes were committed against humanity, and so many deaths, that there can be no winners and losers. Vonnegut struggles with the mass of human death on either side of the war, even though he seems aware that Nazi idealism needed to be stopped at all costs. Vonnegut appears to struggle with the conscience of humanity, and it is up to the reader to decide whether there is any sufficient remedy.

Along with historical discourses, Vonnegut also evokes individuals in the novel that also represent a form of resistance against the norms of society or working for its betterment. These include Lucretia Mott, a social reformer who was an abolitionist and advocate for women's rights. The name given to the freighter the Billy Pilgrim returned to the Americas on was *Lucretia A. Mott*.[34] The deaths of

---

34   Kurt Vonnegut, *Slaughterhouse-Five*, p. 253. Vonnegut uses the middle initial 'A' here when in fact the actual individual's middle initial was 'C' for Coffin. Did he change this for respect of the service men he was alluding to that had survived when so many had died?

Robert Kennedy and Martin Luther King (SF, 268) are both mentioned. Robert Kennedy represented a symbol of American liberalism, a civil rights supporter, and a leading candidate for the democratic presidential candidacy at the time of his death. He was assassinated after addressing supporters after a victory in the California primary elections (1968). Martin Luther King, a leader of the African American civil rights movement, was also assassinated while he stood on a balcony during a visit to Memphis, Tennessee, to support black sanitary public works employees (1968). The fact that both these individuals were assassinated also problematizes what Vonnegut is saying here. Does he want us to believe that fighting for civil rights, the rights of the individual, is pointless because it can only lead to death? Or is he suggesting that we should all lead lives where we fight for the rights of the individual because we only live for a short time, we never know when our own time will come? It is better to fight and die protecting the rights of the individual and freedom, than to live a life of censorship and inequality.

The two assassinations are mentioned at the beginning of the last chapter, which could be considered the epilogue to the novel. Following the mention of these important deaths the reader is introduced to the alien perspective:

On Tralfamadore, says Billy Pilgrim, there isn't much interest in Jesus Christ. The Earthling figure who is most engaging to the Tralfamadorian mind, he says, is Charles Darwin—who taught that those who die are meant to die, that corpses are improvements. (SF, 268-269)

This brings about a sense of confusion in the novel. Vonnegut is careful to present the fact that there can be many ways to engage with war, to engage in different discourses conditioned as absolutes. In the first chapter, he introduces the idea that we cannot change the course of events because they have already happened. Vonnegut introduces us to different ways of understanding what happened and then asks us to question why we are often only taught one viewpoint as absolute, often the socially accepted view of our own culture. Vonnegut suggests that we can therefore change the course of events through changing perception. After the assassinations of two civil rights advocates are introduced to the reader, Vonnegut evokes Charles Darwin, the naturalist famous for his theory of evolution. He fought against the accepted norms of Victorian society, offering an alternative to the widely accepted version of the world, through a scientific method. What is problematic here is that the Tralfamadorians stress that Darwin taught that "those who die are meant to die, that corpses are improvements" (SF, 269). Do the Tralfamadorians suggest that we need to be aware of the untruths we allow our society to teach us, but that in the end it is all pointless because we will die anyway? The human condition is one that none of us will escape from, with everyone dying on their own. Vonnegut never offers us a remedy for the indignity and destruction of war, but there is a sense that if everyone were to start questioning and demanding more information, that we as human beings might be able to change society for the better. We may not live forever but we can make our time on Earth as valuable as possible.

Although Vonnegut includes actual historical events and people in the narrative, the reader must not forget that the text is fictional. Along with the historical points in the novel there exist fictional events and characters too. This adds a deeper element to the dialogic nature of the novel and the heteroglossic interaction that takes place in the narrative. The novel is intensely complex, and Vonnegut needs the mode of fiction to enable him to manipulate conventions and expose the absolutes in our own culture. The individual's experience of war is uniquely complex, and different from the stereotypical views that society generally promotes. Writing a purely factual discourse would not have been enough for Vonnegut: facts, figures, times, and dates do not educate a reader on subjective experiences of what it is like to actively participate in war. In a way, a factual account would have rendered the individuals dehumanized and made it difficult to see what the expense of war is to the individual human. Mary, Bernard V. O'Hare's wife, sums up what she thinks books do to glorify wars at the very beginning of the novel: "war will look just wonderful, so we'll have a lot more of them. And they'll be fought by babies" (SF, 18). The narrator realizes that she thinks "wars were partly encouraged by books" (SF, 19), but both the narrator and Vonnegut do not allow this to happen in the novel. The novel is dialogic and does not offer an absolute truth, it does not allow the "absolutes" that could glorify war.

Vonnegut is conscious of the fact that although he offers many different perspectives, together with points of reference for self-education, there is more to human experience than reading it from books. In offering examples, and creating a multilayered text, he is mimicking the experience of human subjectivity. He is constantly reminding his reader that life is never straightforward, that there are no absolutes. People are often looking for the "movie" ideal of war: They are looking for the great characters, the Schindlers and Anne Franks, and although Vonnegut is not saying these people do not exist, or that they have not done great things, what he is saying is that often these people are the exception. In fact, an individual getting through the war alive and having to live with the consequences of what they have experienced can also be seen as heroic. War is destructive, and it takes its toll on the individual:

> There are almost no characters in this story, and almost no dramatic confrontations, because most of the people in it are so sick and so much the listless playthings of enormous forces. One of the main effects of war, after all, is that people are discouraged from being characters. (SF, 208-209)

The experiences of people are incredibly diverse which makes the absolute stereotypes and ideals of war impossible to accept; however, on the other hand, the essentialism that war promotes makes challenging these almost impossible. The essentialism that culture has promoted of war, in terms of absolute obedience, gives the sense that individuals cannot fight the system. They are the "listless playthings" of culture, and culture is such an "enormous force" that individuals are weakened and made unable to fight back. They believe that they cannot fight back, that they must accept what is given to them, again, much the same as Private Slovik accepted that he would die for being a convicted criminal even though this appears unjust when many others escaped execution. Of course, this again is contradictory, in evoking the carnivalesque nature of the text there are always opposites fighting in juxtaposition for dominance. On one hand, Vonnegut emphasizes the need for the individual to take control of their own perceptions, but on the other, he is stating it is virtually impossible. This appears however to be realistic in terms of its reflection of the difficulties faced by human beings: It is never easy to fight against accepted norms that society perpetuates, often leading to personal sacrifice and hardship. There is no "right" answer to life, it is up to the individual, and they, it seems, can reflect the changing nature of the turnabout of the carnival, by the continual fluctuation of opinions and contradicting ideas.

The fictional characters that Vonnegut includes in his narrative are often seen through a satirical lens: He offers the reader the advantage of seeing what absolute stereotypes could look like in practice, within the war experience, and this relates back to the idea of the carnival costume or mask. When the main character, Billy, becomes unstuck in time he travels back to when he was a chaplain's assistant during World War Two. It is through Billy that Vonnegut introduces the reader to several characters who represent the "ideal" characteristics associated with war. Roland Weary is a character who is presented as "unpopular," from an "unhappy childhood," and "stupid and fat and mean" (SF, 44). Vonnegut uses a sophisticated irony here, as he presents a character who is completely unsuitable for the role of the "war hero," but who, in his own mind, is living that reality:

Weary's version of the true war story went like this: There was a big German attack, and Weary and his antitank buddies fought like hell until everyone was killed but Weary … And then Weary tied in with two scouts, and they became close friends immediately, and they decided to fight their way back to their own lines. They were going to travel fast. They were damned if they'd surrender. They shook hands all around. They called themselves 'The Three Musketeers.' (SF, 53)

Weary believes that he is the ideal warrior, that he is fulfilling the notions that society has conditioned him to believe are the good values of a soldier. Vonnegut describes him as looking like "Tweedledum or Tweedledee" (SF, 50), evoking *Alice's Adventures in Wonderland*[35] (1865) by Lewis Carroll, a fantasy novel filled with anthropomorphic creatures and strange logic. Vonnegut is manipulating the reader with the character of Weary and is alluding to the notions and representations the reader acquires from their belief in society; essentially, he is turning ideas upside down to reveal that they are not as straightforward as society would have us believe. *Alice's Adventures in Wonderland* suggests that the reader needs to assess their own logic, just as the logic of Weary, and his belief in his role as the soldier, needs to be assessed. There is an ephemeral motion to the narrative, one which Vonnegut uses to create a multi-voiced characteristic to the text. The heteroglossic elements come together: With the singular character of Weary, the reader is exposed to stereotypical ideals of war, the notion of impaired logic, and strange decision-making, but also Greek mythology with the introduction of the "dirty picture of a woman attempting sexual intercourse with a Shetland pony" (SF, 51).

The photograph is another heteroglot element in the narrative, and not only a representation of myth, but an introduction of the French photographer Louis J. M. Daguerre.[36] Daguerre was famous for his invention of daguerreotype photography, the polaroid photograph of its time, in the first half of the nineteenth century. Tom Gunning supposes in his text "In Your Face: Physiognomy, Photography, and the Gnostic Mission of Early Film" (1997) that "Uncovering the role that capturing the face played in both cinema and its antecedents traces a saraband between seeing and knowing … which could not only reproduce human eyesight but exceed it"[37] or, that photography was supposedly the ultimate

35 Lewis Carroll, *Alices Adventures in Wonderland and Through the Looking Glass* (The Centenary Edition), Ed. Hugh Haughton, Penguin, 1998, Rutherford, NJ.

36 Helmut Gernsheim & Alison Gernsheim, *L. J. M. Daguerre: The History of the Diorama and the Daguerreotype*, Dover Publications, 1968, New York.

37 Tom Gunning, "In Your Face: Physiognomy, Photography, and the Gnostic Mission of Early Film," *Modernism/Modernity*, Vol. 4, no. 1, January 1997, p. 2, muse.jhu.edu/login?auth=0&type=summary&url=/journals/modernism-modernity/v004/4.1gunning.html. Accessed August 28, 2022.

representation of reality. If there was a photo, it must be true, and the mythic pornography of Weary adds to this element: "Le Fevre replied that there are thousands of myths like that, with the woman a mortal and the pony a god" (SF, 52). The character of Daguerre's assistant, Le Fevre, appearing to be fictitious, also incorporates that interplay of the dialogic nature of the narrative.

Weary further introduces the historical adventure novel *The Three Musketeers* (1844), by Alexandre Dumas. This story, set in seventeenth-century France, incorporates the gallantry and adventure of the three friends, Athos, Porthos, and Aramis who made the motto "all for one and one for all" ("tous pour un, un pour tous") famous.[38] Again, these elements stress the ideas associated with the carnival interplay of stereotypes, and how the war experiences of Billy Pilgrim are interlocked with notions of how things are supposed to be, the illusion of the heroic elements or war, juxtaposed with the reality of living the experience.

Weary's representation is complex and problematic to the reader. He is unsuitable for the role of war hero but represents the common soldier in many ways. He "was as new to war as Billy. He was a replacement, too" (SF, 43), and he did not belong in the ideal world of war. His relationships are portrayed as "crazy, sexy, murderous," (SF, 44) with him "eventually" (SF, 45) beating up people; however, he is instrumental in getting Billy through the early part of the narrative during the war, in the time-traveling sequences. He keeps Billy moving, refusing to leave him behind, later getting "ditched" (SF, 44) by the other musketeers. This upsets his comfortable illusion of heroic comradeship, although he still manages to keep hold of the iconic idealism:

> He dilated upon the piety and heroism of 'The Three Musketeers,' portrayed, in the most glowing and impassioned hues, their virtue and magnanimity, the imperishable honor they acquired for themselves, and the great services they rendered to Christianity. (SF, 64)

He views the stereotype of the comradery evoked by The Three Musketeers with a sense of absolutism. It is the illusion he has been educated to believe in by society and he is not ready to surrender that belief. He endeavors to fulfill the element of what he needs to be, even though it is not really in his nature, and he never questions if it is working for him. Even when the illusion falters, he continues to have faith in it, showing what can happen when individuals refuse to question or challenge what is presented as fact. He blames Billy for his loss, for the sacrifices

---

38 Alexandre Dumas, *The Three Musketeers*, Dover Thrift Edition, 2007, New York.

he has made, as without Billy he may have escaped rather than become a prisoner of war. In a sense, he is Billy's savior at the beginning of the novel, keeping him alive and moving, even though he is extremely sick. Everything the reader knows about him makes them dislike him in many ways: he does not fit with the ideal hero; he does not represent the good in society.

Vonnegut is again suggesting that the reader needs to look deeper, we need to question what our beliefs are and where we have acquired them. Weary, although a relatively inferior character in the novel in terms of Vonnegut's incorporation of him, is integral to the carnivalization that takes place. He is representative of a multifaceted creation, of an ideal, of how a good soldier may behave, yet he is the opposite of gallant and honorable. Even after his death during transportation to the prisoner of war camp, his influence is felt later in the novel because of his belief that Billy caused his death: "Weary, in his continuous delirium, told again and again of the Three Musketeers ... Above all, he wanted to be avenged, so he said again and again the name of the person who had killed him ... 'Billy Pilgrim'" (SF, 101). In seeking vengeance for his death, he sets in motion the very circumstances of Billy's death, his assassination by Paul Lazzaro: "Billy's high forehead is in the cross hairs of a high-powered laser gun ... Billy Pilgrim is dead" (SF, 182).[39] Vonnegut creates characters that are complex and interconnected which mirror the complexity of human life. Although he states, "there are almost no characters in this story" (SF, 208) what he means is that there are almost no characters that represent stereotypical ideals. Weary's actions, for whatever reasons he may have, are justly heroic in many ways although he does not fulfill the traditional sense of the hero. He has many character flaws, is very unlikeable, miscommunicates, and completely misinterprets the situation he is in. Individual human beings are unique, just as no two set of fingerprints are the same. Stereotypes endeavor to render humans definable and predictable, yet the carnival turnabout makes this illusion impossible.

Another character important to the novel is Howard W. Campbell Jr., one of the characters that Vonnegut has created to go beyond novel boundaries. This is another dialogic discourse integrated into the novel, along with the interaction with both factual and fictional events, people, and characters. Howard W. Campbell Jr. appears as the central narrator in Vonnegut's earlier novel, *Mother Night* (1961), and is representative of a "muddying of the waters" of what is morally acceptable and what is not. He is the character who is supposedly working

---

39 Billy's death takes place "on February thirteenth, 1976" (SF, 180), a Friday; traditionally Friday 13th is considered an unlucky day.

as a double agent, an American working as a propagandist for the Nazi party in Germany. He is essentially an American spy, although this is denied by the American government in the narrative. The inclusion of the character offers a sense of authenticity, continuity, and of plausibility to the work. The reader's awareness of the character's inclusion in another novel makes the character appear more believable as he has a personal written history and existence all his own. The dialogic nature of the novel and its ability to problematize everything that the reader encounters are characteristic of how intricate Vonnegut's fictional world is. Campbell is another character able to highlight the discrepancies between society and culture to offer an insight into the human character: "It's that large part of every man that wants to hate without limit, that wants to hate with God on its side. It's that part of every man that finds all kinds of ugliness so attractive."[40] Campbell exposes the juxtaposing sides of war because he stresses, through a disturbing satire, that there are no perfect fixed social ideologies, and that there can be in fact no "right" side in war. When incarcerated for Nazi war crimes in *Mother Night*, Campbell's prison guard, Aryan, is a character with a similarly complex history. Being a Jew in Nazi-occupied Hungary, he secured his own safety by choosing to forge identity papers to become a member of the Hungarian S.S. He was considered a brutal soldier and was given the job of hunting Jews as a reward. This is shocking and grotesque irony where perceived identity is obfuscated to show the reader the complexity of social ideals. Life cannot be considered straightforward and absolute. The inversion of social identity here evokes Bakhtin's carnival atmosphere and the mask of characterization inverts the norm, everything previously perceived is challenged. The name Aryan is significantly used here and denotes the complicated nature of identity. The connotations of Aryan, coming from a European origin, suggests that the character may have looked typically European, enough that he may be able to pass himself off as a Hungarian S.S. soldier with forged papers. The carnival mask is apparent, his papers allow him to wear a mask, to enact the turnabout needed for his transformation. Campbell's character appears to be a pivot for identity in the novel, he becomes the struggle with ideology and the individual.

In *Slaughterhouse-Five,* Campbell is there to augment the need for the reader to examine their accepted view of society and its ideals. He is there to question the principles that American and western cultures value. He could be considered the ultimate traitor, he has given up everything American society considers

---

40 Kurt Vonnegut, *Mother Night,* Dial Press, 2009, New York, p. 251.

important: freedom, democracy, and economic autonomy, in favor of the controlling fascist alternative offered by the Nazi party. He views humanity as able to "hate without limit,"[41] that all people, no matter what their background, have the capacity, in fact the need, to hate. He recognizes that no matter what side you are on, hate is a part of choosing sides. He sees humans as hateful creatures, who seek the approval of God, and who need to have a sense of "good" on their side to convince themselves they are somehow different from all the other haters. He describes the American soldiers as:

> the most self-pitying, least fraternal, and dirtiest of all prisoners of war, said Campbell. They were incapable of concerted action on their own behalf. They despised any leader from among their own number, refused to follow or even listen to him, on the grounds that he was no better than they were, that he should stop putting on airs. (SF, 166-167)

Campbell speaks of Americans in a derogatory manner, and Vonnegut incorporates him into the narrative as a point of resistance to the American dream. The sense of individualism is attacked by Campbell, and there is a suggestion here that if society believes in individualism so aggressively then it can have a destructive effect on behavior, promoting lazy and selfish people. This is another problematic suggestion and appears as a cautionary addendum. Vonnegut appears to promote the value of the individual, he promotes the need for human beings to work together and support each other in a realistic and measured society, a society that values individual human lives. He seems to suggest here that too much emphasis on individual equality renders people unable to function in a positive way; they see themselves as having no need to work with others, so why should they listen to anyone else? Vonnegut consistently presents situations that promote thought in the reader. Vonnegut is provocative, he is challenging the reader to question all the possibilities, yet never giving a definite alternative that he thinks is plausible. This is further evidence that there is no ideal, that there can be no perfect order for humanity.

Later in the novel, Campbell appears again on a visit to the Slaughterhouse to recruit American soldiers to the "The Free American Corps" (SF, 206) a unit designed to fight on the Russian front on behalf of the Germans. This time he appears dressed in a comical way, wearing a "white ten-gallon hat and black cowboy boots decorated with swastikas and stars" (SF, 207), almost the perfect blend

---

41 Kurt Vonnegut, *Mother Night*, p. 251.

of American and Nazi: "He was sheathed in a blue body stocking which had yellow stripes running from his armpits to his ankles" and "a broad armband which was red, with a blue swastika in a circle of white" (SF, 207). Vonnegut portrays him as a confused individual, attempting to blend the national colors and symbols of both the nations he is attempting to represent. This is contentious: What is Vonnegut trying to say with this portrayal? There is a suggestion that both the values and ideals presented by Campbell are equal, that they are equally presented by the character. At the same time, he looks ridiculous, almost clown-like, and his appearance would seem outlandish. This appearance links in well to the idea of the carnival costume and mask that are needed to allow for the carnivalization of the turnabout to take place. Vonnegut wants us to see that it does not matter what side of the war people are on, either side can behave in the same way, as we have already seen with the invocation of war narratives. Campbell is the character that inverts the notions of the ideal American, his carnival costume allowing the reader to see the illusions present in the American national identity. Campbell views his fellow Americans as investing in the illusion of freedom, and in a sense free will, when in fact it has rendered them unable to function as a culture and society at all. They are so busy fighting among themselves that they do not have any freedom. The "free" in his "Free American Corps" is a suggestion that the soldiers might really be free if they follow Campbell, as he could offer them the stability they need against the illusions of culture. Campbell is a character that really underscores the contradictory nature of the text, he makes the reader uncomfortable and challenged by the illusionary perceptions they may have invested in themselves, and he is therefore one of Vonnegut's most powerful carnivalizing characterizations.

Derby is the character that stands up to Campbell because he hates Campbell's disparagement of American values:

[He] called Campbell a snake. He corrected that. He said that snakes couldn't help being snakes, and that Campbell, who *could* help being what he was, was something much lower than a snake or a rat—or even a blood-filled tick …

Derby spoke movingly of the American form of government, with freedom and justice and opportunities and fair play for all. He said there wasn't a man there who wouldn't gladly die for those ideals. (SF, 209)

Derby's staunch rebuttal of Campbell's take on the American way of life suggests that although there are flaws in the system, there are still ideals worth fighting for. Vonnegut wants his readers to be aware of the problems in society, he acknowledges that there are limits to every system. He encourages the reader to consider values that go against humanity, and any ideology that seeks to destroy human lives. He requires the reader to approach anything presented to them as absolute truth with reservation; he wants them to interrogate everything, to understand that there are many alternatives, and everything is not always straightforward. The character of Campbell suggests that the blending of opposites is impossible, or near impossible. No culture or social system is perfect, and we do not have to resort to killing those who do not agree with us. Social debate and discourse are needed to improve the life of the individual, although individuals must still value each other and work together. No one can win in war, too many human beings die. Freedom, justice, opportunity, and fairness appear to be the notions that appeal to Vonnegut, and they are the qualities that he sees as promoting an effective society. Of course, the pacifism that Vonnegut seeks is idealistic, as he has already acknowledged to some extent within the first chapter by suggesting that stopping war within human society would be comparable to stopping a natural phenomenon in nature. What he is seeking is that human society moves toward a culture of "working together." Even if the allies fighting against the Nazis during World War Two can be considered a noble cause, it came at an enormous cost to human life. In Vonnegut's reality, he sees the possibility that in the simple steps of cooperation and understanding of the humans around us, of acceptance and willingness to act with kindness, that war would become an action of the past and not the future. Vonnegut does not deny the need for action, he is suggesting that by acting in a different way, the industrial scale of death does not need to be an inevitability. Again, he is asking us to look for alternative perspectives, to re-evaluate, he is not offering the absolute antidote to war, just our consideration. Robert Hipkiss asserts, "the key reason, and the reason why he tempers irony with sentimentality, is that for one who sees the universe deterministically, as Vonnegut does, there is no blame. There are no villains, and hence, there is no one to be held accountable."[42] Again, the dialogic nature of the narrative problematizes what Vonnegut is trying to say: on one hand, he states that there can be no solution to war, but on the other hand, he suggests that if society works together, it can find a solution. He suggests there are ideals worth fighting for, together with saying that no ideal can be fixed and definite. As Bakhtin asserts:

---

42 Robert A. Hipkiss, *The American Absurd: Pynchon, Vonnegut, and Barth,*. p. 69.

Within this 'great dialogue' [the novel] could be heard, illuminating it and thickening its texture, the compositionally expressed dialogues of the heroes; ultimately, dialogue penetrates within, into every word of the novel, making it double-voiced, into every gesture, every mimic movement … making it convulsive and anguished.[43]

The text is consistently "double-voiced" and complex as the reader grapples with the intertextuality of what Vonnegut is showing us about the nature of war and its representation in society. There have been so many stereotypical characters that do not behave in the traditional sense, and familiar narratives that have been disproven with so many differing perspectives. The reader's only option is to submit to the notion that Vonnegut suggests in the narrative, that there are no fixed and definite ideals present in our human world. It may be an "anguished" realization, but it will allow human culture to change and adapt to a better future.

The Prisoner of War camp that Billy is taken to in *Slaughterhouse-Five* is a microcosm of how society deals with war and the expectations placed on the men within it. Vonnegut continues the carnival duality with the representation of the allied forces, particularly the American and British. When the American soldiers arrive, a British corporal records their names in a big red ledger: "Everybody was legally alive now" (SF, 115). The men did not officially exist until this point when they are formally recorded, before this they are missing and probably dead, they were just another one of the number of people unaccounted for. In a sense, they have no value until their names are written in the book, until they are acknowledged by society, the German soldiers, and the prisoners of war. The English prisoners already in the camp are described as "exactly what Englishmen ought to be" (SF, 120), they were "clean and enthusiastic and decent and strong" (SF, 119), after all, most had been prisoners for much of the war. They appear as the epitome of what idealistic views of soldiers might look like, they were officers and "each of them had attempted to escape from … prison at least once" (SF, 118). Vonnegut is careful here and is suggesting that although these prisoners are in fact the ideal of what people might think soldiers should be like, most of those prisoners had in fact not seen much fighting as they had been "the first English-speaking prisoners to be taken" (SF, 118). Vonnegut carnivalizes the views of war and how soldiers stand up to the test. These men are in perfect form, they are ironically the "wealthiest people in Europe" (SF, 119), as even though they are prisoners, they had lived handsomely from extra Red Cross rations sent in error whilst the rest

---

43 Mikhail Bakhtin, "Dostoevsky's Polyphonic Novel," *Problems of Dostoevsky's Poetics*, p. 40.

of Europe went hungry living among the devastation of war. They are described as working "like darling elves, sweeping, mopping, cooking, baking—making mattresses of straw and burlap bags, setting tables, putting [out] party favors" (SF, 120). Vonnegut is mocking them; they sound like a clip from a fairytale film. They are given the traditionally feminine role of housekeepers and described as "darling elves" evoking the sense of a Hollywood film illusion. They appear to have no understanding about the conditions and experiences of what actual war is. They have lived in relative harmony, and are well taken care of, even "adored" (SF, 120) by their German captors. Even the soap and candles are ironic in this situation of pleasant comfort: The men had "no way of knowing" (SF, 122), but the "candles and soap were made from the fat of rendered Jews and Gypsies and fairies and communists" (SF, 122). Their comfortable, safe, and pleasant environment is false, it is based on lies, and they have no way of knowing that at the time. Representative of how society can force human beings into similar situations, they often have no way of knowing what is happening behind the mechanics of society, only what they are allowed to know.

In juxtaposition, the Americans are described differently, and the Englishmen look "in astonishment at the frowsy creatures" (SF, 123). The Americans are war-weary, they are starving, inappropriately clothed, and both emotionally and mentally numb. An Englishman looks with "pity" (SF, 123) on Billy and says "'My God—what have they done to you, lad? This isn't a man. It's a broken kite'" (SF, 123-124). The English are taken aback by the condition of the new arrivals, but they still do not appear to have a grasp on the reality of the situation. The words "broken kite" makes Billy sound like a broken toy that can be fixed with some tape and made to fly again, it does not cover the experiences and horror he has faced or is yet to face. The Americans represent the experience of war, the individual experiences of living through combat and trying to survive, they are the reality of what war looks like. Even the performance given of *Cinderella* by the Englishmen for the new American prisoners of war is a carnivalization of the situation. The Englishmen are wearing the masks of the carnival, they are taking on the role, not only of the ideal soldiers, but of the characters in the play. The whole experience appears confused, damaged, and malfunctioning, and the turnabout created highlights the absurdity of their situation. It is a microcosm of the structures in society. The whole set is strange to Billy after his experiences and what he has witnessed. The setting is opulent, with a "Dozens of teapots … boiling" (SF, 121), very ironic considering the man mentioned at the beginning of the novel is executed for taking a teapot from the rubble of Dresden. There is so much food, "heaps of fresh-baked white bread on the tables, gobs of butter, pots of marmalade" (SF, 122), so much abundance when these men are so hungry and have been through so much. The war creates destruction and devastation, men are reduced to skeletons, but still stereotypical ideas of war live on. The extremes of society are exposed by Vonnegut, and the reader must see, and experience, the polarization that these ideas created by the differences in the two extremes of prisoners.

Just as the character of Campbell explores the idea of the American persona and the American dream, this episode in the camp also parodies these two ideals to reveal the truth behind the mythical aspiration. The Americans are seen to be the opposite of the ideal, they are dirty and with no self-respect. The English even go so far as to lecture them about it: "'If you stop taking pride in your appearance, you will very soon die'" (SF, 185). The ideals behind the American dream of freedom—opportunity, prosperity, and success—appear appealing if you are at home in America, but if you are caught up in the catastrophe of war they can be quickly forgotten. A German soldier sums up the irony of the situation when he speaks to Billy, dressed clown-like, on his arrival to Dresden:

'I take it you find war a very comical thing.'
Billy looked at him vaguely. Billy had lost track momentarily of where he was or how he had gotten there. He had no idea that people thought he was clowning. It was Fate, of course, which had costumed him—Fate, and a feeble will to survive.
'Did you expect us to *laugh*?' the surgeon asked him …
'And do you feel *proud* to represent America as you do?' (SF, 193)

Billy has no comprehension of his appearance, he is wearing clothes that he has managed to scavenge together, including the silver boots belonging to the Cinderella costume from the prisoner of war camp. As the German surgeon points out, Billy's physical representation is a mockery of everything that America stands for. It is also in that moment that Billy spontaneously time travels to the instance in which his daughter is buying into the American dream, supporting the inversion of the mythical perfect American ideal: "His daughter Barbara was about to get married, and she and his wife had gone downtown to pick out patterns for her crystal and silverware" (SF, 78-79). As she is busy with consumerism, her clown-like father is eroding the very notion of the "American Dream." The play the Englishmen perform, with cross-dressing and role reversal, suggests a similar carnival inversion. The costumes worn defamiliarize the expectations of war and transports the production into the carnival arena. The costumes and role performance represent the engagement of the literal physical carnival. These men take part in a carnival turnabout, and it becomes comical, almost embarrassing. The idea of the soldier is inverted to be considered comical and sad, not just heroic, or exciting: "All the symbols of the carnival idiom are filled with this pathos of change and renewal, with the sense of gay relativity of prevailing truths and authorities."[44]

The representation of the "ideal soldier" is also portrayed by the character of Valencia Merble, Billy's wife, whilst she and Billy are talking in their marriage bed. Ideals perpetuated by the media seem to be particularly assigned to the women in the novel. This is true of the first chapter when O'Hare's wife is concerned about the narrator's need to write about his experiences in the war being governed by a need to be portrayed by actors in a film such as Frank Sinatra and John Wayne: "When the beautiful people were past, Valencia questioned her funny-looking husband about war. It was a simple-minded thing for a female Earthling to do, to associate sex and glamor with war" (SF, 154). Vonnegut takes the opportunity to reinforce how ideals and expectations of war can permeate throughout society and affect the way others might see individuals and affect relationships. The narrator views the perspective of glamourizing and sexualizing war as simplistic. Valencia is seen to be ignorant and simple for not questioning the ideals she has been conditioned to accept. She knows Billy has secrets but does not seem to understand the experiences Billy has encountered when she questions him. She appears to want to know his secrets but does not really grasp the concept that it must be extremely painful and hard for him to talk about. In pressing him, she seems to be the catalyst for another time-travel episode, he is not ready to talk about the war and confront what he has seen.

Vonnegut creates another dialogic element to the text by the introduction of the writer, Kilgore Trout. Trout appears in several of Vonnegut's novels and makes an appearance in *Slaughterhouse-Five*, in a similar way to how Campbell interacts within the narrative. Just as the character of Campbell appears to have more credibility by being able to transcend novel boundaries, Trout also has this function, but with the ability to create narratives himself. This has a particularly Bakhtinian element because the narrative can create a discourse that engages the reader to question the validity of writing itself, and what it represents. The character of Trout fits into the carnival aspect of Vonnegut's novels because he can turn everything the reader understands about the narrative worlds upside down to offer different perspectives. He is a satirical and carnivalizing force that allows

---

44 Mikhail Bakhtin, "Introduction," *Rabelais and His World*, p. 11.

Vonnegut to play with different carnival forms. In a sense using a character such as Trout allows Vonnegut to render human society as a form of narrative itself, that can be shown as unfixed and illusionary. The novel becomes so interwoven and multi-voiced that it questions the nature of reality itself. The elements of fact and fiction have become so heteroglossic, the novel is a site for exploration of reality, it becomes difficult to separate which references are factual, and which are fictional. In a way, the novel feels like it is a factual account because fact and fiction are so closely intertwined, it is hard to distinguish between them. The fictional characters and references appear real, Vonnegut makes it hard for the reader to disconnect from the text and this is representative of what is taking place in society. Our ideas of war are, at times, absolute and arbitrary, yet we tend not to question them because we have been conditioned. Vonnegut is reconditioning us to question everything, and the reader must investigate what Vonnegut is writing in *Slaughterhouse-Five* to examine what is actual and what is imagination. We must research, we must ask what points are made that have a basis in the real world, if there is such a place. The reader is encouraged to re-evaluate reality and seek out what is useful. Even though a character may be fictional, it does not mean that they have nothing useful to contribute. The carnivalization of perception, of recognizing this need, is what Vonnegut is trying to express to his reader. He needs them to accept that the world is full of heteroglossia, the world is a dialogic place where there can be no absolutes. There are too many voices for us not to question the ideals and values we have been taught. The novel becomes Vonnegut's site of resistance, his dialogic discourse of possibility.

The character of Trout disregards novel boundaries in several ways and is believed to be loosely based on the late science fiction writer Theodore Sturgeon, whose *New York Times* obituary recognized the connection.[45] Many have also asserted that the character could represent an alter-ego of Vonnegut himself. In terms of *Slaughterhouse-Five*, Vonnegut uses the character as a catalyst to question the discourse presented by western society. When Trout is asked by the "very pretty" (SF, 217) Maggie White, whether the most famous of his novels, whose summary he makes up on the spot, is real, he replies: "'Of course it happened' … 'If I wrote something that hadn't really happened, and I tried to sell it, I could go to jail. That's *fraud*'" (SF, 218). The character is used consistently to parody and carnivalize what is taking place in society. Trout "was making this up as he went along" (SF, 218) but professes that it would be impossible to write something

---

45   New York Times, *Theodore Sturgeon Dies: Writer of Fantasies*, May 11, 1985, Section 1, P. 17, www.nytimes.com/1985/05/11/arts/theodore-sturgion-dies-writer-of-fantisies.html. Accessed August 28, 2022.

that had not really happened. Vonnegut has incorporated many factual narratives in his novel, he wants the reader to question what is presented as absolute, and Trout is used as an example of this. He says he could go to jail for fraud if he did this, but the reader has already encountered many differing narratives that suggest there are different ways of looking at an event. He is lying about his own writing, having fun at someone else's expense, but he is also a character himself. Vonnegut is highlighting the possibility that all fictions are in a sense fraudulent as there can be no one absolute version of an event. He could be suggesting that all historical narrative is fictional, that it is always from one individual perspective, even though there is always another side to the story. All writing becomes fraudulent and not based on any fixed reality. The presence of Trout's own works in the novel supports the idea that in writing something down it can in some way contribute to its validity. In including the references to Trout's novels, Vonnegut gives the writings a sense of existence and in the same way as the factual references in the text, it gives the narrative a sense of authenticity. This is ironic as the writer and the novels are fictional, but the reader is forced to acknowledge that this is representative of the fictions we tell ourselves that are compounded by our social cultures. The novel is dialogic, and these voices, although fictional, add to the heteroglossia in the narrative to make the reader attentive to the varying degrees of discourses taking place. Whether factual or fictional, all the voices are representative of the challenges faced by society, many individuals with differing backgrounds and experiences coming together. The question of validity becomes irrelevant in the sense that they do exist, and the reader is forced to acknowledge them. In society, when absolutes are defined, voices are lost and narratives ignored. Vonnegut is suggesting that society is complicated, more complicated than the ability to just give one definite social definition, without any acknowledgment that there are other opinions and options. The form of the novel is problematic as the interaction between the different elements come together to create a world where, "all utterances are heteroglot ... functions of a matrix of forces practically impossible to recoup, and therefore impossible to resolve."[46] It is difficult to discern whether Vonnegut accepts that this is an inevitable side effect of incorporating so many voices of complexity in the novel. He could be signposting the fact that there can be no satisfactory resolution to the problems faced by society, and that humanity should just strive to make things better for all individuals, even though it will never succeed. Or he could be suggesting that by

---

46 Mikhail Bakhtin, "Glossary," *The Dialogic Imagination*, p. 428.

accepting that there can be no definite absolute ideals, that acceptance can allow humanity to empathically grow as an advanced civilization where war no longer takes place. In its realization and understanding, it can finally succeed.

The books penned by Trout, and mentioned in the novel, have themselves intrinsic value to the understanding of Vonnegut's stance on society. Among the books mentioned are *Maniacs in the Fourth Dimension* (SF, 132), about "mental diseases [that] couldn't be treated because the causes of the diseases were all in the fourth dimension" (SF, 132), *The Gospel from Outer Space* (SF, 138), about an alien making a study of Christianity and "why Christians found it so easy to be cruel" (SF, 138), *The Gutless Wonder* (SF, 213), a book about a robot with bad breath who is cured, but also "predicted the wide-spread use of burning jellied gasoline on human beings" (SF, 213-214) by a robot that looked like a human being, and *The Big Board*, "about an Earthling man and woman who were kidnapped by extra-terrestrials" (SF, 257). The books are ironic, all bearing some importance and connection to the real world, although obviously fictional. The character of Trout is used to emphasize the flaws in the narrative of society, the fictions that we collectively accept. Written down, the stories appear funny, their titles suggestive of Vonnegut's own feelings (especially in relation to *The Gutless Wonder*, clearly referring to the development and use of Napalm bombs during the Vietnam war), yet these allude to real narratives, real experiences that have taken place. Vonnegut chooses inflammatory novel choices for Trout: He is fictional and can write these pieces without too much repercussion. He is a creative device, used as a devil's advocate, there to point out boldly the discrepancies that human beings should be aware of, the discrepancies often overlooked. In effect, he is a carnival mask that Vonnegut wears himself, for there to be a total carnivalization of social narrative. There needs to be a complete dismantling of every narrative that human beings are exposed to, and in using Trout, Vonnegut is allowed to experiment with different forms of the carnival for the breaking down to take place.

The use of Trout as a Science Fiction writer could also have importance in the novel, as although Vonnegut does not necessarily consider himself as a Science Fiction writer, the choice of subject matter for Trout often appears to have a fantastical nature even though it is based on our relative reality. Vonnegut appears to be suggesting that much of history, when considered closely, can appear farfetched and fantastical on paper. Kilgore Trout is unpopular, his writing bad, but it is his ideas about humanity that are good: "Jesus—if Kilgore Trout could only write! … Kilgore Trout's unpopularity was deserved. His prose was frightful. Only his ideas were good … he writes about Earthlings all the time, and they're all Americans. Practically nobody on Earth is an American" (SF, 140). He writes about the important things: He writes about earthlings, about human beings, and the important things that affect them. He studies religion, "whether or not Jesus had really died on the cross, or whether he had been taken down while still alive" (SF, 260). He considers the ethics of burning people with napalm and examines money and its effects on humanity with a book about a money tree: "It had twenty-dollar bills for leaves ... Its fruit was diamonds. It attracted human beings who killed each other around the roots" (SF, 213). Just as Thomas More's *Utopia* (1516)[47] attempted to address the social problems of the sixteenth century, Vonnegut is attempting to address the problems of the twentieth century, not by suggesting a new world order, but by encouraging people to recognize the problems that the current system has and to understand how those problems came to be. No matter where the reader is, in time or space, they cannot escape their cultural nuances, and in reading Vonnegut they are exposing themselves to the influence of all the discourses present in the narrative. As Bakhtin suggests:

> At any given time, in any given place, there will be a set of conditions—social, historical, meteorological, physiological—that will insure that a word uttered in that place and at that time will have a meaning different than it would have under any other conditions."[48]

The influence of Trout and the discourses evoked by Vonnegut are purposeful in the text: They are not included for decoration, each one brings a condition, whether "social, historical, meteorological, physiological," and the texts create a complexity that mirrors real life. They have been chosen carefully by Vonnegut to represent facets of society; the differing perspectives are there to expose the intricacies of how single-minded thinking can lead to absolutes.

The character of Trout is there as a direct challenger: He does not seem to care much for how he is viewed and simply writes what he wants, often stories that although presented as "fictional" have roots in real-life situations, events, or experiences. Vonnegut uses the character to parody the world around us, and the act of the carnival is there to highlight the inadequacy of social structures. The reader is introduced to their own lives as a fictional narrative, made inadequate and exposed as fraudulent. In this way, the fact that Trout earlier states that "'If I wrote something that hadn't really happened, and I tried to sell it, I could go

---

47 Thomas More, *Utopia*, Penguin, 2003, London.
48 Mikhail Bakhtin, 'Glossary," *The Dialogic Imagination*, p. 428.

to jail. That's *fraud*,'" (SF, 218) even though he is blatantly telling a lie, he is mocking the system. Many of the narratives we accept as "real" are simply just one aspect or one side of a bigger story, they are not the whole truth. We accept fraudulent narratives in society all the time, elements we read in stories or from myths, etc., but "One thing Trout said ... was that there really *were* vampires and werewolves and goblins ... but that they were in the fourth dimension" (SF, 132). Not everything is as straightforward as we think, and there is often a different explanation for a "truth" we have accepted as absolute. Vonnegut loved to play with the possibilities of narrative in society, and he understood that fiction was an element that allowed humans to explore the possibilities without feeling threatened.

Another device Vonnegut employs for the satirical carnivalization of reality is the use of the Tralfamadorians. This device enables Vonnegut to show how the perceptions of the everyday reality in our own society function. He uses the sense of "other" to depict just how farcical and unrealistic the ideas of humans are. The reader can see beyond a human-centric environment of knowledge to look in upon their world, and to see what happens in that enclosed bubble of perception. The readers can begin to discard their absolute experiences and are introduced to an alternative interpretation of their reality. Vonnegut carnivalizes human reality to show how redundant war is and how needless the destructive forces of war are. Billy encounters the Tralfamadorians at several key moments in the novel, and it is through these episodes that Billy's human reaction to the alien interpretation of ideas allows the carnivalization to invert accepted norms.

When Billy starts to travel sporadically through time and is transported to past events in his own lifetime, he becomes "unstuck in time" (SF, 29). It is unexpected and indicates to the reader that events in the narrative will not follow the traditionally accepted perceptions of human experience. This sense of disjointed movement can be interpreted as a voyage through memory, stopping to visit the defining moments that shape and influence human lives. The idea is that human individuals must revisit the events of the past to consolidate and understand the present moment. In this sense, all the moments are connected and simultaneously influence the present, each moment impacting the other. Billy's time-traveling episodes could also be considered an indication of a mental illness or breakdown, the psychological trauma he has encountered as a response to the effects of the war experience:

Psychosomatic responses, indeed, Life, with its torturous vacillation between sweet and sour, sublimity and pathos, has become so unendurable for Billy that he becomes stuporous, his actions somnambulistic, and in an act of total disengagement, he retreats 'upstairs in his nice white house' ... which gives every appearance of being an asylum.[49]

The episodes in the novel where Billy engages in discussion with the Tralfamadorians act as key pivotal moments where the reader is forced to engage and accept the existence of alternative perspectives. For Billy, the moments act as a coping mechanism by allowing him the space to question his own fantastical experiences, and to think through ideas and thoughts. Billy states in the narrative that the Tralfamadorians "didn't have anything to do with his coming unstuck. They were simply able to give him insights into what was really going on" (SF, 38). The presence of the alien "other" allows the reading experience to mimic the experience of the narrative space. Vonnegut uses the alien perspective to help Billy and the reader understand their moment in time and space. It engages the reader's awareness through a comic conceit where they find comparisons in their life situation to the main character, and which forces them to question their own ideas. The Tralfamadorians appear to be present in the narrative, as Billy's experiences with them are vivid and enlightening. However, it is just possible that they may be an illusion, something that has been made up by Billy's mind as he becomes mentally unstable. This is again a carnival interplay within the text by Vonnegut, that many of the beliefs we hold are illusionary, they are humanity's way of making sense of the world we live in. The Tralfamadorians might just be a hallucination of Billy's mind, as he struggles to cope with the mental pressures of what he experienced in the war. They could literally be a metaphor for how human beings assign arbitrary meaning to the world, in order to cope with the chaos.

Regardless of their imaginary status, the Tralfamadorians contribute to the overall carnival atmosphere established by Vonnegut in the novel, highlighted by their comic appearance and the carnival-like elements of their behaviors. They are described as:

> two feet high, and green, and shaped like plumber's friends. Their suction cups were on the ground, and their shafts, which were extremely flexible, usually pointed to the sky. At the top of each shaft was a little hand with a green eye on its palm ... and they could see in four dimensions. (SF, 33)

---

49 Lawrence R. Broer, "*Slaughterhouse-Five:* Pilgrim's Progress," *Sanity Plea: Schizophrenia in the Novels of Kurt Vonnegut*, p. 93.

The Tralfamadorian appearance behaves like a carnival costume; it highlights and inverts the opinions we have of ourselves as human beings. Their appearance is laughable, but at the same time, they can show the reader that humans have become so entrenched in what they consider to be acceptable and normal. They represent the "other" and they allow the carnival turnabout to take place so that we can see the illusions portrayed by our own perceptions. They are funny creatures, having strange behaviors and outlooks on life that seem odd and unrelatable to the human experience. They appear to have a constant need for entertainment which allows them to place Billy in a zoo for amusement value. Ironic, since in many ways they mimic the behaviors of humans, as they too display animals in zoos for their own amusement value. Also, this need is reminiscent of the way in which humanity has increasingly become reliant on the constant social media connectivity of the modern world—human beings also seem to have the desire for a constant stream of entertainment. The Tralfamadorians appear to hold little worth in relation to human life, and again, although their outlook seems strange and different, can they really be considered that different when human beings have been cold enough to kill so many millions of human individuals during wars? The perception of ourselves as human beings becomes problematic because we are revealed to be judgmental and hypocritical, we judge the "other" as unfeeling when we behave in the same way. The Tralfamadorians allow the reader to look in at the perceptions of human experience and enable them to consider it from a different perspective.

The Tralfamadorians highlight the way in which time and events are recorded. Humanity tends to record the events of war throughout history as moments, singular events that happen in a vacuum, and they are subjectively judged by the predominant power of the moment. Walter Benjamin, the German philosopher and cultural critic, asserts in his essay "Theses on the Philosophy of History" that: "To articulate the past historically does not mean to recognize it 'the way it really was' ... It means to seize hold of a memory as it flashes up at a moment of danger [of war],"[50] and that "The nature of this sadness stands out more clearly if one asks with whom the adherents of historicism actually empathize. The answer is inevitable: with the victor. And all rulers are the heirs of those who conquered before them."[51] It is extremely easy for a human being to look back at the discourses produced by events and dehumanize what happened,

---

50 Walter Benjamin, "Theses on the Philosophy of History," *Illuminations*, Schocken, 1969, New York, p. 255.

51 Walter Benjamin, "Theses on the Philosophy of History," p. 256.

almost like the way in which the Tralfamadorians see time simultaneously. These events tend to be frozen moments in time, and the linear aspect of our existence allows these moments to be understood in this way when looking back. Vonnegut is searching, through the novel form, for an understanding of his own experiences in Dresden, and to question what happened there. The events seem to take on an unintelligible quality, that they were based on farcical assumptions made by humanity. The absolute ideals and values conditioned through history into our own earthly cultures have allowed terrible things to happen to individual human beings. Humanity does not appear to have the ability to learn from past cultural mistakes, it is as if there is a complete forgetting of the experiences, and events are just remembered for their dehumanized factual accounts, most frequently remembered by the successful element in the event. There can therefore be no absolute and truthful account of what went before in our history, even though it is generally remembered purposefully in this way.

The Tralfamadorians make the notion of an agreed human history, together with an absolute understanding of historical perspectives, problematic and complicated. To them, moments simply are and there is therefore no need for explanation or agreement. When Billy is taken by the Tralfamadorians he asks, "Why Me?" (SF, 97) and they reply:

> 'That is a very *Earthling* question to ask, Mr. Pilgrim. Why *you*? Why *us* for that matter? Why *anything*? Because this moment simply *is*. Have you ever seen bugs trapped in amber?" ...
>
> 'Well, here we are, Mr. Pilgrim, trapped in the amber of this moment. There is no *why*.' (SF, 97)

The suggestion that a moment "simply is" may be considered an indication that there really is no explanation for events that happen, that somehow the universe just develops that way. The aliens see the question "why me?" as typical for someone from Earth because human beings always must know why something has happened the way it does, even though it is pointless. This causes trouble for the reader. On one hand, Vonnegut appears to be suggesting that we need to question the absolute ideals and values we accept blindly in society, that we in some way need to take back control. On the other hand, the Tralfamadorians appear to be saying that events might just be out of our control on a bigger scale than humanity, that things just happen, regardless of what we try to change. This indicates that Vonnegut also allows the possibility of a world where bad things can just happen. Nevertheless, Vonnegut is still asking us to question what we see before us, suggesting that it is our human instinct to find out "why" something is the way it is, to question everything. Vonnegut implores the reader to question, even if we do not like the answers, or if sometimes there is no answer at all.

The Tralfamadorians see reality differently from the way that humans do; they see time as being simultaneous, all moments happening at the same time. Even if a person is dying in one moment, at the same time, they are alive and happy in another moment. To the Tralfamadorians, humans see time like "beads on a string" (SF, 34), every moment happening in sequence, linked, but cannot be moved in different directions. Time appears both linear and simultaneous at the same time for the aliens, for example, if a Tralfamadorian sees a dead person "all he thinks is that the dead person is in bad condition in that particular moment, but that the same person is just fine in plenty of other moments" (SF, 34). This description questions the idea of linear time, but also questions the human significance placed on the accumulation of power and money, or the act of war. The idea of everything happening together, at the same time, renders much of the humans place value on as pointless. The Tralfamadorian perception of time creates a feeling of meaninglessness, and that a person does not need to care from moment to moment because it is already happening and simultaneously resolved. This is possibly a parody of western materialism, the drive to acquire more, but the moment you own the more, or the "thing," is it obsolete and you need the next thing. In a capitalist consumer society, there is no ethos of "make do and mend," and if something is broken or does not work, then you simply go out and get another. Nothing is important, and nothing holds value because there is always a replacement, another moment. Vonnegut forces the reader to engage with conflicting perceptions so that are made to evaluate their own.

Vonnegut's narrative style also reflects the idea of simultaneous time as he breaks down the form of the traditional linear timeline and manipulates the narrative structure: "Its style was staccato, like a long telegram, he thought, but he felt that at last he had discharged a kind of duty to the past."[52] As the character of Billy is transported in time, the narrative structure jumps from one episode to the next. Vonnegut forces the reader to engage with the Tralfamadorian view of history and reality. This structure could also be reflective of the experience of war, where a soldier may experience traumatic fighting on a front line, then rest days of relative peace, and the next moment being transported to a foreign country as a prisoner of war, or transported home where the war experience becomes

---

52 Charles J. Shields, "A Community of Writers, 1965–1967," *And So It Goes: Kurt Vonnegut, A Life*, p. 213.

redundant. The soldier is experiencing mental and emotional uncertainty and fluctuating stability. This narrative structure is also reflective of memory and the idea of memories flooding your consciousness at unexpected moments. Memories follow no static timeline, there may be a trigger; a special piece of music or the smell of a perfume that encapsulates the essence of a previous experience. Vonnegut's narrative is fragmented and timeless, and there can be no fixed progression because time is no longer a fixed point. When Billy is presented in a Tralfamadorian zoo, both a caricature of government supervision and of restrained or limited human perception, the Tralfamadorians demonstrate the way humans see linear time in a strange mechanical way. It mimics how they see human beings, as limited and intellectually restricted:

> his head was encased in a steel sphere which he could never take off. There was only one eyehole through which he could look, and welded to that eyehole were six feet of pipe ... He was also strapped to a steel lattice which was bolted to a flatcar on rails, and there was no way he could turn his head or touch the pipe ... All Billy could see was the little dot at the end of the pipe ...
>
> The flatcar sometimes crept, sometimes went extremely fast, often stopped—went uphill, downhill, around curves, along straightaways. Whatever poor Billy saw through the pipe, he had no choice but to say to himself, 'That's life.' (SF, 147)

As human beings, examining the way the alien race views our own experiences of time, we see a horrific example of what it is to be human. The reader encounters, possibly for the first time, a sense of how time works for us, in our own dimension, the only one we are capable as humans of experiencing. It appears that the Tralfamadorians are claiming that we have no form of free will, that in effect we are being strapped into a terrifying roller coaster ride that we have no control over. We are rendered powerless and simply must experience what life throws at us. This is like the experiences that many conscripted men experience during wartime and reminds the reader of the experiences of both Eddie Slovik and the fictional characters of Billy and Weary. They have no control, or ability to change, the choices that are made for them. They must simply do what they are told and experience the feeling of helplessness, like how Billy feels on the "steel sphere." This is another example of Vonnegut stressing what society does to people. Absolute decisions are made and accepted without a true understanding of how these affect individuals and their lives. They are then exposed to the destructive nature of war, against their will, and have no control over any of the circumstances. Vonnegut understands that humanity is forced to accept that "that's life," that we have to buy into the ideals that are presented to us because we are conditioned to believe from birth that we have no choice. The Tralfamadorians are a device for Vonnegut to show the reader what humanity looks like from the outside, and he uses this to show the reader that there must be a choice, that there is a possibility to change. He does not appear to accept the unchanging spontaneous time asserted by the alien culture, just as Billy is strapped into the steel sphere, he can be unstrapped and set free. What happens to Billy on the rollercoaster is degrading and grotesque, and so is the experience of war, it is this grotesque nature that Bakhtin states must happen to enable renewal and rebirth to take place: "Degradation here means coming down to earth, the contact with earth as an element that swallows up and gives birth at the same time ... in order to bring forth something more and better."[53] It is through the grotesque realism in the novel, through the suffering and degradation of the human being, that the reader can formulate a new understanding, a better perception of what war is.

Writing, and the importance of differing discourses on events, are important to the novel and this is no different for the Tralfamadorians, who also have their own literature. What we see in their literature is completely different from our own human form; a Tralfamadorian describes the alien literature as:

> each clump of symbols is a brief, urgent message—describing a situation, a scene. We Tralfamadorians read them all at once, not one after the other. There isn't any particular relationship between all of the messages, except that the author has chosen them carefully, so that, when seen all at once, they produce an image of life that is beautiful and surprising and deep. There is no beginning, no middle, no end, no suspense, no moral, no causes, no effects. (SF, 112)

The Tralfamadorians see events in their entirety, all at once, and this means that there is never any need to question because they think they understand everything perfectly. Humanity is subject to a linear time frame, which has educated us to always believe that where there is an effect, there must also be a cause. We always look for this cause, we always ask the "why?" The aliens have no need for the deceptions of society or the narrative we sell ourselves because there is no cause and effect, everything just happens the way it is supposed to. For humans to make something happen, they must have a cause, and in the case of war, the cause must warrant the death of millions. Vonnegut suggests here that there really can be no cause for such catastrophic death, that even the lie, or narrative, society allows itself to believe is not enough to warrant the outcome. If we were to follow

---

53 Mikhail Bakhtin, "Introduction," *Rabelais and His World*, p. 21.

the example of the Tralfamadorians, we would need to see through the absolutes of society, the ideals and values presented as fact. We would be able to see the whole picture, while valuing individuals. This does not offer a complete antidote to the problems faced by humanity, as the Tralfamadorians inevitably always believe themselves correct, also leading to absolutes. Everything is accepted for what it is in that moment, everything happening together means nothing can be questioned, changed, or learned from. The alien culture also accepts absolutes with no question.

The discourses and ideas chosen by Vonnegut also incorporate the ideas posed by reader-response criticism. There is a constant movement in the text which causes the reader confusion and forces them to keep reconsidering what it is the author is trying to convey. The dialogic nature of the novel is paramount, and there is a consistent heteroglossic nature in the text that works to cause much of the uncertainty the reader feels. The reader can assume nothing concrete in the novel; it is clever and confusing. Vonnegut manipulates the notions of absolutes, and the sense that there is a true reality that we all live by. He is simply there to point out the flaws in our own perceptions, and not give us the answers. We look for answers, for absolutes, perhaps a characteristic of human beings, yet when faced with no distinct answer, we continue to question and search, to look for meaning. We must remember, as readers, that our reading experience is influenced by our entire life experiences up to the point we are reading a narrative, influenced by past experiences, people, media, history, etc. Vonnegut implies that there can be no absolute answer. We are constantly questioning and addressing our perceptions, but if there are no absolutes where does that leave us? We interpret texts by the standards of our own experiences; we can never fully understand what Vonnegut experienced during the war, only a way to access some alternative perspectives. We must come to our own conclusions. Stanley Fish asserts in the essay "Literature in the Reader: Affective Stylistics" that the word "meaning" needs to be eliminated because it implies that there is a message or a point to a text. The reader looks to interpret language in order to gain meaning, but the experience of the reader always compromises the moment, and the meaning, the way the author may have intended it to be, is always lost. As soon as the reader engages with the narrative, all original meaning is destroyed because of the experiences that reader brings to the text. The reader can only decode the text within the parameters of their own understanding and all previous experiences, they cannot access the direct experiences of the author. All we can really do for texts is to "permit as little distortion as possible."[54] Vonnegut understands that there is no absolute reality, that each of us experiences something different, affected by our own experiences. He is not prepared to dictate to us how we should respond, he hopes our humanity will lead us to the same conclusions that he has come to. He offers the hope of a new perspective, not the absolute answers. Even though Fish would argue that Vonnegut's intentions in the narrative are irrelevant, it is hard to disregard them completely. Here Vonnegut has transferred his experiences onto the page, for his readers to experience. Yes, the reader interprets them from their own perspective, but it seems unreasonable to disregard them as meaningless considering what they represent. The reader and their perceptions are the desired target, it is up to them to decide how they interpret the information, but without Vonnegut and his dramatic experiences, there would be nothing to interpret, or any way for society to hope for a better outcome.

It is clear throughout the novel that the character of Billy has undergone such devastating experiences that he has almost certainly had a mental breakdown. Indeed, having him admitted to a veterans' psychiatric hospital would serve as confirmation of this, yet ironically, it is Billy who has developed the understanding needed to question: "Billy had committed himself ... Nobody else suspected that he was going crazy. Everybody else thought he looked fine and was acting fine. Now he was in the hospital, the doctors agreed: He *was* going crazy" (SF. 127). Having himself admitted to the hospital is jumbled up with the rest of the timeline in the novel and is representative of the effects that his experiences have cost him. The erratic timeline, although an effective literary tool, is also reflective of how an individual might experience the effort of trying to come to terms with what has happened to them. The effects of Post-Traumatic Stress Disorder (PTSD) can have the effect of flashback sequences. To Billy, these episodes would be very real, and in the act of remembering and experiencing these episodes, he might indeed feel as though time traveling were possible. This is another example of the dialogic nature of the text: Not only is Vonnegut trying to open the reader's mind to the possibility that our perceptions of culture and society are wrong, but he is also trying to give us the individual experience of what it might be like to have to deal with the aftereffects of war.

The choice of writing a fictional based narrative rather than a factual discourse allows Vonnegut the space to give the reader experience. The nature of fiction allows Vonnegut to experiment with literary time and characterization to

---

54 Stanley E. Fish, "Literature in the Reader: Affective Stylistics," *Reader Response Criticism*. Ed. Jane p. Tompkins, The John Hopkins University Press, 1980, Baltimore, MD, p. 98.

reflect what might be going on in a broken mind. It serves as another reminder of what is taking place in the text; to question whether the allowance of ideals and values that enable individuals to be broken should be tolerated. It might also be an indication that men who have experienced war, who have experience beyond the theoretical, might know more than us. That maybe, in allowing Billy to experience everything that he does, he is more qualified to question and advise humanity through first-hand experience, than his mental state might suggest.

The event that Billy remembers and does not time travel to, "He remembered it shimmeringly" (SF, 226), is being in the slaughterhouse the night Dresden is destroyed. This is a direct opposition to Vonnegut who expressed that he did not remember anything about the night personally. The fact that this is the main remembering sequence and not a time-traveling episode reveals the importance of how Billy sees the event. He remembers the explosions as "sounds like giant footsteps above ... The giants walked and walked." (SF, 226). This seems like a near-supernatural event, something that you might expect to find in a fantasy novel like J. R. R. Tolkien's *Lord of the Rings* (1954). This creates an impact on the reader and feels like a direct memory, that this was exactly how the event would have felt to an individual who experienced it. The fact that it is remembered, rather than used as a time-traveling sequence by Billy, expresses respect for the event. The experience was so integral for Billy that he remembers the details; he does not require the confusion and dislocation of traveling through time to experience it. It is hard not to wonder whether Vonnegut did have any recollection of the events, or whether he too, might imagine the events just as Billy describes them. In a way, Billy can remember for Vonnegut, he is able to give representation to the event, to signify just how catastrophic it was. The imagery of giants in the sequence also conjures up the element of the Fairy Tale, and in some ways, the retelling of the event does become a cautionary tale, one which Vonnegut wants the reader to learn from. Again, another act of carnivalization as the memory acts like a literal carnival scene, with the sounds of explosions like fireworks and elements of the fantastical like the Bakhtinian elements in the text.

Professor Rumfoord, another character who appears in a different Vonnegut novel, *The Sirens of Titan* (1959), is forced to share a room with Billy at the hospital, after breaking his leg on a skiing trip. He does not take Billy seriously and believes he has the mental disorder Echolalia, a disorder where a person automatically repeats the vocalizations of a person who might be near them. The professor is writing a one-volume history of the Army Air Force that is meant to incorporate, in a readable form, a twenty-seven-volume history condensed. He was particularly interested in the firebombing of Dresden because it was hardly mentioned in the original twenty-seven volumes. The events in Dresden were kept a secret for many years from the people of America, but Rumfoord is keen to include it as "new" information: "'A lot of them know now how much worse it was than Hiroshima. So I've got to put something about it in my book. From the official Air Force standpoint, it'll be all new'" (SF, 244-245). The irony of course is that it would not have been a secret to Germany, or to those in Europe who would have experienced the aftermath of the destruction in the city. An event on such a massive scale cannot really be considered a secret. The fact that Rumfoord also does not believe that Billy could possibly have been there and experienced it is an indication of how men, having experienced war and its destruction, may have been treated after the event, as mental illness was still heavily stigmatized at the time. They may not have been taken seriously, just as Rumfoord does not take Billy seriously: "Rumfoord had so long considered Billy a repulsive non-person who would be much better off dead." (SF, 245). This episode is also representative of how society lies, or withholds information, from its citizens. This event would not have been a big secret for much of the world having known about it; however, steps were taken to suppress the information because doubts had been raised as to whether the bombing should have taken place. Dresden was a predominantly civilian city, with most casualties being ordinary civilian people, not military personnel. Germany had never thought a mainly civilian populated city would be attacked and, not expecting it, was completely unprepared:

> On the square there were thousands of people standing shoulder to shoulder, not panicking, but mute and still. Above them fires stormed. At the station entrances were mounds of dead children, and others were already being piled up, as they were brought out of the station.[55]

Vonnegut bears witness to the many people that were killed in the city of Dresden during the firebombing, he bears witness to the "extraordinary precision with which residential sections of the city were destroyed, but not the important installations."[56] He is requesting that we all bear witness to the lies society tells in order to allow such destruction to take place, to allow so many deaths.

Death is certainly an experience that Vonnegut is no stranger to, and throughout the novel, the reader is repeatedly exposed to the extent to which the war indiscriminately kills on masses. Vonnegut introduces a motif in relation to

---

55 David Irving, "The Victims," *The Destruction of Dresden*, p. 190.
56 David Irving, "The Victims," *The Destruction of Dresden*, p. 194.

death from the very first page of the novel, "So it goes" (SF, 34) which is repeated after every death, apart from one. This has also become a motif that is also representative of Kurt Vonnegut in modern culture and is also present in many of his writings. An explanation of why this is used is also given in the novel by Billy:

> 'When a Tralfamadorian sees a corpse, all he thinks is that the dead person is in bad condition in that particular moment, but that the same person is just fine in plenty of other moments. Now, when I myself hear that somebody is dead, I simply shrug and say what the Tralfamadorians say about dead people, which is "So it goes."' (SF, 34)

This could be reflective of the human acceptance that they can do nothing to change things, or that's just life, and is a way to cope with the unpredictability of death and living as a human being. There are in excess of one hundred mentions of "So it goes" throughout the novel, which is symbolic of just how much death runs throughout the narrative as a theme. The reader cannot help but notice every single mention of "So it goes," because it stands out and is effective as a signpost. The only death that does not warrant the banner "So it goes" is the death mentioned of the real American critic and editor, George Jean Nathan. Billy stays in a hotel room that had once been his home and refers to the critic's passing as an example of the Tralfamadorian concept of death: "According to the Tralfamadorian concept, of course, Nathan was still alive somewhere and always would be" (SF, 255). There is speculation as to why Vonnegut used this as the only death that is not afforded the motif. It is seen either as a sign of great respect, as he is still thought of as alive somewhere, or as a sign of disrespect because his death is not marked. There is every indication in the novel to suggest even if Vonnegut did not appreciate someone, that he would never disrespect someone's death, he had seen too much death, and valued humanity too highly.

Another motif used in the novel is "*poo-tee-weet*" which signifies the way that nature and life go on even after such destructive forces as war:

> Everybody is supposed to be dead, to never say anything or want anything ever again. Everything is supposed to be very quiet after a massacre, and it always is, except for the birds. And what do the birds say? All there is to say about a massacre, things like '*Poo-tee-weet*'(SF, 24).

Human beings seem very insignificant when nature can keep functioning and continuing to live and thrive, even though "everybody is supposed to be dead" (SF, 24). Vonnegut puts humanity into perspective and highlights that the death of so many is completely needless; it achieves nothing. This motif is used as the ending phrase of the novel, "One bird said to Billy Pilgrim, *'Poo-tee-weet?'*" (SF, 275), as he leaves the captivity of the stable that he is locked into when the war is declared over in Europe. He gets up one morning and the war is over. The significance of the stable is important here as it parallels being reborn, alluding to the birth of Jesus. Billy's own name could also have significance. Billy, being the shortened version of William, descends from German roots and signifies protection, perhaps the protection of humanity. The surname pilgrim alludes to the novel *Pilgrim's Progress* by John Bunyan (1678), the journey of a man seeking spiritual enlightenment. It could also fit neatly into the idea of the carnival rebirth, the period following the carnival upheaval, ushering in a sense of calm and balance back to life.

The last chapter acts as an epilogue to the novel, in the same way the first chapter acts as a prologue. There is a record of many deaths in the last chapter, including the individuals, Robert Kennedy, Martin Luther King, and Charles Darwin. There is also the aftermath of the Firebombing of Dresden where Billy must help to clean up the hundreds of corpses. There is a mention of all the "*324,000 new babies born into the world every day*" (SF, 271), that the narrator supposes will "all want dignity" (SF, 271). Just as is stated in the first chapter one of the closing statements is the mention of the teapot: "Somewhere in there the poor old high school teacher, Edgar Derby, was caught with a teapot he had taken from the catacombs. He was arrested for plundering, He was tried and shot. So it goes" (SF. 274). Throughout this chapter it is evident that there are many discourses that must be considered. In creating the carnivalization in *Slaughterhouse-Five* Vonnegut has created a dialogic text that poses more questions than it does answers, and to a greater extent, it offers no answers at all. The historic discourses, the characters, and the basic structure in terms of time in the novel, all suggest that Vonnegut is encouraging his reader to question and perceive things differently. He questions the idea that there are absolutes, even to the extent that he seems to suggest that there is no difference between the polarizing opposites. It is uncomfortable for the reader; it makes us consider what it really is to be an advocate of a political party or ideological ideal. We must consider whether the two sides of a war are that different after all: thousands can be killed by either side, both sides fighting for what they believe is right. Vonnegut never suggests an answer to the questions he poses; he simply presents the suggestion, to allow us to see there might be a different perspective. What he witnessed in Dresden was carried out by his own side, the allied forces, and he knows better than anyone what atrocities can be carried out in the name of "good." Innocent and unsuspecting men, women, and children were killed horrifically, by a planned event, in their thousands; does this differ greatly from what the Nazis were carrying out at the time? Vonnegut does not suggest this comparison explicitly, and it is a wholly uncomfortable comparison to make, yet the reader cannot help but be led there. Vonnegut makes no judgments, but the suggestion is that every individual human life matters regardless of what side they are on. Does killing thousands of innocent people become right if you are fighting against an ideology that is also killing thousands of innocent people? There is no right answer in terms of the memory and respect of those lives that were tragically lost, and perhaps Vonnegut is imploring us to take that away with us. By caring for the next individual near to us, by acting in the best interests of human beings in general, perhaps it might be the future perceptions that we can change, to make sure we can never get in such a destructive situation again. He does not pass judgment on either side; this does not mean he values one side more than the other, or agrees with any ideology, it simply shows that he sees the huge amount of accumulative death as bad for the future well-being of humanity. If he has learned anything from his cathartic journey, it must be that life always carries on regardless of the horrors that take place, and as life always carries on there is always the possibility to change the future for the better. "*Poo-tee-weet?*"

4

Extrapolation

"The imagination circuit is taught to respond to the most minimal of cues. A book is an arrangement of twenty-six phonetic symbols, ten numerals, and about eight punctuation marks, and people can cast their eyes over these and envision the eruption of Mount Vesuvius or Battle of Waterloo."[1]

*

For Kurt Vonnegut, writing was the core medium through which humanity could examine and understand itself. It is the mode of expression that allows people the freedom to envisage worlds from the future, to explore and examine, and question whether the choices made now are the best for subsequent generations. The most key component in all Vonnegut's narrative creations is the element of the human being, and it is through the exploration of social concepts like Technology, Religion, and War that Vonnegut could consider the effects society was having on the individual. He was desperately concerned, spurned on from his own life experiences, that society does not value individual human beings enough, instead viewing them as expendable. Vonnegut was a great Humanist, he believed that humans were the basis for all moral and philosophical considerations in social

---

1 Kurt Vonnegut, "I Used to Be the Owner and Manager of an Automobile Dealership," *A Man Without a Country*, p. 133.

culture. He knew that human beings have the capacity to build a world that is inclusive and beneficial to everyone, not just the few with the most capital. It is in this way that Vonnegut's writing and social commentary are as relevant today as it was when he first began writing. Vonnegut had a prophet-like ability to read human culture and predict the problems it would face in the future, many of the visions he foresaw are just as relevant in the modern America we see today, as they were in the mid-twentieth century.

One of the most important aspects of Vonnegut's outlook on life was his belief in the value of all human beings, but the reader can see this in action from the comments he made about the people he valued for their friendship and support. This is apparent in the author's note, at the end of *A Man Without a Country*, the last piece of writing to be included with the autobiographical essays, in what would be his final published book before his death. Vonnegut's comments on his friendship with Joe Petro III, his art collaboration and business partner, can function as an example of his empathy and kindness to the reader. The inclusion of the note represents the elements of humanity that Vonnegut had been concentrating on throughout his life, and it is a symbolic representation of the values that he judged to be lacking from governments and leadership. At the core of all Vonnegut's work is the element of humanity, the one founding principle that links everyone together regardless of social status, racial ancestry, or demographics: We are *all* human beings. He saw this rudimentary truth as the potential unifying force that could bring a fragmented, and often destructive, world together. The personal note included in the book reflects the deep affection Vonnegut held for humanity and is a wonderful example of the connections he believed human beings needed with each other to create a better world. Vonnegut refers to his meeting Joe as: "one of the best things that ever happened to me, a one-in-a-billion opportunity,"[2] and this open and warm appreciation of his friendship, and emphasis on the priceless nature of meeting his friend, shows how he considered the possible connections that human beings could make with one another—they are opportunities that can easily be missed. He valued people and their contributions to other human beings, and by adding the note, it was not only a message to his friend, but it was an example of how the reader needs to value those around them: "it seems quite possible in retrospect that Joe Petro III saved my life. I will not explain. I will let it go at that."[3] His name for the partnership, Origami Express, he said was his: "tribute to the many-layered

---

2 Kurt Vonnegut, "Author's Note," *A Man Without a Country*, p. 142.
3 Kurt Vonnegut, "Authors Note," *A Man Without a Country*, p. 143.

packages Joe makes for prints he sends for me to sign and number."[4] Vonnegut describes his own artwork, particularly the work scattered throughout the book, as "samplers suitable for framing."[5] Again, the author's note is reflective of the world that Vonnegut saw himself frequenting with his work, both in terms of his artwork and with his written fictional and autobiographical narratives. He was representing the multi-layered and scattered samples of what is to be a human, his experiences had afforded him the ability to be able to see what was important in life: the connections that human beings are able to make with each other. It appears fitting that Vonnegut's last published author's note should be so indicative of the values he had carefully penned for so many years, a powerful reminder that the people around us contribute to our own success as human beings.

The humanist element is the ever-present component of all Vonnegut's work, and this is clearly apparent in the novels discussed: *Player Piano*, *Cat's Cradle*, and *Slaughterhouse-Five*. Each of the novels navigates the world of possibilities, of a world which could be if humanity does not learn from its past mistakes. Vonnegut has sought to carnivalize the current system of things, to expose the shortcomings that are ever-present in society. In Bakhtin's introduction to *Rabelais and His World*, he describes:

> Rabelais' images to have a certain undestroyable nonofficial nature … No dogma, no authoritarianism, no narrow-minded seriousness can coexist with Rabelaisian images; these images are opposed to all that is finished and polished, to all pomposity, to every ready-made solution in the sphere of thought and world outlook[6]

and this is exactly the realization that Vonnegut's prose achieves. He is not interested in the fixed definitions given to us by government or social traditions, he is interested only in improving what he can see as failing humanity. He does not offer the fixed definitions, the "dogma," or the "narrow-minded" views reflected by society, and he does not seek to re-write dogma from his own opinion. Instead, Vonnegut carnivalizes, he points out the flaws so apparent in our social and cultural structures, and he asks the reader to consider whether there may be better alternatives. Vonnegut does not look to the chosen few to make absolutes for the many, but he looks to the "many" of humanity to come together to work toward a peaceful and enlightened future, where every human being is valued. To give the answers, or to propose a *better* way, would give himself an authoritarian voice

---

4 Kurt Vonnegut, "Authors Note," *A Man Without a Country*, p. 141.
5 Kurt Vonnegut, "Authors Note," *A Man Without a Country*, p. 141.
6 Mikhail Bakhtin, "Introduction," *Rabelais and His World*, p. 3.

which does not sit comfortably with the position he is writing from. He has seen some of the very worst that society has to offer, but he sees that one human alone does not have the capacity to change it. Individual human beings are important, but they need to work together to improve the future. Just as Bakhtin says of Rabelais, that "he cannot be approached along the wide beaten roads followed by bourgeois Europe's literary creation and ideology,"[7] neither should Vonnegut be considered with a traditional literary approach. Vonnegut is also different from the long-established and he pushes the boundaries of traditional political, socio-logical, and literary ideologies. His writing must be approached with an open mind, and one which can see past the traditional elements of literary canon and categorization.

Critics have tended to overlook Vonnegut as a serious writer in past years, instead choosing to view him with stagnant eyes, and often misreading his gro-tesquely satirical style as proof of little moral value or understanding of social culture. In his study of *American Fiction Since 1940*, Tony Hilfer concludes that:

> Kurt Vonnegut ... has been attacked for his tone of coolness and apparent lack of indignation, taken as evidence of political and moral indifference. But the very intensity of this antagonism, and especially the *ad hominem* form it takes of presenting Vonnegut as a frivolously amoral person who sniggers at the horrors of our time, seems to contradict the claim that Vonnegut arouses no moral response, not to mention that Vonnegut's public life is politically engaged and exemplarily humanitarian.[8]

Vonnegut's antagonism to modern American cultural norms and his outspoken denial of corporate capitalist values, coupled with his cutting wit, has allowed him to be portrayed in this way. He does not buy into traditional values promoted by our established social structures and is happy to point out the deficiencies. A close reading of Vonnegut shows that he is an intensely sensitive and humanist writer, who is considering the effects that a war-obsessed and technologically advanced world has on human beings. Vonnegut uses the characteristics of the carnivalesque inversion to create the effect of grotesque laughter. He uses these to reveal the illusion of the cultural norms that the reader is "programmed" to live by, implemented via the controlling powers representative of the socially accepted prevalent ideology. He sets out to reveal the contradictions that we are exposed to

---

7 Mikhail Bakhtin, "Introduction," *Rabelais and His World*, p. 3.
8 Tony Hilfer, "Postmodernism As Black Humour," *American Fiction Since 1940*, Longman, 1992, London, p. 124.

daily. He points out to the reader that we collectively encounter these contradictions on such a grand scale that we have become immune to them. Since birth, we are bombarded consistently with social ideals of how we should live so that we now believe that we are living in the "right" way. Vonnegut uses the carnivalesque to enlighten his reader to consider that there is an alternative to the current perspective they accept. He seeks to show alternative ways of viewing society and to see through government propaganda. The "sniggers at the horrors of our time" that Hilfer refers to are the humorous ways of "holding off how awful life can be, to protect yourself,"[9] and should not be misread as indifference. Vonnegut writes serious social and political commentary for those that are open-minded enough to listen. As mentioned previously in the discussion of *Cat's Cradle*, the ability to joke about elements and issues of society, of human culture, that have the capacity to damage individuals on a devastating scale, allows the reader to consider and understand at a safe distance. The satirical novels of Vonnegut act as their carnival costumes which enables them to see the turnabout in the social order, to see through the imaginary constructs that humanity places on itself.

Vonnegut's use of satire is so effective because it enables the carnivalesque inversion to take place. Throughout Vonnegut's novels, there is consistent use of "other" that can create environments where the reader can look in on social and political ideology. A "two-world"[10] carnival is created by juxtaposing the reader's inhabited world with that of the narrative world Vonnegut has created in his novels. This two-world environment mimics the role of the carnival atmosphere, allowing the reader to partake by metaphorically wearing a carnival mask to render all accepted cultural roles void for a short time: "carnival celebrated temporary liberation from the prevailing truth and from the established order."[11] The humor used by Vonnegut allows the reader to partake in "carnival laughter"[12] that is funny and that feels fantastical. However, the reader cannot help but draw parallels to the sphere that they inhabit themselves, allowing for a realization that the "other" world is not that different from their own, in fact a world possible if society does not change. In effect, the two worlds are joined, or so similar that anything is possible. Therefore, the use of satire that Vonnegut has chosen, and the laughter that it generates, enables readers to become open-minded, they begin to question whether elements in the novel could be repeated, and whether this

---

9 Kurt Vonnegut, "I Used to Be the Owner and Manager of an Automobile Dealership," *A Man Without a Country*, p. 129.
10 Mikhail Bakhtin, "Introduction," *Rabelais and His World*, p. 6.
11 Mikhail Bakhtin, "Introduction," *Rabelais and His World*, p. 10.
12 Mikhail Bakhtin, "Introduction," *Rabelais and His World*, p. 11.

would be a positive step for humanity. A reassessment, or renewal, of the accepted takes place, and the reader allows themselves to become aware of the imperfections of socially accepted ideology:

> To degrade an object does not imply merely hurling it into the void of nonexistence, into absolute destruction, but to hurl it down to the reproductive lower stratum, the zone in which conception and a new birth take place. Grotesque realism knows no other level; it is the fruitful earth and the womb. It is always conceiving.[13]

The critics who misread Vonnegut as immoral assume laughter through satire degrades in a way that renders the subject void or destroyed, leaving behind a sense of humiliation for those that have invested in the subject. They miss the serious intention to reassess the subject in a way that gives it deeper and stronger meaning. Vonnegut himself notes that people can no longer read well, they do not possess the critical thinking skills in order to understand and look deeper into the narratives that are designed to get them to think and question social ideology:

> the act of reading is so difficult. Most people can't even read fast enough to get our jokes, and that takes us out of the mainstream ... we really decapitated ourselves when we gave control to people who were proud of the fact that they couldn't read.[14]

The result may feel too grotesque to some that do not understand the complexity of what is taking place, but "grotesque realism is degradation, that is, the lowering of all that is high, spiritual, ideal, abstract."[15] Vonnegut makes the ideas of technology, religion, and war accessible to everyone, they are no longer seen through the "ideals" that social culture has imposed on them, and the reader can begin to understand what they might actually mean for humanity. This is uncomfortable for a reader who may have dedicated their lives to the ideal that society had their best interests at heart.

---

13 Mikhail Bakhtin, "Introduction," *Rabelais and His World*, p. 21.
14 Vonnegut's comments regarding the popularity of the television and the demise of print he believed led to the lack of ability to read well, From "The Conscience of the Writer, Publishers: Weekly 1971," in William Rodney Allen Ed., *Conversations with Kurt Vonnegut*, p. 44.
15 Mikhail Bakhtin, "Introduction," *Rabelais and His World*, p. 19.

Human freedom, the freedom to think independently and the ability to express views openly, was particularly important to Vonnegut, and he was not interested in social censorship or the constraints that it brought:

> NO DOUBT it was Vonnegut's sensitivity about being dismissed as frivolous or, ironically, too serious and banned by a few school boards that increased his zeal for defending free speech, a conviction that came to define him in the later part of his life as much as his stand against war.[16]

The notion of being "dismissed," of being "frivolous," and even "banned" is often a characteristic of a society that fears what a person has to say. It should be the responsibility of writers to resist and push back on any social narratives that do not fit with the facts. Vonnegut understood that he had a powerful role to present alternative narratives, to engage with human beings, for them to question whether humanity was on the right course. He had seen social narratives presented during the Second World War, and he had experienced that those narratives were not necessarily representative of events that happened. Vonnegut felt obligated to ensure history did not keep repeating itself; people deserved the facts on all social interactions so that better decisions could be made for human culture as a collective. Society should not exist for the benefit of the few rich and powerful.

Another idea that is important to Vonnegut, and one which he uses to highlight the relationship of humanity to social ideology, is the concept of "other." He uses it throughout his novels to access the accepted illusionary norms human beings may be unaware of, and this literary juxtaposition takes on different forms depending on the narrative. This is the carnivalesque turnabout in action: the reader is presented to "other" elements and introduced to possible human futures, futures that are distinct and "other" to their own. Within the three novels previously discussed, the "other" is represented in distinctive ways in relation to the ideas Vonnegut is exploring within human culture.

In *Player Piano*, the novel sets out to create a verisimilitude for what a technologically advanced society may function like, and it encourages the reader to be conscious of the direction that current advancements in technology can lead to. The society is similar, yet "other" enough, to our own world for the reader to make connections and fear for the consequences technology could have for the future of humanity. Technology itself becomes the controlling force that renders most of humanity redundant and unnecessary. If meaning and hope are stripped

---

16 Charles J. Shields, "Dear Celebrity, 1984–1991," *And So It Goes: Kurt Vonnegut, A Life*, p. 370.

from the human condition, if everything that gives people worth and a sense of accomplishment is denied to them, what is left but to give up being human beings? We must use the "other" of technology in this novel to recognize our own humanity and worth in the world, to create societies that celebrate individuals and what it is to be human. Technology can support human endeavors in a positive way, or it has the potential to destroy it entirely.

In *Cat's Cradle*, the idea of the "other" takes on the form of social control through the fundamentalist views of religion and science, and it considers how the differing ideological views might affect humanity as a collective. It explores how the idea of a new and "other" religion, a false religion that is blatantly based on lies, has the capacity to give hope and "truth" to human beings. It also explores the juxtaposing belief of science as an alternative to religion, considering how an unregulated scientific community is allowed to unwittingly destroy civilization. The novel uses the sense of "other" to explore the ideas of fundamentalist opinion, and how if taken to extremes religion or science have the capacity to harm human progress. Both religion and science can support human culture, helping it thrive, or if not kept in balance, have the capacity to render humans ignorant. Fundamentalist opinion, regardless of the ideology, always has an eventual outcome to destroy human life.

Lastly, the idea of the "other" in *Slaughterhouse-Five* is the idea of an alien encounter as a way of seeing outside the social and cultural traditions constructed by humanity. The idea of space travel and alien-human interaction is a conceptual device that is repeated throughout Vonnegut's work. He uses this idea to be able to see the absurdity of society and the restrictions that accepted scientific and sociological identities put on the individual. The reader is encouraged to assess their own understanding of the universe in terms of absolutes. Humanity tends to accept the scientific advancements and understanding of the present as the fixed definition of the future. Human culture can often discount opposition to fixed knowledge as hostile, not understanding that the knowledge of the present might be limited. The knowledge of the universe that humans possess now is just a fragment of the bigger picture of the cosmos. We have so much more to learn and understand about our own place in the world, our own plant, and the physics of the wider universe. We must accept that there are no absolutes, that being a human being in a world that is unpredictable or unknown means that we need to constantly check ourselves to adapt and change. We must be open-minded to all possibilities of knowledge and understanding. We must know that there are always different perspectives and that human beings are restricted by the perceptions of their own experiences, and the limited knowledge of the present.

The idea of the "other," both in terms of the individual and the cultural, in Vonnegut's novels creates satirical laughter that has a grotesque resonance. The suggested "other" is often outlandish in appearance to the reader, and it feels both impossible and probable at the same time. The effect of this being that the "other" can create uncomfortable laughter capable of mirroring reality. They appear at first to be ridiculous but on closer inspection bare a shocking realistic similarity to our world. In a sense they are prophetic glances into a future that could become fulfilled should humanity continue the path it is already on. Vonnegut the prophet is trying to show the individual that they can do something about the dark reality of a world that fights wars and represses society. By using the medium of the carnivalesque he can create satirical laughter that is able to poke fun at the way society conducts itself. A satire of cultural world experience is formed that contradicts global ideals, and in turn, free thought is encouraged.

Vonnegut's faith in humanity is integral to the novels discussed and is one of the founding elements that readers could consider as the most important aspect of Vonnegut's work. This is an interesting point as Vonnegut himself appears to be surprised by the title of Humanist. He discusses in an "Address to the American Physical Society" from his book *Wampeters, Foma & Granfalloons* (1974) that: "You have called me a humanist, and I have looked into humanism some, and I have found that a humanist is a person who is tremendously interested in human beings."[17] He appears stupefied that people categorize him in such as way because to him "Most people are mainly interested in people,"[18] and he goes on to discuss the importance of why writers need to add human beings to literary scenes in narratives:

> "If you describe a landscape, or a cityscape, or a seascape, always be sure to put a human figure somewhere in the scene. Why? Because readers are human beings, mostly interested in human beings. People are humanists. *Most* of them are humanists, that is."[19]

Vonnegut considers himself a normal human being interested in what happens to other human beings, both in terms of individuals and as human culture. He appears perplexed because this does not seem to be an obvious point highlight: Of course, he is interested in human beings and what happens to them, every human being is, or should be. It is obvious to Vonnegut that novels should always be

---

17 Kurt Vonnegut, "Address to the American Physical Society," *Wampeters, Foma and Granfalloons*, p. 122.
18 Kurt Vonnegut, "Address to the American Physical Society," *Wampeters, Foma and Granfalloons*, p. 122.
19 Kurt Vonnegut, "Address to the American Physical Society," *Wampeters, Foma and Granfalloons*, p. 123.

about people, and what happens to people, and for the reader to be interested to learn something about what it is to be human. Vonnegut has lived through one of the worst wars of all time, he experienced first-hand what it was like to exist on the edge of death and witness destruction on a massive scale, both in terms of civilization and human beings. He learned lessons from his experiences, and he sees it as his moral duty to pass on his knowledge in a way that is accessible for other human beings. He found that "a joke was a way to break into an adult conversation"[20] and make people understand.

The line that Vonnegut uses that "people are humanists" and that he sees every novel needing "a human figure somewhere in the scene" reflects the sense that Vonnegut is preoccupied with people. It should follow naturally for him to be interested in the cultural and political spheres that affect those people. This leads Vonnegut to be particularly attentive to the American social and political culture in which he lived all his life. The novels discussed reflect the elements in American culture that Vonnegut was concerned with at the time of writing and throughout his career. Vonnegut sees himself concentrating on ideology in America, and on how that nation could have a positive effect on all countries and people in the world:

> I just think about the United States. That's plenty for me to think about; I don't even think about Canada or Mexico very much. And we had a real opportunity here, and still do, because we're so wealthy, we have so much topsoil, so many minerals. This, at least, could be a very humane place ... we're so rich, yet we don't spend the money on the right things ... [and] people have been free to censor, free to outlaw abortion, free to lynch niggers—up to right now [1987].[21]

Vonnegut considers the founding principles of the United States, of equality and freedom, to be the principles that matter most to the future of human beings. He is seeking to encourage his readers to consider where the shortfalls are within that society and collectively build a better country and eventually a better world:

> Vonnegut's belief in the best socialism has to offer and his criticism of American rugged individualism do not lessen his deep concern for individual humans— and the dignity that all humanity deserves ... In the idealized world of Vonnegut, a society formed to benefit the humanity of all its members is quite distinct ...

---

20 Kurt Vonnegut, "As a Kid I Was the Youngest," *A Man Without a Country*, p. 2.
21 William Rodney Allen & Paul Smith, "An Interview with Kurt Vonnegut: 1987," in William Rodney Allen Ed., *Conversations with Kurt Vonnegut*, p. 278.

While humans should be constantly searching to form those extended families encouraged by Vonnegut, we should also be vigilant in our skepticism of all organizations with ulterior motives tied to monetary wealth or power.[22]

Vonnegut's America can synchronize with the "two-world" carnivalesque nature of his writing. His world, the American society which he strives to push towards a better future, is forced into a symbiotic relationship with the cultures and societies that Vonnegut creates in his novels. The carnival effect of laughter allows the reader to comprehend where those shortfalls are, allowing for the "American Dream" to be dismantled and to create space for it to be re-conceived. All the elements of society, including technology, religion, and war, can be re-imagined for a better American society.

Player Piano is Vonnegut's attempt at showing what a world might look like if society allows technology to progress to a point where human beings are no longer required. Vonnegut's insight into the future was astounding considering that this novel was first published in the 1950s, and the novel is reflective of the types of technology available at the time. He envisioned a world where engineers progressed to such a level that they were able to streamline living, and where the bottom line of the accounting ledger was the only goal society saw value in. The world that Vonnegut could see in the future was a direct consequence of the Second World War. That postwar world concerned Vonnegut, he saw that technology during the war had been propelled forward, and the everyday person was going to be at the forefront of those that it would affect the most. The "two-world condition"[23] in the novel is so important because it shows the polarization of how money and profit can affect a society. The traditional carnivalization where the higher sphere of society and the lower sphere meet to render roles and status temporarily redundant is forced under strain by technological advancement. The lower sphere in *Player Piano* no longer fulfills even the most basic of jobs in society, as machines are much faster and much more effective. Instead, the opposites are forced further apart, the life of "officialdom"[24] making all decisions for those outside in the "extrapolitical"[25] part of society, the officials choosing to believe that they have the right to govern absolutely and that the needs of *all* are met effectively. Those residing in the lower society have all their meaning and belief

22 P.L. Thomas, "Vonnegut's Work," in *Reading, Learning, Teaching Kurt Vonnegut*, Peter Lang, 2006, New York, p. 20.
23 Mikhail Bakhtin, "Introduction," *Rabelais and His World*, p. 6.
24 Mikhail Bakhtin, "Introduction," *Rabelais and His World*, p. 6.
25 Mikhail Bakhtin, "Introduction," *Rabelais and His World*, p. 6.

stripped from them to such an extent that they have no choice but to stage their own carnival. They force civil disobedience, dressed in the costumes and paraphernalia of their choosing, to bring back some form of meaning to influence society:

> *Player Piano* suggests that the ever-increasing mechanization of the modern world may result in a system that will end hunger and war, but at what cost? The novel's answer is that for every advance in efficiency and prosperity people must pay with a loss of personal responsibility, freedom, integrity, and dignity.[26]

The effects of technology do not look any brighter in either *Cat's Cradle* or *Slaughterhouse-Five*, both novels suggesting a world altered drastically by its use. In *Cat's Cradle*, an unregulated scientific community, that Vonnegut appears to be suggesting is trusted unwittingly by society, destroys civilization. Technology is seen in terms of the profit it can generate: "New knowledge is the most valuable commodity on earth. The more truth we have to work with, the richer we become" (CC, 41). Again, Vonnegut's postwar conscience struggles with the concept that technology always brings progress, as he knows what technology is capable of and seems to suggest that scientific research, if left unfettered, can lead humanity down a path they should not be going. He carnivalizes the progress of technology by making it seem farfetched, as with a simple thermos of ice crystals the leader of a country can commit suicide: "the thumb and index finger of the other hand [had], as though having just released a little pinch of something, were stuck between his teeth" (CC, 236), impacting and decimating the wider world in a chain reaction. At the beginning of *Cat's Cradle*, the atomic bomb has already been dropped, and the novel is preoccupied with what could happen in a future that considers this to be a step forward in civilization. Vonnegut knows the cost technology has on civilian life, and the character of Papa understands that science and technology lead to power: "Science – you have science, Science is the strongest thing there is" (CC, 146). The use of technology is just as destructive in *Slaughterhouse-Five*, firstly, by the technology of war encountered by Billy Pilgrim and the effects it has on his mental health, and secondly, by the alien representation of technology. The machine of war, the guns and destructive machinery that Billy encounters, puts his life in danger, and it makes him a witness to some of the most destructive technology of the Second World War: "dragon's teeth, killing machines" (SF, 83). The exposure to such technology, and mass destruction,

---

26 Thomas F. Marvin, "Player Piano," *Kurt Vonnegut: A Critical Companion*, p. 36.

affects his life to the extent that he often becomes incapable of continuing. The carnivalization of mental illness, and the repercussions that the war technology has on Billy, enables Vonnegut to manipulate reality. The alien representation of technology further renders Billy powerless to have any control over what is happening to him. The Tralfamadorians use Billy for experimentation and specimen research, strapping him into "a steel lattice which was bolted to a flatcar on rails" (SF, 147), and locking him up as a zoo exhibit: "Billy was displayed there in the zoo in a simulated Earthling habitat" (SF, 143). Carnivalization allows Vonnegut to satirize the effect of war on Billy; he seems delusional and extreme, often portrayed as having no real grasp on reality, and even less human: "That's not a human being anymore" (SF, 243). The manipulation of time allows snapshots of society in different situations, often showing human beings to be intellectually limited. Vonnegut even incorporates the idea that humans have of being at the center of the universe as ridiculous. Billy assumes human beings have something to do with the end of the universe: "If other planets aren't now in danger from Earth, they soon will be" (SF, 148), but the Tralfamadorians correct him: "Earth has nothing to do with it … We blow it up, experimenting with new fuels for our flying saucers" (SF, 149). Even the technology of the Tralfamadorians is not necessarily safe, and all technology needs to be managed with caution. Vonnegut suggests that humanity must treat technology with care and consideration. There is a need to have some type of system in place that allows humans to regulate themselves for humanity to control technology, and not be controlled by the technology itself.

The idea of having an awareness of unconstrained ideology in our social structures also becomes important in association with the theme of religion in Vonnegut's work. The inclusion of religion as a theme so heavily within the novel *Cat's Cradle* shows that Vonnegut was considering whether humans should follow religious doctrine or incorporate the religious organization into human culture at all. As a socialist, Vonnegut is often quoted as sympathizing with Marxist principles: "Vonnegut's ideology seems to be entirely consistent with Marxist theory, but Vonnegut is no Marxist. Although both Marx and Vonnegut criticize the capitalist system, they have different ideas of what would replace it."[27] The Marxist system considers religion as redundant, describing it as the "sign of the oppressed creature, the heart of a heartless world, and the soul of the soulless conditions.

---

27 Thomas F. Marvin, "God Bless You, Mr. Rosewater," *Kurt Vonnegut: A Critical Companion*, p. 112.

It is the opium of the people."[28] Vonnegut does not submit wholly to this belief; he suggests something different. His acknowledgment in the novel from the very beginning that "'All of the true things I am about to tell you are shameless lies'" (CC, 5) suggests that he acknowledges that religion may be based on lies, or that he feels there may be little truth in religion as it is presented in society. However, his later inclusion in the novel that Bokonon realized that "religion became the one real instrument of hope" (CC, 172) shows that he saw the value that it could have for human beings. Life can be miserable, and the actuality of living in the world day-to-day could be a terrible burden on individuals. Vonnegut suggests that if something makes people better human beings, that if it encourages people to strive to do better for each other and for the world, then it can be considered a positive thing. Vonnegut states in *A Man Without a Country* that: "How do Humanists feel about Jesus? I say of Jesus, as all humanists do, 'If what he said is good, and so much of it is absolutely beautiful, what does it matter if he was God or not?'" [29] The implication here by Vonnegut is that it does not matter regarding the origin of where religion comes from, or what "truth" can be extracted from history, all that matters is whether it gives positive recommendations for humans to live by. It does not matter whether Jesus is God, or from God, all that matters is whether he was a good person and he was influencing human beings for the better. The origin of religion is irrelevant; it is the behavior that it motivates that is important. Religion has the capacity to do both good and bad, and it also has the capacity to give hope.

The satirical exploration of religion is also repeated in *Slaughterhouse-Five*. Christ is often mentioned in an unfamiliar manner as a carnivalizing force, often used by the Tralfamadorians and the character of Kilgore Trout, to highlight the nature of humanity's blind belief in something unprovable. The Tralfamadorians consider religion fundamentally flawed and state: "The flaw in the Christ stories, said the visitor from outer space, was that Christ, who didn't look like much, was actually the Son of the Most Powerful Being in the Universe" (SF, 138-139), and Kilgore Trout later rewrites the death of Jesus from a time-traveler's perspective, "The time-traveler was the first one up the ladder, dressed in the clothes of the period, and he leaned close to Jesus ... and he listened." (SF, 260). Again, Vonnegut is highlighting the point that Jesus was human, and although

---

28 Karl Marx, "Introduction," in *Critique of Hegel's Philosophy of Right*, Ed. Sankar Srinivasan. Trans. Andy Blunden, LeoPard Books: Printed by CreateSpace Independent Publishers, an Amazon.com company, 2015, India, p. 8.

29 Kurt Vonnegut, "Do You Know What a Humanist Is?," *A Man Without a Country*, p. 80.

considered to be the son of God, this again feels irrelevant to the narrative, he "didn't look like much" and was "emaciated" at his death, he was the image of a normal human being. Vonnegut acknowledges that the belief in him as God may be flawed but the important thing about him is that he lived and suffered as any other human: "If he were the son of God, he would not need us. It is because he is a common human being exactly like us that we are here– doing, as common people must, what little we can."[30]

The lack of religion in *Player Piano* is just as important as the inclusion of religion in the other two novels. Here, the lack of religion allows society to invest all its powers and energies in creating a technology-based society that fragments and separates human beings from one another. Society is lacking any moral compass and all emphasis is on the continual progression of the economy. Human beings are rendered useless and redundant, and they ultimately desire something to believe in and fight for: "'If only it weren't for the people, the goddamned people … always getting tangled up in the machinery. If it weren't for them, earth would be an engineer's paradise'" (PP, 332). Human beings need to feel they are contributing to something bigger than themselves; they are never straightforward and simple like machines. Human beings in the novel introduce the human element that cannot be controlled and explained by mechanization, their emotional and spiritual needs get in the way of productivity. Vonnegut's carnivalization of religion looks closely at the need for human beings to have a belief in something, almost a spiritual requirement to live fulfilling lives that mean something. He points to the need for human beings to be a part of a collective, a small community group bigger than themselves for them to function happily in society. He does not believe in God but believes in human beings and the need for them to lead good lives: "I apologize. I am willing to drop the word religion, and substitute for it these three words: *heartfelt moral code*. We sure need such a thing, and it should be simple enough and reasonable enough for anyone to understand."[31]

Just as religion and technology are themes repeated in Vonnegut's texts, so too is the theme of war. Vonnegut's experiences of war obviously had a profound effect on him as a person and forced him to consider many of the elements of social culture human beings have built over time. *Slaughterhouse-Five* is preoccupied with the effects that war has on Billy as a person, and his experiences during the war are reflective of the experiences that Vonnegut himself went through. The carnivalization of Billy's world is symptomatic of the effects that war had

30 Kurt Vonnegut, in "Religion," *Palm Sunday: An Autobiographical Collage*, p. 199.
31 Kurt Vonnegut, in "Religion," *Palm Sunday: An Autobiographical Collage*, p. 184.

on servicemen returning to the comforts of their own homes, that once were so familiar yet now so strange and alien. Experiences of war change people, the familiar worlds that once gave them comfort can themselves become alien and unsafe. The world can feel changed forever by what you have been witness to. As stated before, Billy's time is carnivalized to incorporate the element of becoming "unstuck in time" (SF, 29) that is reflective of his mental state. He no longer knows where he is in the world, or where he belongs, shifting from one situation to the next. His time is erratic, he relives the moments of the war that were traumatic for him, and he endures the experiences with the Tralfamadorians. As a soldier, you have little control over what happens to you, and Vonnegut carnivalizes this situation for the reader by rendering Billy helpless in the time sequence of the novel. Billy moves around in time, experiencing war, experiencing peace, and experiencing the "other" in terms of the alien presence. The text mimics the possible effects that war could have on a human being's mind with the recurrence of memory and reliving moments, reflecting experienced trauma. The effect on the reader is similar, they do not know what to expect. Vonnegut is clear that war is not good for human beings, it harms them individually, and as a community:

> The flicker of recognition that passes between Billy and Russian prisoners is like that feeble light in total darkness, a small source of hope and an affirmation that all is not lost. If we are to avoid wars in the future, we must begin by recognizing that our common humanity is much more important than social and cultural differences that divide us.[32]

Vonnegut understands that sides in war are senseless, that it does not matter what side you are on, people are all just human beings experiencing the same terrible forced circumstances. Human culture should be working together as one body, not segmented by borders and differences.

The presence of war is repeated in *Cat's Cradle*, the beginning title of the first chapter being "*The Day The World Ended*" (CC, 1), and the book that the narrator Jonah is writing being "an account of what important Americans had done on the day when the first atomic bomb was dropped on Hiroshima, Japan" (CC, 1). It carnivalizes the ideals of war by allowing those associated with the machines of war to be rendered short-sighted and ignorant of the harm their inventions can cause. There appears to be no understanding that science and technology contributes unashamedly to the war machine. The efficiency of war can only be

---

32 Thomas F. Marvin, "Slaughterhouse-Five," *Kurt Vonnegut: A Critical Companion*, p. 129.

streamlined if it has the men willing to work on the machinery and technological advancements it needs to always be one-up on its opponents. Dr. Felix Hoenikker is one of those men in the novel, he had little appreciation of human beings as his only interest was in science and new knowledge: "He was one of the best-protected human being who ever lived. People couldn't get at him because he just wasn't interested in people" (CC, 13-14). His lack of care and interest for human beings allows him to carelessly create a second weapon capable of destroying the world, the only difference from the first is that this time it succeeds totally. The ignorance of all the human beings involved in the machine of war can have such a catastrophic effect that Vonnegut is imploring us to take heed. War and the weapons created to fight wars can only lead to destruction.

This destructive force of war is also how the society in *Player Piano* is allowed to develop and alter the world as we know it now. A third world war takes place which makes it necessary for large numbers of human beings to be drafted to fight. Little is known of the circumstances of the war, but the engineers and small group of people left behind must increase the efficiency of factories to make goods for the war effort and everyday life. This necessity later renders human beings useless when those coming back from the front line find that they are no longer needed for the jobs they once worked. War is damaging in many ways to human society, not only on an individual level in terms of mental illness and physical disability, but society in general also suffers. Vonnegut carnivalizes the progression of technology normally associated with war, and makes those advancements normally considered forward-thinking as harmful and damaging to human culture. War should not be able to happen in the first place, and if it does, it should not hinder the ability of human beings to live good and healthy lives:

> to *preparations* for war—addiction to the thrills of de-mothballing battleships and inventing weapons systems against which there cannot possibly be a defense, supposedly, and urging the citizenry to hate this part of humanity or that one, and knocking over little governments that might aid and abet an enemy someday, and so on. I am not talking about an addiction to war itself, which is a different matter. A compulsive preparer for war no more wants to go to big-time war than an alcoholic stockbroker wants to pass out with his head in a toilet in Port Authority Bus Terminal.[33]

---

33 Kurt Vonnegut, "XIV," *Fates Worse Than Death*, The Berkley Publishing Group, 1992, New York, p. 136.

The addiction to war that human civilization seems to have must end for us to prosper as a society, and as a wider civilization on Earth. Without understanding this and being able to move forward from these notions, the outlook for humanity is bleak. Vonnegut is desperately showing his readers what could happen to us in the future. Carnivalization is the means by which he can show us the effects of our actions, we must be able to face up to the consequences if we are not prepared to change.

The carnivalesque inversion that takes place in Vonnegut's novels establishes narratives that are complex and are often suggestive of contradictory conclusions for the reader. He frequently appears to be suggesting a remedy for the shortcomings he finds in society, but at the same time suggests that it too might fall short. For example, in *Cat's Cradle* it is made clearly apparent Bokononism is based on lies, suggesting that religion has no place in modern society, yet it is the only institution in the novel that seems to give any hope. He critiques religion, together with the communist dictatorship of San Lorenzo and the capitalist "*granfalloon*: U.S.A." (CC, 275),[34] both of which he suggests offer no constructive social order to humanity. San Lorenzo punishes crime by Hook: "ALL FOOT PLAY WILL BE PUNISHED BY THE HOOK" (CC, 135),[35] and America punishes its people for daring to have a different opinion: "Minton had been fired by the State Department for his softness towards communism" (CC, 96). It is Bokononism that appears to be the last standing at the end of the novel, it outlives both the representation of communism and the capitalist society, yet it is Bokonon who suggests that the only real answer to world destruction is to effectively commit suicide: "I would make a statue of myself, lying on my back, grinning horribly, and thumbing my nose at You Know Who" (CC, 287). Is Vonnegut suggesting here that there can be some hope in a human organization that offers humanity constructive moral advice, even if that advice is based on lies? Or is he suggesting that there is no hope in any form of human organization? That they are all based on lies and offer no substantive equality for all human beings, and that we should give up reproducing, just as the aboriginal Tasmanians are reported to do in Jonah's discussion with Newt: "they gave up reproducing" (CC, 282). These contradictions are repeated throughout the texts studied and are commonplace throughout Vonnegut's body of writing. He is persuading the reader to think critically about social ideology, not to offer them all the answers.

---

34 Emphasis in original text.
35 Emphasis in original text.

In *Player Piano*, the novel weaves a narrative that focuses on the short-sighted and elitist society that rewards only intelligence. Those at the bottom order of society have no meaning and value to society, other than that they bring a kind of significance to those at the top: "do you know that no manager or engineer would have a job if it weren't for you? [to John Averageman]" (PP, 217). The average man must revolt to try to gain some autonomy back in society: "the systematic replacement of automatic control devices by human beings was to begin" (PP, 329). The revolt is effective in its initial stages, but Vonnegut closes the novel with two main sequences that contradict what has been taking place throughout the narrative. The first is the scene where the people are trying to get the Orange-O machine to work: "Now he was proud and smiling because his hands were busy doing what they liked to do best, Paul supposed—replacing men like himself with machines" (PP, 338), and the second, when the leaders of the revolution decide to hand themselves in: "'To a better world,' he [Lasher] started to say, but he cut the toast short, thinking of the people of Ilium, already eager to recreate the same old nightmare" (PP, 340). Is Vonnegut saying that society has no chance because people will continuously make the same mistakes repeatedly, or that they are willing to surrender their autonomy with no conscious thought? Is he saying that humanity needs to fight back against technology, against the controlling forces that try to govern our thoughts, for us to have any chance at all? To what extent, do we continue to fight even if it fails and continues to fail because there might just be one chance it might succeed? And what is Vonnegut trying to suggest with the Tralfamadorians in *Slaughterhouse-Five* who look upon human beings with pity? Human beings believe that they are significant in relation to the rest of the universe, that they are at the center of everything, but the Tralfamadorians reveal to Billy just how insignificant and stupid human beings really are. Everything that humans believe in is somehow shown to be insignificant and wrong, and the moments in time and history that they consider important are also shown to be misunderstood and incorrect: "'That's one thing Earthlings might learn to do, if they tried hard enough: Ignore the awful times, and concentrate on the good ones'" (SF, 150). Should human beings not dwell on the wars and violence that continually surround them because as the Tralfamadorians appear to point out, humans can do nothing to change what happens: "He has *always* pressed it, and he always *will*. We *always* let him and we always *will* let him. The moment is *structured* that way'" (SF, 149).[36] Or is Vonnegut saying that we should work

---

36 A Tralfamadorian test pilot accidentally blows up the universe when experimenting with new fuels for flying saucers—emphasis in original text.

towards a society that campaigns against war and violence because our time is so short here on Earth, that we should be using it peacefully and constructively, and concentrate on the good things? The texts are complex and often suggest conflicting elements for the reader to consider; life is not straightforward and clear, and Vonnegut knows well that one man cannot have all the answers.

It is clear from the three narratives that Vonnegut suggests everything, yet says nothing, he never outright states in his novels what the reader should be thinking, he is merely pointing out to the reader where the deficiencies might be in society. Each of the novels considered has a futuristic aspect that is suggestive of a foresight that gives power to the reader to change what might happen if they are aware enough. The carnivalization in the novels provides the two-world condition in the narratives for this to take place. Vonnegut believes in humanity, but believes that no one person has all the answers:

> Western Civilization cannot be represented by a single person, of course, but a single explanation for the catastrophic course it has followed during this bloody century is possible. We the people, because of our ignorance of the disease, have again and again entrusted power to people we did not know were sickies.[37]

He understands what is wrong with society, that the ideologies and governments entrusted with our safety and welfare are neglectful, and more interested in personal power and gain, yet he is offering no constructed form to oppose the current system. Vonnegut instead offers ideas and the power of free will. If we collectively, as human beings, work on the failings of society and look closely at how technology, religion, and war have contributed to where we are now in time and space, we may be able to make the future of humanity a more positive place. This open invitation is to his readers and to humanity as a whole; Vonnegut is requesting that we consider all the options, to come up with a new human community that takes humanity's hope and makes it into a better something. Human beings do not thrive when forced into a restrictive environment, and Vonnegut wants us to be able to think freely and bring our ideas together as a collective body of people, in order to work together to make things good. No one person has the ability to do it alone, even Vonnegut with all his insight into human beings has the self-awareness that not even he knows the answers to everything, he can only give his opinion: "I am as full of baloney as anybody, and that anybody who says

---

for sure what life is all about might as well lecture on Santa Claus and the Easter Bunny, and tooth fairies, as well."[38]

This open reading of the texts contributes to the complexity of the narratives and supports the dialogic elements in the material. Vonnegut suggests multiple interpretations in the narrative through his use of the carnival. It allows for the complexity of the human state and shows the reader just how complicated social ideology can be. Vonnegut has never said that it would be easy to rectify the problems faced by society, but in order to make a start we must in some way come to a decision about where the problems lie, and make harsh realizations about our past and present mistakes: "Western Civilization's long, hard trip back to sobriety might begin."[39] The dialogic elements in the narratives include the idioms associated with modern sociological culture and traditional political structures, along with the ideas and social constructs from fictional alien cultures that are different and opposed to everything we believe. These elements work together with the actual experiences of technology, religion, and war of the characters in the texts, the differing ideas brought by the author, Kurt Vonnegut, and the ideas brought to the text by Us, the reader. This makes the text a site for struggle and for challenging our perceptions of our perceived current reality. The reader must consider whether any of their opinions and beliefs have any foundation in actual reality and whether there can be any absolutes. The novel is polyphonic and representative of what it is to be a human being in an overly complex and confusing world. Billy, the main character in *Slaughterhouse-Five*, becomes a symbol representing the reader as they travel through Vonnegut's narratives, never really knowing what might happen to them, or what will happen next. It is this complexity, and this sense of altered reality, that critics have often struggled to understand, but what is essential in understanding Vonnegut's narratives. For him to bring any understanding to our social positions, we must comprehend that everything we have ever been told may not be true. We must challenge the traditional social order for us to have any chance at survival as a species. This has proved challenging for some elements of society but shows that Vonnegut's texts are in fact not the evil heretical texts they were once supposed by some school boards. Vonnegut's novels inspire us to consider where in society we have made mistakes and how to change them for the better. His novels reflect what it is to be human, just as Bakhtin saw in the novels of Dostoevsky:

38 Kurt Vonnegut, in "Religion," *Palm Sunday: An Autobiographical Collage*, p. 180.
39 Kurt Vonnegut, "XIV," *Fates Worse Than Death*, p. 135.

From the viewpoint of a consistently monologic visualization and understanding of the represented world, from the viewpoint of some monologic canon for the proper construction of novels, Dostoevsky's world might seem a chaos, and the construction of his novels some sort of conglomerate of disparate materials and incompatible principles for shaping them. Only in the light of Dostoevsky's fundamental artistic task … can one begin to understand the profound organic cohesion, consistency and wholeness of Dostoevsky's poetics.[40]

Vonnegut's novels may seem chaotic, but they have a "profound organic cohesion, consistency and wholeness" that the reader must look for. Vonnegut values the ability "to say absolutely anything without fear of punishment,"[41] and it is this element of freedom that will allow us to critique, criticize, and improve our human civilization.

Of course, trying to analyze Vonnegut's texts for any form of answer proves difficult in the polyphonic novel, and it is impossible to assert any "truth" or "reality" to what is being suggested. Vonnegut was always very *aware* of the act of writing, which may be more apparent in his later novels, especially in the novel *Breakfast of Champions* where the character of Kilgore Trout is made to become self-aware by the narrator. What he teaches us is to never make assumptions that everything we are told is "truth," he wants everyone to become "self-aware" enough to consider the good and the bad in everything. It makes it very difficult to establish any pure academic and absolute definition of exactly what Vonnegut was saying, but this too was exactly what he wanted to achieve. The heteroglossia in the novels, and in human life in general, allows for the simultaneous juxtaposition of ideas. Vonnegut appears to measure ideas on how they affect human beings, for example, we know that the atomic bomb killed masses of innocent civilians, which equals a bad idea. If each human being assessed the impact of a decision by how it might affect another individual around them, it might have a positive effect in the future. He acknowledges that "No respecter of evidence has ever found the least clue to what life is all about"[42] so how can we expect any different from his novels:

'Oh, there have been lots of brilliant guesses. But honest, educated people have to identify them as such—as guesses. What are guesses worth? Scientifically and legally, they are not worth doodley-squat. As the saying goes: Your guess is as

40 Mikhail Bakhtin, "Dostoevsky's Polyphonic Novel," *Problems of Dostoevsky's Poetics*, p. 8.
41 Kurt Vonnegut, in "The First Amendment," *Palm Sunday: An Autobiographical Collage*, p. 3.
42 Kurt Vonnegut, in "Religion," *Palm Sunday: An Autobiographical Collage*, p. 178.

good as mine … A good education in skepticism can help us discover those bad guesses, and destroy them with mockery and contempt.[43]

On first inspection, the past, present, and future, sometimes appear alike when reading Vonnegut because human beings are continually making the same guesses as to what they should be doing for the best, which seems to offer little hope for humanity. Vonnegut's simple suggestion that we should *think* carefully about any ideas for humanity and the implications they might have for the next generation is important. He realizes that we keep making the same mistakes repeatedly in society, that we are always placing trust in entities that we know to be corrupt. If we are ever to make any changes, then we should consider what our previous guesses, in the past and the present, have generated for the betterment of human civilization. We can use informed guesses to predict what will happen in the future, but we must use our current knowledge effectively and learn from our mistakes:

'Can we spit out all our knowledge? I don't think that is possible. It is something I have often wanted to do. We are stuck with our knowledge, which has seeped into all our tissues. We had better make the best of a bad situation, which is a wonderful human skill. We had better make use of what has poisoned us, which is knowledge.[44]

It is impossible for us to "spit out all our knowledge" but it is possible, just as Vonnegut points out, that we can "make the best of a bad situation," if we listen to one another. On second inspection, Vonnegut does offer hope for humanity, but it is reliant on us all returning "to extended families as quickly as we can, and be lonesome no more."[45] If we can live in closer communities that care for one another, we might have some hope for the future.[46]

So, as our contemporary generation does begin to navigate a changing world where issues such as climate change, pandemic, and war cause emotional and physical hardships, we can look toward Vonnegut for his example of deep faith

---

43 Kurt Vonnegut, in "Religion," *Palm Sunday: An Autobiographical Collage*, pp. 178–179.
44 Kurt Vonnegut, in "Religion," *Palm Sunday: An Autobiographical Collage*, p. 182.
45 Kurt Vonnegut, in "Religion," *Palm Sunday: An Autobiographical Collage*, p. 187.
46 Thomas F. Marvin, "Literary Contexts," *Kurt Vonnegut: A Critical Companion*, p. 20.
   Vonnegut studied under Dr. Robert Redfield at the University of Chicago, who taught that humans had always lived in extended families within folk societies until industrialization broke these communities apart. This has left human beings without meaningful extended groups, and they have become dissatisfied and lonely. This has essentially disabled their ability to make good decisions for humanity because they need these supportive structures to make good decisions as collective community groups.

in human beings. We do not need to be suspicious of each other if we can listen and understand that we are all present in the same circumstances—life on Earth. We can collaborate and engage with each other's ideas to find a solution to the ills that we find in our global problems. We must ignore the seduction of media stereotypes and hatred of "other," and learn to read deeply into the narratives we are presented as fact. We must put individual human beings at the very foundation of our social ideologies, not the corporate purse or mechanics of war, but rewrite a new and positive human cultural ideology for everyone. We must reach for a better and kinder future, inclusive of all human beings. Vonnegut envisioned the potential for America to lead the world and be the guiding force for good, meeting the challenges head-on. Unfortunately, Kurt Vonnegut never said it would be easy …

Bibliography

Primary Works

Mikhail Bakhtin

Bakhtin, Mikhail. *Problems of Dostoevsky's Poetics.* Ed & Trans. Caryl Emerson, University of Minnesota Press, 1984, Minneapolis, MN.

Bakhtin, Mikhail. *Rabelais and His World.* Trans. Hélène Iswolsky, Indiana University Press, 1984, Bloomington, IN.

Bakhtin, M. M. *The Dialogic Imagination.* Ed. Michael Holquist. Trans. Caryl Emerson & Michael Holquist, University of Texas Press, 1981, Austin, TX.

Bakhtin, M. M. & P. N. Medvedev. *The Formal Method in Literary Scholarship: A Critical Introduction to Sociological Poetics.* Trans. Albert J. Wehrle, The John Hopkins University Press, 1991, Baltimore, MD.

Kurt Vonnegut

Fiction

Vonnegut, Kurt, Bagombo Snuffbox, Vintage, 2000, London.

Vonnegut, Kurt, Between Time & Timbuktu, Grafton Books, 1986, London.

Vonnegut, Kurt, Bluebeard, Dell Publishing, 1987, New York.

Vonnegut, Kurt, Breakfast of Champions, Vintage, 2000, London.

Vonnegut, Kurt, 2BR02B, Wildside Press, 2009, Rockville, MD.

Vonnegut, Kurt, Cat's Cradle, Dial Press Trade Paperbacks, 2010, New York.

Vonnegut, Kurt, Kurt Vonnegut Complete Stories, Collected & Introduced by Jerome Klinkowitz & Dan Wakefield, Seven Stories Press, 2017, New York.

Vonnegut, Kurt, Deadeye Dick, Dial Press Trade Paperbacks, 1999, New York.

Vonnegut, Kurt, Galapagos, Dial Press Trade Paperbacks, 2009, New York.

Vonnegut, Kurt, God Bless You, Mr. Rosewater: Or Pearls Before Swine, Jonathan Cape, 1974, London.

Vonnegut, Kurt, Happy Birthday Wanda June, Granada Publishing, 1981, London.

Vonnegut, Kurt, Hocus Pocus, G. P. Putman's Sons, 1990, New York.

Vonnegut, Kurt, Jailbird, Vintage, 1992, London.

Vonnegut, Kurt, Look At The Birdie: Unpublished Short Fiction, Delacorte Press, 2009, New York.

Vonnegut, Kurt, Mother Night, Dial Press Trade Paperbacks, 2009, New York.

Vonnegut, Kurt, Player Piano, Dial Press Trade Paperbacks, 2006, New York.

Vonnegut, Kurt, Slapstick, Dial Press Trade Paperbacks, 2010, New York.

Vonnegut, Kurt, Slaughterhouse-Five, Dial Press Trade Paperbacks, 2009, New York.

Vonnegut, Kurt, The Sirens of Titan, Dial Press Trade Paperbacks, 2009, New York.

Vonnegut, Kurt, Timequake, Berkley Books, 1998, New York.

Vonnegut, Kurt, We Are What We Pretend to Be, Da Capo Press, 2012, Boston, MA.

Vonnegut, Kurt, While Mortals Sleep: Unpublished Short Fiction, Delacorte Press, 2011, New York.

Non-Fiction

Vonnegut, Kurt, Armageddon in Retrospect, G. P. Putnam's Sons, 2008, New York.

Vonnegut, Kurt, A Man Without a Country, Seven Stories Press, 2005, New York.

Vonnegut, Kurt, Fates Worse Than Death, The Berkley Publishing Group, 1992, New York.

Vonnegut, Kurt, If This Isn't Nice, What Is? Advice for the Young: The Graduation Speeches (Kindle Edition). *Ed. Dan Wakefield*, Seven Stories Press, 2014, New York.

Vonnegut, Kurt, Kurt Vonnegut: Letters. Ed. Dan Wakefield, Delacorte Press, 2012, New York.

Vonnegut, Kurt, Kurt Vonnegut on Mark Twain, Spokesman Books, 2004, Nottingham UK.

Vonnegut, Kurt, Love, Kurt: The Vonnegut Love Letters 1941-1945, Ed. Edith Vonnegut, Random House, 2020, New York.

Vonnegut, Kurt, Palm Sunday: An Autobiographical Collage, Dial Press Trade Paperbacks, 2011, New York.

Vonnegut, Kurt. Wampeters, Foma and Granfalloons, Jonathan Cape, 1975, London.

Vonnegut, Kurt, Welcome to the Monkey House & Palm Sunday: An Autobiographical Collage, Vintage, 1994, London.

In These Times Articles

Vonnegut, Kurt, "American Christmas Card 2004," *In These Times*, December 23, 2004, inthesetimes.com/article/vonnegut-xmascard, Accessed August 28, 2022.

Vonnegut, Kurt, "Cold Turkey," *In These Times*, May 10, 2004, inthesetimes.com/article/cold-turkey, Accessed August 28, 2022.

Vonnegut, Kurt, "Dear Mr. Vonnegut," *In These Times*, April 14, 2003, inthesetimes.com/article/dear-mr-vonnegut2, Accessed August 28, 2022.

Vonnegut, Kurt, "Dear Mr. Vonnegut," *In These Times*, February 28, 2003, inthesetimes.com/article/dear-mr-vonnegut3, Accessed August 28, 2022.

Vonnegut Kurt, "False Advertising," *In These Times*, March 24, 2004, inthesetimes.com/article/false-advertising, Accessed August 28, 2022.

Vonnegut, Kurt, "I Love You, Madame Librarian," *In These Times*, August 6, 2004, inthesetimes.com/article/i-love-you-madame-librarian, Accessed August 28, 2022.

Vonnegut, Kurt, "Knowing What's Nice," *In These Times*, November 6, 2003, inthesetimes.com/article/knowing-whats-nice, Accessed August 28, 2022.

Vonnegut, Kurt, "Requiem for a Dreamer," *In These Times*, October 15, 2004, inthesetimes.com/article/requiem-for-a-dreamer, Accessed August 28, 2022.

Vonnegut, Kurt, "State of the Asylum: A conversation between the novelist Kurt Vonnegut and science fiction writer Kilgore Trout on President Bush's 2004 State of the Union address," *In These Times*, February 5, 2004, "inthesetimes.com/article/state-of-the-asylum, Accessed August 28, 2022.

Vonnegut, Kurt, "Strange Weather Lately," *In These Times*, May 9, 2003, inthesetimes.com/article/strange-weather-lately, Accessed August 28, 2022.

Vonnegut, Kurt, "Susan Sontag and Arthur Miller," *In These Times*, March 3, 2005, inthesetimes.com/article/susan-sontag-and-arthur-miller, Accessed August 28, 2022.

Vonnegut, Kurt, "The End is Near," *In These Times*, October 29, 2004, inthesetimes.com/article/the-end-is-near, Accessed August 28, 2022.

Vonnegut, Kurt, "Your Guess Is as Good As Mine," *In These Times*, December 12, 2005, inthesetimes.com/article/your-guess-is-as-good-as-mine, Accessed August 28, 2022.

Interviews

Allen, William Rodney, *Conversations with Kurt Vonnegut*. Jackson, The University Press of Mississippi, 1988, Jackson MS.

Vonnegut, Kurt, "Kurt Vonnegut Judges Modern Society," *Morning Edition*, NPR, Jan 26, 2006, 1:05 seconds, npr.org/templates/story/story.php?storyId=5165342, Accessed August 28, 2022.

Vonnegut, Kurt & Lee Stringer. *Like Shaking Hands With God: A Conversation about Writing*, Washington Square Press, 1999, New York.

Selected Criticism & Texts

Adlam, Carol, Rachel Falconer, Vitalii Makhlin & Alastair Renfrew. Eds. *Face to Face: Bakhtin in Russia and the West*, Sheffield Academic Press, 1997, Sheffield UK.

Aglietta, Michel, *Theory of Capitalist Regulation: The US Experience*, Verso, 2015, New York.

Allen, William Rodney, *Understanding Kurt Vonnegut* (Understanding Contemporary American Literature), University of South Carolina Press, 2009, Columbia, SC.

Ballard, J. G. *Crash*, Vintage, 2004, London.

Barta, Peter I., Paul Allen Miller, Charles Platter, & David Shepherd. Eds. *Carnivalizing Difference: Bakhtin and the Other*, Routledge, 2001, London.

Beauvoir, Simone de. *The Second Sex*. Trans. Constance Borde & Sheila Malovany-Chevallier, Vintage, 2011, New York.

Bell, M. M. & M. Gardiner. Eds. *Bakhtin and the Human Sciences*, Sage Publications, 1998, London.

Benjamin, Walter. *Illuminations*, Schocken, 1969, New York.

Bloom, Harold, Ed., *Modern Critical Interpretations: Kurt Vonnegut's Cat's Cradle*, Chelsea House Publishers, 2002, Philadelphia, PA.

Bloom, Harold, Ed., *Modern Critical Interpretations: Kurt Vonnegut's Slaughterhouse-Five*, Chelsea House Publishers, 2001, Philadelphia, PA.

Booker, M. Keith. *Techniques of Subversion in Modern Literature: Transgression, Abjection and Carnivalesque*, University Press of Florida, 1991, Gainsville, FL.

Bradbury, Malcolm. *The Modern American Novel*, (second edition), Oxford University Press, 1992, Oxford UK.

Brandist, Craig. *The Bakhtin Circle: Philosophy, Culture and Politics*, Pluto Press, 2002, London.

Broer, Lawrence R. *Sanity Plea: Schizophrenia in the Novels of Kurt Vonnegut*, The University of Alabama Press, 1994, Tuscaloosa, AL.

Bruhn, Jørgen & Jan Lundquist. Eds. *The Novelness of Bakhtin: Perspectives and Possibilities*, Museum Tusculanum Press, 2001, Copenhagen.

Bunyan, John. *The Pilgrims Progress*, Dover Publications, 2002, Mineola, NY.

Calvino, Italo. *Invisible Cities*, Vintage, 1997, London.

Carroll, Lewis. *Alices Adventures in Wonderland and Through the Looking Glass* (The Centenary Edition), Ed. Hugh Haughton, Penguin, 1998, Rutherford, NJ.

Chénetier, Marc. *Beyond Suspicion: New American Fiction Since 1960*, Trans. Elizabeth A. Houlding, University of Pennsylvania Press, 1996, Philadelphia, PA.

Clark, K. & M. Holquist. *Mikhail Bakhtin*, Belknap Press of Harvard University Press, 1984, Cambridge, MA.

Cuddon, J. A. *Dictionary of Literary Terms and Literary Theory* (Third Edition), Penguin, 1991, London.

Davis, Todd F. *Kurt Vonnegut's Crusade*, State University of New York Press, 2006, New York.

Descartes, Rene. *Discourse on the Method*, Oxford University Press, 2008, Oxford UK.

Dentith, Simon. *An Introductory Reader: Bakhtinian Thoughts*, Routledge, 1996, London.

Doerries, Bryan. *The Theater of War: What Ancient Greek Tragedies Can Teach Us Today*, Alfred A. Knopf, 2015, London.

Dumas, Alexandre. *The Three Musketeers*, Dover Thrift Edition, 2007, New York.

Edwards, Brian. *Theories of Play and Postmodern Fiction*, Garland Science, 1998, New York.

Endell, Mary. *Dresden: History, Stage, Gallery* (Kindle Edition), HardPress Publishing, 2014, Miami, FL.

Fitzgerald, F. Scott. *The Great Gatsby*, Penguin, 1950, London.

Flanagan, Martin. *Bakhtin and The Movies: New Ways of Understanding Hollywood Film*, Palgrave Macmillan, 2009, London.

Gardiner, Michael E. Ed. *Mikhail Bakhtin*, Sage Publications, 2003, London.

Gernsheim, Helmut & Alison Gernsheim. *L. J. M. Daguerre: The History of the Diorama and the Daguerreotype*, Dover Publications, 1968, New York.

Gold, Herbert. *Fiction of the Fifties: A Decade of American Writing*, Doubleday & Company INC, 1959, New York.

Gray, Richard. Ed. *American Fiction: New Readings*, Wiley-Blackwell, 2011, Chichester UK.

Gray, Richard. Ed. *A History of American Literature*, Blackwell Publishing, 2005, Oxford UK.

Hall Jamieson, Katherine, *Eloquence in an Electronic Age: The Transformation of Political Speechmaking*, Oxford University Press, 1990, New York.

Heller, Joseph. *Catch-22*, David Campbell Publishers, 1995, London.

Hilfer, Tony. *American Fiction Since 1940*, Longman, 1992, London.

Hipkiss, Robert A. *The American Absurd: Pynchon, Vonnegut, and Barth*, Associated Faculty Press Inc., 1984, New York.

Hirschkop, Ken & David Shepherd. Eds. *Bakhtin and Cultural Theory*, Manchester University Press, 1989, Manchester UK.

Holquist, Michael. *Dialogism: Bakhtin and His World*, Routledge, 1990, London.

Holy Bible, English Standard Version (ESV), Good News Publishers, 2007, Wheaton, IL.

Huie, William Bradford. *The Execution of Private Slovik*, The New American Library, 1954, New York.

Hutcheon, Linda. *A Poetics of Postmodernism: History, Theory*, Fiction, Routledge, 1988, New York.

Hutcheon, Linda. *The Politics of Postmodernism*, Routledge, 1989, London.

Irving David. *The Destruction of Dresden*, Ballantine Books INC, 1963, New York.

Johnson, B. S. *The Unfortunates*, Picador, 1999, London.

Klinkowitz, Jerome & John Somer. Eds. *Kurt Vonnegut Jr: The Vonnegut Statement*, Granada Publishing/Panther Books Ltd, 1975, St. Albans, Herts.

Klinkowitz, Jerome. *Kurt Vonnegut*, Methuen, 1983, New York.

Klinkowitz, Jerome. *Slaughterhouse-Five: Reforming the Novel and the World*, Twayne Publishers, 1990, Boston, MA.

Klinkowitz, Jerome. *The Vonnegut Effect*. University of South Carolina Press, 2004, Columbia, SC.

Klinkowitz, Jerome. *Kurt Vonnegut's America*. University of South Carolina Press, 2010, Columbia, SC.

Klinkowitz, Jerome & Donald L. Lawler. Eds. *Vonnegut in America: An Introduction to the Life and Work of Kurt Vonnegut*, Delacorte Press, 1977, New York.

Knowles, Ronald. *Shakespeare and Carnival: After Bakhtin*, Palgrave Macmillan, 1998, London.

Kramer, Lloyd & Sarah Maza. Eds. *A Companion to Western Historical Thought*, Blackwell Publishers, 2002, Oxford UK.

Leeds, Marc. *The Vonnegut Encyclopedia: An Authorized Compendium*, Greenwood Press, 1995, Westport, CT USA.

Leeds, Marc. *The Vonnegut Encyclopedia: An Authorized Compendium*, Revised Edition, Delacorte Press, 2016, New York.

Leeds, Marc & Peter Reed. Eds. *Kurt Vonnegut: Images and Representations* (Contributions to the Study of Science Fiction & Fantasy), Greenwood Press, 2000, Westport, CT.

Lodge, David. *After Bakhtin: Essays on Fiction and Criticism*, Routledge, 1990, London.

Lodge. David, with Nigel Wood, Ed., *Modern Criticism and Theory: A Reader*, Second Edition, Longman, 2000, Harlow, Essex.

Mackay, Charles. *Extraordinary Popular Delusions and the Madness of Crowds* (Kindle Edition), CreateSpace Independent Publishing Platform, 2011, London.

Malpas, Simon. *The Postmodern*, Routledge, 2005, Oxon.

Marvin, Thomas F. *Kurt Vonnegut: A Critical Companion*, Greenwood Press, 2002, Westport, CT.

Marx, Karl. *Critique of Hegel's Philosophy of Right*, Ed. Sankar Srinivasan. Trans. Andy Blunden, LeoPard Books (Printed by CreateSpace Independent Publishers, an Amazon.com company), 2015, India.

Marx, Karl & Frederick Engels. *The Communist Manifesto*, International Publishers, 2016, New York.

May, Keith M. *Out of the Maelstrom: Psychology and the Novel in the Twentieth Century*, Elek Books, 1977, London.

Melville, Herman. *Moby Dick*, Oxford University Press, 1998, Oxford.

Mentak, Said. *A (Mis)Reading of Kurt Vonnegut* (Focus on Civilizations and Cultures), Nova Science Pub Inc, 2010, New York.

Merrill, Robert, Ed., Critical Essays on Kurt Vonnegut, G. K. Hall & Co.,1990, Boston, MA.

McCracken, Scott. *Pulp: Reading Popular Fiction*, Manchester University Press, 1998, Manchester UK.

McHale, Brian. *Postmodernist Fiction*, Routledge, 1987, London.

More, Thomas. *Utopia*, Penguin, 2003, London.

Morse, Donald E. *The Novels of Kurt Vonnegut: Imagining Being an American*, Praeger Publishers, 2003, Westport, CT USA.

Mustuzza, Leonard, Ed., Critical Insights: Slaughterhouse-Five, Salem Press, 2011, Pasadena, CA.

Nollan, Valerie, Z., *Bakhtin: Ethics and Mechanics*, Northwestern University Press, 2004, Evanston, IL USA.

Pechey, Graham. *Mikhail Bakhtin: The Word in the World*, Routledge, 2007, London.

Pynchon, Thomas. Gravity's Rainbow, Vintage, 2000, London.

Rackstraw, Loree. *Love As Always, Kurt Vonnegut As I Knew Him*, Da Capo Press, 2009, Philadelphia, PA.

Reed, Peter. *Writer for the Seventies: Kurt Vonnegut JR.*, Warner Books, 1972, New York.

Roberts, Adam. *The History of Science Fiction*, Palgrave Macmillan, 2005, London.

Schatt, Stanley. *Kurt Vonnegut, Jr.*, Edited by Sylvia E. Bowman, Twayne Publishers, 1976, Boston, MA.

Scodel, Ruth. *An Introduction to Ancient Greek Tragedy*, Cambridge University Press, 2010, Cambridge UK.

Seed, David. Ed. *A companion to Science Fiction*, Blackwell Publishing, 2008, Oxford.

Seiter, Ellen, Hans Borchers, Gabriele Kreutzner, & Eva-Maria Warth. Eds. *Remote Control: Television, Audiences, and Cultural Power*, Routledge, 1989, New York.

Shakespeare, William. *Romeo and Juliet*, Cambridge University Press, 2014, Cambridge UK.

Shields, Charles J. *And So It Goes: Kurt Vonnegut: A Life*, Henry Holt and Co, 2011, New York.

Simmons, David. *The Anti-Hero in the American Novel: From Joseph Heller to Kurt Vonnegut*, Palgrave Macmillan, 2008, New York.

Simmons, David. Ed. *New Critical Essays on Kurt Vonnegut* (American Literature Readings in the 21st Century), Palgrave Macmillan, 2009, New York.

Steinbeck, John. *Of Mice and Men*, Penguin, 2002, New York.

Strand, Ginger. *The Brothers Vonnegut: Science and Fiction in the House of Magic*, Farrar Straus and Giroux, 2015, New York.

Sumner, Gregory D. *Unstuck in Time: A Journey through Kurt Vonnegut's Life and Novels*, Seven Stories Press, 2011, New York.

Tally, Robert T. *Kurt Vonnegut and the American Novel: A Postmodern Iconography*, Bloomsbury Publishing, 2013, New York.

Tanner, Tony, *The American Mystery: American Literature from Emerson to Delillo*, Cambridge University Press, 2000, Cambridge UK.

Thomas, P. L. *Reading, Learning, Teaching: Kurt Vonnegut*, Peter Lang, 2006, New York.

Todorov, Tzvetan. Mikhail Bakhtin: *The Dialogic Principle*, Trans. Wlad Godzich, University of Minnesota Press, 1985, Minneapolis, MN.

Tompkins, Jane P. Ed. *Reader-Response Criticism*, The John Hopkins University Press, 1980, Baltimore, MD.

Vice, Sue. *Introducing Bakhtin*, Manchester University Press, 1997, Manchester UK.

Vonnegut, Mark. *The Eden Express*, Praeger, 1975, New York.

Vonnegut, Mark. *Just Like Someone Without Mental Illness Only More So: A Memoir*, Delacorte Press, 2010, New York.

Vonnegut Yarmolinsky. Jane. *Angels Without Wings: A Courageous Family's Triumph over Tragedy*, Houghton Mifflin Company, 1987, Boston, MA.

Wells, H. G. *The War That Will End War*, Duffield & Company, 1914, New York.

Williams W. E. Ed. *A Book of English Essays*, Penguin Books, 1980, Middlesex UK.

Wyss, Johann David. *The Swiss Family Robinson*, Bantam Dell, 2008, New York.

Journals

Benincà, Elisa, Bill Ballantine, Stephen P. Ellner, and Jef Huisman. "Species Fluctuations Sustained by a Cyclic Succession at the Edge of Chaos," *PNAS*, Vol. 112, no. 20, May 19, 2015, pp. 6389–6394.

Gunning, Tim. "In Your Face: Physiognomy, Photography, and the Gnostic Mission of Early Film," *Modernism/Modernity*, Vol. 4, no. 1, January 1997, pp. 1-29.

muse.jhu.edu/login?auth=0&type=summary&url=/journals/modernism-modernity/v004/4.1gunning.html, Accessed August 28, 2022.

Hanuman, Dr. A. R. N. "Hope and Despair: A Carnivalesque Study of Kurt Vonnegut's *Cat's Cradle*," *The Criterion: An International Journal in English*, Vol. 2, no. 1, 2011, pp. 15-21.

Jweid, Abdalhadi Nimer Abdalqader Abu and Arbaayah Binti Ali Termizi, "Fiction and Reality in Kurt Vonnegut's *Slaughterhouse-Five*," *Research Journal of English Language and Literature*, Vol. 3, no. 1, 2015, pp. 130-141.

Liu, Chien-Chi. "Carnival Rhetoric in Vonnegut's *Slaughterhouse-Five*," *Journal of the College of Liberal Arts, Chung Hising University*, Vol. XXI, 1991, pp. 129-149.

Reed, Peter. "Kurt Vonnegut's Fantastic Faces," *The Journal of the Fantastic in the Arts*, Vol. 10, no. 1(37), Winter 1998, p. 77.

Papers

Augello, Chuck. "Deadeye Dick and the Aesthetics of Accessibility." Paper presented at the Annual Meeting of The Kurt Vonnegut Society, American Literature Association, Boston, May 2015.

Beck, Gunter. "'This Miracle of Organ Transplants and Other Forms of Therapeutic Vivisection': Medicine and Medical Ethics in Kurt Vonnegut's Work." Paper presented at the Annual Meeting of The Kurt Vonnegut Society, American Literature Association, Boston, 29 May 2009.

Curry, Nick and Jeremy C. Ellis. "The Voice of Kurt Vonnegut." Paper presented at the Annual Meeting of The Kurt Vonnegut Society, American Literature Association, Boston, 29 May 2009.

Curry, Nick. "Reflections of Kurt Vonnegut's Moral Universe." Paper presented at the Annual Meeting of The Kurt Vonnegut Society, American Literature Association, Boston, May 2011.

Dunston, Susan. "Vonnegut and Melville on the Great American Con Game." Paper presented at the Annual Meeting of The Kurt Vonnegut Society, American Literature Association, Boston, May 2013.

Farrell, Susan. "The Fraudulent Light in Mother Night." Paper presented at the Annual Meeting of The Kurt Vonnegut Society, American Literature Association, Boston, 29 May 2009.

Farrell, Susan. "Teaching Vonnegut in the Context of Twentieth Century American War Literature." Paper presented at the Annual Meeting of The Kurt Vonnegut Society, American Literature Association, San Francisco, 18 May 2010.

Farrell, Susan. "Vonnegut on the Art of Writing." Paper presented at the Annual Meeting of The Kurt Vonnegut Society, American Literature Association, Boston, May 2011.

Farrell, Susan. "Vonnegut and Biography Roundtable." Paper presented at the Annual Meeting of The Kurt Vonnegut Society, American Literature Association, San Francisco, May 2012.

Hertweck, Tom. "Now It's the Women's Turn: The Art(s) of Reconciliation in Vonnegut's Bluebeard." Paper presented at the Annual Meeting of The Kurt Vonnegut Society, American Literature Association, Boston, 29 May 2009.

Lowman, Nicole. "'Now It Can Be Told: Vonnegut's Breakfast of Champions and Adolescent Readers." Paper presented at the Annual Meeting of The Kurt Vonnegut Society, American Literature Association, Washington D.C., May 2014.

Lowman, Nicole. "Color Was Everything: The American Racial Hierarchy in Vonnegut's Breakfast of Champions." Paper presented at the Annual Meeting of The Kurt Vonnegut Society, American Literature Association, Boston, May 2015.

McNeely, R. Brent. "'The Very Saddest Love Story I Ever Hope to Hear': Faustian Intertextuality in Kurt Vonnegut's The Sirens of Titan." Paper presented at the Annual Meeting of The Kurt Vonnegut Society, American Literature Association, Boston, May 2015.

Perdieu. Zach. "Foucaultian Systems of Normalization in the Early Novels of Kurt Vonnegut." Paper presented at the Annual Meeting of The Kurt Vonnegut Society, American Literature Association, Boston, May 2015.

Privett, Josh. "Sight (Un) Seen: Kurt Vonnegut's Literary Optometry." Paper presented at the Annual Meeting of The Kurt Vonnegut Society, American Literature Association, Washington D.C., May 2014.

Privett, Josh. "'Always-Already Recreating the "Same Old Nightmare': The Function of Ideology in Kurt Vonnegut's Player Piano." Paper presented at the Annual Meeting of The Kurt Vonnegut Society, American Literature Association, Boston, May 2015.

Rackshaw, Loree. "Paradox Revisited in Bluebeard." Paper presented at the First Annual Meeting of The Kurt Vonnegut Society, American Literature Association, Boston, 29 May 2009.

Todd Atchinson, S. "'Like Bugs Trapped in Amber': The Chaos of Composition in Slaughterhouse-Five." Paper presented at the First Annual Meeting of The Kurt Vonnegut Society, American Literature Association, Boston, 29 May 2009.

Van Sickle, Larry. "How To Get A Job Like Mine: Kurt Vonnegut as Corpse Miner." Paper presented at the Annual Meeting of The Kurt Vonnegut Society, American Literature Association, Boston, May 2011.

Websites

Buchanan, Robert Angus. "History of Technology: The 20th Century," The Encyclopedia Britannica Inc. 2016, www.britannica.com/technology/history-of-technology, Accessed August 28, 2022.

Definition of satire from the Cambridge Academic Content Dictionary, Cambridge University Press 2016, dictionary.cambridge.org/us/dictionary/english/satire, Accessed August 28, 2022.

Dickson, Gary. "Children's Crusade." *Encyclopedia Britannica*, March 18, 2018, www.britannica.com/event/Childrens-Crusade. Accessed August 28, 2022.

Hall, Wendy. "Anti-Communism in the 1950s," The Gilder Lehrman Institute of American History 2009-2016, ap.gilderlehrman.org/history-by-era/fifties/essays/anti-communism-1950s, Accessed August 28, 2022.

"The Children's Crusade," National Museum of African American History & Culture, The Smithsonian, nmaahc.si.edu/blog/childrens-crusade. Accessed August 28, 2022.

The Editors of Encyclopedia Britannica, "Player Piano." Encyclopedia Britannica Inc. 2021, www.britannica.com/art/player-piano, Accessed August 28, 2022.

The Kurt Vonnegut Museum and Library, www.vonnegutlibrary.org/, Accessed August 28, 2022.

The Kurt Vonnegut Website, https://www.vonnegut.com/, Accessed August 28, 2022.

The New York Times, "Theodore Sturgeon Dies: Writer of Fantasies." *New York Times*, Published: May 11, 1985, www.nytimes.com/1985/05/11/arts/theodore-sturgion-dies-writer-of-fantisies.html, Accessed August 28, 2022.

The Victoria and Albert Museum, "The History of Musical Etiquette," Victoria and Albert Museum, London, 2016, www.vam.ac.uk/content/articles/t/history-of-musical-etiquette/, Accessed August 2016.

Newspaper Articles

Jack Bell. "Senators May Ask Setup of World Security Council" The Independent-Record (Helena, Montana), 6 August 1945 v. 11 n. 257, 1.

"Truman Tells of Great Scientific Gain" The Independent-Record (Helena, Montana), 6 August 1945 v. 11 n. 257, 1.

Film

The Decision to Drop the Bomb, Dir. Fred Freed & Wilmette III, *Films Inc.*, 1965, *Internet Archive*, Film supplied by PeriscopeFilm.com, https://archive.org/details/90984-the-decision-to-drop-the-bomb-vwr, Accessed August 28, 2022.

Index